D0816139

Ace Books by John G. Hemry

STARK'S WAR
STARK'S COMMAND
STARK'S CRUSADE

A JUST DETERMINATION
(April 2012)
BURDEN OF PROOF
(August 2012)
RULE OF EVIDENCE
(November 2012)
AGAINST ALL ENEMIES
(January 2013)

Writing as Jack Campbell

THE LOST FLEET: DAUNTLESS
THE LOST FLEET: FEARLESS
THE LOST FLEET: COURAGEOUS
THE LOST FLEET: VALIANT
THE LOST FLEET: RELENTLESS
THE LOST FLEET: VICTORIOUS
THE LOST FLEET: BEYOND THE FRONTIER: DREADNAUGHT

STARK'S CRUSADE

John G. Hemry

ACE BOOKS, NEW YORK

THE BERKLEY PUBLISHING GROUP
Published by the Penguin Group
Penguin Group (USA) Inc.
375 Hudson Street, New York, New York 10014, USA

Penguin Group (Canada), 90 Eglinton Avenue East, Suite 700, Toronto, Ontario M4P 2Y3, Canada
(a division of Pearson Penguin Canada Inc.) • Penguin Books Ltd., 80 Strand, London WC2R 0RL,
England • Penguin Group Ireland, 25 St. Stephen's Green, Dublin 2, Ireland (a division of Penguin
Books Ltd.) • Penguin Group (Australia), 250 Camberwell Road, Camberwell, Victoria 3124, Australia
(a division of Pearson Australia Group Pty. Ltd.) • Penguin Books India Pvt. Ltd., 11 Community
Centre, Panchsheel Park, New Delhi—110 017, India • Penguin Group (NZ), 67 Apollo Drive,
Rosedale, Auckland 0632, New Zealand (a division of Pearson New Zealand Ltd.) • Penguin Books
(South Africa) (Pty.) Ltd., 24 Sturdee Avenue, Rosebank, Johannesburg 2196, South Africa

Penguin Books Ltd., Registered Offices: 80 Strand, London WC2R 0RL, England

This is a work of fiction. Names, characters, places, and incidents either are the product of the author's
imagination or are used fictitiously, and any resemblance to actual persons, living or dead, business
establishments, events, or locales is entirely coincidental. The publisher does not have any control over
and does not assume any responsibility for author or third-party websites or their content.

STARK'S CRUSADE

An Ace Book / published by arrangement with the author

PUBLISHING HISTORY
Ace mass-market edition / March 2002

Copyright © 2002 by John G. Hemry.
Cover art by Don Sipley.
Cover design by Annette Fiore DeFex.

ISBN: 978-0-441-00915-2

ACE
Ace Books are published by The Berkley Publishing Group,
a division of Penguin Group (USA) Inc.,
375 Hudson Street, New York, New York 10014.
ACE and the "A" design are trademarks of Penguin Group (USA) Inc.

PRINTED IN THE UNITED STATES OF AMERICA

11 10 9 8 7 6 5 4 3

ALWAYS LEARNING   **PEARSON**

To the many fine military and civilian personnel I had the honor of working with over the years, and especially to those such as Master Chief Milam, Commander Barchi, and Mike Fitzmorris who are no longer with us.

For S., as always.

PART ONE

The Use of the Battle

"*Why should I* care what a mutinous mob has to say? Why should I care what *you* have to say?"

Sergeant Ethan Stark, acting commander of the rebellious American military forces on the Moon, held his temper with an effort. "General, you command the enemy forces occupying part of the lunar surface outside our perimeter. I command the units defending the American Colony. We're not a mob. I am attempting to—"

"If you wish to surrender, I would entertain the possibility."

"We won't surrender. Not to you. Not to anybody. You've agreed to let the part of the Moon's surface under your direct control be used as a staging area for supplies and ammunition to be used against us. We can't permit that."

"You threaten me? You actually dare to threaten me?"

"I'm just telling you we won't allow preparations for an attack against us to proceed without taking action."

Stark's latest words seemed to amuse the enemy general. "I see. So you are just offering friendly advice? Why should I pay more attention to you than to the representatives of the U.S. government? They are paying us handsomely for the use of our facilities. What can you offer in exchange for my turning down such an opportunity?"

"I'm not offering you anything."

"Nothing? You bargain poorly. Perhaps you are, what is the American expression, out of your league?"

"My soldiers are the best combatants on the lunar surface. We're a helluva lot better at playing the game up here than your forces are, General, and we've proved that more than once." The smile vanished from his opponent's face. "Stirring up a hornet's nest isn't in your best interests. You'd be wise to listen to what I'm telling you."

"Listen to you? Or you will do . . . what? You think I am interested in your 'advice'? Advice from a mob with no offensive capability?"

"I repeat; we're not a mob. Maybe we're not taking orders from authorities on Earth right now, but we're still a fully functioning military organization, we're still dedicated to defending the American citizens in the Colony here, and I assure you that we have the ability to launch attacks anywhere, at any time, in support of that mission."

"Of course you can. Attack our defenses, your fighting spirit against our entrenched weapons and soldiers. Just as your friends did. What was it called? The Third Division? Before we ground them into the dust? Have you managed to recover all of their bodies yet?"

Stark's vision hazed red with anger as the enemy commander mocked the deaths of thousands. Third Division had been effectively destroyed during the ill-planned and poorly led offensive that had triggered the mutiny by Stark and the other noncommissioned officers on the Moon. The disaster had been the final straw after decades of poor leadership on Earth and years of seemingly endless war on the lunar surface, the final straw for soldiers who believed they could no longer trust in anyone but themselves. *I risked everything to try to save some of the apes in Third Division, and I'm not gonna listen to some smug, pompous ass make fun of their sacrifice.*

Stark raised one hand, as if pointing a weapon, then plunged it down to break the communications circuit. The enemy General's image vanished, leaving Stark's command center momentarily silent.

Sergeant Vic Reynolds, Stark's friend and chief of staff, kept her eyes on the screen for a moment after it went dark, then glanced over at Stark. "Let's kick his teeth in."

"Yeah. Let's do that."

• • •

Shapes moved against the endless night of space. Blunt objects carrying people and cargo, the convoy of shuttles hung in a ragged formation while a pair of escorting warships herded them toward the lunar landing field awaiting their arrival. There were wolves among the stars, hiding in the dark in wait for fat, easy targets like the supply shuttles.

Alarms sounded as sensor arrays on the warships tracked objects rising from the Moon's surface toward the convoy. The armed shuttles of Stark's tiny Navy lunged at the convoy, even as the warship escorts moved to intercept the threat. New stars winked into life against the blackness, as fire and counterfire blazed between the combatants.

Around Stark, the watchstanders in the command center in the American headquarters complex on the lunar surface worked quietly and efficiently, organizing and feeding information to the huge displays dominating the room. Colored symbols crawled across those displays like geometric insects; red for enemy, blue for friendly. Threat symbology, representing weapons, darted around the larger shapes, which marked warships and shuttles, the spacecraft seeming slow and cumbersome compared with the flight of their weapons. Stark had to remind himself that those spacecraft could move at speeds measured in miles per second, a concept almost too alien for a ground soldier to grasp.

"Commander Stark?" One of the watchstanders highlighted text scrolling in one corner of the big headquarters display. "We're picking up communications from the warships on the common merchant frequency."

Stark squinted to read the words. "Charlie Foxtrot Bravo Two? What's that mean?"

"It's from the Convoy Tactical Signals Code, sir. I guess they haven't changed it. The signal means 'All convoy units remain in formation.' The warships have repeated the message several times."

Stark looked back at the display, where vectors for the supply shuttles continued to shoot off in various directions. "It doesn't look like the convoy is paying much attention."

"No, sir. The warships sound kinda upset."

"According to Chief Wiseman, they shouldn't have expected anything else. It's exactly what she told us would happen."

Weapons burst, creating expanding clusters of heat and debris, while the dueling warships tossed out countermeasures designed to fool radar, infrared, and any other means of targeting them. Stark's search systems lost contact with the fleeing supply shuttles, their vectors fading into estimated tracks as a sector of the forever-night over the Moon grew temporarily opaque to ground-based sensors.

Despite their overwhelming advantage in firepower, the escorting warships hung back, forming a defensive shield for the now-scattered convoy, content to hurl volleys whenever one of Stark's armed shuttles swung toward them.

"Chief Wiseman," Stark called his fleet commander. In response to his communication, a window automatically opened in one corner of Stark's display, showing the face of Chief Petty Officer Wiseman on the command deck of her armed shuttle. "What're those warships doing?"

"Exactly what I expected them to do. They're protecting those supply shuttles. The warships don't know exactly where all the convoy shuttles are anymore, but they're trying to stay between me and them."

"Couldn't the warships defend the convoy better by coming at your shuttles and hitting them hard? You couldn't hold your ground against that. They'd drive you away for sure."

"Hey, Commander, leave the Navy stuff to experts. That's why I'm in charge of your fleet, right? Listen close, mud crawler. Those warships aren't charging after me because of something called physics. You ever study naval tactics?"

"I saw a lot of old vids when I was a kid. You know, slave galleys and sailing ships and stuff. I wouldn't expect that to have anything to do with what you're doing."

"Wrong. We're playing by the same rules up here as those oar-powered galleys did. It's all about limited propulsion resources and momentum. These ships, even my shuttles, are big. Lots of mass. We accelerate slow, relative to things like our weapons, and once we get going in one direction we can't shift to a new course by turning on a dime. Mass don't like changing direction, and unlike ships back on the World, we don't even have water to turn against."

Wiseman tapped some controls, bringing up a small 3-D panel in one corner of the comm screen. "See? Here's the convoy, coming out of one of the Earth's orbital facilities, making a standard approach to the Moon. Standard because it requires the best combination of least fuel and least time." A broad arrow extended outward from the World, curving as it intercepted the Moon's own orbit. "Physics tells those shuttles they need to follow this path to get to their objective on the Moon. We know physics, too, so we know the path they're gonna take."

A short red arrow arced up from the Moon, aiming to intercept the shuttles. "We've got what you'd call a window up here, an area above the Moon guarded by our antiorbital defenses. We pop out that window and make a move at the convoy. The warships try to keep us from getting close enough to nail any of the convoy shuttles, but the shuttles are scattering anyway because they're a bunch of civs hired to haul loads and none of them want to get shot at. Meanwhile, everybody and their friend throws out various junk designed to keep enemies from tracking a target, like the little doppelgänger decoys that pick up emissions from other ships in the area and mimic them. It'll all disperse or deactivate eventually, but for now we've confused the traffic control situation up here something awful. Anybody monitoring this location will be seeing some stuff that ain't there, and not be able to see some stuff that is there."

Stark confirmed Wiseman's statement by checking the confused tangle of symbols on the headquarters display, then studied the 3-D panel again. "Great. But that still doesn't explain why those warships don't just charge at you. You'd have to run, then."

Wiseman grinned. "There's more than one direction to run. We could accelerate straight past them. Risky, but getting hits on us during a high-speed pass would be real hard. So, sure, those warships could come after us, but if even one of my shuttles gets past them, those warships will have the devil's own time turning and accelerating back in the other direction to try to catch it. We'd be in among the convoy's supply shuttles for sure before the warships got back."

Vic Reynolds, standing near Stark, nodded. "So you're saying the warships have some probability of winning, but prefer the certainty of not losing."

"Well, that's their job, ain't it? Killing my shuttles would be fun, but those warships ain't on a hunter-killer sweep. So they're just gonna hold me off and make sure I don't get to the supply shuttles they're charged with protecting. In the process of doing that, though, they've lost track of those supply shuttles in the mess of combat and countermeasures we're generating up here."

"Just like you said they would." During the planning for the operation, Wiseman had been confident. *You want to raid the enemy? Fine. You can't shoot your way in. The only way through their defenses is by confusing 'em and foolin' 'em. Give me an incoming convoy, and I'll screw the situation around so bad the enemy won't know which end is up.* "So you think this diversion is working?"

"We're gonna find out for sure any time now. One thing's for certain, we've generated so much 'noise' up here that anything being quiet is gonna be a lot harder to spot until it clears this area. Keep your fingers crossed."

Out of the confused tangle of dueling countermeasures and battle debris, four supply shuttles fell toward the lunar surface, broadcasting urgent pleas for sanctuary on the enemy landing field nearest their trajectories. One of Wiseman's armed shuttles made an abortive lunge in their direction, quickly shying off as enemy surface defenses locked on and prepared to engage once the armed shuttle came within range. The supply shuttles dropped swiftly, tracked by surface defenses that remained silent as the unarmed supply craft braked hard to make emergency landings on the field.

Lunar dust drifted in fine, slowly falling clouds across the spaceport. Landing fields were regularly swept for dust, but the fine particles always reappeared, drifting down from space or dislodged by the actions of humans nearby. Against the solid black shadows and glaring white of sunlight on the lunar surface, the gray shades of dust hung like a thin, pallid fog.

Now, as always, it hindered the vision of the multispectrum sensors trying to identify the supply shuttles. "Unidentified shuttles," someone called. "Provide your ship identification codes and landing field authorization."

"What?" The supply shuttle pilot responding had a ragged, frightened edge to his voice, speaking too rapidly as he continued. "Didn't copy. Say again. Who is this?"

"This is the landing field controller. I need your ship identification codes. Provide them immediately. Where was your scheduled landing destination?"

"Uh, uh . . . I think, uh, right here. Yeah. This field. We were supposed to land here."

"Negative, shuttle. We have no deliveries scheduled today. Identify yourself and your authorized destination immediately."

"Right here, I tell you! Hey, we almost got blown to pieces and just barely made it down, and you're giving us a hard time! Give us a break! Just let us off-load our cargo so we can get the hell out of this war zone and back to near-Earth orbit where it's safe!"

"Shuttle, do not off-load cargo onto this field without authorization. We have no heavy transport available to receive your loads."

"Don't need it, pal. Our cargo can move on its own. Beginning off-load now." Moments later, cargo bays gaped open on the shuttles and began disgorging armored figures.

"What's going on? Who are those people?"

"Our cargo, buddy! Like I told you."

"We have no . . . are those soldiers? Are you off-loading soldiers?"

"Yeah. That's our cargo. Deliver here. That's what my flight plan says." As the pilot and landing field controller debated, the soldiers swiftly formed into parade ranks and started marching across the field, their formations appearing almost tiny against the dead, gray expanse of the landing field. Almost unnoticed behind them, the shuttles began disgorging four huge black shapes.

"I don't have any delivery notification for soldiers! Get them back on those shuttles!"

"Uh-uh. No way. I almost got killed delivering them, and you want me to take them back? Look, my orders say to drop these military goons off for, uh, security duties here. You got something special worth guarding?"

"We have a considerable quantity of supplies the Americans are staging here for their offensive against their rebellious colony. But no one notified us they were sending . . . what is that?" The first of the black shapes swung majestically out from beneath the shuttle that had delivered it. Nonreflective surfaces only hinted at the massive armored shape as it surged forward across the field in the wake of the soldiers. "Is that a tank?"

"Uh, yeah, that's what the delivery order says."

Send some of my armor along, Sergeant Lamont had urged.

That's crazy, Sergeant Reynolds had rebutted him. *You don't send heavy armor on raids.*

Yeah. Everybody knows that. So nobody'll expect it, right? How much antiarmor weaponry is on ready-alert in a rear area? Most likely none. And if you're dropping big cargo shuttles on the field, they can each carry one of my hogs in their heavy lift slings. Total surprise. Bet ya I can raise a lot of hell before anybody can react.

It might work, Stark had admitted. *But you're still crazy.*

Nah. I'm a tanker.

"Stop them! Stop the tanks and the soldiers. Everybody cease movement. I need to clear this."

"Hey." Sergeant Lamont, in the lead tank, joined the conversation. "I can't leave my gear just sitting out in the open." Stark, tracking the vehicle's progress through the command and control link, shifted his perspective to view the world through the tank commander's display, watching as the armored vehicle's sensors automatically located and tagged defenses and communications points around the landing field. Though Stark had never been inside a tank, he'd viewed the outside world many times from the inside of an Armored Personnel Carrier, and the smooth scrolling past of the barren landscape was just like that from an outside viewer on an APC. "My orders say to deploy my tanks around this field," Lamont continued.

"I've never seen such orders!"

"Well, then, you oughta check with the landing field controller."

"This *is* the landing field controller!"

"Then you must have a copy of our orders."

"There are no such orders on file. Who issued them?"

"They came from your boss."

"My—?" The controller hesitated as Lamont's tanks and the infantry moved closer to the edges of the landing field. "What's the Landing Authority Authorization Order Code?"

"The Landing Authority Authorization Order Code?"

"Yes. The LAAOC."

"Uh, lemme see. Where is that?"

"In the order header! If you military people don't stop moving immediately I'll . . . I'll tell our security forces to stop you!"

"Hey, hey, calm down."

Stark looked over at Reynolds, who was smiling in admiration despite the tension in her eyes. "Lamont can stall like nobody's business," Stark noted. "But he's pushing it, Vic. We need to shoot first or that infantry might get chewed up by the landing field defenses."

"You're right, especially with our troops marching in close order so nobody'll think they're attacking until it's too late. Do we tell Lamont to open fire?"

"I don't want to do that, Vic. The guy on the scene should have the discretion to decide. That's what we always said should happen, right?"

"It's hard to argue with that. We all got micromanaged too many times by people sitting a hundred klicks from the front. It's awfully tempting to try to run everything from here." She waved one hand around the headquarters command center, filled with displays and communications terminals from which officers had once tried to do just that. "This gear makes it real easy to think you're right there on the scene."

"Yeah. Only you're not, so you don't really know what's going down like the people who are there. We don't want to give dumb orders which kill people and lose battles. Which is what the officers we replaced used to do. But Lamont's too cocky. He's having too much fun playing with that enemy controller."

"I agree. He's too caught up in the deception game. Someone watching the bigger picture has to reign him in, Ethan."

"Okay. I get it. That someone would be me, right? I guess that's the right job for someone back here. Lamont, this is Stark."

"Hey, boss. We're doing great."

"Lamont, stop trying to string this guy. Open fire as soon as you're ready."

"You mean like now?"

"I mean like real soon. It's still your call. But don't let him get off the first shot, or I'll rip your head off when you get back here."

"Uh, roger that. Stand by for fireworks."

After several more verbal exchanges with Lamont, the increasingly frustrated and angry controller had apparently reached the end of his rope. "Stop all movement or I will activate our security forces!"

"Hold on. Did you say you needed our LAAOC?"

"Yes, you idiot!"

"Well, I got your LAAOC right here, pal." On Stark's display, he watched threat symbology detach itself from the tank as its main cannon swung and fired in one motion. An instant of shocked silence reigned, then the shell impacted on the main surface communications relay, hurling fragments of rock and metal in all directions. Lamont's other tanks opened fire, raking the landing field defenses even as those defenders frantically tried to bring to bear weapons designed to engage overhead targets, not forces deployed on the field itself.

The neat infantry formations dissolved, armored soldiers scattering into combat dispersal and engaging targets with deliberate skill. Stark switched displays to the camera mounted in an individual soldier's helmet, watching through the eyes of a squad leader as she led her troops into a defensive fortification. Symbology on the battle armor Heads-Up Displays painted lightning-quick detections of armored foes, HUD targeting systems highlighting kill-points as the squad swept forward, pausing only to fire their rifles as they picked off each target. *Wish I was doing that, instead of sitting here. Wish the other noncoms had chosen someone else to lead them so I could still be a squad leader. But I got another job to do now.*

The squad Stark was observing overran the fortification, the remnants of the enemy weapon's crew hastily surrendering. On the squad leader's HUD, points for attaching demolition charges were now illuminated on the heavy surface defenses. The squad broke into fire teams, some guarding the prisoners while others placed the demolitions to ensure the weapons' destruction. *All happening perfect without me calling the shots. This is the way it ought to be. I know from lots of experience that the best thing leaders can usually do is keep their mouths shut and let their people do their jobs. As long as they ain't screwing up, anyway. But man, it's frustrating.*

Something was missing, something that nagged at Stark, so that he automatically glanced toward one corner of the squad leader's HUD, looking for something that wasn't there. The timeline. It had become so routine, a readout linked to the operational plan that informed every individual soldier the second they began to fall behind the rigid schedules devised by planners who likely had never seen the battlefield. A happy green when the soldier was on timeline, most soldiers were used to seeing it in increasingly accusing shades of yellow, orange, and red. Being off timeline was a major distraction for a combat soldier, so Stark and his improvised staff had decided to see what would happen without one. So far, the world hadn't come to an end.

"I read all primary defenses eliminated," Lamont reported. "Whadayya think, Milheim?"

Sergeant Milheim, commanding the ground soldiers from Fourth Battalion on the landing field, took a moment to respond. "Yeah. We're not taking any fire, anyway."

"Well, then, let's start blowing things up!"

"Concur. Fourth Battalion, plant your charges on the targets specified in your Tacs. Keep an eye out for hostile visitors while you're at it." The soldiers of Fourth Battalion scattered even more, heading for locations where their Tactical Computer Systems indicated communications, weapons, and supply equipment should be.

Stark pulled his view back again, scanning the display for indications of an enemy response. Every soldier's suit, every tank, every shuttle contained sensors, and the inputs from those sources were all fed to places like this to be fused together into a single picture. Blue symbols marking Stark's troops swarmed over the field like ants at a picnic. Several small clusters of red enemy symbology sat motionless, tagged with extra symbols, indicating their status as prisoners. At a few sites along the edge of the field, green symbols indicated probable civilian employees of the landing field fleeing for their lives. Stark shook his head. "I don't see nothing."

Reynolds studied the display. "And that bothers you." It was a statement rather than a question.

"Damn right. There oughta be something else in place defending that field. Lamont! Milheim!"

"Yo."

"Roger."

"Listen up. There's something else out there. Keep your guard up."

"I don't see anything," Milheim offered.

"Neither do I. So where would a quick reaction defensive force be that we wouldn't see it?"

"Cargo warehouses," Lamont announced. "Nice, warm, and hidden until they're needed. You think?"

Vic Reynolds nodded and keyed her own response. "I think so. You're right. They'd be under cover and protected from immediate detection and attack."

"Sure they would. I'll swing a couple of my hogs that way. Milheim, I'd appreciate some of your boys and girls coming along."

"Roger," Milheim acknowledged. "I'm sending the two nearest platoons to link up with your armor."

Stark leaned back, nodding in approval as he watched the commands fly across the tactical display and units on the landing field begin the move in response. He hesitated, then glanced at Reynolds. "So did I just do something stupid? Get all nervous and jerk around the troops on the field for nothing?"

"No. Ethan, you may or may not be right about a reaction force being hidden there, but it makes sense. And thinking about that is exactly what you should be doing from back here. You know what it's like in combat. Too much going on too fast. I think the troops out there appreciate your thinking about things they don't have time to focus on."

"Maybe—" Stark began, whatever else he might have said choked off as alarms pulsed on the display.

Two armored cars shot onto the landing field, erupting from a depression near the known warehouse locations, spitting light-caliber shells as they came. Behind the armored cars, a couple of platoons of infantry came dashing out, firing rapidly. Instead of surprising a widely dispersed force, though, they ran head-on into the scratch force Lamont and Milheim had just assembled.

The light rounds from one of the armored cars glanced uselessly off the carapace of one of Lamont's tanks, which swung its turret and spat a single round at the attacking vehicle. The heavy shell decapitated the armored car, striking just beneath its weapon mount and blowing the entire top of the vehicle into a long, high parabola extended by the low lunar gravity.

The first armored car's gun mount was still tumbling in languid flight against the bright stars above when the nearest squad of Milheim's infantry targeted its companion. At close range, the infantry weapons punched through the light armor of the enemy vehicle, riddling it with penetrations. The armored car staggered under the barrage, then ceased firing, its gun mount locked in place, before grounding and sliding to a prolonged halt, atmosphere venting from a dozen holes. A single surviving crew member spilled out, arms upraised in surrender.

The surprised enemy ground troops targeted Lamont's tanks. *Not a great choice*, Stark thought, *but the only chance they've got is to take out that armor fast. Not that they'll be able to do that with Milheim's infantry hitting them.* A single enemy antiarmor round detonated just short of its target as the tank's point defenses scored a just-in-time hit. Then the enemy antiarmor teams started dropping as Milheim's soldiers hit them with a blizzard of fire. Belatedly, the enemy infantry tried to shift targets to hit the other ground fighters, but then the tanks began flaying them with their own secondary armament. A brief scattering of fire from the enemy forces tapered off into nothing, then the enemy began broadcasting surrender messages as individual soldiers stood, dropping their weapons and raising their hands.

"Commander Stark, we got a problem," Milheim reported.

"What's that?"

"I got a coupla platoons of enemy soldiers surrendering here."

"So what's the problem?"

"Do we want 'em?"

"Hell, no." The cargo shuttles had been fully loaded and wouldn't need any extra bodies weighing them down on the way back.

"I didn't think so. What do I do with 'em?"

Stark glanced at Vic, who triggered her own circuit. "Milheim, this is Reynolds. Tell the enemy to leave their weapons and run. Anybody who's slow in doing either gets shot."

"Roger. Oh, man."

"Now what?"

"Got word from one of my squads. There's some American techs here. Private contractors, I think. Do we bring 'em back?"

"Link me to that squad." Stark switched controls swiftly, bringing up vid of the view from another soldier's battle armor. Visible before him were two figures in surface suits, armored only enough to protect them from the lunar environment. Some sort of corporate logo made bright splashes on the left breasts of their suits, looking weirdly out of place against the black, white, and gray of the lunar surface. "They look like civs," he remarked to Reynolds. "What do you think? They might know some stuff we could use."

"They might. But, Ethan, there's a chance we'll lose a shuttle on the way back. We don't want these guys to be on that shuttle, because if they are, we get blamed for causing the deaths of other Americans. American civs, no less. So far, our hands are clean. Let's keep it that way."

"Yeah. Good call, Vic. Milheim? Let 'em go. And tell 'em to run like hell. I don't want them around when we blow away everything on that field."

"You're the boss."

"Hey!" another soldier called over the command circuit. "This is Corporal Yuin. I'm at that big pile of junk to lunar southeast of the landing field. Everybody stop throwing bullets this way!"

Stark tagged Yuin's symbol. "What's the problem, Corporal?"

"The problem is this junk ain't beans and blankets! Sir. It's ordnance. Live ammo. Tons of it. And it ain't covered by anything but some sort of metallic tarp."

"It's on the surface? Almost unprotected? Geez. Thanks, Corporal." Stark pulled back, glaring around the command center. "Have I got a combat engineer in here anywhere?"

Sergeant Tran, responsible for running the command center since the death of his predecessor, Sergeant Tanaka, pivoted and pointed to where one watchstander was raising her hand. Solid and squarish in her build, she almost resembled a bulldozer herself. "Right here, sir."

"We got a big pile of munitions on the surface. You heard that?"

"Yessir."

"Is that as stupid as I think it is? Won't the stuff blow if one of those micrometeorites hits the pile?"

"Not likely, sir. The explosives they use these days are really stable. They'll only blow if the detonator goes off. So maybe if the little rock hit a detonator dead on, maybe then something would blow. That reinforced tarp they're using would stop the small stuff, or at least slow it enough to reduce the chance of an explosion. I wouldn't do it, but you could get away with storing stuff on the surface for a while like that if you didn't have enough covered storage on hand."

Vic leaned forward. "How do we blow it if the explosives are stable?"

"Oh, that's easy. Just plant the explosive charges. They'll make the right kind of bang to set off the detonators and then everything else." The combat engineer paused. "I wouldn't want to be anywhere near that spot when the charges go off. That's gonna be a helluva blast."

"I bet," Stark acknowledged. "Thanks, Corporal. Milheim, tell your people to plant their charges anywhere on that pile and get the hell out of there. Lamont!"

"Yo." The tanker sounded like he was having the time of his life.

"We got munitions lying around in the area I'm highlighting. Got it? Anything big might set them off, so make sure your people don't throw any heavy stuff in there. We don't need anybody blowing the place halfway back to Earth before we leave."

"That stuff's all ammo? Roger. I got an interdict for that area on all my tanks' fire control systems now. If anybody tries to override it, I'll fire them out of my main cannon."

Stark looked over at Reynolds. "They left tons of ammo just lying on the surface? Are they nuts?"

"More likely they filled the local magazines with other munitions and haven't found a place for this stuff, yet, like the corporal said."

"So what if a big rock fell on it?"

"I assume they were planning on hitting any big rocks with the landing field defenses. That would deflect them, anyway."

"Yeah, right. Probably onto the heads of some poor foot soldiers. Where the hell have our former bosses been keeping all this ordnance? We always ran into shortages before." Before, when they'd been obeying their officers' orders through the apparently endless lunar war. Before they'd mutinied and cut themselves off from a system that never seemed to have enough money for bullets or spare parts, but could always afford to send them somewhere where they needed every bullet and part they could get and then some.

Vic shrugged. "Some of it's probably from the strategic reserve stockpiles. It's been long enough since we mutinied for the powers that be to have ramped up ammunition production, though."

"I guess. But they always claimed they couldn't afford lots of ammo. So how're those powers that be paying for the stuff?"

"Ethan? What's the rule about questions?"

Stark smiled despite his tension. "'Never ask a question you don't wanna know the answer to,'" he quoted. "You'd think I was a new recruit." He focused back on the battle scene. "Okay. See anything else to worry about?"

She shook her head. "You've been doing a good job of spotting problems so far."

"Uh-huh. But you're still a better tactical thinker than me." Stark nodded at the display and the scattered symbology on it. "What do you think?"

"I think that if we get hit right now we'd be toast. Our forces are too spread out."

"They gotta be spread out to reach all the targets we want to destroy."

"I know, but—Ethan." Vic pointed a single finger toward her display, the digit jumping across several threat readings. "We're starting to take more fire from the warehouse area. Aimed fire."

"Aimed." Somebody who wasn't panicking, somebody who was keeping under cover. "Some more of that reaction force?"

"No. Reinforcements."

"How can you be sure of that? If we bug out early we might not destroy every target we want to nail."

Reynolds eyed him narrowly, her finger stabbing at the display once more. "The way that reaction force came out, you could tell they were risking everything on a quick hit. And nobody provided covering fire for them when we hit back. These are new. And there could be a company, or a battalion, right behind these guys. Those ridges over that way screen the approach from our sensors so we can't view this area to be sure."

"We knew that. But—"

"But nothing, Ethan. If you were going to hit our forces on that field, how would plan your approach?"

Stark stared at the display, his face growing grim. "Yeah. Behind the screening terrain. Lamont's tanks and that company of infantry are still there. Could they handle anything that comes for a few minutes?"

"Hell, Ethan, you know as well as I do that it'd depend on

what comes! If a bunch of armor and mech infantry comes over that ridge behind an artillery barrage . . . "

"Okay. You're right." Stark blinked, then took another look at his display, deliberately pulling back the scale so he could see beyond the landing field. *I'm getting too caught up in this. Lots of fun, breaking stuff and watching the enemy run.* "Thanks, Vic. Milheim, Lamont, it's getting hot out there."

"Roger," Milheim agreed. " I don't like what's going down by those warehouses. We've achieved most of our objectives. I suggest we get the hell out of Dodge."

"There's still time to hit the remaining objectives," Lamont argued. "We can handle things for a few more minutes."

Stark hesitated, weighing what he saw, what he felt, with what his commanders on the scene were saying. *My guts tell me what the right answer is. Maybe I'm just over-cautious, but . . .* "No. The remaining objectives aren't worth the risk. Get your people back to the shuttles. It's time to leave."

"My tanks can finish the job then bring up the rear . . ." Lamont began.

"Negative. Begin withdrawal now. Expedite." Stark started to call out more detailed instructions, then caught himself. *I told 'em what to do. Now, just watch. Tell 'em if there's a problem.*

"Yessir, yessir, three bags full."

The scattered blue symbols paused in their motion as commands flew to every soldier and vehicle, then began rapidly falling back toward the shuttles. They left behind myriad symbols blinking with threat warnings, explosive charges planted on almost every piece of equipment around the landing field. As the Americans retreated, the fire from the warehouse area grew in intensity, lashing at soldiers trying to hasten back to their shuttles. Heavy shells began falling around them as well, as the enemy finally shifted batteries normally aimed beyond the front to target the field to their rear. "Milheim," Vic commanded. "Put some fire down on those warehouses. Make those shooters keep their heads down. Lamont, can your tanks take out any of that incoming artillery?"

"If the firing angle's right," Lamont responded. "But I'm starting to run low on ammo."

Stark brought up the ammunition status of the tanks, grimacing as he noted how much the armor had already fired off. He briefly wondered about the chances of scrounging more ammo from the massive stockpile to one side of the landing field, and just as quickly discarded the idea. *The way it always works is the stuff we wanted would be on the bottom of the pile. And I don't want my people messing around that mountain of explosives while the enemy drops shells on them.* "Understand. But if you apes don't leave now, all the ammo in the world won't do you any good."

"Okay, we'll keep shooting until we're jacked back into the shuttles. Hope that doesn't make them sailors nervous."

Stark grinned. *Those sailors are probably already plenty nervous because of the artillery dropping around them.* "Who's monitoring the shuttles?" he called to the watchstanders. "How are they?"

"Ready to boost," a private reported. "No damage except some surface scratches from shrapnel."

Stark switched scans again restlessly. The fire from the warehouse area kept growing heavier. So far, no direct cannon fire had advertised the presence of enemy armor, but that had to be close. Blue symbology clustered around the shuttles as the ground troops returned to their transports. Stark fought down an instinctive impulse to order the soldiers to disperse, knowing a concentration of targets was impossible to avoid if Milheim's infantry wanted to board the ships rapidly. The clusters of symbology shrank quickly as the soldiers raced aboard, replaced by tick marks alongside the shuttle symbols indicating numbers onboard. *Go! Go! Go! Get the hell out of there!*

"Got something going on over here," Vic noted. "Shuttle Bravo, what's the holdup?"

"Got a jam in the cargo loading hoist," the shuttle pilot reported. "Trying to clear."

"How long? How long to clear the jam?"

"Dunno. Could be five seconds, could be five minutes. Or longer. This gear is a real bitch sometimes."

Vic looked over at Stark, who shook his head wordlessly. "Shuttle Bravo, forget the armor. Get the tank crew on board with the infantry."

"Roger. Understand I leave the tank and get all personnel on board." It was hard to tell whether the pilot felt relieved or frustrated at having to dump the armored vehicle.

Sergeant Lamont's voice didn't leave any doubt, however. "Stark! You can't leave one of my hogs behind!"

"We don't have any choice," Stark answered. "We can't afford the delay." As if to emphasize his words, enemy soldiers finally began spilling onto the field, evading forward in a last-ditch attempt to disable one or more of the shuttles. "Can't you put that tank on auto or somethin' to help hold those guys off?"

"Yeah." Lamont sounded as if he'd lost a friend. "Okay, I'm putting it on an auto-defend/destruct sequence. It'll raise hell until we take off and then self-detonate its fuel, air, and ammo supplies. Sorry, man." The last words seemed addressed to the forlorn tank as it shot away from the shuttle and began throwing rounds into the advancing enemy ranks.

The last of Stark's infantry tumbled into their shuttles, firing until their weapons were blocked by closing hatches. "All tanks secured!" Moments later, the shuttles blasted upward in a ragged volley, chased by futile shots from the ground. Lamont's abandoned tank ripped off a blistering barrage, staggering as a couple of antitank rounds impacted in the empty crew compartment, then blew apart in a series of blasts that sent shrapnel flying across the landing field and high overhead. Stark, trying not to think about how important every piece of armor was to his forces, watched the projected paths of some of the debris as it flew upward, then snorted a brief, tense laugh. "Looks like Lamont put one of his tanks into low lunar orbit."

"A few pieces of it, anyway." Vic checked the time on her display. "They set the charges for minimum delay to make sure those enemy troops wouldn't be able to deactivate them. Any second now and we should see a lot more stuff heading for orbit."

"Those shuttles are still too damn close. Wish we coulda command-detonated the charges."

"That kind of signal is too easy to jam," Reynolds reminded him. "And fiber-optic cable doesn't unreel well from a shuttle heading off at max acceleration. Hold on."

She'd barely finished speaking when the charges left by Milheim's troops began detonating. Watching the view from a backward-looking camera on one of the fleeing shuttles, Stark saw a section of lunar terrain lift skyward as the huge ammunition stockpile went off in a rapid series of blasts that quickly merged into one massive explosion. Luminosity and infrared scales backed down in swift shifts to avoid being overwhelmed by the glare. "Holy cow," Vic breathed. "How much ammo did they have in that pile?"

"I dunno, but I'm sure glad I'm not on that landing field. I guess we could've saved the other charges. There ain't gonna be nothing left of that field but one mother of a crater."

"Maybe they ought to name that crater after you."

"Thanks. Are the shuttles clear of the blast effects and debris?"

"It's going to be close," Sergeant Tran reported. "There's too much junk flying to track every piece."

"The shuttles are still boosting out at max acceleration," the private who had reported earlier announced. "But they're heading into threat envelopes from enemy antiorbital systems."

"I've got enemy and American warships converging toward the shuttles' projected orbital track," another watchstander reported.

Stark took a second to rub his forehead, trying to fight down the sick feeling in his gut. *Now comes the hard part. Getting away.* "Where's Wiseman and her armed shuttles?"

"Moving to intercept the warships."

"Is she nuts?"

"No," Vic advised. "She's pushing the other deception, Ethan. Making the warships and the enemy think those shuttles are going to follow a suborbital path back here."

"Sure. Right. So when do our shuttles change—." Stark bit off the sentence as acceleration vectors on the cargo shuttles swung around. Attitude jets pushed the spacecraft tails toward the black heavens and pointed their noses back toward the dead Moon below. "Okay. Standby on the artillery." He checked the armed shuttles, watching as they canted wildly as well, arcing their courses around so they were also pointed at the Moon's surface. The displays updated the spacecrafts' courses continuously, the projected paths of the two groups of shuttles now pointing toward each other. Wiseman's armed shuttles were curving in from over the American enclave toward the enemy front lines as the fleeing cargo shuttles headed toward the same location from the opposite direction.

"I sure as hell hope this works," Vic whispered.

"You and me both. Artillery. Sergeant Grace? Execute pre-planned fire mission Bravo Foxtrot."

"Roger. Understand execute fire mission Bravo Foxtrot." Behind the lines the heavy artillery pieces sat within their own bunkers, monsters designed to hurl shells long distances. On the Moon, with only one-sixth the gravity, those shells carried a lot less propellant and a lot more warhead. As Stark watched, threat symbology sprang from the artillery sites, heading for the same area as the shuttles were converging upon.

"You know," Sergeant Tran remarked. "If I were one of those enemy soldiers at that spot, I'd wonder what the hell was coming at me."

"That's the idea," Stark noted. "Wiseman, how's it look?"

"Just keep those warships off my tail." Her face seemed oddly flattened under the force of her shuttle's acceleration. On display, the enemy warships were pushing the edge of the Colony's anti-orbital defenses. A few threat symbols detached from the warships, marking desperate attempts to achieve an improbable hit against fleeing targets at maximum range. "Just for the record," Wiseman added, "I really hate accelerating toward the surface of planets and moons. Understood?"

"I assume you're planning on pulling out before you hit."

"Assuming everything works right, yeah. If it doesn't, I'm gonna be real pissed."

And real dead. Stark checked the converging tracks of cargo shuttles, armed shuttles, and artillery. *Okay. Artillery hits first. Saturates the defenses around that location while Wiseman's shuttles sweep in from the front and the cargo shuttles come in from the rear. Any functioning defenses should automatically engage Wiseman's shuttles because they're an incoming target. Defenses should give the cargo shuttles low targeting priority because they're fleeing targets. Hopefully none of the defenders will realize we're planning on that and switch to manual targeting in time. Those cargo shuttles don't have half the survivability of Wiseman's armed shuttles.* "Cross your fingers, Vic."

"And my toes," she assured him.

Enemy defenses began throwing out rounds to intercept the incoming artillery, but Stark's barrage was too big to be stopped. He'd sat under enough artillery barrages himself to know exactly what would happen while those big shells were hitting the enemy line. Exposed sensors and weapons would be shielded and troops would keep their heads as low as possible. In the case of soldiers in bunkers, it was an almost irrational reflex, since any shell penetrating their underground lairs would be certain to kill everyone whether prone or standing fully upright. But sometimes even irrational reflexes made you feel a little better, made it a little easier to handle the thought of tons of explosives falling all around you.

Wiseman's armed shuttles were maneuvering again, putting everything into pulling out of their death dive toward the surface and converting it into a dash straight over the enemy line. The cargo shuttles were also altering course, jinking as madly under the push of their attitude jets as their forward velocity would allow.

Symbology converged. Stark avoided calling up visual of the artillery hitting the enemy positions. He'd seen it happen a thousand times, and derived no joy from thinking of the soldiers cowering under the bombardment. Wiseman's armed shuttles tossed out weapons of their own, and a flurry of countermeasures, as a scattering of enemy defenses tried to engage the fast-moving targets. At the last instant, a few of the enemy shots sought out the cargo shuttles as they and Wiseman's armed shuttles rocketed past each other. Almost instantly, the armed shuttles fired their attitude jets again, then kicked in their main drives, arcing up once more in a high-g maneuver to curve back inside the American defenses as quickly as possible.

Stark realized he hadn't been breathing and took in a long, shuddering breath as the cargo shuttle symbology lunged toward the American defensive line. *Damn. Did we pull this off? Actually get our people out intact?*

"Got a hit," a watchstander announced as alarms sounded. "Shuttle Alpha."

"How bad?"

"Hull rupture, stabilization systems out, got an uncontrolled tumble. The shuttle's close to the deck. She's got no room to recover."

"Oh, man." Nerving himself, Stark called up vid from the shuttle, jerking involuntarily as his vision suddenly filled with wildly tossing images. The impact of the hit and secondary explosions on the shuttle had thrown it off its smooth trajectory.

Lunar terrain littered with rocks zipped past in flashes of gray and white, alternating with the star-sown blackness of space.

"Gutierrez!" Chief Petty Officer Wiseman shouted over the circuit at the shuttle pilot. "You're too low for autorepair to stabilize that pig. Do it manual!"

"R-roger," Gutierrez came back, his voice shaking, as his body was tossed constantly against its restraining harness.

Stark blinked as Vic deliberately broke his vid connection, then toggled another circuit. Now he could see the shuttle from the outside, captured by ground sensors as it cartwheeled over the Moon's surface inside the American perimeter. Apparently random spurts of heat marked firings of the shuttle's stabilizer jets as Gutierrez tried to halt the tumble by feel. "Is it working?" Vic asked.

"Can't tell. Wait." A heavy burst from two stabilizers and the shuttle seemed to shudder in place, the uncontrolled tumble replaced by a ragged corkscrew with the shuttle's nose yawing in a wide circle. "That's one damned good pilot."

"Yeah. But he can't save it. Too low. And too much forward velocity. When it hits—"

Before Reynolds could finish, the forward stabilizers fired again, shoving the shuttle's nose up and on past the vertical so that the shuttle's main drive pointed forward. The main drive roared, its exhaust throwing up swirls of dust from the nearby surface as the shuttle yawed wildly overhead. The shuttle slowed, shaking under the force of deceleration even as it sank closer to the rocky landscape. A moment later, some portion of the shuttle impacted the surface, shedding pieces of hull as the spacecraft bounced back upward, tumbling out of control once again. "Gutierrez!" Wiseman commanded. "You've done everything you can! Eject! Get your crew out of that thing!"

"No! I've got passengers! I can still—"

The pilot's voice cut off as the shuttle hit hard, hurling rocks and fragments of the ship off to either side, rose slightly, then slammed to the Moon's surface again with brutal finality. The shuttle slid across the rough surface, its progress erratic as the crippled craft rebounded off the larger rocks and bounced over the smaller ones. "Medical!" Sergeant Tran was calling into the comm circuit. "Get a full response team to that site as fast as possible."

"On our way," Medical responded instantly.

Tran pointed to the display. "Four ambulances. I'll have more headed there in a minute."

"Good," Stark approved, angered as his voice shook slightly. "Good," he repeated in firmer tones. "And good job having that medical team on alert. Vic, is everybody else okay?"

She scanned the display, chewing her lower lip, then nodded. "Looks like it. The other cargo shuttles are braking for landing, and Wiseman's got her armed shuttles headed back this way. You going to the scene?"

"Yeah." Once again she'd read his mind. Or maybe she just knew him better than anyone else. "Alert my command APC, okay?"

"They'll be waiting."

Stark ran this time, not worried about decorum. Word of the downed shuttle had spread with the impossible speed of any bad news, so no one questioned his dash to the APC dock. Inside the APC, he pulled himself into the command chair and strapped in with one motion. "You've got the crash site?" he asked the driver.

"Yessir."

"Then get me there fast!"

"Yessir." The driver fell silent, concentrating on his driving as the APC surged into motion. Stark sat silent, his eyes not really seeing the display before him where the cargo shuttles were coming to rest on the American Colony's landing field and Wiseman's armed shuttles were braking to shed velocity after safely regaining the protection of the Colony's surface defenses. He tried not to think, not to worry, knowing nothing he thought or imagined could help the soldiers and crew of the crashed shuttle. But, finally, he prayed, briefly and fervently.

The APC came to a halt near the ambulances clustered around the crash site. Stark checked the seals on his own battle armor before cracking the APC's hatch, then pulled himself through onto the lunar surface.

As always, time seemed to suddenly slow down. Stark dropped slowly, his feet landing gently yet still puffing up small clouds of fine gray dust. Small rocks littered the landscape here, interspersed with a few larger boulders, all as jagged as the day they were birthed, without the smoothing effects of an Earth-like environment to round them off. Figures moved around the wreck and the ambulances, bounding with odd grace from point to point. Stark's HUD automatically tagged the figures, some with medical symbols, some as regular infantry, and some as wounded. The medics weren't hard to spot. Unlike the battle armor of the infantry, the medical personnel wore lighter weight outfits that allowed them to better treat wounded while still in their suits. Medics weren't supposed to need armor anyway, since they weren't supposed to be shot at. Sometimes the enemy actually abided by that rule. Most of the time, the medics practiced trying not to get hit while they tended casualties.

Off to one side, a small pile of armored bodies was marked with the ugly symbol that signified the dead.

Stark moved forward, trying to get involved in the rescue and recovery while simultaneously staying out of the way of people who were doing their jobs just fine without his interference. "Doctor Asad. You in charge?"

The figure tagged by his HUD as Asad turned slightly to nod toward Stark. "That's right."

"How bad is it?"

It was impossible to shrug in a suit, but somehow Asad managed to mimic the motion. "Could be worse. You see the dead over there. Not too many. Very few, considering how torn up this shuttle is. Most of the rest just have the usual abrasions, bruises, broken bones, and such. No big deal fixing them up."

Stark took another look at the grouping of the dead, counting them this time, then looking toward the shredded, crumpled wreck of the shuttle. *Only five. Very few is right. Damn miracle is more like it.* "That's amazing."

"Uh huh. Credit the pilot and his crew, I guess. They must have gotten the velocity on that sucker down quite a bit before it hit."

"Where are they?" Stark looked around, vainly searching his HUD for anyone tagged as flight personnel. "The shuttle crew?"

"Where?" Asad nodded again, this time toward the wreck. "In there. The shuttle came to rest on the crew compartment. We haven't been able to pry the bodies out, yet. Too busy taking care of the living. Might need engineers to open it up, anyway." He paused. "I guess they didn't have time to eject the crew compartment. Too bad."

"They had a chance, Doc. They could've ejected."

"Why didn't they?"

"They were trying to save their passengers."

Dr. Asad stood silent for a moment. "They did that. I'll get them out, Sergeant Stark. I'll take real good care of them. Promise."

"Thanks. Do you need anything else? More people, more equipment, more transport?"

"Have you got anything coming to pick up the soldiers who can walk?"

Stark checked his command display before answering. "Sure do. There's some more APCs on the way. Should be here in a few minutes."

"Then we're fine. Everybody who needs help has got it."

"Guess there's nothing else I can do here, then. Good job handling the wounded. You and your people. Tell 'em thanks for me and all the other grunts."

Another impossible suited shrug from Asad. "That's our job. But I'll tell my people. It never hurts to know you're appreciated."

Stark moved slowly back to his APC, turning to look once more at the wrecked shuttle as he reached his transport. *Gutierrez. And your whole damn crew. Thanks for saving those soldiers. I'll make sure you're not forgotten.* He pulled himself into the APC, sealing the hatch then strapping in, moving with the weariness of great age or great responsibility.

A briefing room big enough to accommodate the official planning hierarchy had no trouble holding Stark's small group for their postmortem of the operation. Sergeant Tanaka had explained the old routine to Stark before she'd died in the failed raid on Stark's headquarters. Generals would be holding down the best seats, flanked by senior planners, backed up by assistant planners, supported by junior planners. Standing against the wall would be the action officers who would do any actual work if such was required. Before each officer at the main table a display would offer instant access to any portion of the massive operation plan being developed; annexes, appendices, annexes to appendices, subsections, sub-subsections, and the ever-popular attachments to any and everything. "They tried to print out one of the oplans once," Tanaka had offered. "Some general insisted on it. But headquarters ran out of paper before the print job finished."

"Were you short on paper?" Stark had asked.

"Heck, no. We had a lot of paper. Reams and reams. Just not enough to print out an oplan. I hear oplans used to be a little shorter, back before they went paperless. Now everybody just copies the last one onto their hard drive and adds on to it. There's probably stuff in there about fighting the Brits during the Revolution. Who'd know? Nobody can read the things anymore, and I don't think anybody tries."

Stark shook off the memory of Tanaka, one more face and name gone from this world, and focused back on the present, gesturing toward the image of Lexington Sector floating slightly above the surface of the table. "Okay, you apes. What went right and what'd we do wrong?"

Vic swung one finger slowly along the arc of low elevations studded with defensive symbology that marked the enemy front. "We got our forces in past there and out again. That's a big plus."

"Yeah, but it still cost us a shuttle. We haven't got a lot of those. Gordo." Stark focused on his supply officer, Sergeant Gordasa. "Have we had any luck trying to get more on the black market?"

Gordasa shook his head. "Too expensive, but more to the point, too tightly monitored. Nobody can figure out how to get one to us without being caught." He offered a small smile. "Now, if you'd brought back all that ammunition you blew up, I might've been able to trade that for one."

"Sorry, Gordo. We were too busy to form a work detail." He turned to Sergeant Tran. "Speaking of that ammo, any problems with all the junk it blasted into space? Any of it gonna fall on us once its orbit decays?"

"No," Tran stated. "It was a surface blast, so most of the debris flung upward came from the ammo itself, and that debris was fairly small stuff. A lot of it, but small. Nothing any of our surface installations can't handle. They were built to deal with small impacts."

"Okay. Stacey." Security officer Sergeant Yurivan, leaning backward in her chair as if half-asleep, opened one eye slightly and cocked it toward Stark. "Any reaction from back home?"

Yurivan yawned. "Nope. Of course, the powers that be ain't

telling anyone about this back home. There's a lot of buzz about the explosion, because you couldn't hide the blasted thing from anyone on Earth who was looking this way, but officially its cause remains undetermined."

Reynolds snorted. "How long does the Pentagon and the government think they can stonewall something like that?"

"If they're being stupid, maybe they think a long time. Or long enough to deal with us first and then keep everything classified until the sun burns out, anyway." Stacey Yurivan smiled. "Oh, yeah. Got an unofficial thanks from a couple of civ contractors who you let run away from that landing field. They say they owe us. Could be nice friends to have."

"Could be," Stark agreed. *I guess that's doing well by doing right, or something like that.* "Chief Wiseman, how're you doing?"

His naval commander made a small face, then waved away the question. "I'm okay. You lose people. It happens."

"You lost real good people," Reynolds corrected.

"That's right," Stark agreed. "You sailors all did great, and that shuttle crew . . . well, they did above and beyond. For real. I made a promise, Chief. They'll be remembered."

Wiseman managed a small smile. "Thanks. And if it's any consolation, I bet people'll be studying how we used those shuttles for quite a while. We wrote a new chapter on raiding."

"Good." Stark glanced over at Sergeant Lamont, who was sitting uncharacteristically subdued. "I guess you're still unhappy about losing that tank."

Lamont spread his hands. "They're my babies, Stark. We can salvage the tank from the wrecked shuttle, by the way, but losing even one piece of heavy armor hurts. We can't replace 'em, you know."

"I know. Not unless Gordo manages a black-market buy of a shuttle. Maybe he can smuggle a tank onto it."

"Why not?" Gordasa muttered. "Just ask Supply to do the impossible. No problem. We deal with CDATs all the time."

Lamont chuckled. Back in the twentieth century soldiers had joked about DATs, dumb-ass tankers. As their tanks grew more sophisticated the DATs had become CDATs, computerized dumb-ass tankers. "Gordo, after word gets out on that raid, my boys and girls will be in the CDAT Hall of Fame. You'll feel honored every time you reject a spare parts requisition from us."

Stark smiled briefly. "Mendo." Private Mendoza, his chin resting on both hands as he watched the others speak, jerked slightly in surprise. "What do you think? We blew up a lot of stuff and ruined that enemy general's day, week, month, and year. Big picture, though, was it worth it?"

"I think, Commander Stark . . . " Mendo visibly hesitated for a moment, then spread his hands over the display. "It depends. On the objective. What do we seek?"

"To avoid getting beat," Yurivan drawled.

Stark wondered if Mendoza would be intimidated by Stacey Yurivan's mockery, but the small private shook his head stubbornly. "That is a very limited objective, though a valid one. But is that our objective, Commander Stark? And is it a wise objective?"

"Why wouldn't it be wise?" Stark asked.

Mendoza paused again, gathering his thoughts. "A defensive strategy can work, but it requires time. Time to wear out the enemy. Too, it requires an enemy who cannot corner you, cannot force a decisive battle."

"We're surrounded here," Lamont noted.

"Exactly. The essence of a delaying strategy is to avoid a decisive battle. It is often called a Fabian Strategy after the Roman commander who used it successfully against Hannibal. Since the Romans had lost every time they fought a major engagement with Hannibal, Fabius simply refused to fight such an engagement, always retreating when confronted."

"What kept this Hannibal from just capturing Rome while Fabius ran away?" Reynolds questioned.

"Rome had fixed defenses. Walls. Hannibal lacked the engines of war necessary to breach those walls. Nor could he settle down to attempt to build them while worried about the Roman army operating in his rear. So Hannibal could not win as long as Fabius refused to fight. Operating in hostile territory far from home, Hannibal's army was eventually worn down and forced to retreat."

"Interesting idea," Stark noted. "But it sounds like this Fabius had time on his side. Which we may not. And he could run away when he didn't want to fight. We've got nowhere to run."

"Just so," Mendoza agreed. "We must wait in one location while our opponents muster their forces against us. Aside from tactical adjustments to the perimeter, we must defend the Colony. We have Rome's walls, but we lack an army on the outside able to threaten anyone besieging us."

"We aren't stuck here," Lamont argued. "We left the perimeter to hit that enemy landing field. Why not keep doing that?"

Mendoza shook his head. "Carrying out that raid required use of deception to bypass enemy defenses. Can another raid such as we conducted succeed again?"

"No chance in hell," Reynolds stated. "I'd hate to be the shuttle crew that accidentally lands on the wrong field from now on. They'll get blown away before they can say 'bad mistake.' There may be another way to get past the enemy defenses surrounding us, but I sure can't think of any right now." Some of the others at the table looked uncomfortable at her words, but no one contradicted Reynolds.

"Then we must be prepared to defend against heavy attacks," Mendoza concluded, "and to somehow hold out until our attackers are exhausted."

Stark glanced around at his staff, all of whom were digesting Mendoza's advice with expressions of varied discontent. "What you're not saying, Mendo, is that our attackers basically have the entire resources of Earth to hit us with, and all we've got is what's on this particular patch of the Moon. Right?"

Mendoza nodded. "We can inflict immense losses on our foes, time and again, and still lose eventually." He stopped speaking, obviously pondering his last statement. "Much like the Carthaginians. Hannibal's people. They defeated the Romans over and over again, destroying armies and fleets. The Romans always came back, though."

"Very cheerful," Stacey Yurivan remarked. "But you're leaving out the political aspect of this, aren't you? Just how willing is everyone on Earth to spend their lives and treasure trying to beat us?"

Vic Reynolds nodded. "That's a good point. Our former bosses, the government and Pentagon, want us beat something fierce. But does everyone else? Especially if the cost rises too high."

"Don't forget the corporations who just about own the government," Sergeant Bev Manley advised. She'd been sitting quietly, one eye on the debate, while she tried to catch up on her administrative duties with the other. "On the one hand, they want us beat, too. On the other, pure revenge won't help their profits any. We make the cost of beating us too expensive, and the corporations should want to make a deal with us. Any word on that yet?"

Yurivan shook her head, then glanced sidelong at Stark. "Maybe our boss's civ buddies can clue him in on that. They worked for corporations before we let them kick their bosses off this rock, right?"

"They did," Stark agreed. "And I'll be meeting with the Colony manager and his assistant later today, to brief them on the raid's results. I'll ask what they know about things back on Earth."

His staff exchanged glances, then Manley put into words what the others were obviously thinking. "Are you sure we can trust them, Ethan? I know they've hung with us so far, and that surprised the hell out of me I can tell you, but they've gotta be feeling trapped right now. If the civs get scared they might try to cut a deal that leaves us hanging."

Stark stared back with a confidence he wasn't sure he really felt. "I trust them. Remember, the civs gave us warning about that raid that hit this headquarters. Warning that probably made the difference in keeping us alive. They've also been giving us matériel assistance. They volunteered their medical facilities to help handle our casualties. And some of them are even enlisting. Right, Vic?"

"Right. Damnedest thing I've ever heard of. You should've seen the expression on the face of the corporal the civs asked how to enlist." The military had grown too separate from society as a whole, too isolated from the civilians it had been formed to protect. A closed club, where military families raised children who joined, while civilians looked on with worry at the people who carried weapons and were willing to kill if ordered. Almost as incomprehensible to the Free Lunch Culture, the military were willing to die, if ordered. "I agree with Ethan. I think we can trust these civs. They've been right behind the front lines for years. They know we're here to protect them."

Stacey Yurivan smiled insincerely. "You'd be expected to

agree with Stark, wouldn't you, Reynolds? You being old pals and all."

"I tell it like I see it, Stace."

Sergeant Gordasa cleared his throat. "I have to agree with Stark and Reynolds. I'm working with the civs a lot to get spares and food and stuff since our normal supply routes are closed off. They're trying to get decent deals, sure, but they're not trying to cheat us. They treat me okay, one-on-one. And the stuff coming in is good quality. Hell, the food's better than we're used to. Verdad?"

Everyone around the table nodded. The soldiers had recently actually been able to identify the source of some of the meat in their meals. "Still and all," Manley persisted, "I've got to ask; what do the civs want? For us to keep protecting them, sure. But why? What are they expecting to be able to do while we do all this fighting?"

Everyone looked at Stark, who scowled back. "Last I heard, there was a lot of sentiment in the civ colony for declaring independence from home. They'd become a new country, and I guess that'd make us that new country's military."

"What kinda country?"

"Like the U.S., I guess. Or how it's supposed to be, anyway. All these civs up here got trapped into real bad contracts with their corporations. They were being shafted something fierce, while the corporate bosses were getting richer, as usual. So they don't want that kind of stuff up here."

"There's nothing wrong with capitalism," Stacey observed.

"No, there ain't, except the same thing that's wrong with any system allowed to run without any checks on it. That's what the government's supposed to do, not be in bed with the bosses, right?"

"The Constitution is sort of silent on that."

" 'Provide for the general welfare,' " Vic recited. "I think that covers it. Fine. Let's assume these civs declare independence and form their own country and even adopt the exact same Constitution we're sworn to protect. How comfortable is everybody with that?"

There was a long silence, finally broken by grumbling from Manley. "We're Americans, damnit. I don't want to be anything else."

"Me, neither," Stark agreed. "But the people running our country don't like us much. We may not have any choice about becoming something else."

Yurivan looked up, grinning suddenly. "That's an angle. The government's been putting out word that we're all criminals and troublemakers, out for anything we can get."

"Good thing none of us fit that description, huh, Stace?"

"If I may finish without further heckling, we haven't had much propaganda of our own to counter that. But we can get word around back home that we're loyal and true-blue and one hundred percent and all, and the only reason we're in trouble is because the bosses don't want us because we kicked out other bosses who were idiots. It could stir up some trouble at home. Maybe get some pressure off us."

Reynolds smiled. "That's a good idea. The civs running the Colony tell us the two major political parties are really running scared that they'll be kicked out of power. If we get word out on what we really feel, that might help that thing happen."

"It might. But these other guys, these political parties that want to clean things up, might not like us any better than the current crop of crooks. Who knows?"

"Campbell might," Stark noted. "The Colony manager. Like I said, Vic and I have a meeting with him later. I'll sound him out on that. Are there any other issues we should deal with here?"

Lamont grinned. "Let's see, we've talked about what our main strategy should be, whether we want to belong to another country, and how good the food is lately. What's left?"

"Locating a replacement shuttle," Gordasa noted, then shook his head in mock despair. "I'll take care of that, and you guys can handle the easy stuff."

Stark laughed along with the others, motioning for everyone to leave, but paused himself as Vic placed a restraining hand on his arm. "Sergeant Milheim. He just made it in. You want him to hang around and provide you with individual feedback or just put it in a report?"

"If he puts it in a report, I'd never find time to read it. Besides, if I call somebody to see me, the least I can do is actually take some time for them once they get here. You can head out, though."

"No problem." Vic left, motioning Milheim in through the door.

"Sorry I didn't make the meeting," Milheim began.

"Don't worry about it," Stark waved away any further apology. "Your people did real good out there. Did you notice any problems with the operation?"

Milheim hesitated, frowning in thought. "No. Nothing comes to mind. I will tell you it was nice not having that damned timeline blinking at us."

"Yeah. I don't think we're gonna use them much anymore. Not to govern individual movements, anyway. You gotta have a coordinated timeline when you're working together, but having one just so people will jump through hoops when the planners wanted them to never did make all that much sense."

"That reminds me, speaking of the old days, it was also nice knowing our action wasn't being broadcast as a vid entertainment. We were all sick of that."

"Damn right," Stark agreed. When the Pentagon had needed to raise large sums of money to fund the lunar operation, some unsung SOB had realized they could use the audio and video feeds from soldiers' command and control equipment to fashion almost-real-time programs for commercial broadcast. Programs that quickly became popular enough to earn a good chunk of advertising revenue. For a time, the need for high vid ratings had played at least as large a role in military operations as the desire for victory. "That'll never happen again. Not if we have any say in it. What about us, though, back here? Were we on your shoulder too much? Was there something we shoulda been doin' that we didn't?"

Milheim shrugged. "You seemed pretty transparent, truth to tell. I kept looking over my own shoulder wondering what was missing, and realizing I didn't have some bozo back at headquarters telling me to take one step left instead of one step right. I liked you keeping an eye on the big picture. That was a good call focusing on the warehouses, and I appreciated being asked my opinion based on my feeling of the scene. No complaints, I guess."

Stark gazed at Milheim, chewing his lip while he chose the right words. "Look, no offense, but I don't know you very well. Good reputation and all that, and you handle your unit real well.

But I don't know if you're the kind of guy who'd tell me to my face if I'd screwed something up. Would you?"

Milheim didn't have to feign indignation. "I look out for my people. If you were doing something that'd mess them over, I'd let you know."

"Good. I knew you took care of your troops. That's why they put you in charge of your battalion, right? Because they trusted you."

"Yeah. Lucky me. At least I didn't get put in charge of the whole shebang like you did."

"Hey, it's not so bad." Stark grinned with obvious self-mockery. "Maybe someday you'll take it over from me."

"No, thanks."

"I'll buy you a beer."

Milheim laughed. "You couldn't get me drunk enough to say yes to that proposition."

"Now, that sounds familiar. I think I've heard it on every date I've ever been on."

Another laugh. "I didn't think you had to worry about dating. Everybody knows about you and Vic Reynolds."

Stark blew out his breath in exasperation. "Everybody but me and Reynolds, you mean. I wouldn't have made her my second in command if we were involved like that. That'd just have been asking for trouble. And it wouldn't have been right. We're tight, Milheim, but not that way."

"Really? How come?"

"I dunno. Just the way it works, I guess. You got a steady girl?"

Milheim smiled. "Nope. My wife would frown on that. Wives get touchy about that sorta thing."

"I'd heard that. Kids?"

"Yeah. They're all up here, thanks to that swap we worked out, trading our old officers for our family members. Come by the quarters sometime and I'll introduce you."

"How are those quarters, anyway?" With the arrival of military families, the Colony had voluntarily begun excavating a large bloc of new residential construction for the creation of an ad hoc 'fort.' "I haven't had much time to check on 'em, and I know they're being built without much in the way of frills."

"They're okay," Milheim temporized. "It doesn't take much

to equal the sort of base housing we're used to, does it? But the kids love the low gravity. They're bouncing off the walls. Literally. Like I said, come by and see it sometime."

"Thanks. When I get the time, I'll be sure to take you up on that."

"When you get the time? I guess it'll be a while, then, won't it?" Milheim sobered abruptly, his mouth tight. "Damn."

"What's wrong?"

"Talking about family. It reminded me, I got to write some letters. You know. To the families of the soldiers we lost on the raid." Milheim closed his eyes for a moment. "One of them had her family up here. Guess I got to tell them personally."

"We got chaplains for that."

"I've still gotta go."

"I know, but you go along with a chaplain." Stark lowered his voice pitch slightly to emphasize his words. "That's an order. You don't need to take that kind of burden all on yourself."

"Umm, okay. Thanks."

"Don't thank me. I gave the orders that sent those soldiers on the raid. I oughta talk to a chaplain, too." *But I won't, because there's nobody to order me to do it, and I'm too damn stubborn.* "How about your wounded? Where're they located in medical?" Stark didn't bother asking if Milheim knew the locations of his casualties, or whether he'd already visited them. He already knew enough about the man to be certain of both items.

"They're in a couple of different bays. Eight Charlie and Ten Delta. Most of them got patched up and sent to their quarters already."

"Good. I'll drop by, too. You need any time off?"

"No. No. I'll do better if I'm working. Besides, I oughta be used to this by now, huh?"

"Milheim, I hope to God neither one of us ever gets used to it."

Colony Manager James Campbell and his executive director, Cheryl Sarafina, were already waiting when Stark and Reynolds arrived at the manager's office. Burrowed out of the lunar surface, like so much else of the Colony, it offered the comforting presence of solid rock walls on all sides and a very thick covering of metal, rock, and dust for a roof. On one wall, a vid screen displayed the view Campbell's office might have had were it located on the surface—black shadow, gray rock, and white light running off to a too-close horizon that gave way to the unending lunar night sky. Campbell had been frugal enough or politically astute enough to equip his office with standard lunar fixtures, lightweight metal desks, tables, and chairs. The office offered no luxury and, at the moment, little comfort for its occupants. "Thank you for coming here for this meeting," Campbell began. "I needed to stay close to the office today."

"That's okay," Stark replied. "Besides, it wouldn't be right for the civ bosses to come to the mil leaders all the time, would it? I work for you."

"Yes." Campbell shook his head, then laughed. "You hold the power to control this Colony, Sergeant. Tell me again why you work for me."

Stark looked offended. "Sir. You're the elected representative of the people here. I work for the people. So I work for you. That's how it's supposed to work."

"So it is. Speaking of which . . ." Campbell nodded in the general direction of the enemy landing field Stark's troops had raided. "I assume the seismic event the Colony recently felt was related to the attack you had previously forewarned me of?"

"That's right."

"I'm afraid that seismic event caught us by surprise. We weren't expecting anything of that magnitude."

"Neither were we. They had more ammunition stockpiled there than we thought. A lot more."

Sarafina frowned. "Are you certain, Sergeant Stark, given the size of the explosive event, that it only involved conventional weaponry? Could any other weapons have been stored there?"

Stark frowned in turn, glancing at Vic, who shrugged as she answered. "I'd seriously doubt it. Mainly because the American authorities wouldn't be eager to leave weapons of mass destruction under the control of a foreign power. But it doesn't hurt to check." She hauled out her comm pad. "Command Center, this is Sergeant Reynolds. Have we done any analysis of the debris from the explosion we triggered?"

"The big one?" a watchstander replied. "Yes, Sergeant. That's standard procedure."

"Are there any indications anything other than conventional explosives were involved?"

"No. There's no fallout registering. We'd have been able to spot the presence of extraneous nuclear material if it'd been blown up with everything else. No null-particle transients detected, either. Everything's consistent with standard explosive and weapons composition, mixed in with a lot of pulverized lunar material, of course."

"Thanks." Reynolds pocketed the device. "Just standard explosives. Bad enough if you're close, but nothing worse than that."

"Good." Sarafina pointed upward. "Our spaceport tracked a great deal of activity during your . . . your . . . action. Warships and shuttles. We weren't expecting that."

Stark shifted in discomfort. "Yeah, well, that was part of our plan, but we didn't want to brief that part because if anything had gotten out, well . . ."

Campbell shook his head, his face stern. "I'm sorry, Sergeant, but in the future you must let us know that kind of detail. My civilians run the spaceport. I won't share anything with them that you tell me to hold in confidence, but I need to know what's happening when they report unusual activity so I can keep them from doing the wrong thing. Do you see that?"

"Yes. Yessir, I do. That makes sense."

"I understand why you didn't trust us with that information, Sergeant, but we need to overcome that legacy of distrust."

Even as Stark was nodding, Vic spoke up. "Speaking of distrust, our soldiers are wondering what the civilians in the Colony intend to do. We know sentiment is very much against the authorities back on Earth, but what are you planning on doing about it?"

Campbell sighed. "It increasingly appears we may have no alternative but to declare our independence. Make a clean break of it and establish our own country."

"As one of our soldiers asked, what kind of country?"

Campbell and Sarafina looked at each other, obviously startled by the question. "Why . . . I suppose the kind of country the United States is meant to be. A democracy. Freedom for individuals. And enough limits on sources of power, public and private, to ensure we retain freedom."

"So you're planning on adopting the U.S. Constitution as your governing document?"

"Ah . . ." Campbell glanced helplessly toward Sarafina, who spread her hands in an equally distressed gesture. "I suppose that would be the model. We might want to tinker with it, but, uh, to be perfectly honest, I don't think anyone's given much thought to that question as of yet."

"We have," Stark advised. "You're talking about the reason for us fighting. I'll tell you honestly, my people won't support a dictatorship, no matter how it's dressed up. They might accept a government built around the Constitution, but they're still not thrilled about it."

Campbell stared back as if now perplexed. "Then what do they want?"

Stark exhaled a brief, humorless laugh. "They want things the way they're supposed to be, with us taking orders from the Pentagon, which takes orders from the government, which takes orders from the people. But they know with the way things are, that's probably not going to happen."

"I see." Campbell held up a hand as Stark began to continue. "I do. Quite honestly. It was easy to think about and talk about independence when the concept was far off in time and practicality. But the closer we've come to being able to form our own country, the less happy I am. We ought to have an alternative, for heaven's sake. We ought to have a means to have our problems addressed by our government instead of being on the receiving end of constant threats and orders to do what we're told, or else."

"I take it negotiations aren't going well?" Vic asked.

Campbell made a face, using one hand to indicate Sarafina, as she shook her head. "No progress at all. We've been in almost constant touch, sent out a lot of feelers for different ways to resolve the issues in dispute, and host regular parties of official negotiators, but we're getting no meaningful replies."

Stark shook his head in turn, not trying to hide his disgust. "The government still won't talk to us?"

"Oh, they'll talk. They'll talk until the sun goes nova. But, as I said, they offer nothing except the standard orders to submit to lawful authority this instant if not sooner."

Sarafina gestured toward the ceiling. "There's no question our parent corporations on Earth are very much behind this. They're insisting that the politicians they paid for make every effort to recover their property up here, and they're backing up those demands with what they call 'patriotic contributions' to help pay for the military options being employed against the Colony."

"You're kidding. The same corporations that avoided paying taxes to support us when we were protecting them are willing to pony up extra bucks to attack us? Am I the only one who thinks that's dumber than dirt?"

"It makes sense up to point. The point at which projected losses begin to exceed projected gains. The corporations would not fund this sort of activity forever given that profit-loss equation, but they also must factor in some noneconomic issues in their decisions."

"Such as?" Vic asked.

"Such as the fact that the corporations have invested heavily in the current occupants of the Congress and the White House. As we have discussed before, loss of the Moon Colony prior to the upcoming election might well result in loss of control of the government by those politicians in the pay of the corporations. Obviously, this would create any number of negative consequences for the corporations."

Campbell pointed vaguely upward, toward Earth, as well. "Don't forget the politicians have their own motivations. At the very least, they have to spin whatever happens as a victory to the electorate. The economy back home continues to sink deeper into recession, apparently due to a combination of the shock of losing the corporate assets up here and the results of all the money being diverted to the effort to defeat this Colony. Or rather to defeat your forces, to give credit where it's due. The government is making a mighty effort to limit information about us to whatever the government wants people to know, but it isn't working."

He stopped speaking for a moment, pondering his next words. "People will put up with a great deal as long as they think the people running things know what they're doing. If they lose that confidence, they start asking awkward questions about many things. There have been demonstrations. Large ones. Officially, those demonstrations involve some sort of un-American radical fringe. Our own information indicates they have consisted primarily of middle-class and blue-collar workers who are, to put it bluntly, fed up."

Vic sketched a small smile. "I'm afraid Ethan Stark appears to have a nasty habit of triggering revolutions."

"It doesn't appear to be heading toward revolution. Certainly not armed revolution. It may all fizzle out, especially if the economy improves a little. But the government has to produce a significant victory up here to have any hopes of justifying its policies toward us to date. If anything, the corporations are more likely to cry uncle when the bottom line suffers enough. Changes of policy are no big deal to them. But the government is another story."

Stark nodded, this time wearily. "They won't quit trying to win, no matter how much it costs everybody else. Will the election back home come in time to make a difference?"

"It's hard to say," Sarafina admitted. "More to the point, there's increasing pressure within the Colony to hold a referendum on independence as soon as possible, and if the sentiment for independence prevails, to announce the result immediately, without waiting any longer in the hope that the national election will make a difference. People are tired of waiting."

"And we're tired of fighting. So what's the time frame here? When would this referendum be held?"

Campbell and Sarafina exchanged looks again. "Potentially within a few weeks," the Colony manager stated. "Any longer than that would require me to actively stall the measure, and quite frankly I've had it up to here with our government."

"You're not alone in that. My old man was fed up with 'em years ago."

"One additional thing concerns us," Sarafina added. "So far the military attacks on us have been . . . what is the right word?"

"Conventional?"

"Yes. That's it. No weapons of mass destruction. There have been software intrusion attempts to destroy our automated infrastructure, but they have all been frustrated. We worry, however, what the response will be if we declare independence? What weapons might the authorities use against us then?"

"They're not going to use nukes or null bombs," Vic advised. "Too much fallout, in every sense of the word. Besides, destroying what's here would defeat us, but wouldn't be a victory for the authorities. They'd have lost the Colony and everything associated with it. That said . . ." She looked over at Stark. "We're a bit worried about what might be coming, too."

"That's right," Stark agreed. "The basic situation when this started hasn't changed. Thanks to a long period of downsizing, and generals and admirals who constantly cut force levels to pay for their latest pet weapons, the military doesn't have enough war-fighters. We were stretched to the max prior to all this, but since then the Pentagon has lost Third Division to sheer stupidity and our First Division up here. That only leaves Second Division to keep our enemies in line, as well as our 'friends' and 'allies', and protect the U.S. from any kind of ground incursion. That doesn't leave any soldiers to try to pry us out of here."

"So, they've been hiring mercenaries and cutting deals with foreign forces," Vic continued. "That hasn't worked. Sooner or later, they'll try something else, and we don't know what that might be."

Campbell frowned. "Surely you can guess what sort of method might be employed."

"Mr. Campbell, if the powers that be were going to do something smart, then yes, I could hazard a pretty good guess. But the powers that be don't have a very good track record when it comes to the concept of 'smart.' If they go the stupid option, every possible card is on the table. Except the nukes and nulls, of course. That'd be above and beyond stupid."

"I've learned not to underestimate the stupidity of some people, but I'll accept your assessment because I simply don't have anything else to go with." Now Campbell looked pained, sharing another look with Sarafina. "My executive assistant and I aren't at all sure about the wisdom of the course we're following, but events don't always allow time for careful evaluation, and circumstances often don't allow every possible option."

It was Stark's turn to frown. He stared toward the floor for a moment as he once again experienced that falling-off-a-cliff feeling, the sense that he was being carried along with events instead of making his own decisions. *And I like making my own decisions. They're not always the right ones, God knows, but at least they're mine.* He looked back at the two civilians and at Vic Reynolds, all of them displaying curiously similar attitudes, as if whatever happened in the future would be something to be endured rather than something to be controlled. None of them seemed any happier with that idea that Stark felt. *There's got to be another way of looking at this. I tried to promise myself, don't get trapped in a sea of bad options. Plan ahead, look ahead. But I'm damned if I can see anything else to do.*

Outside the office, Stark waved Reynolds onward. "You go on back to headquarters if you want."

"What if I don't want?" She raised one eyebrow. "Where are you going?"

"Medical. I oughta visit the wounded from our raid."

"Just them? No one else?"

Stark closed his eyes. "You know damned well there's someone else."

She gripped his shoulder for a moment. "I'm not trying to needle you, Ethan. Just snap out of the denial. I'm glad you're going to check on Murphy, but you and I have both seen the reports. He's still out, and he shouldn't be. But we'll do everything we can. Just don't tear yourself apart over it."

"He's mine, Vic." Stark had come to the Moon commanding his own squad, twelve soldiers who were his personal responsibility. Some of those soldiers had died pretty early. Some had died recently. Murphy had been with the squad a long time. Not a great soldier. More of an easygoing, I'll-get-the-job-done-if-I-have-to sort of guy. Stark had been forced to leave that squad when his fellow noncommissioned officers voted him into command of the entire rebellious military force, but his heart had stayed with those few soldiers. "Maybe if I'd done something different—."

"Ethan, knock it off. You kept that boy alive through a dozen operations. If he pulls through now, that'll be thanks in great part to you as well. Save your guilt for something you couldn't have helped."

Stark glared back at her. "Thanks for the kind words."

"You don't need kind words. You need someone to tell you when you're being an idiot." Vic grinned. "That's me."

Stark managed somehow to smile slightly in return. "And you do it well, soldier. Thanks."

" 'Thanks,' he says. Say hi to Murphy for me."

"I will."

• • •

Medical always felt hushed, always quiet, even after an attack
when doctors and nurses were rushing frantically to save casualties, even when a variety of equipment hummed and roared as
part of that effort. Stark braced himself, then walked down the
hall past the reception desk, his gliding, low-gravity steps even
quieter than usual.

The wounded from Fourth Battalion were still where Milheim
had reported. Even the medical science of the twenty-first century couldn't repair damaged organs, muscles, and bone in a day.
But they were closing in on that goal. The main limit seemed to
be the inability of the human body to absorb accelerated healing
at the same time as it was weakened by the damage that required
the healing.

Everyone perked up at Stark's arrival, managing to broadcast
cheer despite haggard, pale faces. *And why not? If you make it to
medical nowadays, you're gonna live. You're going to be put
back together. Why not be happy about that?* Stark shook hands,
clapped backs (gently), asked about families, praised their unit
and their performance in battle, and in general did all the things
soldiers needed when they were still in giddy shock from a brush
with death.

But when he came to the last wounded soldier, he sat silently
by his bed. The soldier remained sedated, hooked up to machines
that kept him alive, while other machines and his own system
worked to repair damage that would have surely killed the man a
few decades earlier. A few patches of pale skin showed among
the surgical coverings, the plates where machine joined human,
and a few articles of clothing artfully arranged to provide the soldier some modesty. Stark squinted at the chart displayed near the
bed, filled with medical terms he couldn't understand, watching
the tracks of pulse and respiration flow by uninterrupted. *If he
did wake up, right now, what would I say? What would be enough
and not too much?* Finally he whispered "good luck, soldier,"
and headed for another area of medical, where another casualty
awaited him.

Private Murphy had a small room to himself, sectioned off
with lightweight panels. The machines around him hummed and
blinked, reassuring in their steady rhythm. He lay flat on his
back, eyes closed, looking absurdly healthy. Only someone who
knew him as well as Stark could have spotted the thinness of the

skin over Murphy's cheeks, a small sign of the stress his body had recently endured.

At the foot of the bed, holding the status display in one hand, stood a familiar figure. Stark cleared his throat, drawing her attention. "Hi, Doc."

The tired-eyed medic turned, quirking a small smile of welcome. "Welcome back, Sergeant. I can't seem to get rid of you."

"Sorry. But I gotta . . . you know."

She nodded. "Visit the wounded. Of course. When the generals came through here they used to have vid photographers recording the event. I guess that's not your speed, though."

"Hell, no. I already dropped in on the new ones, and now I wanted to see how Murphy was doing." Stark let his anguish show for just a moment. "What's wrong with him?"

"Nothing." The medic rubbed her cheeks with her palms, gazing at Murphy bleakly. "We call it half-life. That's just a nickname. The real term is some big medical phrase, but it adds up to a person who's been fixed up so everything should work, but the body doesn't seem to believe it. It's like we've got something inside that knows how much hurt our body has taken, and after a certain point it decides the game's over."

"I don't get it. He's healthy?"

"Sort of. Like I said, all his organs are functional. But if we shut off the life-support gear they'll fail anyway. Not because they're broken but because they apparently think they're broken."

"Is he—? I mean, you talk like you've seen this before. Any chance Murph will come out of it?"

The medic smiled sadly. Even as she spoke, Stark wondered briefly if she'd ever looked anything but tired and sad. "Any chance? Yeah. Some do. Maybe after a few days. Maybe after a few years. But maybe never. At some point, the relatives have to decide whether to pull the plug. Has the kid got relatives up here?"

Stark shook his head. "Nah. Just me, I guess."

"He could do worse." She paused, staring at Murphy with hooded eyes. "You know, even if he does come out of it, he may not be the same guy. He's been as close to being dead permanent as a human can get. It's not easy on someone."

"I guess not." Stark motioned cautiously toward Murphy, as if afraid to disturb him. "Is it okay if I talk to him?"

"You're the boss. You can do anything you want. It can't hurt."

"Can he hear me?"

"I don't know. Assume he can. I saw a case like this once where the girl's boyfriend showed up and she smiled. Dead to the world, but she smiled." The medic motioned toward Murphy's still form. "He got a girl?"

"Had one. She died during the action that put Murphy in here."

"Tough break. She in the same outfit?"

"Nah. She wasn't mil. She was civ. A colonist."

"Civilian?" The medic's eyes widened in amazement, then focused back on Murphy. "Well, that's a new one on me. Your boy looks mil all the way. That always scares off civs."

"These civs are different. They care about us. We ain't just an exciting vid show for them."

"Yeah. I've seen some of that. Like the way the civ doctors have helped out with our casualties. But, still . . ." The medic's voice trailed off. "Tough break. Real tough." She stepped backward. "I'll leave you alone for a few minutes."

"Thanks." Stark hesitated, then looked directly at the medic. "That girl you just mentioned. The one who knew her boyfriend had stopped by. She ever wake up?"

"No. But she knew she hadn't been forgotten."

Stark walked gingerly toward the hospital bed, then sat carefully, staring for a moment at Murphy's face, the slack expression and closed eyes so similar to those of an exhausted soldier enjoying a deep sleep. "Hey, Murph." He reached into a pocket, extracting a small figurine with a goofy smile. "I dunno if you ever saw this, but it was Robin's. It's called a paca. Just some dumb mascot thing that all the civ women bought years ago. She got it from her mother. My mom has one, too. Small world, huh? Anyway, it meant somethin' to Robin, so I figure it'll mean somethin' to you." He balanced the paca carefully on the nearest table, the figurine's idiot grin focused on Murphy's face.

Stark licked his lips, composing his thoughts before speaking again. "Look, I know I've always told you what to do and usually how to do it, right, Murph? But I can't do that now. I've got no right to. You gotta decide this, if you still can. You're a good kid, led a good life, stuck up for your friends. If you figure you've served a full tour here and it's time to head for a new assignment, well, that's your right. I know you got a lot of friends waiting. Hope so, anyway."

"But if you want to fight a little longer, if you wanta come back, I'll be here. I'll help any way I can. I wish I could do more. I wish I knew for sure what you wanted." Murphy's face didn't alter, except for the slow, even movements caused by his breathing. "Just like everything else in life, I guess. Just gotta do whatever we think is best and hope it's right." He touched one arm gently, as if afraid the limb would break under a firmer pressure. "Get your rest, soldier."

Stark stood as quietly as he could, as if Murphy were merely sleeping and shouldn't be disturbed, then walked carefully to where the medic had waited at a respectful distance.

"Any luck?" she asked, her voice hushed.

"No. You didn't expect me to have any, did you?"

"No. But miracles happen sometimes. If I didn't believe in the occasional miracle, there's a lot of times I'd just throw up my hands and give up. Instead, I keep trying, even when common sense says there's no hope."

Stark fashioned a crooked half-smile. "That's people, ain't it? We just keep trying. Maybe we're just stubborn. Doc?"

"Yes?"

"You think there's someplace else? You know, Heaven or whatever? A better place?"

"I sure hope so. The only ones who know for sure can't talk about it to us."

"Yeah." Stark brooded, his eyes still fixed on Murphy. "I wonder, though. If we think there's a great place waiting for us, and all those people who're gone now are waiting there, too, how come we fight so hard to stay alive? How come we don't give up? How come we fix up sick and injured people instead of lettin' 'em die and go there?"

"Maybe because we don't know, and can't know, for sure. Maybe because people always hate change, even good change. Maybe just because we don't want to leave behind the people and places in this world. Or maybe whoever's running things designed humans to want to stay here as long as possible."

"That'd fit, wouldn't it? But why would anyone make humans want to stay here where it's so easy to make bad choices, where people can get hurt and can hurt other people? That seems kinda cruel. Why do that? What's the point in making us stay here as long as we can?"

"Maybe we're supposed to be learning something while we're here."

Stark stood silent for a moment, then nodded. "Huh. Makes sense. It sounds like you've thought about it."

"You watch enough people die and it sort of comes naturally."

"Let me know if anything changes, okay?"

"Sure. I'll keep an eye on him."

Stark walked slowly away, glancing back just before the curtain fell to block his view. The medic stood beside Murphy's bed, hands resting on the grab rail, her shoulders bent as if under a burden, her head lowered. Somehow Stark knew her eyes would be even wearier than usual.

Artillery dropped shells all around as small arms fire raked the exposed position occupied by the dwindling force of American troops. Private Ethan Stark, clinging to the dirt as if he could somehow will himself beneath it for protection, shuddered in time to the almost constant vibrations of explosions. Before his eyes, battered stalks of grass trembled, their torn stems spotted with blood.

The soldier to Stark's right turned her head, looking straight at him. Corporal Stein, Stark's mentor and the closest he'd ever had to a big sister. But she was glaring in anger now, not at the enemy, but at him. "You really screwed up this time, didn't you, Stark?" Somehow the words came to him clearly despite the thunder of battle.

"Kate? Whadayya mean? How'd I screw up?"

"You led us here, didn't you? Trapped us here."

Stark, already severely stressed by combat, wanted to scream in frustration at the unfairness of the accusation. "I'm not in charge, damnit! This isn't my fault!" Something was wrong. Stark gazed outward, where the tree line from which the enemy had been firing had somehow vanished, been replaced by barren ridges. The grass before him was gone, too, replaced by jagged rocks bearing the same blood. "Kate? What the hell . . . ?" He looked back at her, unable to finish his question.

"We trusted you, Stark. And you led us here. And now we can't even try to run." Stein gestured, indicating her lower body.

Stark stared, sickened, as he suddenly saw her legs were gone, blasted away by one of the incoming shells. He jerked his head, looking away, and found himself facing another soldier to his left. This one lay facedown, within easy reach, but unmoving. As if of its own will, Stark's hand moved to shake the soldier. The body lolled, limp, but the soldier's head flopped to the side. Private Murphy. Still alive. Stark could feel his breath against his hand. But his eyes, his face, were vacant and empty. "You're not dead!" Stark shouted. "You're not—."

He came awake, pulse pounding, his body still shaking from the memory of battle. *Patterson's Knoll. I've refought that damned battle damn near every night since it ended. It was bad enough all those times, but now it's getting worse.* He sat up, rubbing his face, calming his breathing. Major Patterson had led two companies of soldiers too far ahead of everyone else and learned too late that the enemy had more troops and more equipment than expected. Instead of retreating, he led his soldiers to an exposed hill and dithered there, until they were surrounded and slowly pounded to pieces. Stark had been one of three soldiers to survive, by escaping through the enemy lines that night. He'd left behind a lot of dead friends, including Kate Stein.

So now I get to dream of it being my fault. Of being responsible for it all. It's all getting jumbled up. Patterson's Knoll and here. The dead there. The people counting on me here. What the hell am I gonna do?

He thought about Kate Stein briefly, about the lessons in survival she'd taught new soldier Ethan Stark, about what she might advise now. But that led to thoughts of her brother, Grant. The soldier who'd come up here pretending to idolize Stark and had ended up betraying Stark and his troops in a misguided act of revenge. The soldier who'd been court-martialed for that at Stark's orders and executed by a firing squad after Stark had confirmed the court-martial's sentence. *Wherever you are, Kate, I can understand if you hate me now. But I didn't have any real choice. Maybe if you'd still been around when that idiot Grant was growing up, he'd have learned something good from you like I did.*

Stark stood, trying to shove all memory of the old battle and the Steins from his mind. He knew sleep wouldn't come again this night and didn't like the idea of sitting alone in his quarters staring into the darkness. After a long moment, Stark opened the door and headed for the nearest recreation room.

At this hour the small room was empty, of course, the utilitarian metal chairs all vacant. It always took awhile for someone new to the Moon to accept the apparently spindly construction of those chairs. In a typical, but in this case justified, act of economy, the chairs had been built with just enough metal to support a human's weight in gravity one-sixth that of Earth.

Stark grabbed a cup of coffee and sat at one of the small tables. Before him, the built-in display showed a screen saver that painted blackness with splotches of color, like the lights that showed behind closed eyes. Stark gazed morosely at the light display, imagining shapes in the glowing blotches.

Trapped. Yeah, we're trapped. I mean, pity the fools who try to take us, but we can't run. Sooner or later, if they keep hitting us, we'll lose. I've never been that good at math, but I know how battles add up. It doesn't matter how many you've won. As soon as you add in the battle you just lost, it all comes to zero. The victories don't count, then. Just like killing enemies. Kill the first hundred, great. But if the next one kills you, what was the point?

Stark's meandering thoughts settled on that last question. *Reminds me of something. Some guys who stood and died. Who? Where? A face came to mind. Rash Paratnam? He's still alive, thank God. But he told me once about some guys. What was the name? Something like Sports. Spartans. Yeah. Some battle where they stood and fought to the last. Why the hell'd they do that, anyway?*

The answer might not matter at all, but at least finding it would be a diversion from bad dreams and other questions whose answers couldn't be looked up. Rousing himself, Stark activated the display, searching for the battle his friend had once described. *This must be it. Thermopylae.* He read the description, grew intrigued enough to call up the background, then the longer-term results. An hour passed.

Stark had been given the Colony manager's private number, and he used it now. After several rings, Campbell answered, gazing bleary-eyed and disheveled into the screen. "Sergeant Stark? Is there an emergency?"

"No. Not an emergency. There's something I wanted to talk to you about."

Campbell squinted toward the corner of his own screen where the time would be displayed. "Sergeant, you're not much for following normal sleep patterns, are you?"

"Uh, I guess not, sir. Too many nights on duty, I guess. Listen, you ever hear of some guys named Spartans?"

"Spartans? Of course. Ancient Greece, correct?"

"That's right. Well, they fought a battle once at some place I can't pronounce. Thermo something. There were only a hundred of them, sent to stop an invading army."

Campbell shook his head as if trying to shake his thoughts into order. "That would have been the Persians, if I recall right."

"Yeah. Anyway, these Spartans held for a while. Those were their orders. Hold the position. But the Persians had a huge army. So eventually they surrounded the Spartans and killed them all." Stark moved his finger as if pointing to text no longer displayed. "They could've run, but they didn't. They'd been ordered to hold. They stayed and died."

"It was certainly a noble sacrifice, Sergeant Stark, but what—?"

Stark looked upward, seeking the right words. "But it was more than that. All the different Greeks fought a lot with each other. Cities, I guess. So even though this big Persian army was coming, the Greeks weren't cooperating well. But those hundred Spartans changed that. They didn't just buy a little time. What they did was give all the Greeks a symbol. See, they didn't die for themselves. They knew even if the Persians got beat that they'd still be dead. And they could've hung back in their part of Greece and just tried to protect their own territory. But they died protecting everybody. They became a symbol. Something for all the Greeks to rally around."

Campbell nodded, clearly puzzled. "Yes, that would have been important. But why is this old battle important now?"

"Because it tells us something, Mr. Campbell." Stark leaned toward the screen to emphasize his next words. "Something about making good things happen. I'm going to ask you a favor, sir."

"What's that?"

"This vote on declaring independence. I want you to postpone it."

"What?" Campbell shook his head again, as if testing his hearing this time. "Postpone the referendum on independence? Why?"

Stark hesitated, once again searching for the words he needed. "Because we can leave the U.S. and get away with it for at least a while. I mean, the Colony is pretty well off, now that it's not being sucked dry by the corporations back home and by the extra taxes you civs had to pay because you weren't allowed to elect your own representatives to help protect you from that kind of nonsense. Hell, you're rich in resources and specialized manufacturing plants, right? And my troops can protect this Colony for a while. Maybe forever. But we'd be cutting and running, wouldn't we? Taking what we could get and leaving all the ordinary civs back home stuck with the same corrupt politicians and corrupted system."

"You're saying we should stick with a country which is doing everything it can to intimidate, coerce, and oppress us? Why?" Campbell repeated, this time more forcefully.

"There's two things you can do when something's broke, sir. You can throw it away, or you can try to fix it. I know, it seems like the attitude has always been to throw it away. But it couldn't have always been like that." Stark paused, remembering another point. "I've got parents back home still. Civs, like you. I still remember being a know-it-all teenager, being embarrassed by them. But, you know, they were, they are, decent people who want to do the right thing. Most civs are, I guess. Like most mil, too. They've just been convinced that nothing they do can change things. Maybe if they have an example of people who keep trying to change things for the better even when those people could just cut and run and be pretty well set, maybe they'd try, too. And if enough of them decide to try, what happens to the system?"

"You're saying we should stick with the U.S. as an example to everyone else, that by committing ourselves to fix the system we'll inspire others to try? That's a noble sentiment, Sergeant, but I'm not sure it would be responsible of me to make it policy.

I have to think of the people of this Colony. You're asking a lot of them."

"Sir, with all due respect, my people are dying every day to defend the Colony. I'm not asking your people to face that kind of thing. I'm just asking them to stand up and say 'we're not running even though we could.'"

Campbell's expression had closed down at Stark's last words, giving no clue to his inner thoughts. "I appreciate your sacrifices, Sergeant. We all do. But you do realize a declaration of independence would benefit your soldiers as well. As our own country, we can make peace with some or all of the enemy alliance which has been at war with us since this Colony was founded. That would take a lot of pressure off of you and your soldiers. And it would mean my people wouldn't have to live in state of siege any longer."

"I already figured that, Mr. Campbell. But I heard something earlier today that really bothered me. One of my smart advisers told us about how a guy named Hannibal got beat because he couldn't defeat a Roman army that wouldn't fight him the way he wanted, and because he couldn't take Rome while that army was still out there. That made me pretty unhappy, because I figured we haven't got any army out there to make life difficult for the people trying to take this Colony."

Campbell nodded. "There simply isn't any prospect for forming an alliance with other Earth nations. They won't risk the wrath of the United States—"

"No, sir," Stark interrupted. "I didn't mean any foreign army. But everybody back home, the civs who are supposed to be supporting these attacks against us, ain't they an army? If they all refused to back the people who are trying to defeat us, the same people who've been using guys like you and me and every other poor slob up here and back home for who knows how many years, what would happen?"

"I don't know." Campbell stared, so intent that Stark imagined he could see the wheels turning in the Colony manager's brain. "That's a thought, Sergeant. A very interesting thought. And you're right that inspiring such action by the civilian populace back home would require a powerful example."

"So you're gonna do what I ask?"

"I'm going to think about it. No promises yet. I can stall the independence referendum for a short time without creating too much trouble. Outright canceling it is a step I'm not prepared to take at this time."

"I can't ask for more than that."

"Would you, personally, be willing to tell the citizens of this Colony what you've told me?"

"Me? I'm no public speaker. I'm just a grunt. You're the politician."

"Sometimes, when sincerity and believability are at issue, a politician isn't the best speaker to use," Campbell noted dryly. "Do you believe in what you just said enough to go on vid and tell everyone else?"

Stark felt a major headache coming on, but nodded. *Ah, hell. Why do I keep trapping myself into this kind of thing?* "Okay. If I have to, I'll do it."

"Thank you, Sergeant." Campbell glanced ostentatiously toward his clock once again. "I'll call you about this later on. During normal hours. When people are usually awake."

"Sure," Stark grinned at the gibe. "Any time."

"Goodnight, Sergeant."

The screen blanked and Stark leaned back, letting out a long breath. *Now what have I done? Vic is gonna give me hell. . . .* A slight sound near the door to the rec room caught his attention. Looking that way, Stark saw Vic Reynolds leaning against the doorway, her arms crossed and an enigmatic expression on her face. "Oh, hi, Vic."

" 'Hi,' he says. Going off half-cocked again, Ethan?"

"It's the way I work best."

"You occasionally might try thinking and planning things through first. Just for the hell of it." She came in, sitting across from him. "So, you're going to ask the civs not to declare independence. Are you planning to tell the troops that?"

He hadn't thought about that yet, but the answer came instantly anyway. "Yeah. As soon as I talk to Campbell again. Within a few days, I guess."

"Good." The answer surprised him, as did Vic's smile of grudging admiration. "You always surprise me, Ethan. We've been looking for a cause, something to fight for, and most people figured that would turn out to be independence."

"There isn't a lot of enthusiasm for independence, Vic. It's more like something people figured they'd have to do."

"Exactly. Instead, you offer as a cause our own country again. Hang in there because the country needs you to find its way, so the civs will do the right thing once they see you willing to die for it. Not as a vid show, not to prop up corporate profits in some stinking part of the world that happens to be rich in natural resources, but as defenders of what's right." She raised her hands and applauded softly. "Good work, Sergeant."

"Knock it off. I didn't think it through like that. I wasn't trying to figure all the angles."

"You never do, Ethan. That's why people believe in you." She bent her head slightly to one side, regarding him closely. "But to make this one work, you'll have to convince the civs to follow your ideas, too. Can you do that?"

"I dunno." He scowled down at the blank display, where the screen saver was once again painting random patterns. "I'm just a grunt, Vic. When did my job get so complicated?"

"Probably about the time you took it seriously. There aren't any easy jobs, Ethan. Not if they're being done right."

"What was that dumb motto they tried to foist on us once? 'If you're not having fun, you're not doing it right.' Remember that? Well, I haven't been having much fun lately, so I guess that speaks for itself. What are you doing up at this hour, anyway?"

"Ever since that raid hit us here at headquarters I've been waking up at odd hours with an urge to inspect the security posts."

"Nothing wrong with that." The raiders, using access codes provided by Grant Stein, had almost achieved the total surprise they needed. Almost. Neither Reynolds nor Stark had been happy with the amount of luck that had played a major role in saving them that night. "Everything okay?" Vic nodded as Stark yawned. "Then I suggest we go to bed."

"You sly devil, you."

Stark felt his face warming. "That's not what I meant."

"I know. Life's complicated enough without adding something like that." Vic stood, heading for the door. "See you in the morning, soldier. Whatever the future holds, we'll handle it better if we get some sleep between now and then."

• • •

"Commander Stark? The civs are seeing ghosts again."

Stark was into his battle armor and fastening the seals so quickly that he was still blinking sleep out of his eyes as he headed for the command center. The last time the civilian technicians responsible for scanning space above the Colony's landing field had reported seeing a ghost on their scans it had been the only warning that a raid was about to hit Stark's headquarters. Inside the command center, Sergeant Tran and Sergeant Reynolds waited, both armored as well. "Good morning." Outside, the black sky never changed, but by the artificial human clock it was about 0300 now. "How many ghosts? Where?"

Tran pointed at the display, where unknown contact symbology overlay trajectories curving down from space toward the Colony. "Either three or four. The civs notified us as soon as they spotted the ghosts on their scans, and by working directly with them we've been able to tweak our own sensors to get occasional detections."

"Why are they trying this again? The last time the fact that the civ sensors work on slightly different parameters let them see a shuttle that was hiding from our own sensors and warn us. Don't they realize the same thing will happen this time?"

Vic shook her head. "No, Ethan. They don't realize that because they probably never found out the civs tipped us off. As far as they know, we were oblivious until the raid hit our headquarters, after which we did a manual scan looking for the raiders' shuttle and spotted it."

"So they figure they could get away with inserting raiders that way again, huh? Those ghosts don't look like they're heading for the headquarters complex, though."

"They're not, but we can't be sure where they *are* heading. Our systems are still trying to refine their objective, but the hits we're getting on the ghosts are so weak they're having trouble."

"So give me a guess, damnit. Those shuttles will be grounding before long, and I want a reception committee on hand for them."

Vic looked at Tran, who focused on one of his watchstanders. That corporal squinted at the display, tapping in a few commands, which brightened or faded different portions of the ghosts' projected tracks. "Sir, if I had to call it now, I'd say they're headed for the primary power plant."

"The power plant." A high-power fusion reactor, off to one side of the Colony proper, buried and surrounded by berms. "That's it, Vic. They want to grab that power plant. What happens if they do?"

Another watchstander answered. "Slow death, sir. They'll have us and the civs in the Colony by the throat. We can't run things up here off the backup plant and whatever solar cells we can spread."

"Great. And I guess the alternative would be trying to retake it with a firefight around a fusion reactor. Vic, get the on-call units moving to the plant, as fast as they can go. What kind of security does that power plant have, anyway?"

Sergeant Tran indicated a scattering of symbology as he zoomed the display onto the power plant's location. "Military Police, backing up civ security personnel."

Stark checked the symbology quickly. "A squad of MPs? That's it?"

"That's it."

"And there's three or four raider shuttles, you said? They're smaller than the cargo shuttles, so that'd be about a company of attackers?"

"That's our estimate, Commander. The raiders are likely to be elite troops, if the attack on our headquarters was any indication."

"Vic, I want those on-call units at the power plant five minutes ago. Tran, alert all units on the perimeter that we've got something going down and there might be some probes or all-out attacks coming to take advantage of it. Oh, yeah, and get me the commander of those MPs." A moment later, Stark's display popped up a window showing a tense-looking Sergeant. "You in charge of the MPs at the plant?"

"Affirmative. They tell me we've got company coming."

"Looks like it, yeah. What kind of armament have you apes got?"

"We're real light infantry. Rifles and sidearms. That's it."

"What about the civ security people there?"

"Strictly nonlethal stuff. Unless we want to use them for human shields, I'm planning on telling them to stay under cover."

Stark took a moment to check the progress of his reaction

forces. APCs loaded with infantry were converging on the power plant from three locations, while a fourth column consisting of a couple of Lamont's tanks headed that way as well. "Okay. I've got three companies heading to reinforce you, as well as some heavy armor. But the stuff we're tracking is going to get to you before those reinforcements can. I need you to hold that power plant."

The MP sergeant nodded. "I guess after this I won't have to listen to you guys tell us we're not combat troops. But it sounds like we're going to be seriously overmatched in numbers and weaponry."

"I know. There's nothing else there you can use in the way of weapons?"

"Just the particle cannons."

"Particle cannons?" Stark checked his display, punching controls with increasing anger. "I don't show any super-heavy weaponry like that at the power plant."

"That's 'cause they ain't weapons. Technically. There's a couple cannon here to fragment or divert any rocks falling on the plant. But they're only designed to engage rocks. I don't even know if I can train one at a surface target."

"Give it a try." Stark checked the progress of his units again, measuring it against the increasingly firm tracks of the ghosts. "You only have to hold for maybe fifteen minutes, Sergeant."

"Is that all?" The MP tried to smile. "If we make it, I'd sure appreciate having some heavier firepower added to our TO&E."

"You hold that plant, and I'll add a damn tank to your table of organization and equipment if you want one." He looked over at Vic. "Okay. Tell me why such a critical location only has a squad of MPs guarding it."

"I don't know, Ethan. That's how it was when we took over, and it was one of a million things we've never had time to review. According to the system, those MPs and the civ cops are only supposed to provide security against individual nut cases, not a full-scale raid. Oh, hell. Tran, can those particle cannon knock down the ghosts before they land?"

Tran gritted his teeth. "I should've thought of that. Does anybody on the watch team have the answer?"

A corporal nodded. "I know. If those cannon are designed to take out rocks, then they won't be able to engage the ghosts.

They're designed to use active targeting systems to track and hit nonmaneuvering contacts."

"What, you mean, just radar?"

"That's right. They don't need anything else. But if they illuminate the ghosts, the ghosts will alter trajectories, and the cannon fire control won't be able to handle that."

Tran turned back to Vic and spread his hands. "Good idea. Won't work."

"Thanks anyway," Vic replied. "But on second thought we might not have wanted to use them even if we could."

Stark gave her a quizzical look. "Why not?"

"What if they're U.S. troops this time?" Vic asked. "Do we want to knock down shuttles full of American soldiers?"

"Not if we can help it. Could they be Americans?" Stark grimaced at the display as if doing so would give him a better view of the ghosts. "We heard the Rangers had been folded into regular units to try and make up manning shortfalls. Would they send regular troops on a raid like this?"

"We did."

"That's because we're not doing things by the book, Vic. You know the Pentagon. The book says you use special troops for special ops. But there's not a full company of spec ops troops left. That would mean they've hired another batch of mercs from some other country's special forces."

"We hope."

"Yeah."

His comm unit beeped. "Stark? This is Yurivan."

"Hey, Stace. What's up?"

"Just thought you'd like to know somebody's trying to activate some of those worms we found hidden in the system after the last raid."

Stark breathed a sigh of relief. *Those were nasty worms, if I remember right. They would have messed up our combat systems and a lot of other stuff.* "Is there any chance you can locate this 'somebody'?"

"I'm trying, but my hackers say that somebody is covering their tracks real well."

"Is there any chance we missed some worms when we scrubbed the system? Or that any new ones have been inserted?"

"There's always a chance, Stark. If all the lights go out and you start choking to death, you'll know we missed a couple."

"Thanks, Stace." Stark looked over at Vic. "Why'd I make her security officer, again?"

"Don't ask me. It was your idea," Vic reminded him. "But she's awfully good at it."

"I could do without the 'awful' part. Tran, how close are the ghosts to landing?"

Tran checked his display, rubbing the back of his neck. "We'll probably lose the ghosts any minute now when they get too low for multisensor scan analysis. Say two minutes to touchdown, max."

"Two minutes." Stark eyed the symbology on the big display, switching from unit to unit to track the progress of the reinforcements. "And the closest reaction force is at least ten minutes out. Vic, I'm going to bring up vid from the MPs and see if I can help coordinate their defense. They haven't had the combat time I've had. You hustle those reinforcements in and keep me advised of their progress."

"Roger. Everything else around the perimeter still looks quiet."

"Good. I'll . . . wait a minute. Tran, can I transmit to those raiders?"

"Well, there's common frequencies the raiders will surely be monitoring, but you wouldn't be able to transmit any worms—"

"That's not what I have in mind. Get some circuits ready." Stark called up vid for the MPs, seeing through their armor combat systems. Their sergeant had deployed them along the low berm in fire teams, the soldiers lying just beneath the edge to take advantage of what little cover existed. *Not bad.* He checked for the name of the MP sergeant before speaking. "Sergeant Sullivan. Good job on setting up your troops. Have you got everybody on the berm?"

"All but a couple I've got working on something special."

He'll need everyone on the firing line. But he knows that, and he doesn't have time to explain what those two soldiers are doing. So I'll trust him. "Have you given your soldiers guidance on targeting?"

"Uh, no, sir. I figured we'd use highest probability hit criteria, like in the sims."

"The enemy knows that. Once you start shooting, they'll probably send a few people out to draw fire so they can target all your shooters. So designate one or two guys to engage anybody with the highest hit probabilities and have everyone else keep shooting at other targets."

"Yes, sir. Good idea. I guess you learned that one the hard way, huh?"

"You bet." *He's nervous, jawing with me a little to try to hide it.* "I'd like to talk to your troops for a second."

"Sure. I mean, you're the boss."

Stark triggered the circuit to cover the entire squad. "This is Stark. You've got a rough battle coming on. These raiders are likely to be tough, but you've only got to hold 'em a few minutes. They're gonna come at you fast, because they know they've got to take that power plant before any reinforcements can arrive to help you. But they think we haven't seen 'em, don't know they're coming. You guys show 'em different." On Sergeant Sullivan's HUD, Stark watched visual systems tagging anomalies. "Sergeant, that's probably them." The anomalies multiplied as the ghosts closed on their objective, until they reached a point where the shuttles couldn't be hidden anymore.

Four shuttle symbols seemed to flare into existence as the raiders dropped in to a hard landing. Stark winced in automatic sympathy, remembering the physical stress of those high-g's when assault craft braked at the last minute. The craft had barely touched the surface when hatches popped and armored figures came dashing out, heading straight for the berm.

"They're in our armor," Vic murmured. "Mark V model, like the last raiders."

"Got it." Stark keyed the broadcast frequencies he'd had prepared. "All personnel in the raiding force and on your shuttles. We're ready for you. This installation is heavily defended." *At least it will be once the reinforcements get here.* "You're outnumbered and outgunned. Surrender immediately."

The attackers may have hesitated for a fraction of a second, but instead of surrendering, many opened fire while the others came on. The MPs opened up as well, dropping several attackers in the first volley thanks to the lack of cover on the open area around the power plant. But the raiders came on, laying down accurate, heavy fire, which had the MPs ducking for cover.

"Sergeant Sullivan! Tell your soldiers to shift to full auto. They need to put out enough fire to slow those raiders down."

"Yes, sir." The volume of the defending barrage ramped up as the MPs began emptying their magazines.

Stark watched, trying to remain emotionally detached as the MPs took casualties. Within five minutes of the first shot, half the MP squad was either wounded or dead, the survivors beginning to waver under the pressure. "Vic, where's those reinforcements?"

"They're moving as fast as they can, Ethan. We need to buy a few more minutes."

More MPs dropped, rolling back down the berm under the impact of hits. The vid from Sergeant Sullivan's armor hazed suddenly as bullets tore through the suit's systems. On Sullivan's HUD, Stark saw damage markers glowing red as the suit tried to repair the damage. On another portion of the HUD, other markers displayed the damage bullets had done to the man inside the suit. Sullivan himself was still fighting, despite a shattered shoulder, which must have been causing agony every time he fired despite the drugs his med kit was pumping into his body. Stark checked the status of all the remaining MPs, grimly noting their dwindling numbers and depleted ammunition.

"Ethan, the nearest reinforcements are two minutes from the far side of the power plant."

"That's too far, Vic. There's maybe six MPs left still able to fight, and they're low on ammo." On vid, Stark watched the raiders surge forward in a mass dash for the berm. Once they reached it, it would be almost impossible to avoid a battle among the fusion reactor's components. *Now would be a good time for a miracle.*

Stark jerked backward in surprise as a section of lunar soil erupted as if it had been punched by a giant. The eruption traveled in a wavering line, cutting a trench a meter deep as it meandered across the rock then back and forth through the ranks of the raiders, before walking up one side of a raider shuttle. The shuttle split along that line, the two pieces sliding apart in slow motion as the weak lunar gravity tugged their mass into movement. The raiders milled about in shock, their ranks ripped asunder, their charge momentarily halted. "What the hell was that?"

"One of the particle cannon, I'm guessing," Vic replied. "Not much on accuracy, but it sure did a number on things. It almost looked like they were training the thing by hand."

"Can you do that?"

"I wouldn't if I could help it. I just hope none of those MPs got fried getting off that shot."

Those must've been the two guys Sullivan sent on the special errand. On vid, the raiders were reforming under the urging of their officers and began moving toward the berm again despite a scattering of fire from the remaining MPs. "Vic."

"Pull back your scan, Ethan. The cavalry's here."

Stark adjusted his scan, grinning in relief as APCs lurched to a halt at the base of the berm and fresh platoons of his soldiers spilled out. "Make sure they know there's a charge coming their way."

"They know, Ethan."

The first raiders over the top were moving so fast that they were inside the ranks of Stark's soldiers before realizing it. One or two tried to fight, dying in a confused fusilade of fire that had Stark agonizing over the chances that his soldiers would hit each other. Then the reinforcements continued up the slope as more units arrived below them and provided covering fire.

The raiders' charge fragmented and broke as it ran into the fresh troops. They fell back again, this time obviously retreating toward their shuttles, firing as they went, despite increasingly heavy losses as the number of defenders kept growing.

"Ethan, I'm sending the armor and one of the companies of infantry around the side of the power plant. Maybe they can nail those shuttles before they lift off."

"Good idea, Vic. I'll see if I can stop this mess before they get there." Stark triggered the broadcast frequencies again. "All personnel in the raiding force. You are trapped and heavily outnumbered. Surrender now to avoid further bloodshed. You on the raider shuttles, we have you targeted. If you attempt to lift off, you will be destroyed. I repeat, surrender immediately."

Once again there was no visible response to Stark's demand. Most of the raiders continued firing even though they were pinned down now by the intensity of the barrage from the power plant's defenders. Some continued evading backward, trying to reach the relative safety of the shuttles.

Two tanks came around the edge of the berm, pausing momentarily while their main cannons sought targets. Both vehicles fired, their shells streaking straight into the side of the nearest shuttle. The resulting explosions ripped holes through the shuttle's skin, holes that widened as gusts of fuel and gasses blew out from shattered storage tanks. "Vic, tell the armor to lay off those shuttles. I want to try to take the other two intact."

"Roger. Armor, shift to ground unit targets unless the shuttles try to lift." APCs jerked to a halt near the tanks, depositing the third company of infantry to add their fire to that already lashing the raiders.

Stark cursed as he watched increasing numbers of enemy symbology flash with assessed casualty markers. *I wanted 'em dead when they had a chance of winning, but now it's turning into a slaughter.* He broadcast again. "Raider commander. You are wasting the lives of your soldiers. You can't win and you can't run. Surrender now."

This time his words got a response. The remaining fire from the raiders rapidly dwindled to nothing, followed by a reply on the same frequency Stark had broadcast over. "This is the commander of the assault force. My soldiers have been ordered to cease fire. I request you cease fire as well."

"I didn't hear the word 'surrender,' yet."

"Yes. We surrender, damn you."

"Vic."

"Got it, Ethan. All units, cease fire. Alpha and Delta Companies, maintain covering positions. Charlie Company, advance and disarm the raiders. Send one squad to each remaining shuttle to take possession. Chief Wiseman, we need some of your people to bring those shuttles into the spaceport."

Stark checked on the status of Sergeant Sullivan and his MPs again, shaking his head as he read off the casualty count. "Sullivan? Can you respond?"

"Uh, yeah." The combined impact of Sullivan's wounds and the drugs his med kit had pumped into him had left the sergeant only partly coherent. "We held, didn't we?"

"You held. There's medics on the way."

"Good. I'm kinda messed up. Oh, Christ. My people. Look at 'em."

Stark had to swallow before speaking again. "You lost a lot of soldiers, Sergeant Sullivan." Assuming the medics saved every one left alive, the squad had still lost half its number in dead. All of those still alive were wounded. "They did their job. You're the best damn combat troops I ever saw in action." It was a small exaggeration, Stark admitted to himself, but only a small one.

"Thanks. I . . . hell. Good thing we got that particle cannon goin', huh?"

"Yeah. How come I didn't scan the people you sent to do that?"

"We figured we'd have to train the thing manually if we could make it work at all." Sullivan's voice wavered from the effects of shock. "They had to put on special suits for protection from the energy fields around the cannon. Nothing goes in or out of those suits except for a real limited visual display, so they could see what they were doing but couldn't transmit."

"They did great, Sergeant. You all did." Stark saw a medical team kneeling next to Sullivan. "Take a break, soldier."

"Yes, sir."

Stark pulled back from his view of Sullivan, taking in the entire area once again. A swift check of the raider casualty markers showed they had suffered worse than the defenders thanks to the particle cannon and the timely arrival of the reinforcements. Perhaps two-thirds of the raiders were down. Stark felt a sudden coldness inside as a belated thought came to life. "Somebody check and find out if we've just fought Americans." In the rush of battle, no one had stopped to think. Now he waited, sick at heart and afraid for the answer.

"Commander Stark? This is Charlie Company commander. They're not ours."

"You sure?"

"Positive. They got dogtags implanted, but in the wrong place, and our gear can't read them. Maybe I'll get a positive ID once we get a chance to pull their armor off, but they're not American."

"Good." Stark sagged back, fighting down an impulse to tremble with relief. "Good God."

Reynolds eyed him. "What?"

"Vic, I didn't even think about it when we were fighting. I could've been watching other American soldiers die fighting us, and I didn't even think about it."

"You were busy." Stark glared at her as Vic continued. "They fired first. They didn't hesitate to shoot to kill. What were you supposed to do different?"

"Think about what I was doing, damnit. You don't kill people on automatic pilot."

"You do if they're trying to kill you."

He almost snapped back at Vic again, appalled by her apparently cold attitude, then took a deep breath instead. *She's right, on one level. They didn't give us a chance to do anything but fight. But I bet she's stressed out by the chance we might've been trading shots with other Americans, just like I am. She'll never admit it if I'm letting that chance get to me, though.* "You've got a point." Vic looked surprised, then grimaced. "What's the matter?"

"I just had to swallow some words," she replied. "They didn't taste too good."

"I know the feeling. Okay, the past is past. Let's look ahead. First priority after we get the prisoners secured is to do a full review of every critical installation, military and civilian, inside this perimeter and make sure they're all adequately defended."

"I agree. I'll put Bev Manley on it."

"Bev? She's admin, not combat."

"Yes, but she's extremely thorough and will look at everything with fresh eyes. Bev will identify any weak spots."

Stark rubbed his eyes. "Yeah. You're right. We also need to tell Sergeant Gordasa we've had a couple of new shuttles with state-of-the-art concealment gear delivered to us courtesy of the government. Maybe they'll help us smuggle stuff through the blockade."

"I doubt it. The government will know how to defeat its own gear."

"I guess so. Well, maybe they'll come in handy against some of the other people we're fighting up here." Stark shook his head, abruptly aware of the shortness of his interrupted night's sleep. "I need coffee something fierce."

A nearby watchstander jumped to his feet. "I'll get it, sir."

"No, you won't. You'll sit at that watchstation and do the job you're being paid for." He looked out across the entire command center. "You all did good. Good handling the detection, the alert, and everything else. Thanks." Stark stood, glancing over at Vic. "You want some coffee, too?"

"Please. If there's none ready, just bring me back a handful of coffee grounds to chew on."

"I might do that for myself, too." He paused, his eyes drawn by a monitor that displayed an outside view, the Earth hanging in brilliant color against the blackness that surrounded it. "Maybe this latest failed attack will make the government change its mind about defeating us, maybe get them negotiating seriously. You think?"

"Stranger things have happened," Vic sighed. "Are you sure you don't want to try to grab another hour's sleep before the day officially begins?"

"Nah. I got work to do."

PART TWO

Friction

"*Breaking news. The* United Nations, no less, has declared Sergeant Ethan Stark and his followers to be international outlaws." Stacey Yurivan grinned at the other members of Stark's staff as she tapped the display before her. "All member states are authorized to use force against us."

Sergeant Gordasa scratched the side of his head. "They can do that?"

"Apparently, especially if the U.S. of A. is leaning on everybody and promising them major goodies." Yurivan smirked at Stark, who sat, arms crossed, leaning back in his chair with a deliberately detached expression. "I guess your noble initiative of hanging our asses out so we can inspire the citizens back home with our idealism hasn't impressed the government."

"It's impressed them enough to bring about this step," Vic pointed out. "I can't imagine what kind of effort it took to get the UN to come down on us."

Yurivan smiled a little wider. "Established governments anywhere don't care much for revolutionaries, Reynolds. Especially revolutionaries with noble motives. That's just the thing to scare professional politicians."

"Good. That's the point. Anything that scares the system and attracts support for us from the little guys is a good thing."

"The problem with little guys is they don't have enough big

guns. Speaking of which, as I just reported, we're now at war with every country on Earth. That must be some kind of record."

Bev Manley nodded agreement. "I for one am proud. And with Ethan Stark leading us, this might be just the beginning. We may yet encounter an alien species and end up at war with them, too."

Stark shook his head with feigned exasperation as his staff laughed. "With people like you working for me, any kind of disaster is possible. Now, if you apes are done with your stand-up routines, we got business." He glowered at the table's surface for a moment, his face settling into grim lines, before looking up again. "We've finally got some info on how the Pentagon plans on taking us down."

Manley cocked a questioning eyebrow. "They've figured out how to do that without enough trigger-pulling enlisted soldiers?" She glanced at Vic Reynolds for confirmation, but Vic shook her head to indicate lack of knowledge, then focused back on Stark.

"Yeah. They think they've figured that out."

Lamont shrugged. "Why the gloom? I thought they were hiring foreign mercs for that. We can take them. We have taken them. Just like that raid on the power plant. Easy."

"There wasn't a lot of 'easy' involved in stopping that raid. But, yeah, we've stopped everything they've thrown at us so far. I guess sometimes even the brass in the Pentagon can figure out something isn't working if it fails often enough. After we trashed that last batch of mercs trying to set up shop nearby, they settled on another idea." Stark held up a data coin, turning it slightly between thumb and forefinger. "I got this. Don't ask how." Yurivan's smile vanished. "Don't worry, Stace. I know covert collection is your job. I'm not bypassing you. Not on purpose. Somebody sent me this for their own reasons, and that's all I know. Understand?" Everyone nodded, their expressions now a mix of curious and concerned. Stark popped the coin into his unit, holding it so no one else could see the screen even though it showed nothing but a shadowy figure.

The figure on the screen began speaking as if the words were being reluctantly forced out, his or her voice concealed by security recording protocols that randomly shifted tone, timing, and accents. It protected the speaker from identification, but almost guaranteed a headache to anyone listening for long. "Ethan

Stark, you're doing too damn good up there. You've beat everything and everybody up real bad, and now the brass back here can't even dream up fantasies on how to knock you apes down. So they're doin' somethin' so stupid I had to warn you." There was a deep breath, audible to the listeners, then the speaker continued. "They're gonna employ metal-heads. The assembly lines are workin' on 'em right now. Officially the things are called Joint Autonomous Battle Robotic Weaponized Combatants. Even that name's heavily classified, but we're calling 'em Jabberwocks, anyway. From JABRWCs, see? I guess that name fits 'cause they gotta be ugly."

Another deep breath. "I know, you figure you'll take them out like usual by cutting the electronic umbilical, but like I said, the brass are being real stupid. I got it for certain that these metal-heads are designed to operate without a link. Think about that. Especially with all the civs you're protecting up there. It stinks. I don't want any part of it, even if sending you this warning means if I'm caught, we'll get to share the same firing squad." A brief pause, then the words came in a rush. "The shorter this is, the more likely it'll get through. Besides, I don't got much more detail. You'll have to work with what you've got. Beat these things, Stark." The screen blanked.

"Who was that?" Gordasa asked in the hush that followed.

"I'm not sure. Maybe a friend of mine," Stark stated, removing the coin and repocketing it. "He or she took a helluva risk sending me this."

"Metal-heads." Vic let the phrase hang alone for a long moment. "They're actually constructing robotic combatants to attack us?"

Stark nodded. "You heard what he said. Jabberwocks. What's that mean?"

"'Beware the Jabberwock, my son,'" Bev Manley quoted, "'the jaws that bite, the claws that snatch.' It's from one of the Alice stories. At least we apparently don't have to worry about frumious bandersnatchi," she added.

Stark fixed her with a glare. "I got enough problems without adding new ones. Whatever the hell a bandersnatchi is."

"I think that should be 'bandersnatchi are,'" Manley suggested, then winced as Stark's glare intensified.

Gordasa looked around as if seeking enlightenment. "I don't

understand. What was that talk about links and electronic umbilicals?"

Vic moved her forefingers apart on the table surface. "Control mechanisms, Gordo. The bright boys and girls in combat systems development have been trying to build unmanned weapons for who knows how many decades. They never worked, though, because the unmanned weapons always needed a comm link for a human operator to provide the brains for the weapon."

"Artificial intelligence couldn't handle it?"

Stark snorted. "Hell, Gordo, AI still can't even handle supply without human oversight, can it? The systems can never see past their programming. Combat's too unpredictable, calls for too much imagination. It overloads any metal brains they've ever built. Besides, even when the weapon's able to function on its own, you still need to monitor it, get status reports, and stop it from doing something stupid because its little metal brain misreads a line of code."

"Exactly," Vic agreed. "So they've always needed a human calling the shots, or at least looking over the metal-head's shoulder, which meant a comm link. Problem is, the enemy could just jam the link, and then you've got an unmanned weapon with a very limited brain, just sort of running amuck."

"Or," Stacey Yurivan added, "if the enemy was really on the ball they'd copy the link and send in a stronger version."

Sergeant Gordasa nodded in understanding. "Which would allow them to take over the weapon and use it themselves, right? So why not just design a weapon that could fight along predictable lines without a link?"

"Because," Yurivan continued with a smile, "anything that can be programmed can be reprogrammed. Figure out how to insert the new programming, maybe over the air, maybe as a worm, and it takes over the metal-head. Bingo, the enemy's got a bunch of new combat mechs and you've got a big problem, especially if you can't reestablish control because there ain't no link!"

"So why not tell the metal-heads to ignore new programming?"

Stacey's grin seemed almost demonic. "Sure. You could do that. Design an AI that can reject its own programming. Then you arm it. Sound like a good idea to you?"

Gordasa paled. "Dios. It could override all its inhibits. Kill anything and anybody. Is that what the Pentagon is doing now? No wonder Stark's friend was worried about the civs up here."

"Yeah," Stark agreed. "All the old attempts at building metal-heads at least had fail-safes that kept them from going crazy and slaughtering anything that moved or breathed. But if these, uh, Jabberwocks are made to work without links, we can't count on any functional fail-safe mechanisms. And taking 'em over or stopping 'em won't be as simple as messing with their links. So, people, what are we going to do about it? How we gonna beat these Jabberwocks? Any ideas?"

Bev Manley scowled. "There's always a back door, Ethan. I learned that in Administration. Some way to get into a system. I don't care how they design it."

"Probably. I'm not a hacker, but I've worked with enough of 'em. It sounds like they're trying to lock that back door real tight, though."

Vic's eyes narrowed. "If they're really trying to cut the link, it means one of two things. Either they're creating a Frankenstein's monster and handing it heavy weaponry, or they're building in fail-safe mechanisms."

"The link *is* the fail-safe," Stark insisted. "Nothing else would ensure they could exercise direct control or disable the metal-heads if necessary, right?"

Lamont raised a finger. "Unless the people building these things have convinced the brass they don't need a link, that their latest software or hardwire AI inhibits can do the job. I've run into that with automated systems on my tanks. You don't need a human in the loop, the weapon geeks tell me, because the system can think fine by itself. Only it never can, and we end up nurse-maiding it along with everything else."

"Exactly," Vic agreed. "So why would the Pentagon believe it this time?"

"Because they want to! Contractors are always telling the brass they've got a weapon that will cost a buck a copy, require zero maintenance, launch itself, and home in on evil. Then it ends up costing a buck an atom, breaks every time somebody looks at it, and has to be carried to the target by some ground ape. Any-body here think the Pentagon wouldn't buy something that didn't really work as advertised?"

Silence settled around the table for a moment, then Vic nodded. "That's a very good point." She looked over at Stark. "We need to assume we have to develop an ability to kill these things fast and clean."

"Even though they'll be fast and mean," Lamont pointed out. "You know how hard it can be to nail an automated target. They're just faster than us. And you gotta assume redundant critical functions, so one hit won't take 'em down."

"Depends what kind of hit it is, doesn't it?" Yurivan questioned, smiling again.

"You got an idea, Stace?" Stark demanded.

"Maybe. I'm an expert on messing with people's minds, right? So maybe I'm thinking of a new way to mess with a metalhead's mind. Maybe. Gotta check with some people."

"Do it." Stark glared around the table. "Do it careful. Nobody breathes a word about how we found this out." He focused on Chief Wiseman, sitting silent so far. "Any chance at all we can intercept the shuttles carrying these things and knock 'em out before they get here?"

Wiseman made a face. "There's always a chance. Decent chance? No, I don't think so. There's convoys coming in all the time. How do we know which one's have the Jabberwocks? Even if we could find out which convoy to hit, priority cargo like that would be protected by so much firepower my shuttles would be vaporized before we got into range, so even a kamikaze mission wouldn't likely succeed." She glanced around at the other staff members, then back at Stark. "We could lob rocks at 'em, of course. Crater the landing site."

"Rocks," Vic stated. "You mean big rocks."

"Yeah. Flippin' big rocks. Dig a few new craters and put on a fireworks show for the folks back on Earth."

Vic shook her head, looking to Stark for backup. "If we escalate to using weapons of mass destruction here, then the people we're fighting may assume we'd use the same against Earth. And if they believe that, they'll drop enough rocks, nukes, and nullbombs on us to turn this whole part of the Moon into a crater that'll make Tycho look tiny."

Stark nodded. "And the rest of the world will cheer them on, because that's the nightmare we've all managed to avoid so far, right? So, no rocks. Sorry, Chief."

"That's okay. It's not like I wanted to do it."

"Thanks for bringing up the possibility anyway. I need to know every option. Okay, that's all I got. Looks like things may be coming to a head, military-wise."

"What do you mean?" Manley asked.

"I mean either we beat these things or they'll beat us. And robotic combatants cost big time, so the Pentagon must be putting everything it's got into paying for 'em. They won't have anything left to throw at us after this."

Gordasa smiled. "So maybe the Lunar War will finally end?"

"Maybe. Maybe just from mutual exhaustion, but I can live with that. Let's hope when it does end we're all still around." Stark sat silent as his staff members rose and headed out, some talking quietly and the others silent with their thoughts, until only Chief Wiseman was left, hesitating near the door. "You got something else, Chief?"

"Nah. I, uh . . . ."

Stark measured Wiseman's uncertainty, then waved her back to a seat. "Why don't you hang around for a minute? We don't get much time to talk, and I've never gotten to know many sailors."

"Lucky you. Mind if I splice the main brace?"

"If I knew what that meant I'd tell you if I minded."

She chuckled, waving toward the drink dispenser one of the previous commanding generals had ordered installed in the conference room. "It means having a drink. Booze."

"Sure. Have a beer. Get me one, too, if you don't mind."

"No problem."

Stark stared quizzically at his beer after Wiseman brought it. "What's having a drink have to do with . . . whatever you said?"

"Splicing the main brace? Beats the hell out of me," Wiseman admitted, taking a long drink. "It's just traditional to call it that. Like, you know, announcing the smoking lamp is out at taps."

"Smoking lamp? What's that, some kind of light?"

"Beats me. But every night on every ship we announce the smoking lamp is out, and every morning we announce it's lit."

"You don't even know what the thing is and you're turning it on and off every day?" Stark shook his head, taking a drink himself. "I'll never understand sailors."

She grinned back, then turned suddenly somber. "It's tradition, Stark. Don't have to mean a damn thing, and probably doesn't anymore, but it gives us structure. It says we're a warship, says we do things our way, says some things never really change. Hopefully the good things, but you never know." Wiseman stopped talking abruptly, then took another long drink. "Man, this is lousy beer."

"You don't have to drink it."

"I didn't say it was *that* lousy." She sat silent for a moment, eyes suddenly shadowed.

"What's buggin' you, Chief?" Stark asked. "Something's got you unhappy. Anything I can help with?"

"I doubt it." Wiseman smiled crookedly, as if at an inner joke. "I've just been thinking how important tradition can be, even when it don't make sense. You ever worry about that, Stark? That maybe we're tossing out tradition and the whole shebang is going to blow up around us because of it?"

"No. I don't. Not for that reason, anyway. We didn't choose to do this, Chief. We got forced into it." He held up a hand as Wiseman started to speak. "Wait a sec. You're worried about tradition. I understand that. It is important. Damned important. But there's two kinds of tradition. That's what I think. There's traditions that hold you together, that make your unit or your service special in your mind, that keep you going when you ought to give up. Right? But there's another kind of tradition, one that doesn't care about looking out for each other or making things work well or helping you keep fighting when any fool would cut and run. No, that's the kind of tradition that's nothing but 'we did, so you have to do it.' Or 'it's always been that way.' Or 'you have to do it that way, because that's how it's always been done.' Or 'you don't get any input on this because somebody a million miles away already decided it.' You know what I mean. The traditions that bureaucrats in uniform and idiots and sadists use to justify doing stupid things to good people."

Wiseman's smile grew a little crookeder. "I know a few of those."

"You mean the traditions or the idiots?"

"Both." The smile vanished, replaced by thoughtfulness. "You're right. I never really thought about it that way, but that's how it works, don't it? Chief Gunners Mate Melendez, my second in command, he told me once about some old army, the Brits I think, who were trying to get their artillery to fire faster. So the

Brits had some specialists come in to analyze how they fired the big guns, and after they'd watched a few firings the specialists said 'how come those two guys on the gun team always stand over to the side at attention before the guns can fire?' Nobody knew, they just knew you had to do that. They finally found some ancient retired gunner and asked him. Know what he said?"

Stark shrugged. "Can't imagine."

"He said those two guys were supposed to hold the horses," Wiseman laughed. Stark stared back, obviously confused. "The guns used to be pulled into action by horses, and when the guns fired somebody had to hold the horses to keep the bang from scaring them off." She smothered another laugh in a quick drink. "The horses were long gone, but every gun still had two guys ready to hold them."

"Man, that *is* dumb," Stark laughed along this time. "You ever hear Stacey Yurivan's story about some old Russian ruler? Catherine or Kate or something."

"What about her?"

"Seems one spring day she was walking on the lawn of her castle or whatever and she saw some pretty flower that'd just bloomed. So she told her people to put a sentry on that spot to make sure nobody stepped on the flower. Well, maybe a hundred years later some other Russian ruler looks out at the same lawn and wonders for the first time why there's a sentry standing out in the middle of it. Turns out nobody ever told anyone to stop posting a sentry once the flower died, so there'd been a soldier posted there ever since, rain or shine, summer and winter, guarding the spot where a flower'd once been."

"Hah! Sounds like something our own bosses would've done." Chief Wiseman sobered again, sipping her beer slowly, eyes distant. "Yeah. There's dumb stuff. But the good traditions are important."

"The good traditions *are* important. And no matter what else happens, we're going to keep 'em. What got you thinking about 'em? Anything in particular?"

"My birthday." She quirked a small smile at Stark's reaction. "Don't bother singing me 'Happy Birthday.' The only thing I celebrate about birthdays now is the fact that I've survived long enough for another one. No, it just got me thinking about my family. My two brothers joined the Navy, too. Of course. What else you gonna do when your parents are Navy?" She still smiled, but her eyes were looking somewhere into the past. "We'd have some kinda bar crawls when we were in port together. People used to call us the Three Wisemen."

"Used to?"

"Yeah. Joe died when his ship got nailed during a heavy action up here. The USS *John Hancock*. Whole thing blew to hell while she was covering some transports. They shoulda run, but they had to save those other ships, right? We didn't have to worry about burials for any of the crew 'cause there weren't any bodies left to speak of." She took another drink, her face shading into sadness. "They awarded the ship and crew a Presidential Unit Commendation. Posthumously. Fighting their ship to the end in the finest tradition of the Naval Service. All that crap. But they did their duty, didn't they? Good ship. Good tradition. My brother did us proud." She sat silent a moment longer. "Now it's the Two Wisemen. So far."

"Sorry."

"I heard you're the only mil in your family, Stark, that all the rest are civs. That right?"

"That's right."

"Does that make it any easier?"

Stark shook his head, frowning. "Does it make *what* any easier?"

"Ordering people into combat. Knowing some of 'em will die. I mean, since they ain't relatives, and since you didn't grow up with 'em."

"They're still friends. No, it's not easier at all. Maybe harder."

Wiseman smiled again. "Reminds me of another joke, one my grandfather told me. Back when the Russians controlled Poland, in the twentieth century, I guess, some Russian went to Poland and asks a native whether he thinks of the Russians as his friends or his family. The Pole says family, of course, because you get to choose your friends."

Stark laughed. "There's a lot of truth in that, ain't there? But family's still important. Where's your other brother?"

"Wet Navy, now. One small blessing. I won't run into him up here. He always told me I was crazy for staying a space surfer. Said ships ought to float on water, not on nothing."

"I guess he's got a point. The Air Force always said the same thing, right?"

"Yeah, sure," Chief Wiseman snorted. "When they were trying to claim they should control all ops in space. But they couldn't figure out how to build luxury accommodations for their pilots up here, so they left the job to sailors. We're used to livin' miserable." She drained her beer, then stood. "Thanks for listening, boss."

"That's part of the job."

"Yeah. But some people are better at it than others. You ain't a bad boss for a mud crawler."

"Thanks, Chief. You ain't bad for a squid."

"Says you," Wiseman snorted again, then saluted. "By your leave, sir."

Stark stood as well, returning the salute. "Take care of yourself, Chief. Sure you don't wanna talk any more?"

"No, thanks. Besides, I gotta get going if I'm gonna be back with our little fleet in time for eight o'clock reports."

"Eight o'clock? You mean twenty-hundred?" Stark asked, converting the civilian time measurement into military time. "You got plenty of time 'til then."

"No, I don't. The Navy always holds eight o'clock reports at seven-thirty."

"Then why are they called eight—? This is like that crazy lamp thing, ain't it?"

"Sort of. It's a Navy thing. You wouldn't understand." She saluted again, almost cheerfully, then left, practically running into Vic Reynolds on her way out.

Vic glanced curiously after Wiseman. "You guys planning some special op?"

"Nah. Just doing some personnel counseling."

Reynolds sat, looking concerned now. "Does the Chief have some problems?"

"Nah. Just the usual. Worried about things. She needed a little hand-holding and a sympathetic ear. You know the drill."

"The same one I give you every time you get depressed? Yeah, I'm familiar with it."

"That's because you're a decent leader," Stark stated. "I hope I am, too. Thank God we can talk to each other when things get rough."

"I guess. And, speaking of leadership responsibilities . . ."

"Oh, man. Now what?"

Vic pursed her lips in thought for a moment. "How do I say this? We're winning and morale is great, but the troops are edgy."

"Yeah. I've felt it, too. Can't quite put my finger on it, but something's wrong. You got any ideas?"

"A couple." Reynolds leaned back, staring upward where rough metal shielded and armored the ceiling. "Part of it is the old end game question. You've given us a reason to fight, now, besides just surviving, but the problem with holding yourself up as a symbol is there's no way to know if it's working."

"A lot of people are trying to find out, Vic. The demonstrations back home are getting bigger. The government's been tossing mercs at us, and now they're cooking up those Jabberwocks, so you know they're worried. Stacey and the civ security people keep spotting attempts to intrude on our systems or plant worms. Oh, yeah, and the government's propaganda mills keep churning out stories about how horrible we are. If you go by how hard our enemies are trying to beat us and discredit us, we must look like a real threat to them."

"I know. But even if it works, we don't know how long it'll take. We've been fighting up here for what seems like forever already. No one wants to keep fighting a day longer than we have to."

Stark nodded. "I wish I knew the answer to that. Hell, I wish I could end the war right now. All I can say is the civs in the Colony are working like crazy to stir up hate and discontent back home with the government. Sarafina's been keeping you briefed on their efforts, right?"

"Uh-huh. There's no way the government can totally block the civs' ability to download info into systems back on the World, so they can't stop our own propaganda from getting through. But she doesn't know for sure how well any of it's working or if or when it'll succeed, either. But then she's not being asked to be shot at while she waits for the answer." Vic held up a hand to forestall Stark's words. "I know. Cheryl Sarafina's a decent human being, and I respect her judgment, which I never thought I'd say about a civ, but it's a fact. There's a different level of stress. Still, I don't think that issue is entirely the problem."

"Huh. What else, Vic? What're your guts telling you?"

"They're telling me our friends back home are up to something we haven't spotted. Spreading their own brand of hate and discontent up here. Or trying to, anyway."

"Wouldn't surprise me in the least."

"Stacey got anything?"

Stark shook his head. "Nah. She's worried, though, for the same reason you are. Stace figures the spooks back home have got to be trying to cause trouble up here, and she hasn't been able to spot it, not with the tools we've got."

"We could try some loyalty screens . . ."

"No. That won't happen. I start loyalty screens, and it'll hurt us more than anything the spooks are trying to do. I've got to trust my people, Vic."

She nodded, her face unhappy. "I guess you're right about loyalty screens. But some people don't deserve trust, Ethan. This isn't like before, when you could know every person who worked for you in your squad. There's people in this little army of ours that you and I never heard of, let alone know personally. And you know soldiers aren't angels." Vic reached to activate the nearest display panel, punching in some codes. "Like here. We've had almost a hundred grunts hauled up on charges for using that new synth drug, Rapture. Somebody's making it, and somebody's selling it, but we haven't nailed them, yet."

"We will. Stacey's real ticked off about that Rapture stuff. It's the sort of thing she'd have tried running in the old days. Well, maybe not. Rapture can mess up people permanent, right? Stace wouldn't have played that game. But she's still determined to take the dealers down."

"After which some other designer drug will pop up to keep things ugly," Vic noted. "Okay. So, what do we do about the people issue? Try something proactive or wait for something bad to happen?"

"Let's try to think of something proactive. I can't think of anything we haven't already done, but maybe there's something. It's pretty late in the day now to be trying creative thinking. Let's get together tomorrow, say during lunch, and hash out some ideas."

"Sounds good." She gazed at Stark. "Something else bothering you?"

"No. I don't think so. Probably just like you said. The agencies back on Earth have got to be working on something to make us unhappy. I really wish I knew what it was."

Stark had just entered his quarters, trying to decide whether to dig through the virtual mound of paperless paperwork on his terminal, when his comm unit buzzed urgently. "Stark here."

"Commander Stark, this is Security Central." The watchstander sounded breathless, bringing Stark to full alertness as he listened. "There's some sort of situation going down."

"What do you mean 'some sort of situation'? What exactly is happening?"

"Uh, sir, we got some warning messages coming in from two areas. That'd be Chamberlain Barracks and Morgan Barracks. We've also lost remote monitoring signals from the ammunition magazine nearest those barracks—"

"What kind of warning messages?" Stark broke in, aching to leap into action but forcing himself to wait until he could learn more. "Are you talking another raid?"

"No. No sir. I've got no reports of enemy action. These messages are hard to explain. Let me replay one for you, sir." After the briefest pause, a different voice began speaking hastily. "Hey, you guys. Somethin' funny's happenin' here in Morgan Barracks. We got soldiers coming through in full combat gear, claiming there's some new Enlisted Council that's gonna be running things. Says Stark and his gang are just using us so we're taking over. I says who the hell is 'we,' and they looked sorta confused. We told them to get back to their damn barracks, but it looks like they're tryin' to occupy this one. I think they're all Fifth Battalion troops from Second Brigade. You better get—"

"Security, the message broke off."

"Yessir. That's what happened. We've activated the on-call company in that area, but, uh, what are we supposed to do, sir? I mean, are they supposed to attack someone?"

Stark closed his eyes, wishing his lunch with Vic had happened a few days earlier, before apparently being overtaken by events. "One, notify everyone on my staff. Two, put out the word all soldiers should remain in their quarters or barracks unless they get orders from me otherwise. Three, you get the on-call company down to those two barracks and tell them to block anybody trying to take over those locations or seize control of any area without authority. No shooting. Understand? You haven't told me about any shooting, yet, so I assume there's been none."

"That's right, Commander. No reports of firing and no sensor indications of combat."

"Good. So get our own people in place and just block these other guys until we find out what's going down."

Vic broke into the circuit. "This is Reynolds. Get the on-call companies in the adjacent areas going, too. What's the backup battalion in the area?"

"Uh, that'd be Fifth Battalion."

"Okay," Stark acknowledged. *I guess we can't use them.* "Get the next backup battalion closest to those barracks going. And all those on-call companies, like Sergeant Reynolds said. I want a wall of bodies holding in this so-called Enlisted Council."

"Yessir. Uh, what about the magazine, Commander?"

Stark took a slow, deep breath, imagining what panicked soldiers might do around a large quantity of high explosive. "Same thing. Get the exits blocked. But no offensive activity around that magazine. No pressure. I don't want it blowing half the Colony to hell."

"Yessir. Troops are on the way, Commander."

"Vic, meet me in the command center."

"On my way. Does this mean our lunch date is off?"

He grinned involuntarily at the black humor. "I don't expect to have much time for eating in the next few days. Don't forget your battle armor."

"Ethan, I'm a big girl. I know enough to wear battle armor in a crisis. Are you going to remind me to bring my rifle, too?"

"No. But I sure hope you won't have to use it."

The command center felt off-balance, its normal smooth functioning disrupted by an event the watchstanders had never trained for. "Are you telling me I can't get a map of the barracks area on this display?" Stark demanded.

"We're looking for one," Sergeant Tran advised. "That isn't an area we're supposed to have to worry about."

Vic entered, shaking her head at Tran's words. "What about if the perimeter had been penetrated? There has to be a self-defense plan for the military complex."

Tran slapped his forehead. "Of course there is. We'll get it up right away." He hastened to a console, conferring with the watchstander there as they sought the needed planning document. A moment later, the display lit with a 3-D depiction of the Chamberlain and Morgan Barracks. "We'll get enemy activity posted on here real quick, Commander Stark."

"Thanks. But they're not enemy. Let's keep that in mind." Stark fiddled with the controls, frustrated as his instincts urged him to do something quickly but he was forced to wait for more information. "I oughta go there," he muttered so only Vic could hear.

"No. The situation's too confused." Vic eyed the display as red markers began appearing where so-called Enlisted Council activity had been reported. "Ethan, I just remembered something."

"Doesn't sound like it's anything good."

"It's not. Remember who used to belong to Fifth Battalion? A guy named Kalnick."

"Kalnick?" Sergeant Kalnick had briefly served as commander of the Fifth Battalion, before losing the confidence of his soldiers when he tried to undercut Stark's authority and almost disastrously delayed the battalion's response to an enemy breakthrough. After Kalnick's own people voted him out, Stark had sent him home to Earth, not wanting someone he couldn't trust so close at hand. "Why didn't we think to keep a special eye on that unit?"

"Probably because we both thought everybody had gotten fed up with Kalnick. But I bet he still has some friends in Fifth Battalion. Friends who've been keeping a low profile. Speaking of which," Vic pointed to her console, "looks like the Second Brigade commander is calling in."

Stark called up the incoming transmission. "Sergeant Shwartz? You don't look happy."

"I'm not," Shwartz stated. She turned slightly to issue a command to someone near her, then faced Stark again. "I am forced to report that significant portions of one of my battalions are not responding to orders. They have occupied portions of two barracks and the closest ammunition magazine to their location."

"Portions of the barracks?" Vic questioned. "So they haven't been able to take over both in their entirety?"

"No. Only a small portion of Morgan Barracks is being held, even though it appears practically all of Chamberlain Barracks has been taken over. I believe most, if not all, of the mutineers are from my Fifth Battalion. Despite their talk of an Enlisted Council, whatever that is, they don't seem to be garnering extra support. There hasn't been active resistance to this council that I'm aware of, just passive refusal to go along with the mutiny."

Stark couldn't help internally mocking himself. *I ended up in charge because I started a mutiny, and now I got people mutinying against me. Serves me right for setting a precedent.* "First things first, I see the on-call companies moving into position at those barracks. Are you in contact with them?"

"Yessir. But they lack specific objectives."

"Not anymore. Move them up, nice and slow. Fifth Battalion is quartered in Chamberlain Barracks, right? So I'm guessing the parts of Morgan Barracks that are occupied aren't held too strongly at this point."

Shwartz nodded. "That matches with what I can see from here."

"Try to push those Fifth Battalion people out of Morgan. Just move your own people forward, occupying rooms as they go, and see if the Fifth Batt guys pull back. If weapons get pointed, I want the advance stopped. Understand?"

"I understand. No firing. Stop the advance if firing is threatened. What about the ammo magazine?"

Stark scowled, checking his display. "I'm being told there's an unknown number of troops sealed inside. Send a couple of people, no more than that, to knock on the entrance and try to talk them out. Make sure those people are unarmed. I don't want to make the soldiers sitting on all that ammo nervous." As Sergeant Shwartz gave orders to her soldiers, Stark leaned toward Reynolds. "Vic, whadayya think?"

"I think you're doing the right things. Or at least as good as we can do at this point. We need to contain this mutiny and prevent it from erupting into violence."

"That's what I figured. Sergeant Shwartz? I take it you had no warning something like this might happen?"

"No, sir. Fifth Battalion aren't the best motivated troops I've got, but I had no indications of this level of problems. I don't understand why the senior enlisted in the Battalion didn't pick up some signals."

"Sergeant Shwartz, I think you've got to assume some of

those senior enlisted are part of the problem." She looked shocked. "We'll handle that once we've got a perimeter established."

"Sergeant Stark, given my failure to prevent this mutiny from occurring I would understand if you lacked confidence in my ability—"

"I have every confidence in your ability. None of us saw this coming, and I can see you've reacted quickly and correctly to contain the mutiny. You remain on-scene commander. However, if anybody from this Enlisted Council tries to talk to you, patch 'em in to me. We need to handle any talks from a single location to minimize the chance for misunderstandings or crossed wires." Stark looked toward the watchstanders. "Nobody's reported any problems with normal comms into Chamberlain Barracks, have they? Somebody start calling in there. I want to talk to whomever thinks they're in charge."

Over the next hour, the situation slowly stabilized. Under Shwartz's careful prodding, the rebellious Fifth Battalion soldiers fell back from Morgan Barracks, but once the advancing loyal troops reached the entrances to Chamberlain Barracks they found firm defenses had been set up. "The soldiers inside the ammunition magazine are refusing to open up," Shwartz reported. "They say they need orders from that council."

"Don't make them nervous," Reynolds advised.

"They're already nervous. I've got a couple of squads watching the exits from the magazine, but I've pulled them way back and told them to keep their weapons grounded."

"Good move," Stark approved. "Do the same at the exits to Chamberlain Barracks. Let's make sure no shooting starts." *Unless and until we want it to start. What happens if it comes to that?*

As if reading his mind, Reynolds leaned close to speak softly. "Ethan, we need to try to talk these guys out, but we might need to use force."

"I can't. No, this isn't just morality speaking. It's realistic. If I shoot fellow soldiers to uphold my authority, then I've lost it. Nobody else up here will trust me." He glared at her. "And don't bother telling me not to let on that I know that when I'm talking to this council."

"I never even considered it. Speaking of which, I think we've finally got some comms with that council."

A corporal stared out of the screen. He was clearly trying to project calm and confidence, but Stark had enough experience observing people under stress to know the corporal was putting up a front. *He's rattled. And he's got lots of people with weapons listening to him right now. I better treat him like a live grenade. Real careful.* "Corporal? This is Sergeant Stark. Do you represent this Enlisted Council I'm hearing about?"

"Yes. Yes, I do. I'm Corporal Hostler. Sergeant Stark, you, uh, no longer have authority to, uh, issue orders to us."

That sounds like something he's been rehearsing. Maybe something someone else told him to say? "Corporal, the other units aren't following your lead. You can see that. You're alone and isolated in your barracks."

"If you try to retake this barracks we will resist with all . . . with all necessary force!"

"Calm down. I didn't say anything about attacking you. We're on the same side, right?"

"No. No, we're not. You're just out for yourself. You and your gang."

"My gang?" Stark looked over at Reynolds. "You mean my staff?"

"Yeah. Yes. Reynolds and, uh, Gordasa, and, uh, Yurivan and—"

"Sergeant Stacey Yurivan?" Stark couldn't stop from breaking into the corporal's recital. "Come on. Sergeant Yurivan's from your unit originally. She served there a long time, and you all know her. She's nobody's stooge, and she sure as hell ain't mine." The corporal stopped speaking, apparently thrown off balance by Stark's rebuttal. *Or maybe listening to somebody else tell him what to say?* Stark thought again about Sergeant Kalnick and his friends among the senior enlisted in Fifth Battalion. "Listen, Corporal, if you've got a grievance there's a lot better ways to deal with it. If everybody lays down their weapons we can talk about this."

"No! No tricks!"

Real nervous. I hate nervous people with loaded weapons. "I'm not talking tricks, Corporal. Let's just make sure nothing happens that all of us might regret. What is it you want?"

The corporal brightened visibly. Apparently that question was part of his canned presentation. "You must, uh, relinquish command. The Enlisted Council will give orders from now on."

"Give me a break."

"The Enlisted Council represents the true interests of the enlisted personnel. Your, uh, corrupt and, uh, incompetent leadership is over."

"Corporal, the only people your council *may* represent," Stark replied, carefully emphasizing the 'may,' "are some soldiers in Fifth Battalion. I will not break faith with every other soldier up here by giving in to your demands."

Corporal Hostler gulped. "We, uh . . ."

"Where are your senior enlisted, Corporal? Where are the sergeants from Fifth Battalion?"

"They're . . . all under arrest. Hostages." The words came quickly, almost too quickly.

Stark glanced over at Reynolds, who shook her head skeptically, then he spoke with a mix of calming and authority. "Let's take things one step at a time. First, I have to know any hostages are safe. Second, I need your people to evacuate that ammunition magazine they've occupied."

"No! That's our ace! You wouldn't dare do anything as long as we hold that magazine!"

"Listen, Corporal, if somebody blows that magazine, either on purpose or *by accident,* it'll cause one helluva lot of damage. And kill everyone inside the magazine, as well as a lot of people outside it. A lot of your fellow soldiers. You don't want that, do you?"

"It's . . . our ace," Hostler insisted, his confidence waning once more.

"I can't let you hold this Colony hostage. I can't let you hold the lives of a lot of your fellow soldiers hostage. There's too much chance somebody'll make a mistake that you and me and everyone else will regret. You understand, right?" Stark waited a moment, letting his statement sink in, speaking again only after Hostler's eyes reflected growing worry. "I can talk. I don't want shooting. But I can't let you hold on to a magazine full of ammo. If somebody on your side screws up, or somebody on my side, a lot of soldiers could die. A lot of civs, too. I don't expect you to care about the civs, but how many of your buddies are you willing to see blown to hell?" Hostler started to reply, then bit his lip, his eyes straying slightly to one side. *So, like I thought. You're not in charge, are you, Corporal? There's somebody talking off-screen, and you're listening.*

"Uh, Sergeant Stark, we don't want to risk any of our, uh, fellow soldiers, either. But we need something to make sure you don't attack us."

"I'll give you my word."

"Uh, no. We need, uh, a hostage. Somebody important."

Stark didn't have to look around to know Vic was vigorously shaking her head at him. "You can't volunteer for that!" she hissed.

"Why not?"

"Because you're in charge! Who makes decisions if you're a damn hostage?"

Stark screwed up his mouth as if he'd tasted something bitter, then glowered at Corporal Hostler. "You got anybody in mind?"

"Yessir. Sergeant Reynolds. You provide her as a hostage, and we'll withdraw from the magazine."

Keeping his face carefully composed, Stark looked over at Vic, but instead of answering him she leaned into the vid camera and nodded. "Done. I'll be at the entrance to your barracks in fifteen minutes. Do you need any assistance communicating with your people inside the magazine?"

"No. We're talking to them." Hostler grinned in relief, then looked anxious again, his eyes once more indicating he was listening to someone off screen. "You come here unarmed, Sergeant Reynolds. No weapons, no armor."

Reynolds pursed her mouth in disdain. "Of course. I'll be there, unarmed." Hostler broke the connection, leaving Stark staring at Vic. "Come on, Ethan. Private conference." She led the way to a briefing room just outside the command center, where no watchstanders could overhear their words. "I know you don't like this, Ethan, but it's necessary." Stark looked mutely at her as Reynolds unstrapped her sidearm, laying it carefully on a table nearby. "Keep an eye on this for me, will you?"

"Vic, I—"

"Save it." She looked straight at him. "I agreed to be the hostage for two reasons. First, because I'm sure those fools wouldn't agree to give up the magazine for any other hostage. Second, because it gives us an edge. A big edge."

"An edge."

"You know what I mean, Ethan. Those apes," she stated with a wave in the general direction of Chamberlain Barracks, "think you won't let me get killed."

"Which you might be! What if they panic? What if the enemy hears about this and tries a push and everything falls apart? What if they just decide they can demand anything they want as long as they got you as a hostage?"

Her expression didn't alter. "You stop them, Ethan. You stop them. You take them down."

"And they kill you."

"And they kill me. That's our ace in the hole, our edge, if we need it, Ethan. They don't think you'd let me get killed in order to save everyone else up here."

The ice he'd once felt fill his body had come back, so his limbs felt frozen in place, yet Stark could still speak, though only in a hoarse whisper. "I would if I had to. To save the others. I'm responsible for taking care of them, Vic."

"I know. Nobody else knows you'd do that, but nobody else knows you as well as I do." She reached out one hand, slapping his shoulder lightly. "There's no time for speeches. Do what you have to do, Ethan." Vic turned to go. "If the worst happens, I'll see you in hell."

"Sure."

"Hell's likely to be real crowded, but I'll try to save you a seat."

"You do that." The ice filling him broke, thoughts tumbling through his brain. *How can she joke about this? Because she's scared to death, you idiot. Vic's going into a life-and-death situation without any weapons, without any armor, depending on me to handle things right and get her back, and I don't exactly have a perfect record in either respect.* "Vic." She paused, not looking back. "I'll get you out of there."

"You do your *job*, soldier. That's what matters." Then she was gone.

The transfer took place almost too smoothly, Reynolds standing at relaxed parade rest at one of the Fifth Battalion barricades as the mutineers evacuated the magazine and Shwartz kept her loyal forces calmingly out of sight. Stark watched on vid as Reynolds was escorted by the mutineers into the barracks, feeling simultaneously empty and full of dread. *Now what do I do? I don't know. What would Vic advise? She'd tell me to talk to my staff. Let the civs know what's happening. Keep people informed so I'm not indispensable, and so they know the situation's under control. Okay. Let's get on it.*

Half a day dragged by, then a full twenty-four hours. Corporal Hostler, looking increasingly ragged from tension, kept repeating his demands that Stark step down from command. The failure of other units to follow Fifth Battalion's lead had apparently thrown off the mutineers' plans, but they showed no signs of surrendering despite that.

"Alright, people." Stark's staff, augmented by Sergeant Shwartz, the Colony manager, and another civilian Stark had never met, sat around the conference table looking as if they hadn't slept for more than a day. Which was appropriate, Stark noted to himself, since they hadn't. "What've we got?"

Sergeant Shwartz gestured toward her display. "I've been canvassing the other senior enlisted in Second Brigade on who in Fifth Battalion might be behind this Corporal Hostler and so-called Enlisted Council. We have some good candidates, but we also have quite a few people we're certain wouldn't take part. We have to assume they're hostages, just like Sergeant Reynolds."

Sergeant Stacey Yurivan checked the list. "Good assessment. When did you have a chance to put this together?"

"I just used my copious free time," Shwartz replied, trying to stifle a yawn.

Stark nodded. "You've done a good job keeping things stable around that barracks. What about you, Stace? Any leads on who's behind this?"

Yurivan made a face. "I'm sure our good buddy Harry Kalnick is behind this, like you guessed, but I can't find any footprints and probably won't be able to find any until we get at the stuff inside Fifth Batt's barracks."

Bev Manley shook her head. "I met that guy a few times. Kalnick's competent, I guess, but he's no evil genius. Could he have had any help in bringing this about?"

"I'm sure he had help. I'm sure some professional knuckle-draggers from certain national agencies have been using our boy

Kalnick as a means to an end, though Kalnick might believe he's pulling the strings. But proof of that is likely to be real hard to come by." Yurivan tapped her screen again. "But, good-news-wise, it doesn't look like we're dealing with a full Battalion of malcontents. The guys in Intelligence have been adding up the numbers of soldiers seen when the mutineers tried to take over, and it doesn't add up to anywhere near a battalion. Maybe two companies worth of grunts, more or less."

"Surely they held back some soldiers," Gordasa argued.

"We thought about that." Yurivan nodded toward Sergeant Shwartz. "The mutineers manning the barricades haven't disabled the IFF systems on their battle armor."

"IFF?" Colony Manager Campbell asked.

"Identification friend or foe," Stark explained. "It's a system that makes sure you don't shoot at the people on your side by telling you who's enemy and who's friendly. How's that helping, Stace?"

"Because you can query a suit's IFF to get an individual identification, without alerting the suit's wearer. Didn't know that, Stark? Most people don't. So Shwartz's people have been monitoring the mutineers manning the barricades. Based on the turnover of individuals, we're talking maybe six platoons worth of soldiers actively involved in this little party."

"Two companies," Stark mused. "That ain't great, but it's a lot better than a full battalion. Good work. Anything else?"

Yurivan smiled like a cat digesting a canary. "My little idea for handling the Jabberwocks turns out to be doable, and it may also allow us to take down these mutineers without hurting anybody." She paused to relish the surprise radiating from most of those present. "You can tell me how brilliant I am later. For now, I think Mr. Campbell can fill you in."

Campbell shook his head. "I know just the bare bones. This is the expert." He indicated the man sitting next to him, an individual who at first glance seemed small in stature until you realized he held himself small. "This is my head of Nano-Research and Development, Doctor Gafton. He has some important information."

Doctor Gafton blinked a few times before speaking. Even though no one had to wear glasses anymore, Gafton somehow looked as if he needed them. Focusing closely on Stark, the doctor began speaking. "Mr. Stark—"

"Sergeant," Stark interrupted.

"Sergeant?"

"Yeah. Sergeant."

Gafton blinked again. "Mr. Sergeant—"

A strangled sound came from one end of the table as Sergeant Manley attempted to hold in laughter. Stark glared at her, then back at Doctor Gafton. "Sergeant is my title, Doctor."

The doctor's face creased in puzzlement. "My netlink informs me 'sergeant' is a low-ranking position of limited responsibility. The commander of a large force should be titled 'general.'"

Stark glanced over at Campbell, who shut his own eyes for a moment in seeming exasperation before replying. "Doctor Gafton doesn't get out much, I'm afraid. Doctor, Sergeant Stark is the commander of our military forces."

Before Gafton could say anything else, Stacey Yurivan raised an accusing finger toward him. "You've got an active netlink implanted? Despite the danger?"

Gafton grimaced, then nodded. "It is necessary. I could not coordinate our work without an implant. Of course, the risks are severe despite all the security measures provided, but I must take those risks to fulfill my duties."

Stark glanced from Yurivan to Gafton. *What's that about? Nobody else seems confused. I'll have to ask Vic later. If there is a later.* He shied away from the thought. "So, what is it you've got to tell me, Doctor?"

"The nanobots you have requested are in final design testing and should—"

"I requested nanobots?" Stark looked around the table. Everyone else looked back with blank expressions, with the exception of the smug smile on Sergeant Yurivan's face.

"Yes, you did. Absolutely. A special order."

"Tell me about it, Doc. What do these nanobots do?"

More blinking. "What you requested, of course."

"And that would be?"

"Internal reprogramming and system disabling of a complex, autonomously operating robotic entity. I must admit the requirement that the nanobots had to be delivered using a high-velocity penetration device made the design process a little tricky even with current nanotechnology, but once we established a cushioning medium—"

Stark stopped the flow of words with one hand slapping onto the table with the sudden shock of a rifle shot. "You've designed nanobots to knock out robots?"

"Ah, well, the specifications indicated reprogramming was also desired, but since we know nothing of the hardware or software to be used in the original programming, we cannot build enough options into the nanobots to achieve that function."

"But the nanobots will stop a robotic combatant?"

"Certainly. They will seek out command junctions and interrupt control signal flow. Simple jamming seemed the most reliable concept to pursue, though there is a backup short-out of power relays function which will also be employed." Doctor Gafton peered around as if trying to assess whether his words were understood. "In basic terms, the robots will suffer the equivalent effects of a human exposed to a nerve agent such as sarin."

Manley leaned forward. "How can you be sure they'll work?"

"There is no guarantee of success, pending the outcome of experimental trials. There are a number of variables we must deal with. The degree of shielding of command junctions, the power of command signals which are to be blocked, the presence or absence of defensive nanobots designed to stop or repair internal sabotage—" Gafton stopped in mid-sentence, his expression thoughtful. "Mind you, defensive nanobot systems have not been utilized prior to this time, so we have no reason to expect their presence. This nonetheless represents an uncontrolled variable."

"So we can't be sure they'll work until we use them?"

"Ah . . . yes. Unless you can acquire a working model of the targeted robotic entity to conduct tests upon, that is correct."

"Great." Stark didn't have to exaggerate the level of praise in his voice. "Not perfect. I wish we could try them out beforehand, but that'll give us a real leg up on these Jabberwocks." He looked first at Yurivan and then back at Gafton. "But how exactly does this help solve our mutiny?"

Gafton blinked once more. "I was asked if the nanobots and delivery device could be modified to deliver a disabling function to a standard military battle armor system. The modifications were fairly simple."

It took a moment for the implications to sink in, then Stark grinned. "We've got a way to insert worms into battle armor?"

"Worms?" Gafton questioned. "The slang term refers to destructive software. The disabling function in question will be achieved by nanobots taking all movement, weapons, and communication systems into inoperable status."

"Damn." Stark smiled at Yurivan. "Stacey, I'm glad you're on our side. Can I equip people with these delivery systems right now?"

Gafton shook his head once. "No, not now. Twenty-four hours. In twenty-four hours, plus or minus four hours to allow for unexpected developments, I can provide you with approximately two thousand individual delivery devices manufactured according to the custom specifications for shoulder-employed anti-personnel launch mechanisms."

Stark glared at the doctor for a moment, then shifted his gaze to Sergeant Gordasa. "That sounds like Supply talk. What's he mean?"

"Bullets," Gordasa explained. "He's talking two thousand rifle rounds."

Gafton nodded twice. "That is what I said."

"Two thousand." Stark pondered the number for a moment. "That's enough to load the magazines of maybe a company of loyal troops. I'll find one and—"

"You've got one," Stacey advised. She was clearly enjoying herself immensely.

"Thanks, but I'll want to evaluate—"

"You'll like this particular company. Trust me."

Stark nodded, trying to keep his feelings from showing. *Great. Vic's a hostage, so I have to place my trust in the likes of Stacey Yurivan. I sure hope I'm doing the right thing.*

A few hours later, Sergeant Sanchez saluted Stark, his face as composed and emotionless as ever. "It is good to see you again, Commander Stark."

"Knock it off, Sanch. We're old buddies. You don't need to be formal with me. Your company really volunteered to go in with me?"

"I could not have stopped them," Sanchez assured Stark. Something that might have been a smile flickered on the edges of his mouth, then vanished.

"I bet not. Hell, Sanch, it seems like yesterday that you and me and Vic were all squad leaders in the same platoon. But it also seems like forever. I hated leaving my own squad. I'd led those apes for years."

"It was you who triggered the mutiny which deposed the officers in our division," Sanchez reminded him. "Had you not done that, the senior enlisted would never have had the opportunity to elect you to command the entire force."

"I guess with Vic Reynolds being held hostage you get to be the one to remind me of past screw-ups that I'm still paying for, huh? I tell you, Sanch, there's times I wish it'd never happened."

A too-brief-to-be-readable expression flickered across Sanchez's face. "I am certain there are many in Third Division, those saved by your actions, who feel differently."

"I sure hope so. You're leading the company in with me, then?"

"Unfortunately, no. I must grant that duty to its appropriate holder, the current company commander."

Stark tried not to show disappointment. *That's right. Sanchez got bumped up to battalion commander. I oughta know who the company commander is, blast it.* "Who is that now, Sanch? Anybody I know?" He'd known everyone in the unit, once, but there'd been battles since then, and a few replacements.

Another flicker of a possible smile. Sanchez had grown a lot more expressive in the last several months. "I believe so." He turned slightly, waving someone forward. "You remember Lieutenant Conroy?"

Conroy saluted Stark smartly. "Good afternoon, Commander Stark."

Stark returned the gesture, fighting down a smile of his own. "You got the whole company now, huh, Lieutenant? How's it going?"

"Not bad. A little testing and pressure at first. A few soldiers were surprised to see me."

"I bet. I sure never expected any of our old officers to volunteer to stay up here, under my command."

"There weren't exactly a lot of us. Sixteen total, if I recall."

"Sixteen's a lot," Stark noted, "when you consider it meant working for me and guaranteeing a court-martial if we lose. But I was grateful you stayed. We needed some good officers around to remind people how important you are. When you're doing your jobs right, that is. So the troops haven't given you too much trouble?"

"There were some interesting moments. I just had to remind them I was still an officer. We get along fine, now."

Stark nodded, thinking of how tough some of those moments might have been from enlisted personnel with healthy heads of resentment against an officer corps that had usually been concerned with promotion instead of leadership. "Well, Lieutenant, you know the situation. I guess you've got to rescue me again."

"The last time I did that they took my platoon away and made me a desk jockey." Stark had stayed behind after a risky raid, acting as a rear guard to enable the platoon to escape. Conroy's participation in an unauthorized relief operation to save Stark's life had earned her the enmity of superiors who weren't interested in risking expensive equipment to save one pain-in-the-neck sergeant. "But things are a little different this time," Conroy noted. "I think you'll be happy with the new commander of your old platoon. I'm sure you remember Corporal Gomez."

"Cor—?" Stark broke off his exclamation. *I'll be damned. Anita Gomez, commanding a platoon. Best corporal I ever had. Bet she keeps those apes sharp.* "How'd you talk her into that?"

"I didn't. She volunteered. Maybe she'll tell *you* why. When's the operation going down?"

Stark gestured the two to seats, then paced back and forth. "We need the special rounds for our rifles, first. These are non-lethal rounds. They'll disable the battle armor of anyone shot with them." Neither Conroy nor Sanchez could hide their curiosity. "The special rounds shoot nanobots into the armor, and the nanobots break stuff inside. But they're still manufacturing the rounds for us. After the special ammo is ready, we'll mount the op during the next available downtime. Meal, sleep, whatever. I'm worried about hostages, and I'm worried these mutineers might get desperate and start shooting at us."

Two nods as Stark continued. "We're facing about two companies' worth of soldiers total. That's bad odds for an attack, but they'll be spread out and hopefully won't have any clue about the special rounds we'll be firing."

"A single hit anywhere should disable the soldier?" Conroy asked.

"Right. The barracks has a standard layout. There's three main entrances; two for personnel access and one heavy cargo dock. I'll lead one platoon in the primary entry, and the other two platoons will take the other two." He saw the disapproval register instantly on their faces. "Yeah, I know. I'm not supposed to be leading a combat op, and that's what this might be if the mutineers start throwing live rounds back at us. But if I'm walking in from the front, maybe they'll surrender without shooting at all. I figure the risk is worth the chance to end the mutiny without bloodshed on either side."

"Your rationale seems solid," Sanchez noted, "but Sergeant Reynolds will still give you hell for it when the operation is over."

"No doubt. Any other questions?"

Conroy sighed. "I guess I should lead one of the other platoons in the same way. Seeing a lieutenant apparently walking calmly toward them might cause some serious hesitation on the part of the mutineers. Maybe enough to get past their barricade without shooting."

Sanchez managed a temporary questioning look. "Calmly, Lieutenant Conroy? You will be walking calmly?"

"I said *apparently* calmly. Besides, you know the Infantry School motto: Follow Me."

Stark laughed. "Yeah. Easy to say, ain't it? Until somebody's pointing weapons at you. Okay, there's not much else to say right now. Lieutenant, we're going to load floor plans for the barracks into the Tacs of each soldier. We can't afford to brief them all before the op goes down. We can't risk the mutineers getting a warning."

"I understand."

Sanchez made a gesture, which in another person would have registered as a powerful frown. "You intend loading a detailed plan into the Tacs and not briefing the soldiers prior to that? This does not sound like the Ethan Stark I knew."

"No," Stark replied. "No, it doesn't and no, that's not the idea. You'll get the floor plans. You'll also get what little we know of troop dispositions, mainly where the barricades are at the entrances. It'll be up to individual soldiers to get in there and take down the enemy." Stark grinned. "Maximum individual initiative. Does that sound like the Ethan Stark you knew?"

"Absolutely. It should be an interesting operation. Lieutenant Conroy and I will hold her company in readiness until we receive word from you."

"Thanks. And Lieutenant? Please let Corporal Gomez know I'm really looking forward to working with her again."

"Certainly, Commander."

Stark sweated out the full twenty-four hours Doctor Gafton had projected, plus three of the plus-or-minus-four-hours fudge factor Gafton had added on. When the ammo arrived, he examined the rifle magazines doubtfully. "They're sealed magazines. How can we be sure they're really nanobot rounds?"

Doctor Gafton offered up his characteristic eye blinks, then pointed to the magazine Stark was holding. "They are labeled with the appropriate ammunition designation."

"What if the label is wrong?"

"It shouldn't be. That would create problems."

Stark exhaled, looking toward Sergeant Gordasa. "Gordo?"

Gordasa smiled, gesturing to indicate the crate of rifle magazines. "I double-checked. Broke open a couple at random to verify contents. That cost you two magazines and forty rounds of this special ammo, but I figured it had to be done."

"It did. Thanks, Gordo. You're my kind of supply officer." Stark palmed his personal comm unit. "Sanch? Get Conroy and her people over here. We got some ass-kickin' to do."

Less than half an hour later, Corporal Gomez stood stern-faced before Stark, her hand held at a rigid salute. "The platoon is ready for action, Sargento."

Stark looked down the line of soldiers, noting familiar faces who were trying to suppress grins. He returned the salute. "Good to see you, Anita. We gotta get together more often."

"Maybe when we ain't getting' shot at, huh, Sargento? We gonna kick these mutineers' butts?"

"That's right." Stark waved all three platoons into seats, briefly explained the nanobot rounds, discussed the probable number of mutineers, then called up the floor plan for the Chamberlain Barracks and pointed out the barricades. "That's about all we know. You all have a copy of this floor plan in your Tacs."

"The tactical plan in there, too?" asked Sergeant Rosinski from Third Platoon.

"No." Stark waited a moment for the reaction to wind down.

"There ain't no plan, because we don't know enough to make one. So here's what you apes do. You go in there. You spread out and disarm everybody. If anybody starts shooting, you take 'em out with the nanobot rounds."

"But, where do we go?"

Stark waved at the floor plan. "Wherever you need to go. Listen, I'll explain so you'll see why I'm doing this." It was a habit Stark had been criticized for in the past, by officers annoyed at the time it took him to explain orders that his squad should have been executing without thinking about them. "Put yourself in the enemy's place. Somebody's attacking. What's the first thing you do?"

A pause, and then Corporal Gomez answered. "You figure out where they're putting most of their effort. The main attack, *sí*? So you send reinforcements to stop it."

"Right. Suppose instead of a main attack you've got about a hundred soldiers all moving independently?" Another pause, then soldiers around the room began smiling. "That's the idea. You're all vets. Break into fire teams, go individual if you need to, and spread out to check out every room of that barracks. Your rifles will be loaded with flash-bang grenades to help confuse anybody who needs confusing, and we'll be pumping some smoke into the barracks through the vents to hinder visibility a little. Not too much smoke, because we don't wanna suffocate anybody not in armor, but enough to help."

"So what are we doing while our troops run around by themselves?" Rosinski demanded.

"You're keeping an eye on them," Stark advised. "Somebody's gonna run into trouble. Maybe trapped, maybe facing too many defenders. You watch for that on your scans, and direct help where it's needed. Look, I know this is unconventional as hell, but we need two things to make sure we rescue the hostages without harm. The first is surprise and the second is speed. By spreading you guys through the barracks by every route possible we should be able to maintain both. Any questions?"

A corporal from First Platoon raised his hand. "We'll all be in the same armor as the mutineers. How do we know who's who?"

"We've tweaked the IFF in your outfits to give a special return so you'll know who other members of the company are. Any armor without the tweak that queries you will get a standard reply, so that should help confuse the bad guys a little. Hell. I almost forgot something real important. These nano rounds ain't lethal to anybody in armor. They shouldn't even penetrate the armor. But if you shoot one at an unarmored soldier the least you'll do is shock their nervous system bad. Don't fire at anybody who's not in armor."

"What if they're shooting at us, Sarge?" Private Chen from Stark's old squad asked.

"Then you get close enough to hit 'em over the head and take their weapon away." He saw the order didn't meet with great enthusiasm. "Sorry, people. That's the way it's gotta be. None of those mutineers are gonna be KIA because of something we did. And, yeah, in case you're thinking that's easy for me to say, don't forget I'll be right in there with you. I'm leading Second Platoon in. Walking through the front door."

Reaction rippled through the company, the members of Second Platoon grinning with delight. Then Conroy stood. "I'll be leading in First Platoon. The same way. Rosinski, you get Third Platoon all to yourself."

"Lucky me. I gotta walk in, too?"

"That's up to you. How's your command presence feel today?"

"It's been better. But it should be enough to handle a bunch of apes from Second Brigade."

"Good," Stark grunted. "Anything else?"

After a long moment, another corporal stood. "Sergeant. I gotta tell you, some of us are worried about these, uh, special rounds for the rifles."

"They'll work, Corporal. They've been tested on battle armor. Don't worry about that."

"With all due respect, that's not the worry." The corporal looked around, licking his lips at the stern, questioning expressions on the faces of the senior enlisted. "Some guys are wondering . . . well . . ."

"Spit it out."

"How do we know these ain't normal lethal rounds and we're going in there to really take down these guys permanent?" the corporal blurted.

Stark held up a hand to suppress the angry murmurs that followed the question. "I take it my word ain't good enough?" The corporal gulped, but shook his head. "Well, you got guts to ask that question. Who else is worried about that? Show me hands. I mean it." Slowly, hesitantly, another score of hands raised. *Twenty. Twenty-one counting the corporal. I can't afford to leave that many people out of this op. The odds are too bad as it is. How can I reassure these guys? Breakin' open another magazine wouldn't convince them. What would? Oh. Well, if you gotta, you gotta.*

Stark took four steps to the side, away from the display, sealed his armor's face shield, then turned to face the other soldiers again, spreading his arms out slightly. "Okay, you apes are worried about the nano rounds killing your buddies. So shoot 'em at me." Stark could feel the incredulity radiating from the company. "I mean it. I trust 'em enough to let you pump rounds into me if you want to. I can't give you any more assurance than that." *And Anita, for God's sake don't you shoot the first soldier who raises a weapon at me.*

No one did. The corporal grinned, nodded, and sat down. "That's good enough for me."

"Good." Stark raised his face shield again, relieved that he didn't have to worry about fitting himself into another set of battle armor on short notice. "Now, let's kick some butt."

"In a gentle, nonlethal fashion?" Sergeant Rosinski asked.

"Hell, you can beat on 'em all you want, 'Ski. Just don't shoot any of 'em if they ain't in armor."

Everything looked deceptively quiet at Chamberlain Barracks. The mutineer barricades resembled the piles of furniture dumped in the hallways whenever the solid lunar rock floors in the living quarters were resealed. It was just past normal dinner hour, when everyone should be relaxing. Stark glanced back at his platoon and smiled with an odd degree of contentment for someone about to walk head-on toward fidgety mutineers packing rifles loaded with bullets that would kill. "You ready, Corporal Gomez?"

"*Sí.* Feel's good, don't it? All us together again."

"Damn right. I wouldn't want any other squad, any other platoon with me, not if I could choose from anywhere and anytime." He felt a bit awkward after saying that, as if it were too much, but the truth behind it reassured him.

Stark checked the time, counting down the last seconds on his

HUD. "Okay, everybody. Let's go. By the numbers." Gomez was right. It felt good, leading a small body of soldiers again, responsible for only a limited number of bodies in a limited area.

Stark unsealed his face shield, raising it fully so his face could be seen. Holding his rifle at loose port arms, he began walking toward the main entrance of the barracks. Above the door, an embossed image of a soldier, wearing a high-necked uniform adorned with stars on the collar, gazed severely downward, his big mustache seeming to droop in disapproval of the activity inside. *So that's Chamberlain. A general, I guess. Wonder what he did, and when he did it? I oughta find out, someday.*

The mutineers manning the barricade had noticed Stark's slow, casual progress. Rifles came up, aiming toward him. Twenty paces behind, the platoon followed, not in formation, not dispersed for combat, but ambling along in a nonthreatening manner. At the other entrances, he knew, Conroy and Rosinski were doing the same thing.

"Halt!" The command sounded firm enough, but Stark kept coming. "Halt! We'll shoot!"

Stark didn't halt, continuing his steady, measured pace, but he began talking. "This is Sergeant Ethan Stark. You know who I am, and you know you can trust me. I don't care what somebody else might have told you. I won't lie to you. Put down your weapons and nothing has to happen." Some of the rifle barrels wavered. "We've got plenty of real enemies out there. We don't need to be fighting each other. If you guys have got grievances, you'll get a hearing. I promise."

"He's lying!" The corporal apparently in charge of the barricade rounded on his troops. "You can't trust him. He's just out to be dictator, over our bodies! Our blood! How many of you have lost friends in one of Stark's little wars?"

The weapons aimed at Stark drifted a little further, none directly aimed at him now. *That's it. Keep 'em talking. I'll just keep walking. Any second now they'll notice the platoon behind me....* "I don't start wars, Corporal. I end them. I'm trying to end the one we've been fighting up here. I don't see how fighting each other helps anyone but our enemies." He was almost at the barricade, measuring the hesitation among the mutineers. *A couple more steps—*

"Nail him!" the corporal ordered, but his fellow soldiers hesitated, looking at each other. The corporal cursed at his troops, then leveled his rifle at Stark. *Okay. Game over.* Stark jumped forward and to the side, keeping just high enough to clear the barricade, his rifle swinging to line up on the corporal as Stark fired a short burst directly into his target. He pulled his face shield shut as he dropped on the far side of the barricade, landing on his shoulder and bringing the weapon to bear on the mutineers from the back.

The near-silence of a moment earlier shattered into a million harsh sounds as some of the mutineers tried to target Stark while others returned fire at the members of Stark's platoon. The shock of rifle fire echoed from the walls, oddly disturbing to soldiers who'd grown used to combat in the airless silence of the Moon's exterior. Flash-bang grenades exploded with disorienting light and concussion effects. Most of the mutineers simply broke and ran, some leaving their weapons. Amid the confusion, Stark lay flat where his jump had landed him, carefully targeting each mutineer firing a weapon. Bullets sparked off the wall near his head, throwing chips of rock out in tiny sprays, then the soldier responsible stiffened and fell as Stark's own rounds caught him and froze his battle armor. *Love those nanobots.* His HUD screamed a warning, highlighting a mutineer fumbling with her weapon, and Stark dropped that one as well.

As quickly as it had erupted, the firefight ended, any remaining mobile mutineers dropping their weapons in surrender. "Anita! Detail a guard for these guys. Let's go!" Stark ran down the hall, his armor's microphones picking up the sounds of mutineers fleeing before him and the clatter of most of the platoon following in his wake. "Spread out when you hit intersecting corridors. Keep 'em guessing." He came up against a corner, breathing heavily, taking the barest moment to pull back his scan to see how the other platoons were doing. Rosinski's was apparently stalled near the loading dock, but Conroy's force was streaming into the barracks just like the platoon with Stark. *That's one damn good lieutenant. Shows what you can do if you train an officer up right.*

Stark went around the corner, hunched over and moving fast. Shots spanged into the rock around him as he rolled to the far wall. Behind him, other soldiers followed, returning the fire. He felt a thrill of fear, knowing he was too exposed, but unable to fall back without drawing more attention. *Been out of tactical ops too long. Gotten rusty. Didn't think this one through.* The only thing saving him was the apparent reluctance of the mutineers to risk being hit. They were keeping down and firing without aiming carefully.

"Sargento, you okay?"

"Yeah, Anita. But I ain't happy. Is there anybody in position to get behind those mutineers?"

"*Sí.* Any second now." A flurry of shots ahead of Stark, and then firing ceased as the small pocket of mutineers surrendered to the soldiers hitting them in the flank.

Stark surged back up despite the little voice in the back of his head insisting that he was being an idiot. *Gotta get to Vic. If they're gonna shoot anybody, it'll be her.* Another scan of the barracks as he ran down the hall along with a small group from Second Platoon. The symbols crawling through the 3-D representation of the barracks were frustratingly confusing. As Stark watched, a scattered patch of symbols tagged with First Platoon's ID converged on the red symbology representing the mutineers that were keeping Third Platoon tied down on the loading dock. The red symbols fell away rapidly, some freezing in place and marked as incapacitated, others lost as they ran into halls and rooms where the individual sensors on the battle armor couldn't spot them. "Corporal Gomez."

"*Sí,* Sargento."

"You've got some people close to the central comm relay for the barracks. If you take that, we can see anywhere in here again."

"I'm on it."

It was a very good thing to be able to trust someone so absolutely in combat. Stark put the comm relay out of his mind as he studied the diagram again, letting some of the other soldiers dash past him. *Okay. Figure a big room so they can minimize the number of guards. A big room with only the two exits required by fire code.* There were four possibilities, all briefing rooms. Stark headed for the nearest, watching for any surprises. He was alone now, the other soldiers from Second Platoon scattered in search of targets.

A pair of armored figures came around the corner. Everyone

pointed weapons, but the tweaked IFF pronounced them members of First Platoon. "Sergeant Stark?"

"Yeah." Even as Stark answered, his HUD bloomed with new symbols as the barracks comm relay began forwarding data from every room to his battle armor. "You guys getting the full picture now, too?"

"Yessir. Hey, there's a couple of those Fifth Batt guys one room down."

"You take 'em. I'm heading the other way."

"No problem!" Stark left the others, heading down the hall with more confidence now that his HUD showed what must be most of the mutineers. *I can't assume somebody hasn't worked some bypass on their room's sensors.* Soldiers did that, to cover up illicit activity, or just the presence of a visitor sharing legal but intimate activity. The briefing rooms all showed blank, not bypassed, but openly disabled. *So they* are *being used to hold people. And those people got unhappy enough about that to knock out the sensors. I'll bet that ticked off the 'Enlisted Council.'*

A briefing room far from Stark blossomed with detections, as some soldiers from Third Platoon burst in. "This place is full of privates," one reported. "Unarmed, looks like."

"Was the door locked from the outside?" Sergeant Rosinski demanded.

"That's affirmative, Sarge."

"'Ski," Stark broke in. "It looks like maybe a company worth of enlisted in there. Those'll be some of the ones who didn't go along with the mutiny, but keep an eye on them until we're sure. There's probably another company locked up in another one of the briefing rooms. You copy, Lieutenant Conroy?"

"I copy. Any sign of the senior enlisted?"

"I think I'm about to find some," Stark replied, pausing outside the room he had been heading for. Inside, he could hear shouting, some of it amplified by battle armor and in the angry, panicked tones of a person who thought they were losing control of a situation.

Stark came through the door in a rush, sweeping the room with his rifle as he moved. In front of him, an armored figure hesitated, its IFF tagging it as a mutineer. Stark put a short burst into it, then pivoted to focus on where Vic Reynolds and a couple of other sergeants were struggling for the weapon of a second guard. "Get clear!" Stark bellowed over his outside speaker, and as the sergeants dropped away obediently Stark planted two rounds in the guard's armored chest. The guard tried to bring his own weapon around, then fell.

Stark scanned the room again, carefully, but saw no other threats. "Vic? That the only other guard?"

She was staring at him with a mixture of shock and outrage. "You just shot them both? That casually? What the hell—?"

"I asked you if those were the only guards, soldier!"

Vic stopped speaking, then nodded. "Yes. Those were the only two."

"Good." Stark checked his HUD for any signs of other mutineers in the area, but the few red symbols still active were some distance away. He leaned over the second guard. "Don't get all in an uproar, Vic. He ain't hurt for real." Unsealing the guard's face shield, Stark revealed a sweating face with wide eyes. "Mind you, if this clown had killed anybody in here, I might've left him in his armor until he starved to death."

Private Billings from Stark's old squad came storming in, her weapon at the ready, then halted, sweeping the room. "You okay, Sarge?"

"Yeah, I'm okay."

"Wow. Thanks. Corporal Gomez would've eaten me alive if anything'd happened to you."

"What? Explain that."

"Uh . . . well, Corporal Gomez told me to stick with you no matter what and make sure you didn't get hurt. But I lost you during one of the firefights. You move awful fast for an old guy, Sarge."

"Thanks a lot. You and Gomez oughta know I can take care of myself."

"Okay, Sarge. Um, they're doing a sweep through the rooms, so I guess I should—"

"Yeah. Go ahead. And, Billings?" She paused in mid-step. "Thanks. I mean it. See you around."

"Sure thing, Sarge." Billings headed out of the room, already back in combat mode as she reached the hall.

Vic was on one knee, examining both guards. "Their suits are disabled. What the hell kind of bullets are you using?"

"Something special we were putting together for some guests

we're expecting. They turned out to be handy for this little mess, as well." He glared at her. "Thanks for the vote of confidence."

She flinched. "I'm very sorry, Ethan. I should have known you wouldn't have done that, not unless it was absolutely necessary."

"Yeah, you should have. Who're the rest of you guys?" They seemed to be mostly sergeants, with a scattering of corporals.

One strode forward. "The senior enlisted from Fifth Battalion. Most of them, anyway. We owe you an apology, too, Stark. This never should've happened. We should've seen it coming, and we should've stopped it."

"We'll figure out how it happened later. You said you're most of the senior enlisted? Where's the others? The only guy I've talked to is a corporal named Hostler."

"Hostler? Oh, man, wait'll I get my hands on that sorry little sack of—"

"Lieutenant Conroy," Stark called over the command circuit. "Anybody pick up Corporal Hostler yet?"

"Yes, Commander. One of Rosinski's people caught him trying to sneak out of the barracks. He's currently in Sergeant Yurivan's custody."

"Yurivan? How'd she get him so fast?"

"She came in with me, Commander. Showed up at the last minute and said she ought to walk along with me since she was from Fifth Battalion originally and probably knew the soldiers manning the barricade. It worked. We took the barricade without a shot. After that, things got hot, though."

"So I saw. I think I've got all the loyal senior enlisted in here. Anybody else you pick up was probably in on the mutiny." Stark scanned his Tactical display one more time, noting the lack of ongoing combat, then unsealed his own face shield and raised it so he could speak directly to the soldiers in the room with him. "You guys'll have to wait to work over Hostler, I'm afraid. Sergeant Yurivan's got him at the moment."

"Stacey?" The Fifth Battalion sergeant grinned. "Oh, man. Hostler ain't gonna enjoy that." His smile faded. "But he ain't behind this. Not enough brains and not enough guts. Nobody's told us, but we figure at least some of the sergeants who ain't in here with us were involved."

"By any chance are any of these missing sergeants friends of a guy named Kalnick?"

"You got it. We wanta talk to them, too. Unless Stacey's planning on working them over when she's done with Hostler."

"I'm sure she's looking forward to it, but I'll see what I can do. Speaking of which . . ." Lieutenant Conroy entered, along with four soldiers from First Platoon, escorting several sergeants. "Where'd you find these?"

"A couple were in battle armor. After we disabled it, we pried them out to bring them to you. The others were hiding in one of the conference rooms. I guess that was their headquarters."

"Do tell." Stark lowered his face shield long enough to check his HUD. "I read all rooms secure and no remaining resistance. You concur, Lieutenant?"

"Yessir."

"Any casualties?"

"A couple wounded and four disabled by friendly fire. The mutineers mainly fired wildly, from what I saw."

"Me, too." Stark switched circuits. "Sergeant Shwartz, Chamberlain Barracks is secured. Send in the Military Police on standby to take custody of the building and our prisoners. Oh, yeah. Nobody's hurt except a couple of our people who were wounded. Tell anybody and everybody that." Another switch, to the command center. "Sergeant Tran. Broadcast to all locations that the mutiny has been ended, order has been restored, and none of the mutineers were injured." *Not seriously, anyway. Though I'm not taking bets on what might happen when these sergeants get their hands on some of those mutineers.* "Get the word out." He turned to Lieutenant Conroy. "Turn over the building to the MPs and put your company on liberty. Turn 'em loose as fast as you can."

"Commander Stark, standard debriefing—"

"We'll do a debrief later, Lieutenant. I need your soldiers out and about boasting how they took down these mutineers without hurting any of them."

"Ah." Conroy nodded. "I understand." She moved away, passing on Stark's orders to her platoon leaders.

Stark finally focused on the bedraggled sergeants who had been behind the mutiny. "Game over, ladies and gentlemen. You should've known better than to listen to Kalnick." A couple of them jerked in involuntary reaction. "Yeah, we know he helped start this. Now you're expecting to get the hell kicked out of you and then some firing squads, right?" Faces settled in lines of fear or determination, depending on the individual. "Well, I ain't gonna give you the satisfaction. That'd make you martyrs, wouldn't it? No, you're going to be locked up. Anybody who sings about the people behind this gets better treatment. Anybody who doesn't, gets forgotten in their cells for a while so I can deal with more important things. Forgotten by me, anyway. I'm sure Sergeant Yurivan will want some interviews to help you pass the time. Is that clear? Think about it."

Stark began turning to face the other sergeants, then pivoted back. "Oh, one more thing. If even one of my people had been killed as a result of this nonsense I'd have personally torn you all apart." A group of MPs entered, their leader saluting Stark. "Get these people out of my sight. Lock 'em down tight."

"Yessir. Uh, we're going to need a list of the charges against each individual. That's paperwork required by the stockade."

"You'll get one." He faced the other Fifth Battalion sergeants, not trying to hide his regret. "I hope you'll all understand that we've got to go through everybody in this barracks and make sure they weren't involved in the mutiny. I don't expect anyone in here to have problems proving that, but I have to keep you in the barracks until we've done the investigations. There's a sweep going through now searching for any weapons or stragglers from the guys who fought us. After that, you guys can go back to your quarters. We'll let you know when you can move about freely again. Any questions?"

None of them looked happy, but no one objected. The Fifth Battalion sergeant who'd spoken to Stark stiffened into attention and saluted. "We understand. We do ask that we be consulted on the new leadership for the battalion."

"New leadership?" Stark shook his head. "Whoever set this up was good enough to keep it hidden from everybody. You guys who didn't go along with the mutiny can expect to return to the same positions you've held, unless I get reports of anything especially negative about any particular individual." *And I know you'll be trying ten times as hard to do your jobs well to help make up for this mutiny happening under your noses.* Motivation was motivation, and Stark had no intention of throwing away people who had every reason to work hard in the future.

Relieved smiles spread across the faces before Stark. "You won't regret that, Stark. I knew that crap they were trying to tell us about you wasn't true."

Vic cleared her throat. "Am I confined to the barracks as well? You said everyone here was to be interviewed."

Stark gave her a level look. "No. Since you weren't here when the mutiny started, I guess we can assume you weren't involved. Now, I've gotta get back to the command center to make sure any fallout from this mess is handled right." He headed out without waiting for her.

Vic caught up before he left the building. "Ethan, I said I was sorry. It was unpardonable of me to berate you in front of the other noncommissioned officers, and inexcusable for me to fail to focus on your proper concern over the possible presence of additional guards."

"What about thinking I'd gun down fellow soldiers like I was taking a walk in the park? You sorry for thinking that?"

"I already said so. But you are a very hard man when you think you have to be, Ethan Stark."

Stark had never seen Vic look so contrite. *Maybe she'll feel guilty and cut me a little slack for a while.* "That's okay, I guess."

"Now what the hell were you doing leading this operation in person?"

That sure didn't last long. "I had good reasons. But the biggest one was that I wasn't gonna send people into a fight to maintain my authority without making a last personal effort to shut the mutiny down without a fight. And if it came to a fight, I was damned if I'd let someone else run all the risks."

"Ethan . . ." Vic rubbed her forehead, looking pained. "Oh, hell. What can I say? That's how you are. It'll probably get you killed some day, and I'll be there saying damnit-I-told-you-so, and they'll build a monument to you because you died doing something so flipping noble and self-sacrificing."

"Don't you ever let them build a monument to me."

"It'll be a big one, Ethan. Fountains and towers and pillars and a huge statue of you gazing up at the heavens—"

"Don't you dare!" He gave her a smile. "How was it in there? Bad?"

"It wasn't good. They thought they had you over a barrel. I could tell by the way the guards were acting. There's something about being locked up under guard, Ethan. Something ugly."

"I bet. I'm glad you made it out in one piece."

"Me, too."

Stark reviewed the last of the paperwork relating to the mutiny. Yurivan's interrogations had produced plenty of results, but all of them had ultimately led nowhere. Contacts who had encouraged the mutiny turned out to be people who apparently didn't exist in any record system and couldn't be found. Kalnick's name had been used freely, but actual evidence against him simply didn't exist. *Well, we knew the people working against us were professionals.* The mutineers had been promised many things, most notably amnesty for themselves for any acts relating to the original rebellion led by Stark, and extensive external support once the mutiny was under way. The external support hadn't materialized, either because the mutiny had been so limited or because the support had never actually been planned.

The mutineers had been carefully screened, with many of the privates given administrative punishment if their participation had been minimal. That left maybe thirty soldiers in the stockade for charges ranging from leading the mutiny to firing on the force Stark and Conroy had led into the building. *What am I going to do with them? I don't want to hold that many court-martials, but I don't want them all locked up indefinitely. That wouldn't be right or legal. Hmmm. I bet there's still plenty of family members of soldiers up here that we can swap them for, if the authorities back home are still willing to deal. That'll get them off my hands and get us some more people we do want, which won't hurt morale any.*

His comm unit buzzed. Stark closed out the mutiny records with a sense of relief then keyed his display to receive the incoming call. The screen cleared to show the face of Colony Manager Campbell, looking more than a little bemused. "Sergeant Stark, I assume you're aware that one of the official shuttles has just arrived for the continuation of our talks, not that we're expecting any results."

"Yes, sir. I knew one was coming in. The last I heard it didn't

have any military representatives so I didn't need any presence at
the meeting. But there is something we need to raise."

"Oh? What's that?"

"That mutiny I dealt with. I've got thirty soldiers who were
too heavily involved to just let off easy, and I don't want them
stuck in cells up here. Can you guys work another swap like we
did with the officers?"

"Certainly, Sergeant Stark. It's not too late for me to raise that
during our talks. Thirty, you said? I'm sure we can get something
worked out. But I called you because the official shuttle brought
a visitor along. An unexpected visitor."

Stark raised his eyebrows. "Somebody I need to know
about?"

"I assume so, Sergeant. He says he's your father."

Thirty minutes later, Stark stood fidgeting at Sentry Post One
at the main entrance to the military complex. He'd put on a clean
uniform, and Vic had gone over it to make sure he looked decent.
"It's not every day you meet your dad," she remarked.

"Vic, I haven't seen my dad since I enlisted in the mil. He was
mad as hell at me, told me I was an idiot to join, and we hadn't
even talked after that until about a year ago. Since then it's only
been a couple of pieces of mail."

"I know, Ethan. So what's he doing here, on the official shuttle with the latest batch of nonnegotiators?"

"I guess I'll find out in a few minutes."

"Do you need me along? Never mind. You wouldn't know
until you meet him. I'll be in the command center if you want
me."

"Thanks." Now Stark was waiting for a man he hadn't seen in
person since Stark had been barely out of his teens. A small
group of figures appeared down the hallway leading to the sentry post. Stark recognized Cheryl Sarafina first, leading the
group. In the back, he saw two Colony security guards who had
accompanied Campbell in the past. Finally, as the group got
closer, Stark recognized the man they were escorting, holding
onto an arm or shoulder whenever he wobbled in the low gravity. The group came to a halt before him, and Stark stood tongue-
tied, having completely failed to think up in advance some way
of saying hello in person to his long-estranged father.

The silence stretched for a long moment, then Sarafina smiled politely, as if she recognized what was going on. "Sergeant Stark. This is your father."

The innocuous words broke the ice. Stark reached to shake his father's hand. "Dad. Good to see you."

His father took his hand, moving with the exaggerated care of someone new to lunar gravity who mistrusts his every move. "Good to see you, son."

"You have a good trip?"

"Not bad. I've had worse."

Sarafina seemed to be fighting down another smile. "I can tell this is a very emotional moment for you both. We'll wait here for your father, Sergeant Stark."

"Okay. Thanks. I appreciate you bringing him in." He held out his hand to his father again. "Do you, um, need a hand with balance or anything?"

His father waved the hand away, though his expression was uncertain. "I think I can manage. Try to keep your speed down, though."

"No problem." They moved past the sentry post, the sentries on duty snapping to attention and rendering salutes as Stark passed. He returned the salutes with unusual care. "He's with me," Stark assured the sentries.

They went a few paces in silence, then his father spoke. "Why did they do that?"

"Huh?" Stark glanced over at his father, puzzled. "Do what?"

"That jumping up and saluting stuff. Did they do that for you?"

"Sure. That's standard military courtesy."

"I see a lot of military people passing each other, and they aren't doing that."

"They did that with me because I'm their commander," Stark explained.

"The boss, you mean. So you're the boss here? Of how much?"

"Uh, everything." Stark gestured to take in the hallway. "This place. These people. Everybody and everything military that's defending the Colony."

"Everything?" His father looked around, an unreadable expression now on his face. "Well."

"Yeah." *I gotta get Vic. This is too clumsy. We don't know how to talk. But, then, we never did.* "Let me show you the command center first."

"Alright." His father followed obediently through the hallways, occasionally raising his eyebrows as a passing soldier saluted Stark.

Stark palmed the access to the command center, trying to avoid looking at the new metal of the door that remained a painful reminder of the raid on his headquarters that had cost a number of lives. "This is, uh, the command center."

"So you said." His father peered around. "Pretty impressive gear. Some of it looks like it's been damaged, though. Surely it's not secondhand?"

"Uh, no. There was an attack here. Right here. We had to fight it off behind these consoles. They've been repaired since then. Like the door."

"Oh." His father seemed momentarily at a loss for words. "I remember, now. We heard about it."

"Ethan." Vic came forward. "You have a visitor?"

"Yeah. This is my dad. Dad, this is Vic Reynolds. She's a real good friend. She's also second in command here and a real good tactical thinker."

"A pleasure," his father beamed, leaning slightly to look at Vic's shoulders where her stripes were displayed. "You are also an, uh, sergeant?"

"That's right."

"But you are my son's assistant?"

Stark flinched at the term but Vic merely smiled. "You might say that. My main job seems to be trying to keep him out of trouble. It's an endless task."

"I imagine so! You and I can probably swap some hair-raising tales about that. You sent Ethan's mother and I a letter once, didn't you?"

"I did." She smiled again, then hooked a thumb toward the door. "Why don't we go somewhere quiet to talk, Ethan?"

"Sure." *I don't believe it. Five seconds with him and she's got my dad talking like he's an old friend.* "After you."

Vic led the way to the rec room nearest Stark's quarters, getting coffee as the others sat. His father peered around at the small space and its rock walls. "This is where you work?"

"Sometimes," Stark admitted. "My room's just around the corner from here. It's about the same size."

"Really? As a boy, you always complained your room was too small. This is smaller than that."

Stark felt himself flushing at the memory. "I bitched a lot more than I should have. You and Mom did a helluva lot for me. And taught me a lot of important things."

"I guess we did, though I admit I can't recall just when we taught you to stage revolutions and overthrow governments."

Stark winced. "I can't blame that on you."

"Don't look at me," Vic added. "It's not my fault." She turned to Stark's father, face serious. "I'm sorry, sir, but I must ask you something directly. What brings you here? The government has banned unofficial travel up here, yet you arrived on the shuttle bringing an official negotiating party."

"I was wondering when someone would ask me that." He stared at the floor for a moment, his face reflecting anger. "To put it simply, I'm here to try to convince Ethan that he should give up. Surrender. Accept whatever offer he gets from the government before anyone else gets hurt."

"I see. You don't appear to be happy with that mission."

"I'm not. I happen to be very proud of what my son has done. I've had to spend my life kissing the butts of people who think they're better than me. My son has now kicked those butts nice and hard. And from all I've been able to tell, he didn't do it to get anything for himself, but just to help others."

An awkward silence reigned for a moment. "Hell, Dad," Stark noted, "you never let people walk on you."

"Yes, I did! I'm doing it now by coming here! Not that I had much choice. Your mother's ill. I'm sorry. We hadn't told you. You have enough to worry about, and you'd probably think it was a government trick anyway. No, she's in pretty bad shape, but it can be treated successfully. High odds of remission, they say. If the treatment is approved. Do you know who has to approve the treatment, Ethan?"

"Let me guess."

"Correct. A government official. They'll do it, they say, but I was told it would certainly expedite any decision if I came up here and begged you to give up."

"Bastards." Stark slammed one fist against the wall, oblivious to the blood spotting his knuckles afterward. "I guess Mom's just one more little guy who doesn't count, except when the bosses can use them. Well, hell, tell the government you begged me on your knees and I refused to listen at all. I mean it. If they think they can get to me through Mom they might try some other games with her treatment."

"You're probably right," his father sighed, noticing his coffee for the first time and taking a drink, then twitching in involuntary reaction. "This stuff is awful. This is what you have to drink thanks to the blockade?"

"Nah. This is what the government always gives us. Standard military coffee."

"You ought to try the beer," Vic suggested. "It makes the coffee taste good by comparison."

"I'll take your word for it." Stark's father took another cautious sip, then shuddered. "Well, I've had my say, and I'm sure you want to get rid of me, now."

"No," Stark protested. "Dad, I know you've only got a little while, but you don't have to rush off."

"Thank you." He glanced around, puzzled. "Is it safe here? We've been told you're under siege, your defenses crumbling. But, none of you seem worried at all."

"We're worried. No one knows how things will work out in the end. But we're not crumbling. No way. We've taken everything the government's thrown at us so far and broken it into little pieces."

"There was a tremendous explosion on the Moon a few months ago. A lot of people saw it. The government said it was in the Colony, but there's a lot of people who claim the explosion was outside the Colony."

"It was. We caused it. Blew up a lot of ammunition the government had sent up here."

"You did?" His father laughed. "Serves them right. So, you're safe? You've defeated every attack?"

"I don't want to make it sound too cut and dried. We've been lucky a few times," Stark hedged. "Sometimes it's been pretty close. And we've lost people."

"Lost them? How?"

It took Stark a moment to realize his father truly didn't understand what the term 'lost' meant in the case of a soldier. "Killed, Dad. They've been killed fighting up here."

"Oh." Stark's father ducked his head to hide his embarrassment. "I'm . . . I'm sorry. I really didn't—"

"I know. That's okay."

"But you still seem confident, if I'm any judge of people. Everyone I've seen here seems confident."

Stark pondered the statement, then shrugged. "Yeah. That's right. Truth be told, I think we could grab a lot of extra territory if we wanted it."

"Extra territory?" Stark's father's eyebrows rose, then lowered into a frown. "But the military situation up here has been stalemated for years. That's what the government kept telling us. Were they lying?"

"No. Not about that. It's just the way we were fighting, the way they were telling us to fight, that kept us from breaking the stalemate. Everything was too rigid, too preplanned all to hell and gone, too much micromanagement of the guys with weapons from people way behind the front line. When we got rid of the people behind the front, and managed to survive long enough, we figured out how to do it better."

"I'm not sure I understand. You mean you can, what's the word, command better now?" His father leaned forward, intent on the question.

Stark rubbed his forehead, arranging his thoughts. "Everything's been top down in the past, Dad. You know, just like in civ, uh, civilian jobs. The big boss tells little bosses who tell littler bosses who tell somebody else until you finally get to the apes who do the actual job, and then they're expected to do exactly as told. Oh, there's always talk about letting the guys doing the job have a lot of input, but it never happens much because too few bosses want to share information or authority. It's been that way since forever, I guess, and maybe it had to work that way because only the big boss could collect all the data and maybe understand what was going down."

His father frowned again, this time thoughtfully, then nodded. "Of course. Every system I've seen functions the same way. They collect information and funnel it to what you call the boss, which is whoever is allowed to make decisions. Then the boss uses the same system in reverse to tell everyone what to do."

"But why does some guy at the top have to decide everything?" Stark stood, pacing back and forth as he spoke, the long, low lunar-gravity steps carrying him almost across the room with every stride. "Maybe in the old days, yeah, that had to happen. But now every grunt can know as much as the guy at the top. They've got access to the same data, even though the bosses are usually trying to block them from seeing it because they claim low-level guys can't understand things. We're mushrooms, right? Keep us in the dark and feed us crap."

His father laughed. "I hadn't heard that one before."

"But you know," Stark continued, "maybe now a low-level guy like you or me can understand some or all of that information better, because we're right there where things are happening, not somewhere way behind the front where you can't feel stuff."

"Feel stuff?"

"Yeah. You know. It's not what you're being told, or what your sensors say, it's how the troops feel, how the enemy's reacting, how the ground feels to you right there. And you can't get that through a data stream. No way." Stark paused, his hands moving as if forming his words in the air before him. "So we tried it different. We've let the guys on the scene call the shots. Change the plan if they want. Go for what seems best."

"But . . . I thought the purpose of a plan was to achieve a desired end."

"It should be! But the plan always turns into the be-all and end-all. A little thing like the objective gets lost in all the planning, and everybody ends up worrying about jumping through every hoop in the plan. You can plan something to death, Dad. Until you've got everything every person has to do spelled out, right down to the times when they get a latrine break. Then you ask them what they're trying to accomplish, and all they can do is point to the plan. "

"Hmmm." His father looked toward Vic for her opinion.

"It may sound crazy," she assured him, "but it works. The whole historical basis for military action has been massing defending forces against whatever point the enemy is attacking. If the attacking force is moving forward as dozens or hundreds of autonomously operating units, yet thanks to our technology is able to still coordinate the actions of each one of those units when necessary, it makes it almost impossible to identify the main attack. It's like trying to stop water with your hands."

"Right. Because there isn't a main attack," Stark elaborated. "We tried this in its purest form during an, uh, recent problem up here. Put a bunch of troops into a building held by hostile forces and let them just run where they liked. The bad guys tried to organize a response but couldn't figure out where to react."

"I see," Stark's father replied, though his tone remained doubtful. "I take it you're saying you can now defeat any other military force?"

"I think so. Yeah. If we wanted to."

His father looked even unhappier. "And your primary enemy now is the U.S. government."

"I guess so."

"Then I suppose you're planning to attack that, aren't you?"

The question caught Stark by surprise. He was sure his reaction showed on his face, but he denied it verbally anyway. "I ain't doing that. I'm not launching any attacks on the U.S."

"If he did," Vic added, "I wouldn't help him."

His father pursed his lips, eyes searching Stark's face. "You know you can't win that way. I may not be some military hotshot, but I know sports, at least. If all you do is let the other guy try to win while you only try to stop him, sooner or later that other guy *will* win."

"Dad, sometimes winning ain't worth the price you'd pay for victory. Those people, the civs back in America, they depend on us to protect them. They've done one lousy job of saying 'thanks' in the past, but that don't matter. I'm not gonna win this war if it means hitting them. Or if it means hitting the government that they're still supporting. It sucks, but that's all there is to it. Pardon my language."

"We're all adults here, son. What about your people, then, Ethan? What about all the soldiers who are following you? You realize you're possibly condemning them to an endless and ultimately losing war?"

"Yeah." Stark stared back stubbornly. "I've always kept the faith with the people I'm responsible for. In this case, that means I can't lead these apes into an attack on our home and feel I've done what's right. And we're all responsible for keeping the faith with those civs, to protect them. Nothing we've done so far really hurts the Constitution, and that's what we're sworn to up-hold. If we go in to physically take down the government, we've ripped up that piece of paper. I won't do it, and I won't lead other soldiers to do it. If they don't like it, they can choose another boss."

His father smiled. "That was the big question in my mind, and in the minds of a lot of other people back home. What's this Stark guy have in mind? And I didn't know, son. I knew the boy who left home a long time ago, but I wasn't sure how he'd changed. Now, I know. I'll make sure a lot of other people know, too."

Vic chuckled. "It sounds like the government's plan to use you against Ethan is going to backfire."

"It does, doesn't it, Ms. Reynolds? Serves them right."

"Uh, Dad," Stark advised. "That should be sergeant. Sergeant Reynolds."

"I'm sorry! I just have trouble seeing such a nice, young lady as being in the same line of work as you. Uh, that is—"

"Don't worry, Dad. I know what you meant."

"Me, too," Vic stated. "'Nice, young lady,' huh? You've got a real perceptive father, Ethan."

"Sure. He just thinks that because he's never seen you lead a squad of ground apes as you shred an enemy force into little quivering pieces."

"A girl has a right to have some fun in life, Ethan." Vic checked the time on the nearest display. "I think we need to let you go, Mr. Stark. I'll escort you back to the landing field so you can catch that shuttle when the official delegation leaves."

Stark shook his head. "Vic, Cheryl Sarafina's waiting at Sentry Post One to take him back to the shuttle. I oughta go along—"

"No, you don't." She pointed a firm finger his way. "You don't go near an official shuttle that's packing who knows what possible weapons. I'm not offering our enemies that attractive and valuable a target. Now say good-bye to your father."

"Yessir," Stark grumbled. "Sorry, Dad. Vic's right."

"She sounds a lot like your mother."

"Don't say that. I'm really glad I could see you. Say hi to Mom, and tell her I really hope she's well soon. I hope every-thing works out so I can get down there again. Someday."

"I think if anybody can make that happen, it will be you. If not, at least you tried. Good luck." They shook hands again, then his father was gone. Stark sat for a long time afterward, sipping the cold, bitter coffee before him, until Vic returned and sat down again.

She glanced over at the monitor he'd activated, displaying a view of barren lunar landscape without signs of human activity. Dead rocks. No air. Dust. "You seem depressed. That view isn't going to help things."

"No, but it's not hurting, either. I've been thinking. Something came up while you were a hostage of those mutineers. I meant to ask you about it right away but then forgot."

"So ask."

"The civ scientist who developed those special rounds for taking out the Jabberwocks. He had an implant that tied him in to his lab's net. That seemed to spook a lot of people, including Stacey Yurivan, and she don't spook easy." Stark stopped speaking as he watched Vic's face seem to ice over. "Obviously it ain't something you like, either. What's the deal? Why does talk of implants make everyone act like they've been snakebit?"

She turned her head enough to frown in his direction, then gazed back out over the dead lunar landscape again. "I guess you wouldn't know. Not with being raised as a civ. Everybody in the mil does, but it happened a generation ago, and I don't expect civs ever heard much about it. Classified forever, you know. But it's the sort of horror story mil kids learn and don't forget."

Vic's tone held less warmth than the emptiness outside on the surface, causing Stark to shiver involuntarily. "What was it?"

The reply was a long time coming, then Reynolds spoke with flat, emotionless words. "They created a special experimental unit. All the latest super gizmos to enhance everything. Implants in all the best places. Infrared sensors in the eyes, stuff to speed up reaction time, stuff to keep the heart pumping fast and furious, stuff to boost muscle strength, stuff to fix injuries from inside real fast. Super soldiers. They really kicked butt the first couple of times they went out. Then the opposition figured out what they were up against and cooked up countermeasures."

Vic's words halted again. "Countermeasures?" Stark prodded.

"Yes. Anything that can be programmed can be reprogrammed, right? I remember we talked about that during the meeting where we heard about the Jabberwocks. Well, every im-

plant has instructions programmed or hardwired in that tell it
how to do its job."

"Like the metal-heads."

"Like the metal-heads. So the opposition manufactured
nanobots. Lots of them. They're cheap. Some were designed to
open holes through suit filters to let other nanos in. The guys with
the implants breathed in the others. Some nanos reprogrammed
implants. Some fused with the hardwired stuff and took them
over."

Stark shivered again. "No."

"Yes. They died in different ways, depending on which nano
viruses activated first. Some of the soldiers went blind, then their
hearts stopped. Some had their nervous systems short out."

"Jesus." The single word encompassed a prayer for long-dead
soldiers who'd never had a chance. Stark took a deep breath as
Vic stopped speaking once more. "They all die that way?"

"Not all of them. A few further back realized what was happening. Knew they were doomed. They killed every one of their
stricken fellows they could target, then they turned their weapons
on themselves."

"Oh, my God." Stark shuddered, trying to block the image
from his mind. "No wonder. So how come our use of nanobots
seems to be new to a lot of people?"

"I imagine because people stopped using targetable implants.
And our armor is self-contained, you'll notice, so the nanos used
back then couldn't enter through any filters. The technology to
fire them into a target and keep them functioning didn't exist earlier, either. So people stopped using them, and thinking about
them. Until now."

"Vic, pardon me for asking, but you seem to take this harder
than the others. Like it's personal. Did you—?"

"Don't go there, Ethan."

"Okay." He stared at the wall helplessly, knowing he didn't
have the words he needed. "Uh, so why don't civs have implants?"

"I thought a civ would know." She shifted her head to gaze at
him. "But I bet the reason got suppressed to avoid copycat problems."

"I dunno. Like I said, I never thought about implants that
much. Or heard much about them."

"No one's encouraged to think about them. In the case of civs, it was the Joker Virus. That happened well before the nanobot massacre. I read about it in a classified study. Basically, way back when a lot of science types had implants that allowed direct comms between their brains and the net. Remote programming and stuff. But that junk has to work two ways if it's going to work at all. Some psycho hacker with a grudge against college professors put together a computer virus inspired by his favorite comic book character. It ran through the comm link and added a subprogram to their brain implants that started sending commands into part of their brains. All the profs started laughing so hard they spasmed to death. There'd been hacker games with viruses before, like one that made people with implants act like they were drunk, but nothing like the Joker Virus. After that, nobody wanted implants. Police and emergency personnel even had their communication implants removed. Those were only for back-and-forth communications, but everybody started worrying you could mess up brains with sound pulses or something." She stared toward the view of lunar emptiness. "So, now you know."

"You keep telling me things I don't really want to know. One of these days I'll figure out I should stop asking."

"Maybe. I'm not holding my breath until then."

"Thanks." Stark brooded along with her for a while, his thoughts cascading randomly. "Vic, you think we'll ever build something we can't destroy or turn into a weapon? Something humans won't figure out a way to mess up?"

"No. That would mean we were better at creating things than we were at destroying them. As far as I can tell humans are just too damn good at destroying things for that to ever happen."

"You know, people wonder why, if there's aliens from other stars out there, they haven't contacted us. Maybe the aliens are afraid."

"You might have something there. Humans might be the hands-down best at destroying things." She paused. "I guess it's good to be the best at something, but that's not the 'something' I would have picked."

"Me, neither." Stark reached a decision, leaning toward the vid screen and keying in a command. The ugly, blasted lunar landscape vanished, replaced by a green meadow, dotted with

flowers and framed by trees lit by an unseen sun. In the fore-
ground, a multitude of cute, fluffy bunny rabbits frolicked.

"What in the hell is this?" Vic demanded. "It's revolting."

"Nah, it's cute."

"I *hate* cute. Can't I be moody in peace?"

"No. Either snap out of it, or I'll make you watch the bun-
nies."

"Sadist." Vic suddenly started laughing. "You realize that the
next time you're moping around I'm going to call up this same
scene."

"No, you won't. I have it locked under my own access code."

"You planned this? Ethan Stark, I swear I'll get even."

"You can try." He gripped her hand for a moment. "You're always telling me not to live in the past. That's good advice."

"I know. And thank you. But I'll get even anyway."

Stark stared at his message queue, dreading one from medical
tagged for his personal attention. He almost avoided looking at
it, then noticed the incongruous presence of a smiley emoticon at
the end of the originator line. The message turned out to be extremely brief, just three words, yet it held more meaning for
Stark than all the novels he had ever read. *"Private Murphy's
awake."* It only took a second for Stark to recover from his shock
and head for medical.

Even though it was past normal working hours, the tired-eyed
medic was waiting for him, a ghost of a smile on her face. She
wagged her head toward Murphy's bed. "Miracles happen. You
owe one to the Big Guy upstairs."

"I owe that Big Guy a lot more than one. Can I see Murphy?"

"Sure. He's healthy. He's been healthy. But he's probably still
a little disoriented, and he's definitely weak from lying in bed so
long. There's only so much passive exercise you can accomplish
on a body. So take it slow."

"Got it. Thanks, Doc. Thanks more than I can say."

"I didn't do it, Sergeant. Your boy there did. Thank him."

Stark walked quietly to the bed, but his footsteps were still
noticeable. Murphy turned his head to look, smiling when he saw
Stark coming.

Stark sat carefully next to the bed, studying Murphy's face.
The soldier appeared to have aged, the seemingly perpetual boy-

ish curves in his face somehow now flattened into the harsher planes and angles of maturity. His smile, too, wasn't quite the same. It seemed slightly restrained, as if Murphy had seen too much to ever give in to simple joy again. "Hey, Murph. Welcome back."

"Hey, Sarge." Murphy's voice sounded rusty from disuse. "They tell me you came by a lot when I was out of it."

"I visited a few times. Not often enough, but, you know, there's been a lot goin' on."

"Yeah, Sarge. I understand. I guess I had everyone worried."

Stark nodded, smiling. "You sure did. You've overslept before, Murph, but never that bad."

"Hah! Same old Sarge, huh?"

"Mostly. I've got a few more scars, inside and out. Just like you, I expect." Stark left the last sentence hanging, offering Murphy an opening if he wanted to talk about his experience.

He did. Murphy licked his lips nervously, then glanced upward. "I did a lot of thinking, Sarge, when I was out of it. A lot of talking."

"Talking? Who'd you talk to, Murph?"

"Her. Mostly."

Stark fought to keep his face fixed in a calm expression. "You mean Robin?" Murphy's civ girlfriend, killed in the raid on Stark's headquarters, which had also nearly killed Murphy himself.

"Yeah, Sarge. I know she's dead. I did my best to save her, but I guess that wasn't good enough."

"Murph, you personally nailed a whole group of those raiders. You did more than anyone could have imagined doing."

Murphy looked embarrassed by the praise. "I wanted revenge, Sarge. I wanted to get even. At first, I was like, gonna kill 'em all once I woke up. She told me that was wrong."

Stark nodded.

"And she was right. Any idiot can pick up a gun and try to kill people. Oh, sure, some people are real good at it, but it don't prove nothin'. Right, Sarge?"

"Not if you're killing just to kill."

"Right, Sarge," Murphy repeated. "So I'm gonna do different. I'm gonna spend the rest of my life tryin' to save people. Like you, Sarge. I never realized before, all the risks you took for us. How hard you worked to keep us alive. I wanna do the same."

"That's nice, Murph." Stark hesitated, looking down for a moment, then gazed back up at Murphy's anxious face. "It's a real good thing to wanna do with your life. But it's hard, Murph. Real hard, sometimes. Takes you places you don't wanna go. Makes you do things you don't wanna do."

"Like you, Sarge? But that's the point, ain't it? Doin' what you wanna do is the easy way. She told me, make it matter. Make it mean somethin'. I'm gonna do that, Sarge."

Stark stared back wordlessly, remembering his own past, the dead scattered across the surface of both the Earth and her Moon. His unit dying on Patterson's Knoll, Corporal Kate Stein among them, ordering him to safety with her last breaths. His own vow to save others the same fate. And now Murph had his own Patterson's Knoll to carry around inside judging his every action. *It ain't fair to the kid. He wasn't the greatest soldier under the sun, but he was a good kid. Now the kid's gone, I think. But I can't change his mind. Not gonna try. I know how it is. Only thing I can do is keep watching him and help him handle it.* "That's a real good goal in life, Murph."

"Sarge? Last I knew, the squad needed a new corporal, what with Gomez moving up. Can I apply for that?"

Stark blinked in disbelief. "Sure you can."

"Of course, Corporal Gomez, I don't think she'll want me. But I'll show her I can do it, Sarge. I'll work as long as I have to, to convince her I can do that job. Not as good as you and her, but I can do it."

"Sure," Stark repeated. *And someday you'll have a squad, Murph, and after that maybe a platoon. And you'll never sleep peaceful again, worrying about every soldier in them.* "I'll talk to Gomez. She's platoon leader, now."

"Huh? Wow. That's kinda amazing. I bet you're proud of her."

"I'm proud of all of you, Murph. When you getting discharged from here? They tell you?"

"Not yet, Sarge. I gotta do a lot of physical therapy to get my muscles back and all, and they wanta check me over careful." Murphy grinned with a flash of his old mischief. "They wanta check my head, too, I bet."

"I don't think you have to worry about that, Murph." Stark

noticed Murphy sagging backward. "You're still pretty worn out, huh? I'm not gonna stress you any further. You get some rest, get those workouts going, and get back to your squad. I'll be keeping an eye on you."

"Thanks, Sarge." Murphy relaxed, lying flat but watching Stark as he walked out.

Stark pulled out his comm unit as he headed back toward the command center. "Corporal Gomez. You busy?"

"No, Sargento. What's up?"

"Murphy's awake." Stark paused to let her absorb the news. "He's okay."

"*Gracias, Dios*. I'm gonna tell the squad, Sargento."

"Wait. Before you go, I got a request to make."

"A request? Anything you want."

"Murph wants to try out as corporal in the old squad." Silence. "Hello? Anita?"

"Uh, *sí*, Sargento. Uh, Private Murphy, you know, he's not the, uh, most professional and dedicated guy in the world. I mean, corporal? Murphy?"

Stark suppressed a smile. "I know exactly what you're thinking. But I've talked to Murphy since he woke up. He's changed. Grown a lot. And he wants to work for the job."

"If he wants to work, he sure as hell has changed. He volunteered to be corporal? *Verdad?*"

"Yeah. I'm asking you, as a personal favor, to consider it. Take a look at him when he gets out. See how he does."

"Uh, okay, Sargento. For you. You judge people pretty good, so if you think he can handle it . . ."

"I think he might be able to handle it, yeah. Like I said, Anita, he's changed."

It took a moment for her reply. "Sargento, that almost sounded like you weren't too happy Murph has changed."

"I'm happy he's back, and I'm happy he wants more responsibility. But I think I'm gonna miss the old Murph every now and then. Who'd have thunk?"

"You miss the old Murph too much, and I'll come over and screw a few things up for you. Then you'll feel like he's back. Okay, Sargento, you got a deal. I'll take a look at him. Right now, I wanna tell the rest he's okay."

"Sure thing, Anita. Say hi to them all for me."

Stark paused in his progress, then altered his path, ending up at Sergeant Reynolds's room. "Vic? You got a moment?"

She rubbed her eyes. "It's late. I hope you're not calling a staff meeting."

"Not that. I need to tell you, Murphy's awake."

Vic brightened. "That's great." Then her face slid into skepticism. "So how come you're so subdued? What's up? He okay in the head?"

"Yeah. But." Stark explained his conversation with Murphy. "You see. He's gonna have a tough road."

"Right now, he sounds a lot like someone else I know."

"Guilty as charged."

She grinned. "After all this time you've got yourself a son, Ethan. In the spiritual sense, anyway. You ever think it'd be Murphy?"

"No. The universe sure has a funny sense of humor, don't it? Anyway, Vic, I got a special favor to ask. A big one. If anything happens to me . . ."

"Don't worry, Ethan. I'll look out for Murphy if anything happens to you. Promise."

"Thanks. Means a lot."

"*Nyet problema.* It's been a while, but I reckon I remember how to handle a kid."

Stark glanced at her, unable to hide his surprise. "You got a kid, Vic?"

Instead of answering him, Reynolds yawned, then looked at her watch. "Man, it's late, and I've still got some stuff to do before I hit the sack. See you tomorrow, Ethan."

"Sure." Stark watched her with curious eyes for a moment, Vic outwardly cool as she worked, then waved farewell and left. He wandered through the headquarters complex for a while, checking on things, speaking to soldiers standing watch in different areas. Finally entering his own room, Stark sat heavily for a moment at the desk where his monitor displayed work still awaiting his attention. *Hey. I just realized. This system gives me access to the personnel records, and I have the command clearance to look at personal histories on anyone. I could find out anything I wanted about Vic's past. No more mysteries.* His hand reached, one finger tapping the key that sent the machine into hibernation. *But I ain't gonna. Maybe I ain't learned near enough in this job, but I have learned that one of the most important things about being in charge is not doing some of the stuff you could do if you wanted to. If Vic ever wants to tell me, she will.* Stark took advantage of the low gravity to launch himself into a roll/push that deposited him in the bunk, coming to rest on his back, staring upward at the metal sheet that covered lunar rock, which was covered in turn by a thin layer of dust. Above that, endless emptiness opened into forever. Stark gazed at the imagined vista of eternal darkness and smiled. *Screw you. I'm still here, and my rules matter.*

It was easy for the days to run together, for time to pass almost unnoticed in the grind of everyday events, especially in a place where the very idea of a "day" had been imported by humans from somewhere else where the sun actually rose and set once every twenty-four hours. Stark came back to his room after watching a company run through some tactics Vic had been working out to deal with Jabberwocks. He removed his battle armor wearily. *It looked good. It oughta handle those monsters. We think. How are we gonna know before they get here and start shooting at us?*

His door annunciator chimed. Stark, still standing, took one long step to open it. "Mendo? What's up?"

"Commander Stark." Private Mendoza hesitated, glanced down at the old-fashioned paper-printed book he held in one hand, then looked back at Stark with renewed determination. "There is something I should discuss with you. If you have the time."

"Sure." *Mendo volunteering information. That's new. But then, his dad told me Mendo would rise to the occasion if I gave him a chance.* "Come in. Sit down."

"Thank you, sir." Mendoza waited until Stark sat down in front of his desk, then took the room's other chair. He held out the book so Stark could see the title, handling the book as if it were a precious, fragile item. "This is an ancient history text."

"I can see it's pretty old."

"No, sir. I mean it was written millennia ago. One of the first histories in human record. It is about a series of wars."

"The first history we've got and it's about wars? That figures."

Mendoza smiled, relaxing in response to Stark's humor. "Yes, Commander. The book's title is *The Peloponnesian War.* It was written by a man named Thucydides."

"Sorry. Never heard of it."

"The war was very important at the time," Mendoza insisted. "It was fought between alliances led by the city-states of Athens and Sparta."

"Sparta? I know about them. Thermo . . . ?"

"Thermopylae?"

"Yeah. That battle where just a few of those Spartans held their line until they died. It inspired all the other Greeks to fight together. They the guys you're talking about?"

Mendoza nodded, though he had trouble hiding his surprise that Stark had known even that much about ancient Greece. "Yes. Exactly them. That battle at Thermopylae took place long before the Peloponnesian War."

"Okay. I guess that makes sense, if the Spartans and the guys from Athens were fighting each other in this war you're talking about. So why do I need to know about this book?"

Mendoza paused for so long Stark felt a stab of impatience, but he waited until the private started speaking once more. "This was my father's book, Commander. He had made many notes in the margins. They are fragmentary, but I have been reading them, and I believe I should tell you of the conclusions my father had reached."

"Lieutenant Mendoza, your dad, he knew what he was talkin' about. Anything he came up with I'd like to know."

"You understand the notes are not complete," Mendoza cautioned, "but the main arguments are fairly clear." He pointed to the book. "Briefly, long ago the city of Athens had become extremely powerful. So powerful it did whatever it wanted, and no one could stop it. Finally, Sparta and most of the other cities in Greece went to war with Athens, but they could not defeat it."

"Hmmm." Stark rubbed his chin. "Sounds familiar. Like here, right? The U.S. of A. is big dog on the World and pretty much does anything it wants. Everybody else just had to put up with it, until we tried to grab the whole Moon, too, and then they all combined to try to stop us up here. Is that what you, your dad, that is, was driving at?"

"Yes, Commander." Mendoza's face glowed like that of a

teacher with an apt pupil. "But the Athenians finally went too far. As part of their aim to become all-powerful, Athens attacked the mighty city of Syracuse."

"Ain't that in New York state? It's not that old."

"No, Commander. The original city of Syracuse, in Sicily. It is in the Mediterranean." Mendoza gathered his thoughts, then plunged ahead. "Syracuse, powerful though it was, could not defeat the Athenian attack alone. It called for help from the Spartans. The Athenians in turn sent more reinforcements. But the Athenian commanders were chosen for their political loyalty and skills, not their military prowess. After a long campaign, the Athenians were defeated. The entire army and fleet they had sent to attack Syracuse were themselves destroyed or captured. Athens never recovered from the loss of so much. A few years later, it was decisively defeated, and it never regained the power it had once held."

Stark stared at Mendoza after the narrative halted, eyes narrowing in thought. "That sounds familiar, too. A bit, anyway. So your dad thought the American attempt to seize the Moon was like these guys from Athens trying to take out Syracuse?"

"Yes, Commander. Overreaching at the height of power. Here, too, strong reinforcements were sent to try to win the war. They failed."

"Yeah, but there's no chance we're gonna fail, Mendo. Nobody's gonna take this Colony. We'll hold it 'til hell freezes over."

"But that is the point, Commander." Mendoza indicated the book again, excitement animating his features. "You will hold. You are in command. My father believed in the wake of General Meecham's failed offensive we would have lost the Colony, and every soldier up here, exactly as the Athenian expeditionary force was destroyed at Syracuse. That is, we would have but for two things."

"Two things? What's that?"

Mendoza hesitated again, then pointed toward Stark. "You are one, sir."

"The hell. What's that supposed to mean?"

"My father's notes indicate he believes our former senior officers were as incompetent as those of the Athenians at Syracuse. He had reached the conclusion that Meecham's offensive might have led to the loss of the entire Colony due to our lack of faith in our commanders, the hesitation and confusion among those same commanders, and our heavy losses. All these combined to create conditions under which an enemy counteroffensive might have prevailed, or at least seized such territory as would have left our position here untenable."

Stark frowned, remembering moments of fear and uncertainty. "Like it was right after we took over? We almost lost then, when the enemy hit us hard and the line crumbled. But I thought that was 'cause we didn't know for sure what we were fighting for right then."

"That was part of it, certainly," Mendoza agreed. "But had Meecham and the other officers remained in command, would our forces have had any stronger motivation?"

"Hell, no. You know that. We wouldn't have had any motivation at all. Not after watching what they did to Third Division. Somebody like Meecham wouldn't have had a snowball's chance in hell of rallying the troops."

"Just so, Commander. The only thing that could have prevented disaster here, as at Syracuse, would have been a dynamic commander, one trusted by the army and able to rally them after a series of serious setbacks."

"That didn't have to be me," Stark demurred. "Any good leader could have done it."

"No, sir," Mendoza objected, his normal reticence lost in the cut and thrust of the argument. "It had to be someone able to overcome the habit of obedience, able to act when action was required. Only you could do that."

"I don't . . ." Stark's words trailed off as he stared into space, remembering the day Third Division had been effectively destroyed during General Meecham's ill-conceived and ill-executed offensive. Thousands of soldiers dying in increasingly futile assaults on the enemy defenses surrounding the Colony, while the aghast lunar veterans of First Division looked on from their positions on the American perimeter. *Everybody else seemed to be looking to me to do something, and nobody else acted until I did. Why was that? I never wondered before.* "Why'd your dad think that about me?"

"Because you did not join the military until you were a young adult." Mendoza gestured toward one wall of Stark's room. "Just about everyone else in the military, such as I, grew up in military families, on forts or bases. Obedience, following the rules, were inculcated in us from our earliest childhoods. It was part of life. For you, such rules were far looser. Just for example, as a child, you were not required to stand to attention when the national anthem was played. You made choices about many things, for better or worse."

Stark felt a sense of dislocation as the conversation brought him back to another talk years before, on a troop transport on the way to the Moon. "Pablo Desoto and I talked about that once. How different growing up was for me compared to him. You remember Pablo, don't you, Mendo?"

"Of course, sir." Corporal Desoto had died early on in the lunar war, hit dead-on by a heavy artillery shell. There'd been no body left for his friends to grieve over. "Then you understand? Your early experience with making many such decisions meant you could finally act when you thought it necessary, where those of us indoctrinated in obedience from youth could not. Unlike those of us who grew up within the military, you lack an automatic deference to and respect for authority."

"I'm an American. If I wanted to respect authority, I'd be something else." It made sense to Stark in that way something does when it both fits events and feels right. *I'm nothing special, but I did grow up different. Is this one of the things we lost when the mil became so professional people literally grew up into it? The ability to say "no" when you really have to? Is that what all that 'citizen-soldier' crap really comes down to? Having people in the mil who can tell their superiors to go to hell when it really matters? Or just having the superiors know their people could do that if they push too far or too hard?* "Let's leave that for now. You said two things. One was me. What was the other?"

"Technology. The command and control systems which allowed everyone to know of your actions." Mendoza leaned forward, one extended forefinger tracing patterns in the air as if an HUD combat display hung there. "At Syracuse, a single, low-level leader in the Athenian army could have made no difference. His unit would have followed him, a few soldiers in the whole army, but no one else would have known of his actions and orders. That one small unit could not have survived. But, here, your assumption of command could occur almost instantaneously thanks to the manner in which every soldier is knitted into the command and control system."

"Sure. Our command and control systems were designed to allow senior commanders to dictate every action of their subordinates, and that's exactly how they've been used by senior officers who wanted to tell everybody exactly how to do everything. But we've been figuring out to use the systems our own way for a long time." Stark didn't know which unknown sergeants had first arranged for covert comm circuits to be laced into the command and control systems so the senior enlisted could talk among themselves without the officers being aware of it, but tricks like that and unauthorized back doors into the command scan levels had been available as long as Stark had been using the systems.

"Just so. It enabled you to bypass the top-down chain of command, to instantly coordinate your actions with other small unit commanders all around the perimeter. Those command and control systems can be used by any junior personnel, allowing them to know things only the highest levels of the chain of command could once know. It allows them to act with tremendous speed and flexibility while easily coordinating their actions. This is how you could successfully assert command in a matter of minutes without significant disruption of our forces."

Stark nodded. "You know that's how we've been using the command and control gear in operations. Trying out just that sort of thing."

"Yes, sir." Mendoza grew so excited his hands began sketching pictures in the air again. "I have been following the tactical and operational innovations you have been using in combat. It is almost like the Roman Legions at the height of their capabilities. Their tactical deployments emphasized an open, flexible formation, able to adapt to whatever enemy formation opposed them. Rome's enemies were locked into rigid formations, which worked only against similarly rigid foes." He grew calmer. "You remember, soon after you took command, when the enemy attack threatened to break our line? You could use the same systems to rally our troops at every location at once. You see, Commander? This could not have happened before. The fact that it could happen here is all that saved the Colony."

Stark stared into an empty corner of the room. "I think you're right. We were brittle enough as it was. First Division had been fighting too long up here. Watching Third Division get sent into a meat grinder for nothing had us all ready to quit, didn't it? We wouldn't have held if the enemy had hit us hard, because we wouldn't have been able to care anymore." He remembered the enemy push soon after he took command that had nearly ruptured the front line irreparably. Rallying the troops had been critical, and had nearly been beyond him. "And if America had lost Third Division and First Division, that would've been almost two-thirds of its existing ground forces. Not to mention all the ships that might've been lost trying to evacuate personnel or in a last-ditch attempt to save the Colony. And with the Colony gone for sure all at once, the economy would have tanked just as fast, not sorta slow like it has been. It would've been like those guys from Athens, wouldn't it? Pushing too far, committing too much, and finally getting their butts kicked so hard the rest of the world could take them out."

"I believe so, Commander. As long as the status of American forces on the Moon remained uncertain, as long as the loyalty of the Colony remained undecided, the rest of world would not perceive enough weakness to unite in a full push to dethrone the last superpower. In summary, my father believed your actions saved the United States from its own overextension, but those actions alone could not have made a difference without modern command and control systems."

Like so much advice from Lieutenant Mendoza, and from his son, it made sense. The only major problem Stark had with the explanation was the role he played in it. *So I'm this big special guy, huh? Saved the Colony, and the country, and all my pals.* He had felt it, sometimes, after a successful action, the sense that he could always do it again, that victory was sweet and defeat unthinkable. *I don't need anybody encouraging me to think that way. But I can't be the first or only guy to have thoughts like that.* "Mendo, you know a lot of history besides this Greek stuff. There's been a lot of generals that won pretty much all their battles, right? What happened to them?"

"I'm not sure I understand your question, sir."

"I mean in the end," Stark explained. "These generals were good. Good enough they won battles, anyway. What happened in the last chapters, though?"

"Ah. I see." Mendoza thought, frowning as he focused on the question. "There are basically two categories of such generals, Commander Stark. Some generals take their victories, but stop. Something prevents them from overreaching. General George Washington was one such. He was not the most brilliant commander of all time, yet he knew his limits and won his war. Then he refused many chances to become dictator or king of the United States."

"No wonder we put him on our money. What's the other category?"

"Generals such as Napoleon, or Alexander, or Julius Caesar. They won battles, then kept reaching for more. More conquests, more titles. Eventually, they reached too far. Napoleon made himself an emperor, then lost a huge army in Russia, and never recovered. Alexander pushed his soldiers to the ends of the known world, and eventually they mutinied. They wanted to go home. Alexander's empire was so big it could not be sustained, and it fell apart as soon as he died. And, of course, Caesar was set to declare himself dictator when assassinated by those who feared his ambition."

"Huh." Stark sat, lost in thought for a moment, remembering fragments of nameless battles on nameless fields. "That's the choice, ain't it? You either get so full of yourself you push too far and get cut off at the knees, or you take a reality check and hold yourself back from what you figure you could do. There's always one more mountain, right? Sooner or later, you either stop trying to climb them or you fall off one." He thought a moment longer. "Like those guys from Athens."

"Yes, Commander. Exactly like the Athenians."

"You'd think war would be like any other job, the more you do it the better you get at it. But it doesn't work that way, does it?"

Private Mendoza nodded. "Clausewitz stated that this was because of friction."

"Friction?"

"Yes. This was the term Clausewitz used to describe the many problems which bedevil any commander. All of the difficulties, the missteps and misunderstood orders, the equipment failures, the unforeseen events, the unpredictable actions of the enemy or of the weather. In short, everything which separates the theory of war from the actual experience of fighting."

"Sort of like that mutiny we had in Fifth Batt? Nobody expected that."

"Yes. Just that sort of thing."

Stark nodded, letting out a long breath. "Yeah. That stuff never lets up. And sooner or later, some of it's bound to trip you up." *I just gotta have enough guts to walk away from some of the mountains in front of me, that's all. Sounds easy. But I'm sure better commanders than I am have decided to climb just one more mountain.* "You still talk to your dad, Mendo?"

Private Mendoza ducked his head to hide his expression at the reference to his father, Lieutenant Mendoza, who had died helping defend this same headquarters complex. "I pray every night."

"Good. You tell your dad from me that you're doing one helluva good job of keeping your commander's head screwed on straight."

"Thank you, Sergeant. I'm sorry. Thank you, Commander."

"You call me whatever you want. And I happen to like being called Sergeant."

Whatever else he may have said was interrupted by a voice from his comm unit. "Commander Stark? This is the command center. There's a situation developing upstairs that you might want to watch."

"A situation?" "Upstairs" meant something going on far above the Moon's surface, at orbital heights or beyond. "Tell me more."

"It looks like there's some civ shuttles trying to sneak in past the blockade." Stark nodded to himself. There were a number of things that brought premium prices if smuggled into the Colony, and a number of items whose value far exceeded their weight in gold if smuggled out. Not to mention the orders for essential spares that had been carefully floated in places where black marketers could be found. "But they might not make it. The Navy's spotted them and is moving in."

That could create a lot of problems, including the possibility that the Navy warships might try to pursue their prey inside the Colony's antiorbital defenses. "Got it," Stark acknowledged. "I'll be right there." He turned to Private Mendoza. "Mendo, I'm afraid I'll have to cut this short. Looks like some more friction just hit the fan. Thanks for coming by, and thanks for all that stuff you figured out. It'll give me a lot to think about." He hesitated for a moment after Mendoza left, habit urging him to don battle armor, then shook his head. *I won't need that for something going on upstairs, and those situations tend to develop awful fast. I'd better get to the command center quick.*

The huge main display in the command center was focused on the "situation" in space. Stark pulled back the perspective on the view so he could see the huge arc of the Moon's surface in relation to the spacecraft symbology crawling through the emptiness above it, then focused back in on the shuttles again. Sergeant Tran came up, nodding in greeting. "Commander Stark, those shuttles are going to have problems getting down here. See those warships?" Large symbology tagged with warship identifiers displayed huge acceleration vectors, their projected tracks running into those of the shuttles.

"Yeah," Stark agreed. "Looks to me like those warships are gonna get to the shuttles before the shuttles get inside our orbital defenses." He studied the tracks of the shuttles for a moment. *Something's missing. What? Oh, yeah.* "Tran, those shuttles must know the Navy's seen 'em, right?"

"Sure. There's no way they could avoid spotting those warships with the Navy piling on that kind of speed."

"So, if they've figured out the Navy's seen 'em, there's no sense trying to hide. Why aren't they running? Trying to get inside our defenses before the Navy can get to them?"

Tran frowned. "That's a good question."

"We have any idea what they're carrying?"

"No, sir. We checked the command system as soon as we spotted those shuttles. There's nothing in there on them."

Something about the reply seemed ominous to Stark. It shouldn't have. Shuttles trying to run the blockade didn't tell anyone they were coming and didn't broadcast their cargo manifests. *But this worries me. Those shuttles aren't acting like blockade runners. Maybe they're Trojan horses? Putting on an act so they can get inside our defenses while the Navy pretends to chase them? But then why aren't they doing a better job of acting like blockade runners?* "Tran, notify Vic Reynolds of what's going on and ask Chief Wiseman to get her armed shuttles hot."

Sergeant Tran looked back at Stark, clearly surprised. "Sir?

This happens every now and then. This particular situation's not routine, but—"

"I know. Call it a gut feeling. Somethin's really wrong here. I want us ready to react if we have to." Tran nodded and hurried off to make the calls. *Now I'll owe Wiseman another beer for making her crew up those shuttles of hers.*

The Navy warships had piled on even more acceleration, pushing the intercept a little farther outside the Colony's defenses. For whatever reason, the shuttles still hadn't reacted. Stark was studying the display so intently he wasn't aware Vic had entered the command center until she spoke beside him. "What's up?"

"What you see." Stark waved toward the display. "Blockade-running shuttles, apparently, getting chased by the Navy."

"I see that. Nothing unusual. I'm wondering why you put the armed shuttles on alert. That's unusual."

"Yeah." Stark rubbed his chin. "I dunno. Those shuttles ain't running, and they ought to be. Right?"

"I would if I was them."

"Maybe their cargo is really fragile? Something that can't handle a sudden acceleration? I wish I knew what was in those shuttles."

"Whatever it is can be replaced," Vic noted with a shrug.

"Commander?" one of the watchstanders signaled. "The Colony manager is calling. He says it's real urgent."

"Great," Stark grumbled, keying in the connection. "Another complication. Stark here."

Campbell spoke quickly, without his usual greetings. "Sergeant, are you aware there's a group of shuttles trying to land here?"

"Yeah. We're watching 'em now." Symbology crawled slowly against the vast backdrop of the main display, the barest slice of the Moon's huge arc now glowing down and to one side as the display angle shifted to maintain a picture of the entire situation. "I wouldn't put any bets on their chances of getting down here, though. There's some heavy Navy units moving to intercept, and our gear says they'll close on the shuttles before our defenses can cover 'em."

"That's what our orbital systems are saying, too, but that's wrong! Those Navy ships should be letting those shuttles through."

Stark fought down an immediate blistering response, instead just staring back at Campbell. "Why? Are you saying these shuttles are officially scheduled?"

"Of course. You know we've been negotiating with the government. This group of shuttles was cleared, but the Navy warships are reacting like they're blockade runners. I'm very worried."

"Me, too. If these shuttles were cleared and scheduled, how come my people didn't know they were coming?"

"You didn't? I . . . don't know. The government negotiating effort was reorganized not long ago, but they should have—"

"Mr. Campbell, my people haven't heard about these shuttles. If the military here didn't get the word, it's pretty safe to assume the military up there didn't get told either. That'd be why the Navy's assuming those shuttles are blockade runners and reacting accordingly. Tell the shuttles to explain to those warships what's happened. They might get held up for a few orbits, but—"

"They've been trying to tell the Navy they're an approved mission! But the warships just keep coming. You know they're authorized to destroy any shuttle trying to run the blockade!"

"They wouldn't ice somebody trying to surrender." *Would they? What kind of orders have they got?*

"The shuttle pilots think they might. They're scared. Too scared to stop, I think."

Stark looked to Vic for advice, but she just spread her hands in exasperation. "Sir, I don't know what I can—"

"Sergeant." Campbell slowed his speech with an obvious effort, speaking with care. "The 'cargo' on those shuttles are humans. Relatives of people in this Colony, trying to rejoin their husbands, wives, fathers, and mothers. Do you understand?"

"Ah, hell. There's civ passengers on those shuttles? Kids and everything?"

"Yes, Sergeant."

"And you knew they were comin' in now?"

Campbell closed his eyes before he spoke. "Everyone was supposed to have been informed."

"Well, that is one helluva nice surprise, sir. Just for the record, somebody forgot to inform the people with weapons, and that's causing some real problems. Okay, I'm getting my own shuttles up." He gestured again, highlighting the four symbols that represented his own little fleet then swung his thumb up. Reynolds nodded and began calling commands into another circuit. "But, the odds are real bad. Those warships are closing for intercepts outside our defenses. My shuttles won't be able to prevent that. The best I can do is try to divert the warships' attention while your shuttles try to get the Navy brass to call off their sharks."

"I understand. Please, Sergeant, protect them."

Stark stared momentarily, caught between anger at the lack of warning and surprise at the naked plea, then nodded. "That's our job, sir. We'll do our best. But we'd have had a lot better chance if we'd known in advance that this was going down."

"I understand."

Vic looked as if she'd just bitten into something sour. "I guess I was wrong. Some cargo can't be replaced. I wonder which idiots failed to get the word out that kids were coming in through the blockade?"

"Beats the hell out of me. I'm gonna get me a piece of those idiots' hides when this is all over. Right now, we've got another job."

"Hey," Chief Wiseman called in. "What's up? We gonna bail out those smugglers?"

"They ain't smugglers, Chief," Stark advised. "It's a pre-approved run, but nobody got the word, so the Navy's going after them. We might have to save their butts. Can do?"

"Can't do. My shuttles can't hold off cruisers."

"Chief, there's civs on those shuttles. Family types. Kids."

"Aw, for . . . then they oughta surrender now. If there was a good chance, I'd say different, but . . ."

"Roger. The civs are trying to call off those warships, but they're worried about the Navy's orders."

"I would be, too. We know standing orders are that any blockade runners are toast."

"Right. So get up there. Just in case. Maybe you can run interference if worse comes to worst and help those shuttles get inside our defenses."

"I sure hope it doesn't come to that. We're on our way. Man, I'm getting too old for this much acceleration."

Stark grinned, then lost his humor as he studied the display. Acceleration vectors had suddenly jerked on the civilian shuttles, angling longer as they boosted their main drives. "What the hell? Somebody up there's panicking. Those fools are trying to outrun the Navy ships. Tran, ask Campbell if he's gotten through to the government side, yet. If those warships don't get called off soon, we're going to have a really ugly problem."

"Something's happening," Vic noted, peering at the display. "Are the warships firing weapons?" A half-dozen smaller objects had detached themselves from each Navy cruiser and begun accelerating toward the shuttles at even higher rates than the warships had been maintaining. The combat identification system quickly slapped symbology over each object, with an "unknown" tag prominent.

"Negative," the orbital systems watchstander replied. "I'm trying to ID the objects now, but those are way too big to be torpedoes."

"Maybe the cruisers are launching their own armed shuttles," Vic suggested.

"Those are too small for shuttles," the orbital systems watchstander objected. "And there's too many of them. Cruisers can't carry that number of shuttles."

"Then what are they?" Stark demanded. "Chief Wiseman?"

"Yup." Over the comm circuit she sounded close, so that Stark had trouble remembering her shuttle was actually approaching orbit even as they spoke. "What's coming off those cruisers?"

"I was hoping you'd know."

"Not me. I've never seen anything like those, and my onboard combat systems can't provide an ID, either."

Stark glowered at the symbology that represented the new spacecraft, watching them slide into rigid formations as they boosted away from their cruiser mother ships. *I've seen something like that before. What? Something about how they're moving . . . damn.* "Vic. Were you in Operation Ice Storm?"

"No. Fortunately. I heard it was pure hell. Why?"

"The way those new ships are moving reminds of something." Stark swung his arm across the symbology as the small craft homed in on the blockade runners. "The Air Force tried some new uncrewed aircraft in that op. Latest and greatest thing. Robotic with a special tight, scrambled link. Some of 'em crashed, some got suicided when they started shooting at friendly forces, and the rest were nailed by enemy defenses. But they moved like that."

Vic stared at the display. "Like that. You're sure?"

"Yeah. Real precise. No hesitation or bobbles when they moved in formation. Just like that."

"Navy metal-heads. Autonomous robotic combatants designed for space combat. I guess your friend didn't hear about them."

"Can't fault him or her for that." Stark keyed Wiseman's circuit again. "Wiseman. Those new shuttles or whatever that the cruisers launched. They're metal-heads."

"What? You sure?"

"Sure as I can be without cracking one open."

"Oh, man. Things just got bad, mud crawler. Things just got real bad." Stark frowned as he watched the course/speed vectors for Wiseman's shuttles on the main display suddenly lengthen and shift. "Heading for intercept," she reported.

"Intercept? Negative, Chief. Pull back. You can't engage all those things with four shuttles."

"Yeah. I know. But those things are headin' for the shuttles full of kids, ain't they? I gotta stop 'em."

"We're trying to straighten this mess out, Chief. The Navy's not gonna push an attack once it realizes those shuttles have kids on board. There's no reason—"

"Wrong," Wiseman interrupted. "With all due respect. Sir. I'm guessing these Navy metal-heads are like the ground ones we got word on. No control link. So we got metal-heads on the loose and ordered to attack those shuttles. You sure they're gonna understand surrender? Sir?"

"Oh, God."

Stark looked over at Reynolds, who shook her head in anger. "She's right, Ethan. Those civs are being targeted by things smart enough to kill them, but possibly too stupid not to kill them if they don't have to. Maybe that's why the shuttles are running, now. Maybe they've heard rumors about those things. Maybe more than rumors."

"Campbell said the pilots were scared. Now we know why. Tran!" Stark spun and shouted in one motion. "We can't wait any longer for word to get to those warships through official channels. Get on a direct circuit to those cruisers. Tell 'em the shuttles are full of civs. Including kids. Tell 'em the shuttles were officially scheduled but we're ordering 'em to surrender anyway. They gotta call off those metal-heads."

"Yessir. Immediately. We'll use the universal distress frequency." That frequency was reserved for life-threatening emergencies, but this case arguably fell into that category.

Stark took a deep breath, trying to calm his suddenly adrenaline-charged system. *Nothing I can do from here. Just try to get the word to the right people and hope they do the right things.* "Vic, call Campbell and tell him what's going down. If he's got anyone who can make sure those shuttles stop running, he better get them talking fast." Intercept vectors were shifting only subtly, now, the Navy metal-heads arcing in on intercepts guaranteed to nail the fleeing shuttles outside the range of the Colony's defenses.

"Is that the best advice?" Vic wondered. "Given what they're up against, how do we know that wouldn't just make those shuttles sitting ducks?"

"I don't know! But at least if they surrender those cruisers should help protect them from the metal-heads."

"Commander," Sergeant Tran reported, "the civilian spaceport reports the shuttles have acknowledged orders to stop fleeing from the Navy, but refuse to alter their courses. The Navy ships have definitely received our messages, but have not responded to them."

"This could be incredibly ugly," Vic murmured. "Are the shuttle pilots being stupid or scared, now?"

"Maybe all of the above. Hell, if I had those things coming after me . . . Tran, what'd Campbell say?"

"He's threatening the shuttle pilots that he'll arrest them and confiscate their ships if they don't surrender to the Navy. But Campbell thinks they're going to try to outrun the metal-heads. He says the pilots sound scared to death and are screaming for us to protect them from the metal-heads."

"So why'd they run in the first place with cargoes of kids? If they hadn't, maybe the Navy wouldn't have launched the things. Stupid. Stupid. Stupid. If I get my hands on those guys . . . and on those sorry bastards who were supposed to notify everyone about those shuttles coming in . . ."

"For what it's worth, Campbell looks like he feels personally responsible."

"A fat lot of good that'll do anybody."

"The cruisers are transmitting something," Tran reported. "Can't pick it up. The beam's too tight. Looks like they're trying to call off their metal-heads."

Stark exhaled in relief, then waited with growing anxiety as the robotic combatants continued on course. "So why ain't the metal-heads breaking off?"

"Autonomous means autonomous," Vic noted. "Like we feared. Somebody did a story about this a long time ago. *Fail-Safe* I think it was called. Some weapons got launched by accident and no one could figure out how to recall them."

"What happened?" Stark wondered, his eyes fixed on the display.

"Some cities got blown away."

New symbology blossomed to life, radiating out from one of the Navy cruisers. "Now what's happening?"

"One of the cruisers is firing," the orbital systems watchstander reported.

"Those bastards are shooting at the shuttles?"

"No, sir. She's firing on her own metal-heads. See the weapon trajectories? They're trying to stop those things the hard way."

"Good for them." It couldn't have been an easy decision for whoever was in charge of that big ship to make. A commander interested primarily in protecting him or herself would have waited until the metal-heads actually committed an atrocity before firing, thereby ensuring any board of enquiry would exonerate them. But that wouldn't do the civ kids any good. "They getting any hits?"

"Uh, no sir. Odds are very low. Their weapons are in a tail chase. Low relative velocity so the metal-head point defenses are taking them out." On the display, weapons symbology blinked out time and again as it neared the metal-heads.

The civilian shuttles accelerated once more, pushing their lunar approaches into danger readings. If they didn't slack off their speed soon, they'd be unable to brake in time for a safe landing.

"Going in," Chief Wiseman announced, startling Stark.

"What the hell do you mean?" He searched for the four symbols representing her armed shuttles, catching them with vectors arcing up from the Moon to a point somewhere between the fleeing civilians and the metal-heads. "Those metal-heads have got to be too heavily armed for you to slug it out with. There's too many of them. Break off. Get back here."

"Sorry. Didn't copy your last."

"I said get back here!"

"Say again?"

"Wiseman—!"

"Engaging enemy." Weapon symbology separated from the armed shuttles, shooting past the fleeing civilian shuttles and adding to the confusing mass of vectors filling the display. As Stark watched, all the weapons converged on the two nearest metal-heads, overwhelming their defenses. The two metal-heads were momentarily blocked from view by the detonation detections, then blossomed into expanding spheres of metal fragments and gas.

"That's two," Tran stated. "But she fired every weapon on her shuttles to get them."

The remaining metal-heads came on, still focused on the civilian shuttles. "They're not going to let go," Vic stated. "Those damned things are going to keep after those civ shuttles until they blow them to hell."

Stark saw the acceleration vectors on three of Wiseman's shuttles change as they altered course, angling back toward the Moon, but the armed shuttle carrying Chief Wiseman kept heading for intercept with the metal-heads. "Wiseman! What the hell are you doing?"

"Gotta get those things' attention," Wiseman noted, her voice strained by the acceleration of her shuttle. "Draw them off the civ shuttles before they reach engagement range. And that's any second now." A moment later, the symbology of her shuttle seemed to glow twice as bright.

The orbital systems watchstander stared at the display with a slack jaw. "She's . . . she's turned off all her countermeasures and is transmitting on every frequency."

Stark didn't need that information interpreted. "That's making her shuttle stand out like a target on a firing range." Survival in battle often came down to not being noticed. Countermeasures were designed to hide things that might make weapons notice you, and systems were kept passive to avoid sending out signals that weapons could lock onto. Chief Wiseman was deliberately drawing the maximum possible amount of attention to her shuttle.

Vic's hand was on his shoulder, her eyes sick. "That's the idea, Ethan. She's turning her shuttle into a decoy, to draw off the Navy metal-heads. They're bound to start shooting at her now, instead of those helpless civilian shuttles."

"A decoy." Stark clenched his fists in frustration. "A weapons magnet. Wiseman!"

"Here."

"Break off! That's an order! Reactivate your countermeasures and get out of there!"

"Got a job to do, ground ape." The Chief sounded oddly calm, though Stark could detect the tension underlying her tone. "Gotta shield those civ shuttles. Damn the torpedoes. It's a Navy thing."

"We've told the cruisers to break off! They know the civ shuttles' cargo includes kids. They're trying to stop their metal-heads."

"Stark, those metal-heads aren't breaking off action, and those cruisers can't stop 'em. Not in time. I'm gonna hold these space bugs as long as I can."

It all sounded so familiar. Stark gazed helplessly at the display, where the metal-heads had altered trajectories and spat out a swarm of threat markers that were converging on Wiseman's shuttle. He remembered his own stand to hold off pursuit of his platoon. Ages ago, and yesterday, it seemed. A miracle had saved Stark that day. A miracle in the form of reinforcements arriving at the last moment. *And I ain't got nothing else to send up there to save those squids. Please, God, if there's anything you can do for that crazy sailor, please do it.*

Alerts sounded, pinpointing Wiseman's shuttle. "They're taking hits, Commander," a watchstander sang out. "Incoming weapons are getting past their point defenses."

"Chief Wiseman, that's enough! You've delayed the metal-heads! Break off!"

"Receiving reports of cascading damage," the watchstander continued. "Critical system hits."

"Wiseman! Get the hell out of there! Wiseman!" A hand on his shoulder brought his attention back to the command center, back to Reynolds mutely pointing to the marker on the main display. A blossoming cloud of debris dominated scan for a few moments, its heat and fragments showing up brightly against the dead space all around. Then the scan system corrected for the noise, screening out the debris to concentrate on threats, and the remains of an armed shuttle and her crew vanished from the display except for a bright marker warning of hazardous wreckage radiating out from the center of the explosion.

"Hell," Stark breathed. "Good-bye, Chief. Now, there's only one Wiseman left." He slammed one fist onto the console before him. "Get the rest of those armed shuttles back down here now!" On the display, the fleeing civilian shuttles were closing rapidly on the boundary of the Colony's antiorbital defenses. The metal-heads were still in pursuit, but their initial volleys of weapons had gone after Chief Wiseman's shuttle, and the brief battle had delayed them just enough to shift intercept points inside the Colony's defenses. "Those stupid bastards are gonna make it now, aren't they?"

Vic measured the vectors for the civilian shuttles with her eye, then nodded. "Looks like it. If the metal-heads keep coming, we can take them and anything they fire at the civ shuttles with the Colony's defenses. Chief Wiseman bought them the time they needed."

"She paid too much. Tell Campbell I *want* those pilots the in-stant those shuttles touch down. They're gonna pay for costing us a damn good ship and a damn good crew. And I'm gonna want to talk to Campbell about this. About losing good people and risk-ing kids' lives just because some idiots couldn't send the right notifications to the right places. I'm gonna want to talk." He paused, gritting his teeth. "And tell Chief Gunner's Mate Melen-dez he's not second in command of our naval forces anymore. He's in charge, now."

"Yes, sir," Tran responded. "Anything else, sir?"

The Navy robotic combatants were still coming, seemingly oblivious to the Colony defenses in their pursuit of the civilian shuttles. "Yeah. Tell the antiorbital defense guys I want those metal-heads blown into so many pieces that God Himself couldn't put 'em back together again."

• • •

He sat in his darkened room, a cup of coffee forgotten by his side, staring at nothing. "Ethan?" Vic stood in the door, waiting for his permission to enter.

"Yeah. Come on in."

"Thanks." She sat heavily, something weariness and sorrow could achieve even in lunar gravity. "I've confirmed that every metal-head followed those shuttles down and every one was blasted by our defenses. They won't be going after any more kids."

"Great. Maybe the damn Pentagon will rethink how smart it is to use the flipping things."

"I wouldn't bet on it." Vic bowed her head. "Wiseman and I never got along that well, but she was a real professional. I'm going to miss that squid."

"Me, too. But maybe I needed this. Maybe I needed to fall off a mountain."

"Fall off a mountain? What does that mean?"

"It means maybe I needed to be reminded how much it costs to win or to lose. And maybe to be reminded I can't make anything I want to happen come true just because lots of people take orders from me."

"If you say so. Ethan, you've always cared about the people who work for you, and you've kept your head on pretty straight despite being in charge."

He shook his head, looking away from her. "Yeah, but. There's so many of 'em now, Vic. So many people. It's not easy. You lead a squad, it's easy. By comparison. You know every guy in it. You know their names, their faces, the names of their wives and husbands and boyfriends and girlfriends, the names of their kids. Every one of them is an individual. We've got a bunker to take down. Who do I send? There's a sniper out front. Who's the steadiest shot? Everything you do is based on who they are."

Stark took a long, deep breath, staring into a darkened corner. "But up here, at headquarters, they're all symbols. And you don't know them. Not really. Maybe a face here, a name there, but otherwise it's just so many hundred or thousand privates, so many corporals, so many sergeants. They ain't people anymore, not in your head. They're units you shove around on a big map to do things for you. Vic, if you're a squad leader and you lose five soldiers it rips you up. Almost half your squad is dead, and you'll be writing to their families to say 'damn, I'm sorry.' But from here? You can lose five hundred and not really feel it, 'cause you don't know them, don't see them die, and they're just a few. Just a few compared to all the other people you're moving around."

Vic sat silent, as if sensing Stark had more to say.

"And that's just combat! Vic, at headquarters you got people falling over themselves to do stuff for you. You're the boss. Get him some coffee, get him a beer, make sure he's got a comfy chair, make sure he never has to wait for anybody else and everybody's waiting for him. And if he gives some order that screws over the people under him, well, hell, you do it anyway because he's the boss. After a while, if you're not real careful, you can start thinking that's the way it ought to be, that you're somethin' special and the treatment you're getting ain't special, just what you deserve."

Stark finally looked at her, his mouth a thin line. "It's a helluva corrupter, Vic. Your soul disappears in little pieces, and you don't even know it's gone or even realize what you sold it for."

"I see. That's why Wiseman's death isn't affecting you at all." He glared back at her, but Vic continued, her voice scathing. "Ethan, if you'd let all this get to you like you're saying, then you wouldn't be so torn up by losing Wiseman and her crew. You'd cry some crocodile tears in public, then set up some grand ceremony to say great things about her sacrifice at the same time as you maneuvered to take credit for what Wiseman did. And if anybody raised any questions about screwups, you'd appoint an investigation with a wink-and-nod mandate to cover up what went wrong and blame any problems that couldn't be covered up on somebody else."

Stark sat silent for a long time, looking down at his hands where they lay clenched in his lap. "That's not the way I work, Vic. You know that."

"Duh. So do the troops. Why do you think the troops like you, Ethan? Excuse me, they *respect* you, which is a helluva lot more important. They think a lot of you because they know you care more about them than you do about yourself. Or your precious career."

"They're just grateful I haven't killed 'em. How's that for a great job? As long as you don't kill too many of your own people, you're a goddamn genius and your soldiers love you. Am I wrong to think maybe I oughta be judged by a different standard than that?"

"What standard do you want to be judged by? You command combat troops, Ethan. They have to be willing to sacrifice themselves, and you have to be willing to sacrifice some of them. It's a weird bargain, I grant you, but there's a lot of different ways to handle it. Getting the job done while taking minimal casualties is something to be proud of."

"That's the other thing." Stark gazed morosely downward.

"The other thing? You're depressed because you keep winning? Ethan, you'll never cease to amaze me."

"I'm serious. Winning too much can be dangerous. I was talkin' to Mendo a while back, and you know what he told me? All the big shot generals in the past, even the very best, a lot of 'em got to think they could win regardless of the enemy and the terrain and the fortifications and the weather and everything else. So they all ended up doing something stupid. Not just ordinary stupid. Spectacular stupid. And thousands of their soldiers died for nothing, and maybe they ended up losing the war they were supposed to win."

"That's called a reality check, Ethan."

"So how come their troops have to be the ones who get blown away when the generals get their reality checks?"

"I don't know. Are you asking me why the universe isn't fair?"

"I guess I am." Stark raised his head, determination replacing the moodiness of a moment before. "I'm grumbling about things not being fair like I'm some private just out of boot camp. Okay, maybe I can't fix a lot of stuff, but I can change things right here and now. First I'm gonna tell Campbell if he wants our trust he damn well better trust us in return. Then I'm gonna make sure everyone's sacrifice up here matters, Vic, and I'm gonna make sure heroes like Chief Wiseman get remembered. Maybe get a monument built, maybe get something big named after her. What do you think?"

"I think losers don't get to build monuments or name things, Ethan. Only the winners get to do that."

"Then I guess I'm gonna have to make sure we win."

PART THREE

Ends and Means

Stark sat grimly in his chair, his bearing for all the world like that of a man before a firing squad. Off to one side, Vic sat facing him with a cheerfully encouraging expression. Stark took a moment to glower her way, then tried to fix a more positive display on his face. *You promised. That's what Campbell kept saying. You promised you'd talk to people if I asked you to. So here I am waiting to go on vid. I'll probably say something so stupid they'll show it in reruns 'til hell freezes over. They won't call 'em bloopers anymore. They call 'em Starks. Just watch.*

Vic gave him a thumbs up and received another glower. "You'll be fine, Ethan." Another display not far from Vic showed Colony Manager Campbell sitting with studied calm at his own desk, waiting patiently for the interview to begin. "Just think of it like you're talking to your troops."

"Sure. Did you find out anything about how the commercial vid networks are planning to get this interview to the people back on Earth? The government will jam it for sure."

"They'll try. The vid networks have a pretty impressive setup, Ethan. The interview will go out as a scattered, broadband, frequency-hopping transmission, each little piece of it tagged to be relayed by any receiver within line of sight."

"That's a lot of receivers. But if all they pick up is government jamming it won't amount to a hill of beans."

"Yup. I said it's a scattered transmission, broken into a gazillion little packets, each repeated any number of times and carrying sequence tags. Unless the government jamming puts out a nova's worth of noise, it won't be able to catch them all. Not that the government could afford to do that, because it would shut down all communications. Imagine how that would play on the World. Anyhow, when the packets arrive at a receiver with the right software installed, they fit themselves back together using the sequence tags and you've got yourself an intact interview."

"Huh. That's neat stuff. It's like that story about the monster that breaks into little pieces to get into any place, and then re-assembles itself and eats everybody. How come the networks are going to so much trouble to help us?"

Vic grinned. "They're not doing it to help us. They're doing it because the ratings promise to be huge, and those ratings let the networks set their ad rates."

"I shoulda guessed. As long as it helps us, though . . ."

A voice spoke from the air. "Interview will begin in five, four, three, two, one. Mark." An image appeared before Stark, as if the woman were sitting in a chair just to his front. The vid personality smiled with bright insincerity at Stark, then slightly to his side. On the vid broadcast, Stark had been told, there would be a split screen, as if he and Campbell were sitting side by side. As far as a viewer was concerned, they and their interviewer would all appear to be in the same room. In fact, the vid personality was located in a shuttle far above the lunar surface, close enough so that light-speed lag wouldn't inhibit the interview but far enough that the blockading warships wouldn't be able to physically interfere until the interview was over.

"Good morning." The vid person's voice had the same cool perfection as her clothes and hair. She looked, Stark thought, like a diamond. Very attractive, but hard and sharp enough to cut glass. He saw Campbell nod and heard the Colony manager's answering greeting out of a speaker. Stark simply nodded, trying his best to smile back without making the gesture a grimace.

The vid personality looked over to the other side, addressing an unseen audience. "This *interview* is illegal, according to our government, *but* we have taken steps to ensure the American people are informed on this critical *issue*. We are speaking this morning to the *two* individuals responsible for mounting the first large-scale rebellion against the federal government in two centuries. This event is *important* enough, in our opinion, to override the government's attempts to censor whatever they have to say. The First Amendment, after all, has *yet* to be repealed." She essayed another smile, apparently to signal ironic humor, then focused on the Colony manager's position.

"There is *one* overriding question on the minds of the American people, a question we *have* sought the answer to since this rebellion began. What do you *want*, Mr. Campbell?"

"I want the rights of an American," Campbell answered. "All the inhabitants of the Lunar Colony want those rights. The right to vote. The right to be represented in the national legislature. The right to petition the government for redress of wrongs."

"You are *claiming* these rights have been *withheld* from you?"

"They certainly have. We have been denied every right due an American citizen. All our attempts to gain these rights have been summarily refused."

"The *government* has stated the Lunar Colony has been *kept* under martial law as a necessary element of its *defense*."

"I'm sure our military commander has something to say about that. Sergeant Stark?"

"Yes. *What* do you say to *that*, Sergeant Stark?"

The vid personality turned to face him, smile fixed in place. Stark tried to project confidence, despite his growing irritation with the interviewer's odd habit of emphasizing random words in her sentences. *Maybe she thinks it helps keep her viewers awake. Maybe it does.* "Ma'am, the civilians in this Colony have been allowed to exercise all their rights to self-government recently, and the Colony is as well-defended and secure as it ever was. There's no conflict between the exercise of their civil rights and our mission to defend the Colony."

"*But*, order clearly broke down *during* your mutiny, didn't it?"

"No. We maintained order at all times. We couldn't have successfully defended the Colony if we hadn't maintained order." Vic was pointing to an exaggerated smile on her face. *Okay, okay. I'll try to stay friendly.*

"*What* are you defending the Colony for? What is it *you* seek? Mr. Campbell, you say you *only* want the rights of any American, but many people believe you *really* want to set up your own country, *taking* with you all the things which American taxpayers *have* spent vast sums to place upon the Moon. As *an* American, do you believe you have the *right* to simply take items of great value for your own?"

"No." Campbell's voice stayed calm, reasonable, as if he were still working to belie the government's prior claims about his mental stability. "The only Americans who think they have that right are the people who run our big corporations and occupy high political office." He paused to let the barb sink in. "We have repeatedly offered to discuss a means of compensating for any items of value up here. We have repeatedly stated our desire to work out wage agreements which do not leave us in a state of effective serfdom. Negotiators from the government, with corporate representatives at their elbows, have refused to even discuss these issues."

The vid personality maintained her bright smile, even though it seemed increasingly out of place. "*You* did not address my main question, Mr. *Campbell*. Do you plan to seek independence *for* the Lunar Colony?"

There was a moment's hesitation, then Stark saw Campbell sigh in a gesture just subtle enough to avoid charges of stage theater. "At this time, it is certain a majority of the citizens in the Lunar Colony would support a declaration of independence. I want to emphasize we have been driven to this state by the actions of our own government, including government-sponsored attacks on the Colony which have resulted in the deaths of civilian members of the Colony."

"The government *claims* such deaths were actually *caused* by mutinous military personnel—"

Stark's anger was still flaring when Campbell broke into the question, his face working with passion. "That's a lie. The military people up here have died to protect us. They have died protecting us from attacks by our own government! One of my own assistants, an unarmed civilian who couldn't begin to defend herself, was killed by mercenaries hired to attack us. Mercenaries whose rampage was stopped by Sergeant Stark's soldiers. Every citizen of the Colony would gladly entrust their lives to any of the military personnel up here."

To Stark, the vid personality seemed subtly satisfied by the fiery exchange, no doubt pleased by the thought that it would boost ratings for the interview. "*Every* citizen, Mr. Campbell? Surely there *is* some difference of opinion."

"Yes. Absolutely. I want to emphasize we are operating as a democratic government up here. So, yes, there's still a significant minority who want to remain under the authority of the United States, but frankly I'm facing increasing pressure from the rest of the colonists to make a full break." Campbell's attitude had shifted as he spoke, so that he now seemed to be sharing a dialogue with the vid personality and her audience. "That means a formal declaration of independence. Begin governing ourselves, the way Americans should be allowed to. Have a strong voice in their own government. Get out from under our corporate masters and the band of corrupt politicians who only exist to serve them." The dialogue had imperceptibly shaded into a populist declaration, delivered with earnest conviction.

Stark barely kept himself from smiling. *That guy is one helluva politician. In the best sense of the word. I hope I'm right about that "best sense" stuff, anyway.*

The vid personality smiled some more, apparently taking time to reorder her thoughts as the interview temporarily slid out of her control. "Why *haven't* you done so, Mr. Campbell. What *is* stopping you from doing what you claim is right *and* just?"

"I don't know." His words seemed to shock the personality enough to generate a nonsmiling reaction. "It sounds attractive. And as you say it sounds just. And right and proper. So, why don't I want to do it?"

"Well, *that* is, I'm sure our *government* would contest such a declaration most vigorously—"

"Sergeant Stark's soldiers can defend us. Isn't that right, Sergeant?"

Stark nodded. "Yes. *No* one will take this Colony *by* force." *Damn. Now she's got me doing it.*

Campbell plowed onward, his voice almost beseeching now. "The authorities back home refuse to treat us as if we have legitimate complaints. Every legal alley is closed to us. All they do is threaten us. Why are they afraid of us? Why are they afraid to grant us the rights guaranteed by the Constitution?"

"Mr. Campbell—," the vid personality began speaking in a vain attempt to regain control of the interview.

"They don't deserve to win, do they? They don't deserve to

lord it over people like us. That's not how things are supposed to work in our country. So, why don't I want to declare independence?" Campbell repeated, his tone half-helpless and half-angry. "What possible reason can I have for continuing to try to work for a peaceful resolution in which we stay a part of the United States? It can only be because our country can be, should be, so much more, and none of us want to give up on our country."

The vid personality waited a moment to ensure Campbell had finished. She'd apparently decided his speech would generate better ratings that her questions and seemed almost disappointed when the Colony Manager stopped speaking. "If I *may* be frank, Mr. Campbell, there are *those* who say you have no choice. That you *are* being coerced."

"Coerced? By whom?"

The interviewer's eyebrows rose dramatically. "By the *military* forces surrounding you, of course. You could *not* even consent to this interview unless this military person was *present.*"

"I'm sorry, but I'm the one who wanted Sergeant Stark present in this interview. I had to insist."

"In *that* case, why *are* you present, Sergeant Stark?"

"Because I take orders from Mr. Campbell."

The simple reply seemed to throw the interviewer off balance again. "It is *well* known you have a very large military force under *your* command, Sergeant Stark. It is still *Sergeant*? You have not *promoted* yourself?"

Stark felt his face reddening as Vic gestured urgently for him to remain calm. "I have no authority to promote myself, ma'am. Officially, I'm still a sergeant, and that's what I'll officially remain. As for the size of the military force under my command, that's got nothing to do with my following Mr. Campbell's orders. The military takes orders from civil authorities. Mr. Campbell is the civil authority for the Colony."

"But you *have* a very large armed force with which to enforce *your* will, Sergeant Stark."

"That's got nothing to do with it. The military doesn't give orders. It takes them."

"My audience *is* surely aware of the many unsourced reports available via uncensored media in which you are quoted as saying you would not attack your *own* country. Do you know *the* source of those reports, Sergeant Stark?"

Dad. I guess you got the word out about our little talk. And it sounds like it's been giving the government some trouble. Way to go. "Yes, I think I do."

"And will you tell us the name of that source?"

"No. "

"Then *how* is my audience supposed to judge the trustworthiness of *those* reports?"

Stark smiled in what he hoped was a reassuring fashion. "They're true. You can take that directly from me, now."

"Then you *are* willing to publicly foreswear *any* intentions to attack the United States?"

"What?" Stark couldn't suppress his shock at the blunt question, but Vic's approving smile must mean showing his reaction had been the right thing to do. "Hell, no. I mean, I'd never order an attack on the U.S. Never."

But, the *government,* Sergeant Stark? What of an attack *on* the government?"

"No. I won't attack the government. The government represents the people. It's supposed to, anyway, and I won't attack the American people. Never. It's like Mr. Campbell said."

"What Mr. Campbell *said?* To *which* exact statement do you refer?"

"He said that's not how things are supposed to work. And he's right. Maybe if we belonged to some other country, things'd be different. Maybe then the military would be giving orders instead of taking them. But the USA is supposed to be better than that. Better than it is right now. I can't change that. Not with military force. And I won't. But I sure as hell will defend the rights of people like Mr. Campbell and his fellow citizens to try to change things."

The vid personality raised her eyebrows again, looking toward the unseen audience. "Sergeant Stark, do you honestly *believe* one man can make a difference?"

"I sure as hell have."

Campbell was still chuckling when he called Stark after the interview. "Remind me never to debate you, Sergeant."

"You'd run rings around me." Stark, still out of sorts from dealing with the vid personality, didn't try to hide his discomfort.

"Not at all. You certainly caught that interviewer flat-footed."

"I just said what I meant."

"They're not used to that, Sergeant. Believe me. However, that's not why I called. I need to talk to you, one-on-one, fairly soon."

"A private meeting?" Stark looked questioningly toward Vic, then nodded to Campbell's image. "Fine. I can be there in about an hour."

"Excellent. Until then." The screen blanked, then shifted to Stark's prior setting, displaying a section of the lunar landscape.

Stark's questioning face changed into a frown. "I wonder what's up. Vic, has Sarafina told you anything unusual is coming down?"

"You mean 'unusual' besides constant threat of attack from our own country? No. Maybe he wants to apologize again for not warning us those blockade runners were coming with civ kids on board."

"He can apologize all he wants. I've told him the only thing that counts is knowing we'll be kept informed in the future about that sort of thing. I'd also like to get my hands on those shuttle pilots, but Campbell says he has to handle it in civ courts."

"You could lean on him, Ethan. He'd give them up if you made it clear he had to."

"Oh, sure. I'll use my military power to force the civ authorities to do what I want. Just this once, because it's really important. No way. I figured out some time back that the road to hell is paved with stones saying 'just this once because it's important.'"

"Don't get testy. I happen to agree with that sentiment."

"Then why did you suggest I do it in the first place?" Stark asked.

"I'm just keeping you honest. Especially just before you go talk to a civ by yourself. But it's probably nothing big. Maybe Campbell wants to talk philosophy with you."

"Oh, that'd be great, wouldn't it? I think I've had enough philosophical discussions for a while."

Vic took a chair near Stark, leaning back and putting her feet up with a sigh. "Funny how your feet hurt from running around up here just like they do back on Earth. So how many philosophical discussions have you had recently?"

"A couple." Vic raised an eyebrow at him, so Stark relented. "Okay, there's been one with you. You know, after we lost Chief Wiseman. Just before that, I had a long talk with Private Mendoza."

"Ah, yes. You referenced that once during our talk. What'd Mendo have to say, anyway?"

Stark studied the emptiness displayed on the outside view even as he summarized the historical background of the Athenian expedition to Syracuse. "The bottom line was Lieutenant Mendoza thought we almost lost everything up here after Meecham's offensive. Mendo thinks, or his dad did anyway, that this time was different because of our command and control gear. It let us take over when our leaders lost the bubble."

"I guess it did." Vic peered into the darkness as if seeking the object of Stark's attention. "You started the ball rolling, everybody else figured it out pretty quick, and we all acted to take charge, and then everybody could turn to you for orders right away. No delays, no confusion."

"Right. Which couldn't have happened a short while ago. Anything I'd have done would've been, uh, isolated. Nobody would've heard until way later."

"That makes sense, but you and Mendo are missing something. The command and control gear helped set up the situation, too, Ethan. Why were people willing to follow your lead? Because you had a reputation, based on what you'd done." She waved a hand to forestall Stark's objection. "It doesn't matter what you said, it doesn't matter what the brass said, people could check it out for themselves on the system records. They'd all *seen* you in action. They knew what you'd done. All of which meant they figured they could trust you."

"And stick me with this lousy job."

"Which you've been pretty darn good at." Vic canted her head thoughtfully to one side. "The bosses built all this command and control gear so they could tell us what to do and know everything we were doing. But when they did that, they gave all of *us* the means to know what kind of job our *bosses* were doing, as well as the means to know everything they knew, and then we used the same gear to get rid of them when they screwed up. Talk about poetic justice."

"Whatever that is."

She smiled. "The same thing that got you elected to be commander after you'd spent a career giving your commanders trouble."

"Then I don't like it much." Stark stared into the black again.

Vic followed his gaze once more, her grin fading into exasperation. "What the hell are you looking at?"

"I'm not looking at anything. I'm looking for something."

"Fine. What?"

"I don't know."

When he reached Campbell's office, Stark saw the display on the wall there also carried an outside view of the surface. Campbell followed Stark's gaze. "You know, Sergeant Stark, when people first got here those displays almost always defaulted to recorded views of things like rivers, lakes, and forests. Nowadays, though, it seems every time I walk into a room the views show the lunar surface. Why do you suppose that is?"

Stark shrugged. "I'd guess it means we're starting to think of the Moon as our home."

"That's what I was thinking. If so, it would certainly be a monument to the ability of humans to bond with any environment."

"Sir, I was in Minnesota once during the winter. If people can be happy living there, then I figure the Moon's not that far different."

"Not much colder, that's for sure. And no wind chill to worry about." Campbell laughed, then sobered. "Would you like some coffee?" He waved toward two cups sitting on the table. "I'm sure it's better than what you get in the military complex."

"I'm sure it is." Stark took a cautious sip. "Not bad."

"Thank you. The coffee grown up here is regarded as an ultra-expensive luxury on Earth, you know. Not because it's better tasting, but just because it's from here." Campbell took a drink himself, then put his cup down. "I suppose I should tell you why I needed to see you. Briefly, I've been able to maintain some political contacts back home. Not everyone there is happy with the way things are developing. They've given me some important information."

Stark, measuring Campbell's mood, braced himself for the worst. "What's that?"

"There was quite a furor over the performance of the Navy's new weapons against those blockade runners. Fulminations in the Senate, investigative panel in the House, all the usual nonsense. But this time people were truly concerned, not just posturing." Campbell referred to his notepad, shaking his head. "After all, these . . . uh . . . autonomous robotic combatants attacked civilians. We transmitted our records of the incident down to numerous sources on Earth, so there couldn't be any doubt that the uncrewed devices had gone after shuttles full of family members and failed to respond to an attempt at a recall." Campbell closed his eyes. "Once more, let me express my deep and abiding appreciation for Chief Wiseman's sacrifice. The fact that my own failure to inform you in advance of the attempt to smuggle in children contributed to her death is inexcusable. I *will* keep you informed in the future, just as I've asked you to keep me informed."

Stark sat silent for a moment before nodding. "I can't ask for more than that. Chief Wiseman chose to do what she did, but maybe she wouldn't have had to if we'd been able to plan things in advance."

"We're still working on trusting each other, aren't we, Sergeant? Do you still want the shuttle pilots turned over to you for legal action?"

"Huh? Are you serious?"

"If that's the only way to make amends, yes."

Stark hesitated. *I could do it perfectly legal. A trial and all. But, it'd mean soldiers with weapons hauling off civs in handcuffs. And civs sitting in a military stockade. I was a civ when I was a kid. How would I have felt about that back then?* "No."

"No?"

"No. You just talked about trust. I'm not going to make civilians trust me by hauling some of them off at gunpoint and throwing them in a military stockade. No matter how I justify it legally. You keep those pilots."

"Very well, Sergeant. I just wish there was some way to commemorate Chief Wiseman's sacrifice. She is by far the most highly regarded person on the Moon at this time"

"Yeah. Soldiers and sailors tend to be highly regarded once they're dead, don't they? But if you really want to do something else, I've got something I've been thinking about."

"What would that be?" Campbell asked.

"I want to name something after Chief Wiseman. And another shuttle jockey named Gutierrez. They both died saving people. I want them, and their crews, to be remembered special. Is there anything on the Colony . . . ?"

Campbell thought a moment. "There's the spaceport."

"I thought that had a name."

"It does. Nobody uses it. They named the thing after a very powerful and very corrupt politician who happened to control a lot of purse strings when it was being built. I think it would be not only appropriate but also just to rename it the Wiseman-Gutierrez Spaceport."

"You can do that?"

"I could try doing it by dictate, but that might arouse some principled opposition. We don't need anyone acting dictatorially up here. Instead, I'll put it out for a referendum. I think I can safely guarantee its overwhelming passage."

Stark grinned. "Thanks. Thanks a lot. Of course, that'll be one more thing the bosses back home won't like."

Campbell returned the grin. "To hell with 'em. You see, Sergeant, I'm picking up a few phrases from you."

"Your Mom should've warned you about hangin' out with people like me."

"She did. She also told me not to besmirch the family name by going into politics." Campbell's smile faded. "But I need to finish what I was telling you about the fallout from the engagement between the blockade runners and the Navy's robotic combatants. The Navy's version of the robots have, with great publicity, been pulled out of action for retesting and rework. Word of the existence of an Army ground combat counterpart to the Navy's robots was also leaked somehow. The Pentagon and a very large and influential group of defense contractors assured all and sundry that the Army's robotic combatants do not suffer from the same problems and will work perfectly in combat."

Stark shook his head. "They never change. I just wonder how

they'll blame operator error for whatever goes wrong with these Jabberwocks when there ain't any operator?"

"Jabberwocks?"

"That's our nickname for the ground robots, sir."

"Oh, I understand. I suppose we might as well christen the Navy robots Bandersnatchi, then."

"Uh, yeah." *I must be the only guy on the Moon who doesn't get that joke.* "It sounds like we're still gonna face the Jabberwocks, then, and they'll be just as deadly and just as nasty as the ones the Navy used."

"Yes, Sergeant. My information indicates the, uh, Jabberwocks are already being prepared for shipment to the Moon."

"They are?" Stark didn't try to hide his surprise. "Where are they shipping 'em? Any idea?"

Campbell walked to his display, bringing up a map of the lunar surface centered on the Colony. "Over here. You see? There's sort of a large valley whose broad end faces our Colony. I suppose it's actually a crater of some sort, but it looks like a valley to me."

"I know it. There were some attacks in that area early on during the war." Stark's finger moved over the map, reliving troop movements seared into memory. "It looked like an easy approach because there wasn't any terrain on the front line to aid the defenders. It looked that way to people reading maps in the rear, anyway. Once we got troops into there we found out any soldiers trapped in that valley got chewed to pieces from defenses on the rims to either side. We call it the Mixing Bowl."

"The Mixing Bowl. Do soldiers nickname everything, Sergeant?"

"I'm sure there's something we don't, but I can't think of it just now." Stark leaned closer, studying the map. "Yeah. That's what I remembered. The Mixing Bowl is a natural dividing line. It's on the boundary between sectors occupied by the forces of two members of the enemy alliance. Two of the biggest and toughest ones, to boot."

"Well, Sergeant, those two big enemies of ours have apparently cut a deal with Washington. My political sources inform me that substantial numbers of U.S. military forces will soon be occupying that position. The enemy forces will pull back to allow the U.S. forces to occupy the area and then attack us from there."

"You're kidding." Stark mentally ran through his defenses facing that sector. "What does substantial numbers mean? Do you have any specifics?"

"I'm sorry. I don't."

Stark rubbed the back of his neck, contemplating what he knew of the remaining strength of the U.S. military. *Third Division got gutted. First Division is up here answering to me, not the Pentagon. Second Division is understrength and committed all over the world trying to protect corporate investments and, oh-by-the-way, the U.S. of A. itself. That doesn't leave anything. More mercs? Would even the Pentagon be stupid enough to entrust killer robots to soldiers for hire?* "I'll get my people onto this. Maybe we can find out something."

Campbell studied Stark. "You're thinking of something now. Can you share it?"

"I'm thinking about Athens and Sparta, sir."

"Athens and Sparta? I remember your reference to Thermopylae, but what about this brings those Greek city-states to mind again?"

"I'm thinking about Syracuse, Mr. Campbell. I'm wondering what would have happened to the Athenians if, after they'd been beat bad there, they tried attacking it again." Campbell listened, his eyes questioning. "I mean, it still took a while for Sparta to beat Athens even after Syracuse, right? But what if Athens had gone back again, committed what was left of its forces, and lost those, too?"

Campbell pondered the question for a long time while Stark gazed at the map. "Athens would have been defeated much sooner, and much more completely, I think. The Spartans and their allies, who were exhausted from the war, would have retained considerable strength. Later, when Alexander the Great tried to conquer Greece, perhaps the Spartans could have stopped him. Or at least delayed him a great deal. And that would have meant the Persian Empire would have lasted longer, or perhaps not fallen to Alexander at all. In the long run . . ." Campbell looked dazed. "I can't think through everything that might have resulted." His eyes suddenly grew alarmed. "You're saying you think that's what the United States is doing? Falling off the cliff that even Athens at the height of its pride avoided?"

"Yes, sir. That's what I'm saying. Maybe we've been big too

long, been able to do what we wanted when we wanted. The idea that we can't lose just isn't there. Or maybe it's just that our leaders are so obsessed with staying in power that they'll let the country go down the tubes rather than admit defeat. Instead, the leadership is betting the mortgage in the hope that they'll draw an inside straight this time."

"I read once that toward the end of the last century someone predicted a major crisis would affect the United States in this century. I never thought it would be because we're too powerful."

"Hell, if you're weak you watch where you're going. It's big, strong people who walk into holes because they don't think they need to be afraid of anything and never look around."

"That's true. I have a confession, Sergeant Stark. I never thought of you as a deep thinker. I didn't imagine you could think this situation through in this manner. No offense."

"None taken. But I didn't think it all up. One of my people told me about Athens and Sparta and stuff. It didn't take a genius to put two and two together."

Campbell nodded. "Listening to your people takes more smarts than you may appreciate, Sergeant. Many managers never do that."

"I'm not a manager, Mr. Campbell, I'm a leader. And I never regretted letting my people talk to me. Oh, sometimes I gotta tell 'em to shut up if they're clueless and won't take a hint, but usually it doesn't hurt, and sometimes it helps a lot."

"I can't argue that." Campbell sagged back into his chair, the motion oddly graceful in low gravity. "This complicates things."

"I thought they were already plenty complicated."

"They are." Campbell picked up his pad, tapping in a few commands to bring up a map of the Earth's Western Hemisphere. "But now we face the real possibility that winning here could cause America's total defeat on Earth. Can we live with that?"

"I don't know. But, sir, can we live with losing? Not you and me personally, I mean, but the consequences for everybody else. I'm not just thinking about the hundred Spartans now and being a big example, I'm thinking about our government winning by using Jabberwocks and Banda . . . Bander . . ."

"Bandersnatchi."

"Yeah. Them. If the government wins using those, the Pentagon won't invest in people anymore. Hell, the bean counters at the Pentagon have always wanted to get rid of human bodies if it could help them afford a few more toys. So they'll just buy more Jabberwocks to defend the country and to send out to other places to break things when the government or the corporations want that done. And Lord will they break things. Will that be our, what's the word, legacy? A U.S. military made up of robots that obey every order without question?"

Campbell kept his eyes fixed on the map. "I can't help wondering how long it would be before someone gave those robots orders to help them take over. You wouldn't have obeyed such orders, would you, Sergeant?"

"No human military personnel would, sir. We're all sworn to defend the Constitution. We have a legal and moral requirement to refuse any orders contrary to that."

"But, then, you're not robots, are you?" Campbell zoomed in the scale, so his pad showed only the continental United States now. "I find us on the horns of a serious dilemma, Sergeant. We can't afford to win, and we can't afford to lose."

"So what're my orders, sir? I can't decide this alone. What do you want me to do?"

Campbell brooded for a moment longer, staring into the depths of his map as if he could see the people represented on it. "I want you to defend the Colony, Sergeant. I want you to defend *my* people. But I also want you to do your best to minimize any damage to the welfare of the United States, and minimize any damage to her ability to defend herself."

"Hah! Piece a' cake. Yessir. I'll do my best, but I've got to tell you, it's gonna be hard to fight someone and look out for their well-being at the same time."

Campbell grinned. "If anyone can do it, you can, Sergeant."

"Thanks large. I can't wait until I tell Vic about these orders."

"You should tell her soon, and I'll have to tell my assistants." Campbell reached to seize his cup of coffee. "This is where we're supposed to toast our future victory, isn't it, Sergeant? That's what happens in all the old vids."

"Uh-huh. So what do we toast when we're not sure we want to win?"

"I think, Sergeant Stark, that we should toast the right thing.

It's been a long time since the right thing has happened. Let's toast that; that whatever outcome occurs, it be the right one."

"Sure. Whatever that turns out to be." They tapped their mugs together, then drank the rest of their coffee, their faces grimacing at the bitterness.

"We have to do *what?*" Vic pretended to slap the side of her head a couple of times as if her hearing had gone bad. "Win without beating our attackers? Is that what you said our orders are?"

"Pretty much." Stark indicated the display where he had called up a map of the Mixing Bowl region. "You got any thoughts?"

"None I care to share at the moment. That sounds like the sort of order General Meecham would have issued." Vic paced across the room in a low-gravity glide grown instinctive through years of lunar living, shaking her head as she did so. "Ethan, we have to have a mission definition which doesn't require us to do two mutually exclusive things."

"Vic, I explained it to you. There's good reasons for giving us that mission." Stark raised both hands palm up in a gesture of helplessness. "I need you to help me do that."

"Are you under the bizarre impression than I'm some sort of warrior goddess who can grant you a prayer regardless of the laws of nature?"

"No, but I figure you must be one of the priestesses for that goddess. Maybe you can put in a good word for us."

She threw up her hands. "You're hopeless. I'm going to call a staff meeting. Maybe Lamont will have some crazy armored tactic that'll help. Maybe Gordo will be able to order a miracle through the supply system. Are you coming?"

"In a few minutes. I got word there's a civ visitor in my office."

"A civ visitor?" Vic's mouth worked as if she were tasting the words and finding them not to her liking. "What kind of civ visitor?"

"I don't know." Stark held up his hands to forestall her next words. "Yeah. Be careful. I know that. The guy got screened by security for any weapons."

"Okay. You're a big boy. See you in a little while. Maybe this visitor is bringing a brilliant plan for achieving our mission objectives."

A short time later Stark stood appraising his visitor. Not just a civilian, but a civilian with that sleek, well-groomed look that bespoke a generous salary. *Either a corporate exec, not too high up an exec because he's doing this job himself, or a lawyer.* Stark fought down his initial negative impression, shaking the visitor's hand, then seating himself at his desk. "What brings you here, Mr. . . . ?"

The civilian smiled with that carefully cultivated authenticity that meant the smile was probably fake. "Jones. Frank Jones."

"Mr. Jones." Stark used one knuckle to surreptitiously tap a button on his desktop that started the room's recording devices. He kept his expression fixed as a small warning light visible only from his angle announced that his visitor was equipped with something that was jamming those recording devices. *Jones? Gimme a break. Now, who's this phony working for?*

Jones made a smiling examination of Stark's office, nodding admiringly toward the display screen and its depiction of the lunar surface. "This is a nice office. I see you're not the sort for ostentation."

"Mr. Jones, I'm pretty busy. What is it you want?"

The smile shifted slightly, still pleasant but more businesslike now. "I have an offer for you, Sergeant Stark. I understand 'Sergeant' is your preferred form of address?"

"That's right."

"Sergeant Stark, my employers are concerned about costs. I'm sure you understand."

"Just who are these employers, Mr. Jones?"

Jones's smile shifted again, very subtly invoking a shared interest. "Sergeant Stark, you now have experience with managing a large group of individuals working toward common goals, much as a corporate executive does. I'm sure that experience will aid you in understanding and appreciating the problems my employers face."

"I still haven't heard who these employers are, Mr. Jones."

"That isn't important, Sergeant Stark. No, really. What matters is what my employers are willing to offer in exchange for some small cooperation on your part."

Stark raised one eyebrow. "Just what kind of cooperation do your employers want, and why?"

"Why?" Jones now appeared to be sharing a subtle joke with Stark. "If costs exceed profits, the bottom line suffers, Sergeant Stark. Overhead expenses must be kept within appropriate limits. To put it bluntly, war is an overhead expense, an expense which in this case is having too large an impact on profit/loss projections."

"I see." *Corporate, then. This guy represents one or more corporations. More than one, I think. He keeps referring to his "employers."*

"Of course you do. Now, in order to reduce overhead, cut projected losses, and bring profit projections back within the sort of limits favored by the financial community, my employers need to regain control of their facilities up here as well as the means to import new employees who are willing to abide by their contracts. You, Sergeant Stark, are critical to that happening."

Stark raised both eyebrows this time. "It's nice to know I'm important."

"You are very important. Executives recognize talent in other executives. They look out for each other. All my employers ask is that you cooperate in their achieving their goals."

"Cooperate?"

Mr. Jones clasped his hands in his lap, serious now, lapsing into obvious bargaining mode. "Ideally, you create the conditions for a rapid return of assets to my employers."

"You mean I'd have to arrange for the Colony to surrender."

"Surrender scarcely seems likely under present circumstances, does it? No, Sergeant Stark, you've done your job very well. So well that only a defeat of the forces defending the Colony would accomplish our goals."

"You want me to arrange for the military forces I lead to be defeated?" Stark marveled internally that he'd been able to keep his voice so bland while he was seething inside.

"It doesn't have to be that extreme. Security codes compromised, perhaps, or a worm inserted into surveillance systems to fool their monitoring devices. You could end this war very quickly, and that would, naturally, reduce the chances of any further soldiers dying in this sadly misguided struggle."

"I see. Tell me again why I'd want to do this."

"Why, shared interests with my employers, of course." Frank Jones leaned forward slightly, a small smile that implied shared confidences now on his face. "Nonetheless, Sergeant Stark, my employers are willing to reimburse you for your cooperation. Of course."

"Of course."

"Now, I realize a million dollars isn't what it used to be, and your services would be of some value. Therefore I am authorized to offer, purely as a fee for your professional services, the sum of one hundred million dollars. Placed within whatever bank account you choose, of course."

"Of course." Stark fought to keep his face and voice calm. "That money wouldn't do me much good when I'm dead, would it? The government wants me. It wants to court-martial me and then hold a nice firing squad."

"We know that. Certainly, you have to, ahem, 'die' so as to satisfy the legal authorities. It's all fairly simple. You are taken to the location of your choice, given a new identity to go with your new fortune, and someone else's body is left here and identified as your own."

"Won't this 'someone else' object to that, Mr. Jones?"

"Oh, no, no. Not at all. Bodies are always available for the right price. We'd just find someone who had died of natural causes and substitute their body for yours. A few bribes and data substitutions in the forensic labs, and the DNA is proclaimed yours. It's all very simple."

"I bet it is. How can you be sure someone will die when you need it?"

"People die from natural causes all the time, don't they?"

"Yeah. They do." *Who was it that said every form of death could be listed as heart failure? Natural causes, hell.* "I've got to admit, Mr. Jones, that's a lot better offer than General Meecham offered me some time back."

Jones's smile shaded into a smirk. "You can't really expect to find good deals in the military."

"I've heard that." Stark leaned back, finally letting his face harden. "Let me clue you in on something. I'm not interested in your offer. Not now. Not ever. There's some things, and some people, that can't be bought. Not even for a hundred million bucks." Jones nodded politely but his confident smile didn't waver. "What I just said doesn't seem to bother you."

"Well, no, of course not. I've heard variations on it many times, so I know what it really means."

"And what would that be, Mr. Jones?" Stark's voice had become so quiet that Jones had to strain slightly to hear.

"Why, the opening gambit in negotiations for a higher payout, naturally. We don't have to play games. My employers recognize that your position is somewhat comparable to that of a chief executive officer of a corporation, and therefore a compensation package similar to—"

Stark leveled a finger at Jones, his face so stern that the corporate representative's voice choked off in mid-sentence. "That's where I draw the line at listening to any more of this crap. No, you little pissant, I am not like one of your CEOs. I don't bail out with a big pile of cash when stuff goes wrong. I don't sacrifice lots of low-level people to compensate for my own mistakes. And I sure as hell don't betray the trust of people who have placed their lives in my hands." He reached out one hand, this time openly tapping the desktop comm panel. "Security Central, this is Stark. I need a couple of military police to escort Mr. Jones outside the headquarters complex. And I need you to notify Ms. Sarafina in the Colony manager's office that her security people might want to talk to Mr. Jones." Jones's smile finally vanished as his face paled.

"You want us to hand this civ over to the civ Colony security, Commander?"

"That's right. But I want to make sure those civ security guards are accompanied by Ms. Sarafina. Understand?" Guards could be bribed. Stark had no intention of handing a prisoner who could casually speak of hundred-million-dollar payouts over to a couple of doubtless underpaid and overworked security personnel.

"I understand, Commander. I'll have the MPs there right away."

"Good. Make sure one of them's the watch commander." Having a senior noncommissioned officer along might not prevent an attempt at a bribe of the military police, but it would make it harder.

Jones was shaking his head, looking both stern and serious

now. "Sergeant Stark, this is really unnecessary. We can work out a deal without employing threats. But if my employers hear of this, they may well withdraw their offer completely. You must—"

"Don't tell me what I have to do." The tone of Stark's voice hit Jones like a punch, so that the smooth civilian sat silent for the couple of minutes it took for the MPs to arrive. "Here's your prisoner. I know he got swept for weapons before he came in here, but he's got antibug gear on him. Maybe he's got something else we didn't detect. Watch him. Don't listen to him."

One of the soldiers looked Jones up and down with a scornful expression on her face. "Do we need to cuff him, sir?"

"Nah. If he tries to run, catch him and bounce him off the nearest wall a few times. Try not to break anything important if you do that, though."

"Yessir. Anything important on him or on the wall?"

"The wall."

"Yessir." The MPs left, Frank Jones between them with an expression of bafflement finally replacing the false geniality.

Stark sat a moment longer, then keyed his comm unit again. "Sergeant Yurivan? I need to talk to you, Stacey."

Yurivan seemed oddly subdued as she answered. "Good. I need to talk to you, too."

"I can meet you at the staff meeting that Vic's going to call—"

"No. We need to talk privately. Sir. I'll be there in a few minutes."

"Fine." Stark broke the connection, studying his desk as if its surface held the answer to Yurivan's mysterious words. *Is there another mutiny in the works? Has Stacey found another spy? Or worse, does she know there's one but not who it is?*

He'd just finished briefing Campbell on "Frank Jones" when Sergeant Yurivan arrived. "Hi, Stace. Have a seat." Ending the call, Stark leaned back, letting his curiosity show.

Yurivan sat slumped in her chair, gazing sourly at Stark until he finally gestured toward her. "Okay, Stace, what's the deal? Why the private conference and the nasty expression?"

"I want it private and I feel rotten because I'm about to do something I'll probably hate myself for."

"Stace, you try to kiss me and I'll slug you."

The reply brought a grin to Yurivan's face. "Stark, there's some things even I'd never do, and that's one them."

"Thanks. So spill it. I haven't got all day."

She looked angry again. "I need to tell you something. I've been talking to a guy named Maguire."

"Maguire? Don't know him. What unit is he in?"

"He's not in any unit, Stark! Maguire's head of the CIA. You know, boss of Spook Central."

"I know what the CIA is. So, what'd this super spook Maguire want?"

"What do you think he wanted? He's been trying to convince me to turn on you guys. Help the authorities back home take you down. All for a nice payoff and a new identity down the line."

"Huh." Stark rubbed his chin, staring thoughtfully at Yurivan. *I wonder how many other people in this Colony are being pitched recruitment offers by various covert types?* "I didn't know the head of the CIA did recruitment stuff personally."

"Neither did I. I guess I'm really special."

"You're special, all right. The fact that you're telling me this must mean you didn't bite on the deal."

"Nah, I didn't bite. Listen, Stark, I do things my own way, and I don't mind working deals, but I never shot anybody in the back. And I won't. Not that I wasn't flattered by the offer."

"So, if you turned it down, why are telling me?"

The anger was back, though Stark couldn't tell if it was aimed at him or somewhere else. "Because I talked to him. Okay? Sooner or later, you may hear about it. Sergeant Yurivan's been talking to the other side. Maybe negotiating. And then you'll want my head on a platter."

Stark nodded. "By telling me now, you're protecting yourself. Okay. I understand that. But what the hell are you so mad about? Sorry you turned down the offer?"

"Hah! I warned you before, Stark, don't try to psych me. I'm mad because I'm just waiting for you to fire me."

"Fire you. Because . . . ?"

"Because you can't trust me now! Why do I have to spell it out?"

"Because I'm stupid, Stacey. Spell it out. You told me about it. Why don't I trust you?"

She stared back, as if disbelieving, then laughed. "You are

something else, Stark. Fine. How about if I lied? How about if I did take Maguire's offer?"

"Why would you tell me about it if you had?"

"To protect my butt if you found out later I'd been talking to the enemy. 'Oh, yeah, Yurivan told me about that. It's okay.' See?"

"I see. Did you have to learn to think this way or did it come naturally?"

"It's a gift. So let's get it over with, Stark. Fire me. Lock me up. Whatever. I'll get by."

"I'm sure you will. You'd probably be running the entire stockade from inside your cell within a week." Stark leaned back, smiling. "So I've got to fire you because the CIA sent someone to knock on your door. What if that was the whole idea, Stace? Or part of it, anyway?"

"Huh? What do you mean?"

"Spread distrust. If you bought the deal, then great. They got an agent just where the need one. But if you don't, then I can't trust you just because I don't know what really happened, and I gotta fire you anyway, so I lose somebody who's good, damn good, at protecting me and every other ape up here. Either way, Maguire's knuckle-draggers win, and we lose. Right?"

It was Yurivan's turn to nod, grudging admiration on her face. "Yeah. I hadn't thought of that. Good one. You still surprise me, Stark."

I wish people would stop telling me that. "Thanks. I think. Besides, you're not the only one getting offers, Stacey. I just had a guy try to buy me out. That's why I called you."

"A buyout?" Yurivan sat up, intrigued out of her mood. "Who was offering the deal?"

"He never said, directly, but I'm sure his 'employers' are some or all of the corporations trying to get their assets up here back. He talked like a corporate type, anyway. Tried to flatter me by comparing me to some high-level corporate manager."

"Now, that wasn't very smart. How much did he offer you?" Stark shrugged. "A hundred mil."

"A hundred million dollars? And you turned him down?"

"Wouldn't you have?"

"Uh . . . let's not go there. Where's this guy now?"

Stark checked the time. "Probably getting acquainted with a jail cell in the Colony detention facility."

"I'll bet that isn't as comfortable as a business-class resort."

"Probably not. Hey, maybe that guy worked for Maguire, too. I mean, he never mentioned his employers. He just implied they were corporate."

This time Yurivan shrugged. "It's possible, but not every questionable character in the world works for Maguire, you know. A lot of them, I'm sure, but not all of them."

"Including you." She smiled at his statement. "I'll say it bluntly, Stace. I trust you. God knows why."

"You said it yourself. You're stupid."

"That's right, I did. But even if I was smarter than everyone else on the Moon you could still scheme rings around me. Right? That's why I offered you the job of security officer in the first place. And I ain't got any complaints about the way you're doing that job. Well, maybe you could be a little less insubordinate every once in a while, just for the hell of it, but otherwise I'm happy."

She nodded, her face calculating. "What is it you want, then, Stark? We just forget about this?"

"No. We file reports, on my guy and on whatever contacts you had with Maguire."

"Good idea. Then we should tell everybody about them."

"Everybody? Why?"

"Because, if we announce we've been contacted and have turned it down, then anybody else who gets contacted will know we're watching for any more of that. They'll be a bit more scared of accepting a buyout, or whatever deal they're offered."

"That's a good idea." Stark eyed her appraisingly. "You certainly know a lot about this kind of stuff. Spying and security and everything. Just what kind of junk were you involved in before all this started, Stace?"

"Me? I'm still a virgin, Stark. Pure as the driven snow."

"Sure you are. And I bet you'd be willing to sell me that snow at a substantial discount."

"If you're buying, you can have a one-time special good-deal just for you. And the snow's guaranteed to stay frozen until it melts."

"Get out of here, Stace. I'll see you at the staff meeting."

"Yes, sir, Commander." Yurivan stood, saluted with mocking precision, then left marching to a cadence only she could hear.

Stark lay near the defensive perimeter around the American Colony, studying the view ahead through his face shield. Scan highlighted brief detections of enemy forces moving behind their own lines, and the occasional movements of friendly forces to either side of and behind him. Not far to Stark's right, a concealed bunker holding a squad of soldiers formed the linchpin for this small area of the perimeter. Inside that bunker, he knew, the soldiers would be monitoring every tiny movement, every tiny emission, every tiny anomaly for signs of enemy action. If those signs added up to an enemy probe, weapons concealed in the lunar terrain around Stark would open fire, hurling grenades and high-velocity explosive projectiles toward anyone foolish enough to test their defenses. On the other side of the area between the opposing forces, similar enemy bunkers and weapons lay in wait for any moves by Stark's forces. The stretch of lunar terrain between the defensive lines had been dubbed the dead zone long ago, an all-too-appropriate name for any soldier trying to move across it.

It had been quiet for some time now, just minor probes by each side to keep the other side worried. Stark didn't want to lose soldiers testing enemy defenses that had claimed too many lives already, especially when the long-term American goal of taking control of all the Moon's real-estate had been abandoned when Stark took over. The enemy, for their part, had been hurt badly by their own attacks on the Colony perimeter over the years and had recently learned some very nasty lessons at the hands of Stark's newly flexible and unpredictable forces. Lunar war, never cheap, had sucked the combatants dry. It had been a quiet born not of victory or defeat for either side, but simple exhaustion of soldiers, national treasure, and ideas.

But the quiet wouldn't last much longer, not once the work Stark was observing had been completed.

Much of the activity was screened. Armored bulldozers had scraped up rock and dust from positions occupied for countless years and piled them into a berm closing off the open end of the Mixing Bowl. The berm's height didn't match the valley walls to either side, but it was good enough to block direct observation of the valley's surface. Tremors within the berm had been analyzed by Stark's technicians, who had concluded that prefabricated defenses were being hurriedly buried within the berm, along with strings of sensors to allow unimpeded surveillance of Stark's forces. There was at least one tunnel beneath the berm, the technicians advised, possibly more, with only a thin opening remaining in place to screen its location until whatever needed that tunnel was ready to come forth.

Shuttles came down, bright spots of light curving through the blackness overhead, raising thin, slowly falling dust clouds from the new landing strip carved from the surface of the Mixing Bowl's valley. Their flight trajectories came within extreme range of the Colony's own weapons, but Stark hadn't attempted to engage them. He didn't know what, or who, made up the cargo for each shuttle, and had no desire to score a hit on a shuttle packed with American troops.

Stacey says her sources claim the Pentagon's dropping a reinforced brigade from Second Division to provide security for the Mixing Bowl base. How many people does a Brigade Combat Team add up to? I know Second Division was understrength. If they packed people into one brigade, that probably means there's only about one full-strength brigade-equivalent left back on Earth. Maybe less. How can they take that kind of risk? Even with all our super hi-tech gear, one brigade can't defend the entire country. What if some of our long-term enemies back home decide this would be a perfect time to march a division of soldiers over the border and into one of our cities? What'll we do, nuke the city to get 'em out?

Stark knew full well he could have received the same pictures, analyzed the same sensor readouts and gazed at the same view of the Mixing Bowl activity from back at the command center. But he lay among the scattered rocks of the perimeter and watched the activity in person, thinking and absorbing information. *I need to know how this terrain feels. How the situation feels here. Before all hell breaks loose in the form of Jabberwocks.*

"Ethan?"

"Yeah, Vic."

"I take it you're not seeing anything we haven't seen before."

"Nope." He smiled, then moved just enough to see slightly back and to his left, where Vic Reynolds also lay in battle armor.

"The Jabberwocks are going to come out of that tunnel. There's probably more than one tunnel, too."

"That's what I figured. When they blow the tunnel entrances, we'll know they're on the way."

"Right. Of course, the dust and gravel thrown up by the entrances being blown will help screen the Jabberwocks' advance." Vic fell silent for a moment. "What if the nano rounds don't work, Ethan? What if we have to handle these things the hard way?"

"Then we'll kill 'em the hard way."

"No slogans, Ethan. I'm thinking we need to be sure every weapon shooter is ready to switch to standard rounds the instant we say so."

"Good idea. We'll make sure everyone knows that." Stark watched the work a little longer, trying to sort out the emotions he was feeling, then uttered a brief laugh as he identified at least some of them. "Hey, Vic. You wanna hear something funny?"

"I could use a little humor about now."

"I don't mean 'funny' ha-ha, I mean 'funny' strange." Stark studied the Mixing Bowl work as he spoke. "I'm looking at everything goin' on over there, and I'm thinking: 'Alright. That's how we do things.'"

"Excuse me?"

"That's how we do things. Americans. We build stuff. Look at it! Moving dirt, throwing together structures, doing big things. It's kind of cool, ain't it? We're Americans. We build stuff."

"Ethan, you're hopeless. I hate to break your bubble, but the only reason they're building stuff over there is so they can come over here and break stuff. Including you and me."

"I know. I know. So what's all this making *you* think about?"

Vic spoke meditatively, as if she were still thinking through her ideas. "A couple of things. Stacey handed me some new information just before we came out here."

"Good or bad?"

"Is it ever good? She has it reliably that some of the bodies in the Second Division Brigade over there were brought in from other units."

"We knew that. They had to pull them from the other brigades in the division."

"No, Ethan, I mean units from outside Second Division. There's a number of survivors from Third Division in there."

"Third Division." Stark stared across the distance again, remembering the shattered remnants of Third Division, rescued by his mutiny, then sent home if they chose. Most had chosen that, including Stark's old friend Sergeant Rash Paratnam. *Rash, you turned me down flat when I asked you to join us. Hell, you almost bit my head off. But, then, your sister had just been killed and I'd been the one to tell you about it. Now, you might be over there. What if we end up in each other's rifle sights? Maybe I* am *in hell.* "Any names?"

"No." A pause. "I had some friends in that unit, too. But it gets worse."

"I'm not sure I want to know."

"Those people from Fifth Battalion. The mutineers we sent home in exchange for some more family members of people up here. They're with that Second Division force, too."

"Why the hell they'd do that? You think they're volunteers?"

"I seriously doubt it. They probably got sent because they're lunar vets, Ethan. That kind of experience is seriously lacking among those Second Division troops."

"You're probably right. Damn. We were already wondering if we'd be able to shoot at other Americans. Knowing some of them personally doesn't help things."

"But we know they're willing to shoot at us. They did during the mutiny, anyway."

"Yeah." Stark ran through the Fifth Battalion soldiers in his head, trying to remember each of the thirty soldiers who had been too heavily involved in the mutiny to be let off lightly. "No. Knowing all that doesn't help much. You said a couple of things, though. What's the other one?"

"I'm starting to wonder if we've missed something important about these Jabberwocks."

"How do you mean?"

"Laying here, looking at that dead zone they're going to cross, I started imagining how our orders would have been laid out in our Tacs. The brass would have spelled out every step we were supposed to take. Right?"

"I won't forget that soon. We've figured the Jabberwocks would just have some sorta super Tacs to do the same thing."

"But that's important, Ethan. Think about it. We always had strict orders laid down in our Tacs; do this, go here, do that. The Jabberwocks are going to have the same sort of thing, right?"

"Sure."

"But when we ran into something unexpected, something the Tacs didn't allow for, what would we do?"

Stark couldn't shrug in his battle armor, but he made the gesture mentally. "Improvise. Work around it. Whatever . . . I think I see what you're driving at."

"Uh-huh. The brass has always wanted soldiers who didn't think, who just followed orders to the letter. Okay, they've got them at last in the form of these Jabberwocks. And the fact that there's no link means the Jabberwocks are going to be dependent on their Tacs for their courses of action."

"So if we screw up that planned course of action?"

"Bingo. They're going to have to think for themselves. We may not have their reflexes or speed, but I'll lay you odds we can handle combat situations better than any AI they could pack into those things."

Stark studied his scan, viewing his own defenses in the area and the lay of the terrain. Exact positions of defenses were rarely identified, but the Jabberwocks had to be programmed to attack the general locations where bunkers were known to be. *Yeah. We can mess with whatever a Jabberwock uses for a mind. Can't hurt. Might help a lot.* "Thanks, Vic. I'm glad you're on my side."

"Ah, shucks. I bet you say that to all the girls." Stark saw Vic's symbology begin moving backward. "For now, I think I'll get out of immediate range of the enemy. Are you coming?"

"In a few minutes." Stark lay on the ridge, in his battle armor, on the dead surface of the Moon, watching the preparations in the Mixing Bowl to attack his forces, and feeling perfectly at home.

If meetings could solve every problem they faced, Stark reflected, then there shouldn't be any problems left by this point. "This is likely to be the last staff meeting before the big attack goes down. I want everyone to think, real hard, about anything we haven't considered. Little things or big things. What kind of questions do we need answered?"

Stacey Yurivan smiled vacantly, affecting a spaced-out voice. "Why are we here?"

"To make my life difficult, Stace. I take it you have nothing new to report?"

"Not really. The demonstrations back home are getting bigger. Everybody apparently liked hearing you confirm the earlier reports that we weren't planning on dropping into D.C. to party hard. That was a decent job planting those reports to set the stage for your interview, by the way."

"Thanks. The government helped me do it."

"So I understand. Apparently it hasn't been able to prove your father's connection to the reports, though. Still, the whole mess is putting more pressure on the government to put up or shut up. They're promising to end the rebellion and recover this Colony by the end of the month."

Vic checked the calendar on her display. "That only leaves them about a week."

"Very good, Reynolds. Have a donut. Yeah, I can't imagine the generals that are running this op are pleased to have the politicians localizing their attack date. Ummm, what else? There was another big drop in the stock market because some of the countries whose contracts with corporations have been enforced by American soldiers are taking advantage of the lack of said soldiers to renege on the contracts. Just the usual political, economic, and social turmoil."

"Commander Stark?" All eyes shifted to look at Private Mendoza. "I have been wondering if our countermeasure against the Jabberwocks may not already be known to the government."

"The nano rounds?" Stark frowned. "Why do you say that? I mean, no security is perfect, but we've kept the nano rounds pretty quiet."

"Yes, sir. But the fact that we put down the mutiny without killing any mutineers has been widely discussed within the Colony. It has even been transmitted to Earth by various means and reported by the vid stations there. And, of course, we sent some of the mutineers back to Earth. Even though they lacked direct knowledge of the weapon we used to disable their armor, they could have described the effects."

"That's right." Stark rubbed his chin, gazing around the table. "Has there been enough information in any of that to clue the

Pentagon in to the fact that we used nanobots to disable the mutineers' battle armor? Stacey? Vic?"

Vic shook her head. "We don't know. But, if there was, the Pentagon may have had an unusual attack of common sense and realized that if we could use nanobots against battle armor, we could also use them against Jabberwocks. They might already be working on countermeasures. Mendoza, I sure wish you'd thought of this earlier."

"I am sorry, Sergeant Reynolds, I only just—"

"That's okay, Mendo," Stark broke in. "We won't get down on you because you just thought of something the rest of us never did. So, worst case, assume Mendo is right, and the Pentagon knows about the nano rounds. What'll they be doing?"

Lamont spread his hands. "Working on countermeasures. What else?"

"Sure. What kind of countermeasures? The Jabberwocks already would've been armored and camo'd as well as possible. What could they do to stop nano rounds?"

There was a babble of replies as his staff hurled suggestions. "Spaced armor? Would that work?"

"No. How about improved point defenses?"

"Against rifle rounds? No way. Maybe make 'em faster, harder to hit at all—"

"They can only do that by taking off armor! Why would—"

The debate subsided as Bev Manley rapped the table. "You're forgetting something, people. If the Pentagon has figured out we used nano rounds, they might have made some of their own. We might be facing that weapon, too. Which means we have to figure out how to defend *ourselves* from it."

Vic rubbed her forehead as if fighting off a headache. "This just keeps getting worse."

Stacey Yurivan smiled. "We could handle it the traditional way the brass deals with stuff that might interfere with our plans. Pretend it's not there and keep the plan unchanged."

"Thanks, Stace. Keep chiming in with those helpful observations." Vic glared around the table. "Okay. Assume we're defending against nano rounds. How would we do it?"

An uncomfortable silence stretched for long moments, until Lamont made another helpless gesture. "You've got to assume you're going to get hit, sooner or later."

"Fine," Stark agreed. "So, you're hit. How do we handle that? How can we stop nanobots from freezing our battle armor?"

Sergeant Gordasa waved one hand. "Do you know what this sounds like? To me? It's like an infection. Little bugs that get inside you and screw everything up. You can't stop the bugs from getting inside. So if you can't stop the bugs from getting inside, how do you stop them from doing a lot of damage once they are inside? Some kind of, uh, nano vaccination or nano-antivenom?"

Vic turned to Stark. "Gordo's right, Ethan. We have to think of these things as sort of like a medical problem. But a vaccination doesn't seem workable, not with the time we've got. I'm not even sure how that could work. Hunter-killer nanobots inside the battle armor? Lamont, you're our best equipment expert."

"And I never heard of anything like that. I mean, you'd have to figure out IFF of some sort for the nanobots so they could identify intruders, nanoscale weapons of some type, a way to get the killer nanos to the infection site. All kinds of stuff. I don't see how we can invent something like that in less than a week, let alone install it in our armor."

"Me, neither. How else do you counter the nano rounds if you're thinking in medical terms?"

Stark turned to his comm pad. "None of us are likely to know that. But maybe I know someone who might have some answers." He punched in a code, waiting until his screen cleared to show the face of the tired-eyed medic. She seemed to be standing somewhere in one of the casualty wards, the shapes of life-support equipment vaguely visible in the background.

"Good afternoon, Sergeant Stark. Private Murphy's been released. He's been pursuing physical therapy on an outpatient basis for a while now."

"Thanks. I knew that. But that's not why I called. I need your medical expertise to help with a question."

"Sure, but I'm no Nobel laureate. What is it?"

"Suppose you got a virus. One with no cure, and it's moving real fast. What do you do?"

Hey eyes widened. "You certainly dream up some cheerful scenarios, Sergeant. I need to know more about this virus. What's the point of entry into the body?"

"Uh, any point. Through the skin."

"I see." For the first time in Stark's acquaintance with her, the medic seemed upset. "Sergeant, if you're researching bioweapons, me and every other medical specialist will be out of here on the next shuttle. That's over the line."

Stark shook his head. "Geez. I'm sorry. That's not what we're doing. No way. This isn't a real virus. It's mechanical. Works against equipment."

"Mechanical? You mean like a computer virus?"

"Sorta."

"A computer virus moves along circuits at the speed of light, Sergeant. You can counter the infection, but not stop it."

"Okay, we're not talking a worm or something like that. This would be, like, nanobots?"

"Oh. Like the nanos we use sometimes. Those move through the system a lot slower." Mollified, the medic pondered the question. "Fast moving virus, no cure, entry at any point. There's only one thing you can do, Sergeant. Amputate."

"Amputate?"

"Yup." The medic quirked a humorless smile. "Seal off the infected area before the infection gets to something critical. The only way to do that, using a human analogy, is to amputate the infected limb. Real fast. Of course, if the infection has entered through the head that option's not going to help much."

"I can see that."

"What you really want is antibodies to counter the infection. That beats amputation any day. Even though we can grow limbs back these days, it's not a lot of fun."

"I understand."

"There's also the snake bite approach if the infection is entering somewhere on the abdomen. Cut it out and suck it out. I don't know how practical that'd be here, though."

Stark winced at the matter-of-fact description, then nodded. "Thanks, Doc. I appreciate the information."

"No problem."

Stark looked around the table. "Everybody copy that? Can we amputate part of somebody's battle armor if it gets a hit from a nano round?"

Bev Manley scowled at the table's surface. "They had to scratch plans for auto-amputate devices built into the battle armor at the knees, elbows, hips, and shoulders. No soldier would wear the stuff for fear the auto-amputate gear would malfunction."

"I can understand that." Stark was unable to totally suppress a shudder. "But we're not talking physically removing a limb. That's a nonstarter."

Vic had called up an internal battle armor diagram, studying it carefully. "You could, theoretically, seal off a section of battle armor. But it would have to go beyond just shutting off circuits and stopping the flow of fluids and gases. There'd have to be some way of physically blocking anything trying to crawl through any crack."

Sergeant Gordasa nodded. "Something real small trying to crawl through a real small crack. You'd have to, uh, do something like the blood does. Clot. Seal it off that way."

"Can we modify suits to do that?"

Lamont shook his head. "I guess I've got more experience with equipment than anyone here, but you've all done maintenance on your armor, right? The stuff we've got ain't designed for that kind of clotting system. It'll seal external penetrations okay, as long as they're small enough, but sealing off some internal section so nothing can get by? You'd need firewalls in there, to help isolate the sections. You'd need some mechanism for rapidly transporting whatever does the clotting, say special nanobots or just sticky foam. You'd need a detection system that could spot an infection and localize it darn near instantly so it could be sealed off."

Vic indicated the schematics before her. "None of that sounds impossible."

"It's not. I'm not sayin' you can't do it. What I'm sayin' is you'd need something designed to do all that. You can't shovel it inside the existing designs, not without completely rebuilding them. And if you're gonna do that, you might as well build a whole new battle armor designed from the ground up to handle that threat."

"He's right." Stacey Yurivan looked around the table triumphantly. "Something I picked up is finally making sense. I've heard some vague rumors about a crash program by the Pentagon to design new battle armor. Those rumors started soon after the Fifth Batt mutiny got put down."

Vic leaned over the table as she fixed Yurivan with a hard look. "Why didn't you mention that before?"

"Because, Reynolds, I've been trying to confirm it. I don't pass along every rumor that crosses my desk."

"So, how long have we got? When will this new battle armor be fielded?"

"Do I look like a Pentagon weapons geek? I predict the new armor will come on line years late and many millions, or billions, over budget. Beyond that, who knows?"

Stark waved one hand to interrupt the argument. "Stace, if that battle armor was anywhere near ready, wouldn't you have gotten some firmer word?"

"Yeah. I'm sure I would have. It won't show up tomorrow, or the next day, or the next week."

Lamont grunted as if a sudden thought had hit him. "The Jabberwocks. They'd want to do the same modifications on those. But that'd take time, too. They can't have been designed to handle the nano threat, any more than our armor was."

"Good point. Stace, have we seen anything to indicate retrofits to the Jabberwocks?"

"Nope." Yurivan twisted her face slightly as she considered the question. "That'd cause enough of a flap that we'd have heard something. I bet somebody's raised the question, but those Jabberwocks have got to be really complicated. A from-the-ground-up redesign to counter a nanobot threat would probably require basically scrapping them and rebuilding the things. Just like the battle armor."

Gordasa nodded again. "That would require new parts, new specifications, new training. Which would all take a lot of time, and a lot more money, *verdad?* Yet the authorities back home don't have much of either."

"Right, Gordo." Stark nodded in turn. "Campbell says the government figures they've got to win this campaign before the election or they'll lose their hold on power, and then a bunch of people eager to fix the system will start taking some long looks at stuff that's been kept hidden. There's no way the government could postpone action long enough to install the kind of fix we're talkin' about."

"Sounds familiar, doesn't it?" Vic remarked. "There's problems with the gear, but we've got to go ahead anyway. How many times did we get sent on that kind of op?"

"So, they'll do it again. And hope we don't have nano rounds to use against the Jabberwocks. Do they even know we know about the Jabberwocks?"

"They know we know they're working on them," Yurivan advised. "The politicians spilled that. But they don't know if we know they're operational and here to be used against us now."

"That helps. I guess. Well, at least this discussion solved the original question, even though we had to circle back to it. We figured out what kind of defense the Pentagon would have to use, then figured they probably can't use it in the time they've got."

Gordasa pointed at Private Mendoza. "But that still leaves another question he raised. Worst case, what if the nanos don't work? What will we do?"

Stark grinned. "Then we fall back on the traditional means of dealing with hostile, armed individuals. Generous quantities of high-explosive and high-velocity metal, delivered with the necessary degree of accuracy."

"Now you're talkin'!" Lamont looked positively wistful. "Call me old-fashioned, but I prefer the tried-and-true methods of destroying things. All these kinder and gentler means of fighting wars just waste time."

The alert came just after midnight a few days later. Stark had been lying in his bed, unsuccessfully courting sleep, when his comm unit beeped. "Commander Stark, this is the command center. Sensors facing the Mixing Bowl are detecting high levels of subsurface movement, including apparent excavation activity."

"Thanks. Notify Sergeant Reynolds. Activate the reserves and get 'em moving. Put all sectors on alert. Somebody else might try hitting us in another area while they think we're busy at the Mixing Bowl."

Stark was fastening the last seals on his battle armor when Vic called in. "Ethan? I'll join you in the command center."

"No, you won't. I'm taking the command APC out there so I can judge the situation in person."

"Ethan Stark, you never mentioned this plan before!"

"That's because I didn't want to argue about it and now we ain't got time. Look, Vic, I'll be a little ways back from the front, with the APC right there and the reserve combat units all around me."

"You can command just as well from back here."

"No. Not with something new. I need to watch these Jabberwocks, get the full feel for their attack. I can't do that from far away." He grabbed his rifle, heading for the door. "I'm on my way."

Stark could hear Vic's sigh even over the circuit. "All right. Just try to keep your head down, soldier."

His APC was waiting. Stark entered through the side hatch, resolving for umpteenth time to get that hatch sealed so that the APC's armor and camouflage would once again be intact. Any general who couldn't climb through a standard belly access hatch didn't deserve the job of commander, in Stark's estimation. Strapping on his harness, Stark jacked into the APC's internal circuit. "Okay, driver. Let's go hunt some Jabberwocks."

"Yes, sir." The APC driver's reply lacked enthusiasm, either because of the late hour or because he didn't relish the thought of being close to combat. The vehicle surged into motion, the driver taking it through the fairly smooth surface areas of the Colony, then out into the rougher terrain beyond.

Stark studied the display before him, even though he'd already examined that stretch of the front so often he could see it in his sleep. *No actual Jabberwock detections yet. No tunnel entrances blown yet. Those apes from Second Division should have realized that needing to finish the tunnels at the last minute would provide us some extra warning time. Hell, they probably did realize it and got overruled by whatever Operations and Plans genius came up with the tunnel idea.*

Stark had long ago selected a site for his mobile command post a little way back from the front, just behind a low ridge whose gentle curve betrayed its origin in a long-ago meteor impact. The APC came to rest, parked exactly on the designated spot, and Stark popped the hatch.

He scrambled cautiously up the slope, even though his command scan told him there were still no Jabberwock detections and no enemy fire was incoming. *Like we guessed. No artillery preparation or cover fire. They're probably counting on surprise. Not just surprise at the time of attack, but surprise at the Jabberwocks. Too bad for them.*

"Ethan." Vic spoke calmly, just as she always had when commanding a squad on the front line.

Stark could see her in his mind's eye, standing in the command center before the huge display, analyzing the situation. The thought gave him considerable comfort. "Here. How's it look?"

"Like you see on your display. I'm not spotting anything unexpected as of yet. The reserve forces are moving up and should be in position within another few minutes."

Stark checked his scan, nodding with satisfaction as he watched the symbology representing four battalions of soldiers reaching their positions. It had been a risky decision, committing so many battalions right here, but guarding against a possible attack elsewhere around the perimeter seemed less important than maximizing the force available where they knew the attack was coming in. Stark took a moment to review the advancing forces, noting Fifth Battalion of Second Brigade among their number. They'd volunteered for the assignment, eager to prove themselves after the shame of the brief mutiny. He watched their movements a little longer, noting something unexpected. "One of those reserve outfits seems headed straight for me."

"That's right, Ethan. I'm positioning one of the reserve units near your location. Just in case you might need them."

"One of the reserve units? Which one?"

"Bravo Company. Second Battalion. First Brigade. Lieutenant Conroy commanding. Sergeant Sanchez and the rest of the Battalion will be nearby. Happy?"

"Couldn't be happier." Stark had a feeling he knew which platoon of Bravo Company would end up camping on his doorstep. He relaxed, watching the front, imagining he could actually see the subsurface activity still being reported by their sensors.

"Sargento?"

Stark grinned. "Corporal Gomez. Damned glad to see you."

"Same here, Sargento. We got orders to stick to you tight as a whore's hot pants."

"Let me guess where those orders came from. Okay. If I gotta have a guard detail, you guys are who I want."

"*Gracias,* Sargento."

Stark took a moment to check the status readouts of his old squad, enjoying the sensation of once again being just a squad leader checking on his peoples' status. "Murphy? Are you in shape for this?"

"Yeah, Sarge. I can handle it fine."

Stark started to move on to another soldier, then noticed something else tagged to Murphy's data. "Acting corporal? You're acting corporal for the squad, Murph?"

"That's right, Sarge. Corporal Gomez, she said she'd give me a chance."

"I hope you're doing your best at it."

"Sure thing, Sarge. Corporal Gomez says I been doing okay."

Stark barely repressed a surprised exclamation. Corporal Gomez's "okay" was equivalent to fulsome praise from others. "That's good to hear." He felt a sudden urgency and dropped plans to speak to each of the other soldiers from his old squad individually. "All you apes. I'm damned glad you're here with me. I don't know for sure all that's gonna happen, but I do know we're gonna kick some robot butt. Anita."

"*Sí,* Sargento."

"I may get awful busy, dealing with stuff all along the front. Watch my back."

"You don't have to tell us that. That's why we're here. We'll watch your back, front, and flanks. Don't worry."

"I won't." A moment later his suit alarms announced activity not far from the entrance of the Mixing Bowl. Stark used his HUD's built-in view magnifier to zoom in, seeing geysers of lunar rock and dust flying skyward as the entrances to several tunnels blew open. He switched to the command circuit, speaking to every soldier along this part of the front. "Okay, you apes. It looks like they're coming. We're ready for them. I want your best from everybody out there. There ain't any soldiers anywhere as good as you apes, and there ain't any robots that can come close. Let's see what it takes to turn a Jabberwock into junk."

A brief period of silence and peace descended. The reverberating shockwaves from the explosions were masking any detections of Jabberwock ground movement, and the devices themselves were apparently too far away to be spotted by other means. Rocks and dust fell languidly back toward the moon's surface, their movement so slow as to seem grudging, as if the debris was annoyed at having its long rest on a dead world disturbed by human interlopers. Stark waited, aware of the presence on either hand of solid, veteran soldiers, drawing comfort and confidence from that knowledge to armor himself against fear of the unknown.

Tentative alerts began flickering on Stark's HUD as the Jabberwocks advanced, marking brief detections by sensors emplaced along the front. Here a ground vibration was noted, there a splash of infrared, in another place movement against a static backdrop. "Vic, how many do you think are coming?"

"Ethan, the detections are so fragmentary so far—"

"I know. But I'm feeling there's not a lot in this wave. The detections are too scattered for there to be a whole lot of those things coming."

Stark waited patiently for the few seconds it took for Vic to balance his impressions against her own. "I agree, Ethan. This looks like a probe, to find and fix our defenses for the main attack."

"Good. We'll nail these from the existing front and hold off on Papa Romeo." They were counting on Papa Romeo, the code word for the plan they'd cobbled together from guesstimates, assumptions, and their cumulative combat experience to counter the Jabberwocks. But they had to wait for the right moment to implement that plan.

"I concur."

Stark tried to relax, breathing evenly. Combat always brought tension, but fighting an unknown foe, an unknown and inhuman foe, had increased the level of stress. When he was sure his voice would be relaxed and confident, he keyed the command circuit again. "All personnel. This looks like a probe. Let's give it a bloody nose."

The detections were growing stronger even though they remained brief. Stark's armor tried to correlate the snatches of data to build a picture of the Jabberwocks, but couldn't manage anything remotely reliable as of yet. Detections popped into and out of existence whenever a Jabberwock had to clear cover for a moment in order to advance. *Damn, they're fast.*

His armor target alert chirped as sensors zeroed in on another Jabberwock when it briefly skittered into the open, its legs almost a blur. The big combat systems back at headquarters, correlating all the readings so far, projected an estimated picture of the creature onto Stark's HUD. *Jeez. We thought they'd be about man-size, but the things are almost half as big as an APC.*

"Stark? Lamont here."

"Yeah." Stark checked the origin of the call, seeing that Lamont occupied one of the tanks nestled in among the reserve units. "Whatchya got?"

"Check this out." A small window popped into existence on one corner of Stark's HUD, playing out vid transferred from his armor commander. "This happened a couple of seconds ago opposite me. Watch that bug." On the display, a Jabberwock scuttled into view on the flank of a small crater, then hesitated in mid-scuttle as it seemed to grab for balance before dashing forward again to vanish behind more terrain. "See that?"

"I saw it. What's it mean?"

"It means those Jabberwocks are top-heavy, buddy. That one almost overbalanced. And if the ugly bugs have stability issues, they can't move as fast as they should be able to on rough terrain. It'll make 'em easier to target."

"Thanks, Lamont." Stark studied the estimated picture of the Jabberwock on his HUD, details still blurry but the main features growing firmer as combat systems tied in every sighting to add to the depiction. *Eight legs, six arms, too damn big, and top heavy. I guess that's what happens when a soldier gets designed by a committee.* He paused, trying to decide whether to broadcast the top-heavy information to all the defending soldiers. *It might make them overconfident. But if they don't know, they might override their targeting systems if the aim points look screwy. Better trust my people.* "Vic, did you hear Lamont's last?"

"Roger. You going to pass the word?"

"You do it. Those things should slow down a bit every time they reach a difficult patch of terrain. That's the time to nail 'em."

"Works for me. I'll inform all personnel."

"Commander Stark?" Stark checked the ID on the transmission, seeing it came from the commander of the company occupying the defensive line near the center of the attack. "How close do we let those things get before we open fire?"

I guess I can't tell people to wait until they see the whites of their eyes. Not against something without eyes. "I want to minimize their chance of reporting back. Let them get close, then open up."

"How close, sir?"

Stark suppressed an aggravated response. *Not her fault. Everyone is still used to being told exactly how to do the job instead of just what to do and using their own experience.* "Sergeant, you can see the terrain and know the targeting probabilities from your positions a lot better than I can. You shoot when you figure you can nail those things."

"Yes, sir."

Closer. Stark checked the scan to see where the Jabberwocks were getting closest to the line, then switched his view to that from the nearest bunker. The detections were getting firmer and longer, but firing solutions were still frustratingly brief. Stark shook his head, watching how quickly the Jabberwocks were flitting from cover to cover. *Fine, you bastards. Hide all you want on the way in. The last stretch before the bunkers has been cleared. It doesn't have any cover. Then we'll see if you can outrun bullets.*

A Jabberwock loomed into the bunker's view like a monstrous spider out of a bad vid from the last century, its legs blurring as the robotic combatant lunged forward. Stark could now see its multiple arms were outfitted with a variety of weaponry, the barrels and firing rails tracking in search of targets.

The bunker commander had apparently had enough. Chain guns erupted in a brief volley from three locations, spitting streams of bullets at the point where targeting systems said the Jabberwock would be when the bullets got there. Incredibly, the robot managed to avoid the first volley, its legs dancing wildly as it checked its advance and jerked to one side. Unfortunately for the Jabberwock, one of the chain guns kept firing, walking its rounds straight onto the curved shell of the robot. Sparks flew, bright against the black shadows all around.

Stark watched the Jabberwock spin, its own weapons targeting the chain guns. *Man. They're hard to kill, just like we feared.* Then the robot slowed, hesitating as it seemed to lose use of several legs. Two more chain gun bursts caught it dead-on as the Jabberwock staggered, then it froze and fell. *One down. How many does that leave?*

Stark pulled back, checking his scan for activity at the other points where Jabberwocks were testing the defenses. Five others were already knocked out, and as Stark watched, the symbols representing another two ceased motion and were tagged with "kill" markers. Silence settled over the line, the defenders' weapons quiet and no detections marking the presence of other Jabberwocks. *Did we knock 'em all out, or are there some still hiding and watching?* "Vic, do you think that was every Jabberwock in the probe?"

"I think so. There might be some playing possum and surveilling the line, though. Our systems can't be sure how many individual Jabberwocks were spotted on the way in. The only way to know for certain would be to send out patrols and see if they find anything."

"I don't need to know that bad." Somewhere inside the Mixing Bowl base, Stark knew, a lot of officers and probably some contractor technical representatives were trying to analyze what had just happened. The Jabberwocks had surely been knocked out quicker than the attackers had expected. Would that be laid at the feet of luck on the defenders' part, or blamed on the small number of Jabberwocks employed in the probe? Either way, the next attack would surely be stronger.

"All personnel. We stopped 'em cold. Our special rounds worked like a charm. Expect more strength, a larger number of Jabberwocks, in the next attack." Stark studied the field of battle, waiting for some indication of what form the next attack would take.

"Incoming," his suit alert system announced. Stark checked his HUD, watching the tracks of incoming artillery fire headed for his front line. Long-range defenses opened up as the artillery shells came closer, nailing some so that they burst over the empty dead zone between the combatants, but some shells made it through, thundering into the lunar rock with massive loads of high explosive, or tossing out gales of submunitions to seek targets among the rocks below. *That's gotta be cover for something. Yup. I don't believe it.*

"Here they come again," Vic reported.

"I see 'em, Vic. Hell, you can't miss 'em." At a score of points, Jabberwocks suddenly leaped into view, Stark's HUD instantly locking in on the emissions from their rocket-assist packs. *Jump rockets. The same suicidal garbage they've been trying to hoist on us for years. I guess the Jabberwocks are too stupid to tell the weapons designers to pound sand.* The Jabberwocks jinked slightly as they flew, attitude jets trying to confuse any targeting solution.

Jetting low above the surface, the Jabberwocks shot forward, perfect targets against the empty lunar horizon, until they reached the engagement zone for Stark's soldiers. Despite the artillery barrage, the defenders had no trouble locking onto the incoming robotic combatants nearest them. Stark switched to visual for a moment, watching as the nearest Jabberwock ran into a concentrated barrage of fire that stopped it in mid-flight, broke its armored shell into a hundred pieces, and hurled the pieces in all directions. Stark switched back to scan, viewing the red markers that displayed the destruction of every other flying attacker. *Too bad we wasted nano-rounds on those.* "All personnel. If any more of those things try to fly in, use normal ammo on 'em."

"Yessir," one of the bunker commanders acknowledged. "If it flies, it dies."

Stark grinned, enjoying the lack of any sense of guilt. *We're not killing anybody. We're just junking machines. We could do this all day and not pick up any bad karma.*

"Ethan, that was too easy."

"They were stupid, Vic. That's why it was easy."

"The next one won't be. Count on it. They've lost too many of those things. What did our old officers do when a squad couldn't take a position?"

"Throw a platoon at it, then a company, then a battalion."

"And they've figured out flying in is a lot less survival-enhancing than walking in. The next attack will be on the surface, and there'll be a lot of them."

"Good assessment." Stark scanned the area, weighing his options. *Do the Papa Romeo now or wait? Wait. Just a little. Can't leave it too long, though.*

Detections sprang to life once more, fractional and blindingly brief, but in much greater numbers. Stark watched the symbols flick on and off like a meadow full of fireflies. *A feint? Or the real thing?* "Vic? What do you think?"

"This looks like their main push. Those things are too hard to spot to count exactly, but there's a lot of them coming, and the approach tactics match those used by the first probe."

Stark scanned the front, watching the brief detections pop in and out on his HUD, letting his instincts judge the situation. "Yeah. I agree. All units. Execute Papa Romeo. Repeat. Execute Papa Romeo."

Papa Romeo, a half-joking name for the operation, using the phonetic letters that stood for Pretend to Retreat. The units along a large section of the front facing the Jabberwock attack began falling back rapidly, fire teams alternating their movement to cover each other in case of an unexpected dash by the Jabberwocks. Bunkers emptied with a rush as the squads occupying them set the systems on automatic passive defense and dropped back with the other soldiers.

Stark watched closely for any sign of panic, any sign the false retreat might turn into a real one. Dangerous, to start soldiers retreating. It could be hard to stop them. It was a difficult maneuver, one that even veterans might fail if something unexpected rattled them along the way or some rumor of disaster swept the front. But Stark's troops, perhaps bolstered by their recent success with annihilating two Jabberwock attacks, showed no signs of wavering. As the soldiers reached prepared positions along a rough arc bending in from anchors along the existing front, they took up a new defensive line.

Stark had just thoroughly scrambled the tactical situation the Jabberwocks were programmed to confront. It had been Vic Reynolds's suggestion, to leave the established front line the attackers were expecting to face and set up a new line behind it. The new line bent inward, as if a giant had taken a huge bite out of the existing front line. At the points where it joined the old line, new bunkers had been added and strong forces were massed to resist any pressure.

"Vic, activate the minefields." Stark envisioned her back at the headquarters complex, keying in the code that turned numerous scatterings of small rocks into fields of death. They wouldn't stay active long, just a few days, even if they weren't deactivated by remote, but it would be long enough.

Stark checked his scan, smiling with grim satisfaction as he reviewed the status of his defensive line. The attacking Jabberwocks would encounter no resistance from the old front line, as the bunkers on automated passive defenses would fire only if fired upon. But once they penetrated the indentation in the line, they'd take fire from three sides, while covering terrain on which they weren't programmed to confront fixed defenses. If they'd been human attackers, Stark would have felt a surge of pity and sorrow at the waste of life about to occur. Against the Jabberwocks, he gleefully anticipated the destruction of the attackers.

The firefly-like flickers of detections continued, the Jabberwocks coming on with eerie precision. They slowed slightly as they reached firing positions near the old front line. Stark zoomed in on one area, watching as Jabberwocks alternated their scuttling progress. *They're covering each other as they advance.* The implication hit almost instantly. "Vic. I think there's about twice as many Jabberwocks coming as we thought. Only about half of them are moving at a time."

"Damn." Stark knew Vic had aimed the curse at herself. "I should have realized that before you did. I'll make sure scan reflects that."

The number of possible contacts on Stark's HUD multiplied with dismaying speed as the tactical systems reacted to the new instructions. *If I don't like it, and I knew it was coming, everybody else must be even unhappier.* "All personnel. The Jabberwocks are advancing, alternating with each other. That's why you're suddenly seeing a lot more contacts. Stay sharp, but stay frosty. There'll be a lot less of 'em in a few minutes."

The Jabberwocks reached attack positions, then continued forward, dodging and weaving with their inhuman speed. A bunker just to left of the center of the attack opened fire as Jabberwocks literally ran over it. There was a brief fusillade of fire, the bunker triggering its defenses while Jabberwocks swarmed onto the location and poured their own barrage onto every firing point. Stark watched, his eyes hard. *Like a bunch of fire ants massing onto some poor clod who got in their way.* The insect-like movement and attack patterns of the Jabberwocks were unnerving to Stark, even after seeing many destroyed.

The bunker fell silent, its weapons destroyed and the bunker itself breached. Stark scanned the front slowly. The Jabberwocks had paused in their advance, as if satisfied with their conquest. *Come on, you ugly bastards. We've got a little reception waiting for you.* But the robots stayed passive, apparently content to occupy the front. "Vic, we've got a problem."

"So I see."

"We can't wipe them out if they stay along the old line. How do we get them advancing again?"

"Ethan, they swarmed all over that bunker when it fired on them. Maybe if you open up from the new positions, they'll come after you."

"That's not a bad idea. Lamont, tell your hogs I'd like them to see how many of those bugs they can squash from here."

"That's a roger! Let's see how they like heavy incoming." Fire erupted from a dozen points along the new defensive line as Lamont's tanks opened up with their main guns. The Jabberwocks seemed to watch the large shells coming, then stepped aside rapidly to avoid impact points. A few fired back, the tracks of antiarmor missiles blazing in toward the tanks. Given the range, Lamont's tanks easily took out the missiles with their own point defenses. "They ain't coming, boss. And I can't nail 'em from this distance. Maybe if I mounted particle cannons as my main batteries, but not with a shell's time of flight. Those Jabberwocks just dodge too fast."

Great. We never figured the stupid bugs would just sit there. Am I going to have to attack? I could lose a lot of people that way, but I can't leave the Jabberwocks in possession of the front line. Sooner or later, some of the human soldiers from Second Division will move in there, and then I'll have a major headache figuring out how to retake the positions. "Vic, I'd really appreciate another idea. The faster the better."

"Fine." Stark knew her anger was directed not at him, but at the Jabberwocks. "Let's think through their programming. Our old officers handled it. What would they have told us to do?"

"Ummm, lessee. Take the position. Hold the position. Exploit . . . that's it. Vic, if those bugs see us running they'll come after us."

"That's risky, Ethan."

"I know. Get new positions drawn as fast as you can. Fall the front back to where the reserve forces are."

"Which puts you on the front line again. Did you plan this?"

"Vic, damnit—"

"Don't worry. You've got your positions. Here's the download."

Stark took just a moment to glance at the new line Vic had thrown together. *Man, she's good.* "All units. This is Stark.

We've got to let the Jabberwocks see us retreating, so they'll try to chase us. You're getting new positions downloaded now. On my word, I want all the designated units to stand up, wave their arms, and start falling back fast. No panic, understand? If anybody tries to run past their assigned positions I will personally find you and kick your butt into orbit. Now, go!"

All along the back arc of the new front, soldiers stood up in plain sight of the Jabberwocks, turned, and began running. Stark fought down a chill of apprehension. *That looks entirely too real to make me comfortable. Stop when you reach your new positions, guys. Stop.*

Down on the old line, the Jabberwocks seemed to be watching, then abruptly surged into motion all at once like a school of fish. *Alright! Come to papa, you little monsters, you.* "It's working. They're coming. All reserve units, you're part of the front now. Let's take 'em."

Stark felt a presence nearby, turning to see armored figures lying on the slope to either side. His old squad, ready to defend him. He had to resist the urge to review their positions personally. *Not my job anymore. Let the squad leaders do their job, let Anita be the platoon leader.* He felt a separation, not for the first time, from the people and command position he'd always loved.

Stark had delegated control of the artillery to Vic, leaving her the authority to call in missions and removing a major distraction from his own job of overseeing the defense. Now he watched as his HUD highlighted a barrage arching in from his rear. The Jabberwocks were still hard to individually spot and track as they scurried among every bit of possible cover, but the general movement and location of the robotic combatants could be discerned from the trend of brief detections.

Defensive fire blasted out from the Mixing Bowl base, trying to screen the advancing Jabberwocks from the incoming shells, but it was unable to penetrate far inside the Colony's own perimeter. Most of the shells made it through, falling with deadly force among the attackers.

The artillery fell toward the middle and rear of the area covered by the Jabberwocks, herding them forward even as concentrated blasts of gasses from exploding shells battered the robots, fragments of metal sliced into them, and individual submunitions sought out the fast-moving Jabberwocks to sting them from above. Torn mechanical spider shapes staggered forward or in dizzy circles, while others became briefly mobile torches as ammunition or fuel supplies caught fire. The Jabberwocks left a plain littered with wreckage as they swarmed forward, unheeding of their losses.

Stark smiled again, baring his canines as he saw Vic's artillery mission had herded the Jabberwocks toward the minefields. More giant bug shapes shattered as antitank mines ripped them apart. The Jabberwocks began firing, clearing the minefields by the painstaking tactic of shooting at every rock in their path. Humans couldn't have maintained that accurate a barrage while moving that fast, but the Jabberwocks could.

Clear of the minefields, the Jabberwocks came on. Stark caught his breath as he totaled up the numbers still in motion. *Good Lord. How much did the government spend to buy all these things? Better not let 'em get any closer before we start hurting them serious.* "All units. Ladies and Gentlemen, let 'em have it. Open fire."

An arc of fire blazed to life on three sides, hitting the Jabberwocks from the front and both flanks. Most of the fire missed, the mechanical bugs moving so quickly that combat systems couldn't correct aim points fast enough. But so many weapons were firing that the front ranks of Jabberwocks collapsed into frozen uselessness.

Despite the volume of fire pouring from three sides into the indentation in the front, the Jabberwocks kept coming, their scuttling shapes passing over the bodies of fallen robots like a horde of alien monsters. *I wondered what it'd be like to meet something that wasn't human. Well, we've met 'em, and we're fighting 'em. Figures.* He checked his scan, watching the wave of Jabberwock symbology closing swiftly on the improvised defensive line. "Vic, watch for any penetrations."

"I'm watching. They're too close to you now for more artillery. I don't want to risk a short round hitting our own line."

"Understood. We'll take 'em one-on-one." Stark raised his own rifle, watching aiming points spring to life on his HUD as the linked targeting system activated. He fired carefully, picking his targets from the highest hit probabilities, cursing at the number of shots that missed as a Jabberwock used its inhuman speed to dart forward. The Jabberwocks were firing back, blasting off aimed shots without pausing, their accuracy still fortunately confused by the human soldiers' active and passive defensive systems and by the amount of explosion-generated noise created by all the weapons being fired.

A wave of Jabberwocks hit the center of the improvised line, running straight into a massive barrage of fire that dropped every one short of contact. But more scuttled forward, laying down rapid shots that forced Stark's soldiers to take cover or die.

One of Lamont's tanks, its massive beetle-shaped carapace almost invisible against lunar shadow, found itself confronting a pair of Jabberwocks. The first opened fire immediately, its small-caliber rounds glancing off the tank's armor in a brilliant cascade of sparks. The second Jabberwock, slightly back and to the side of the first, paused for a fraction of a second while a heavy anti-armor weapon dropped from the robot's internal magazine onto a firing rail.

The tank's secondary cannon roared, cutting the first Jabberwock in half with a hail of shells. Its turret was swiveling to target the second bug when the antiarmor missile shot out. Point defenses opened up, not scoring a direct hit but diverting the missile slightly. The tank staggered as the missile hit home in a noncritical area, spraying fragments of armor. Then the tank's main gun steadied and fired. This close, even the Jabberwock's speed didn't allow it to dodge the heavy shell. The robot simply vanished as the shell penetrated its armor and exploded inside, leaving the stumps of eight metal legs falling into dust littered with the wreckage of war.

"Hey, you ground apes! How about a little covering fire here! It's gonna take me forever to fix the hole in that tank!"

Stark fired again even as he called out orders. "Ground soldiers. Screen Sergeant Lamont's armor. You can nail the Jabberwocks while they're trying to target the tanks."

A Jabberwock reared up nearby with shocking suddenness, dull metal and rapidly moving limbs rendering it a vague shape out of a nightmare, as it loomed against the endless black of the lunar sky. Stark was still bringing his rifle up when the soldier nearest him screamed in a combination of pain and rage, her suit broadcasting multiple penetrations as the Jabberwock fired a burst into her. Still screaming, the soldier fired on full automatic, her rounds winking in wild pyrotechnics off the head and carapace of the Jabberwock. The bug staggered, wobbling as other soldiers and Stark added their fire, its legs hunting frantically like a spider caught under a boot heel, then froze and fell over in a slow-motion collapse.

Stark reached the wounded soldier first, her fingers still spasmodically tightening on the trigger of her empty weapon. "Take it easy. It's dead." *Billings. Damn.* He scanned her medical readout, then tagged her symbol for high-priority response by the medical teams. "Looks like you'll make it." *If the medics get here quick enough.* "Hang in there." *Please.*

"As long as I killed that bastard," Billings spat, then collapsed from the load of drugs being pumped into her by her suit.

"Ethan."

"Yeah, Vic."

"I'm getting individual Jabberwocks breaking through on the left. I'm moving APCs to intercept."

"Get some tanks with those APCs." Stark fired again as he lay near the badly wounded shape of Private Billings, determined to guard her. "They can't take the bugs alone. The Jabberwocks are too tough and too heavily armed."

"Roger. I'll have to pull the tanks off the line. Everything's committed."

Before Stark could answer, another Jabberwock jerked into view not far away, firing with four of its arms as it skittered toward them. Two brief bursts caught it on the head and side, then a lucky shot with a grenade knocked off two legs. The Jabberwock wove back and forth for a moment, firing erratically, then dropped.

"Good shooting, Caruso." Corporal Gomez, all business. "Chen, get yourself a couple meters over so you can cover the Sargento and Billings better. *Dios!* Here's another one."

Stark cursed as the nearby soldiers engaged another Jabberwock, pulling his scan back so he could see the entire situation again. The dancing symbology that marked split-second detections of Jabberwocks made it hard to evaluate how many were left, but the number of kill symbols indicated they'd knocked out or destroyed scores. "Go ahead and pull the armor, Vic." A sudden chill ran over him as he realized the move might be misinterpreted. "All units. Armor is being pulled off the line to reinforce a reaction force. We are not falling back."

His fear that the movement of the tanks would be misunderstood appeared misplaced as some unknown soldier immediately replied. "Hell, no, we ain't!"

Stark focused back on the immediate area, noting the absence of close-in targets. Symbols marked a half-dozen disabled Jabberwocks scattered close to his position. The nearest soldiers were prone in the thin dust, firing single, carefully aimed shots at Jabberwocks still advancing against other portions of the line. *Like those things that went after the blockade runners. Single-minded. Keep going after the target until it's destroyed.* The flickering detections were few now, most on the left, some behind the line. Infantry was scrambling off the line, alarming Stark until he realized they were moving to target the Jabberwocks who'd made it through the defenses.

APC symbols converged on one of the Jabberwocks. Stark switched scans to view the action through the APC gunner's view. On the APC's targeting system, he could see the hunted Jabberwock's symbology flash there/not-there as the bug dodged rapidly among the rocks. A moment later, a nearby APC shuddered as the Jabberwock poured fire into it, the armored vehicle sliding to the surface while broadcasting damage alarms.

The other APCs fired, raking the area around the Jabberwock even as it continued to fire at the wounded APC. The robot sidestepped too fast to follow, trying to avoid the defenders' fire as it maintained a fanatical focus on destroying the APC it had targeted.

A tank hove into view, its weapons searching for the Jabberwock, then locking on. The Jabberwock, finally satisfied with the damage wrought on the stricken APC or perhaps sensing a new threat, spun to attack the tank, but as it did so, several rounds hit home from different angles. Staggering to one side, the Jabberwock frantically tried to regain its balance, temporarily unable to evade the incoming fire. A moment later, the bug was riddled by APC fire, then its broken carcass was slapped to one side by a cannon shell from the tank.

Stark pulled his view back again, breathing heavily from the stress of action. One or two Jabberwocks were still moving, still coming onward, but first one and then the second froze. A final burst of fire into the immobile remains followed, then silence fell as the defenders vainly sought new targets.

We did it. Good God in Heaven, we did it. Human soldiers, one. Jabberwocks, zero. "Vic, I read the attack stopped dead."

"I concur. No movement apparent. I'm deactivating the mine-fields so our forces can reoccupy the front line."

"Roger. Get those units moving." He paused, tasting something bad in his mouth. "I'll need a casualty count."

"You'll get one."

Stark spun to see where he'd left Private Billings, sagging with relief as he saw her being carried to a waiting ambulance. "She gonna make it?"

One of the medics answered without halting his careful ma-neuvering of the mobile stretcher. "Yes, sir. She'll be stabilized within a couple of minutes."

"Thanks. Anita?"

"*Sí*, Sargento."

"How many?"

A pause, whether to count or to compose herself, Stark didn't know. "One dead. Two wounded, one of those serious."

Stark extrapolated that, comparing the number of Jabber-wocks they'd personally nailed against the number of casualties suffered by Gomez's platoon. *Maybe we didn't lose too many.* "They done good, Corporal Gomez. You've kept 'em real sharp."

"*Gracias*, Sargento. We gonna go after that base now?"

"I'm not planning on it." Stark walked slowly back to the command APC, wishing once again that the vehicle had been armed so that its firepower could have aided in their defense. *One more thing I gotta do someday.* "How's it look, Vic?"

"Reoccupation of the front line is proceeding without any trouble, except for that one bunker that the bugs nuked. I'll put some armor near there to cover the gap." He could hear the relief in her voice, the winding down of tension ratcheted up by the re-cent battle. "So, Ethan, 'thou hast slain the Jabberwock'?"

He looked over the barren lunar landscape, back toward where the headquarters complex lay buried beneath the ancient rock. "What?"

"'Thou hast slain the Jabberwock.' It's a quote, you oaf. From *Alice through the Looking Glass.*"

I guess that's where that Bander-whatsit stuff comes from, too. "How come you remember something like that?"

"They were my favorite books when I was a little girl."

"That's a surprise. That's like, *Alice in Wonderland,* right? Some little dressed-up Brit girl? You liked that?"

"I liked the idea of a girl wandering around exploring strange, new worlds on her own. What's wrong with that? Mind you, I always thought Alice should have been more heavily armed before she started on those expeditions, just in case any of the weirdoes she met happened to turn out hostile."

"Now that part ain't a surprise." Stark checked his scan again, pulling it far back to see a good section of the front. His laughter died as Stark stared at a corner of the scan showing activity behind the enemy lines. He centered the display on it, focusing the scan. "What the hell's going on?"

"Where? Let me see your scan. You mean that stuff on the flanks of the Mixing Bowl?"

"Yeah. I mean that stuff." Scan provided only a scattered picture at that range, showing those traces of enemy activity that could be spotted across the distance, but increasingly large concentrations of enemy symbology seemed to be easing into position, carefully screening themselves from the official American forces occupying the Mixing Bowl. "What are they doing? Are they planning to throw enemy forces against us, too?"

"Ethan, if those enemy units were going to be used against us, they'd be more concerned about screening themselves from us, not from the official forces. Look at their movements. When there's a choice of screening terrain, they're choosing the route that masks them from the Mixing Bowl."

"Why? What the hell are they doing?"

"They're getting ready to hit the official forces. Look. To the south, too. We haven't got as good a view there, but something's going on."

Stark tried to rub his face, his armored hand slapping against his face shield instead. "A double-cross. Why now?"

"Why now? That's easy. Think about it from the enemy's perspective. The official American forces hit us, we hit back, both groups are weakened, then the people that don't like any of us hit what's left in the Mixing Bowl and roll over it. After that, they hope, they hit the defenses here, which the Jabberwocks have already softened up, and take the Colony. One, two, three strikes and we're out."

"Damn. We can't let that happen."

"No, I don't expect we can. How do we stop it?"

"We've got to help 'em. The guys in the Mixing Bowl. They don't have enough forces in there to hold off surprise attacks from both flanks. Not in that terrain."

"No, they don't. Think carefully, though, Ethan. No matter how we try to help, we're going to have to open our defenses here. We're going to have to commit forces that may get shot at by both those enemy forces and by the Mixing Bowl defenders. Worst case, we'll be seriously weakened. We might lose the Colony trying to save the official force. And if we do save them, they might still try to take us."

"Yeah." Stark stared outward, above the barren black/white/gray of the lunar terrain, outward to where the white and blue bannered disc of Earth hung in the blackness, memories cascading through his mind yet somehow leaving a single clear thought. "Yeah. I know all that. But I'm an American, Vic. We all are. The idiots running the country can't change that no matter how much they screw up everything else. And for once, for damned all once, I ain't gonna let everybody else pay for the dumb things our bosses decided were smart. We're gonna save those apes in the official force, and we're gonna see 'em safe home, so they can look out for the civs on Earth like they're supposed to."

"And if those apes thank us by taking over the Colony? Our troops won't fire on Second Division soldiers, Ethan, not even to save themselves. You know that."

He took a deep breath, eyes still fixed on Earth. Somewhere on that ball, somewhere beneath the white clouds, everything he'd been raised to care about waited on his decision. There wasn't any ice filling him this time, just a steady warmth that seemed to come from somewhere other than his suit's heating system. "Yeah. I know that, too. What else can we do, Vic? We got orders from the Colony leader, remember? Don't let the official force get blown away. Those are our orders and our priorities. And those orders make sense, Vic. What's the alternative? Leave home without anybody to defend 'em? If this much of Second Division gets trashed, what's left couldn't defend the borders. The guys who are double-crossing 'em up here will go after our country back home sure as hell. We took an oath, Vic. Protect the Constitution. Nothing we've done yet has really violated that. Home, the Constitution, they've been safe. But if we let those apes die, if we let everybody with a grudge against the U.S. of A. walk in to take whatever piece they think they're owed, what then? It'll all be over. I won't let that happen, even if I have to walk by myself over there and fight on my own."

"You won't be alone, Ethan." After a brief pause, she continued. "We've got one ace we can play. Stacey just notified me she managed to plant it."

"Plant it? Plant what?"

"Remember the worm Stace found in our systems after the raid on our headquarters? The one that would've mirror-imaged our IFF so our friends looked like enemies and vice versa? Her computer geeks were able to modify that worm so the watchdogs in the official systems shouldn't recognize it and so it'll make us look just like them on their IFF."

"No kidding? That's one nice worm."

"Stacey thought it might come in handy. With that, I can load a battalion on shuttles and shoot them over the front. Drop that battalion where it can help stop the surprise attack. That's not enough, but it should do the job until somebody else can get over there."

"Do it. Thanks, Vic. For setting this up, and for agreeing with me on doing this."

"Don't thank me, you idiot. I spent my whole career hoping for a leader who cared more about ideals than their own self-interest. So I got you. Serves me right. Let's try not to get killed."

"Deal."

He stood next to the APC, pondering what his decision might do to the soldiers who had trusted and followed him to this point. *I'll tell 'em what I'm doing and why. They deserve to know that.* "All units. This is Stark. We've spotted enemy forces moving to attack the Mixing Bowl on both flanks. They're planning on nailing the apes from Second Division and then maybe coming after us here. We'd be safe if we just stayed here behind our lines, but the Second Division grunts won't stand a chance without our help. I'm planning on helping them. That might mean the official force can take us down afterwards. But at least they'll be alive and able to help defend the U.S. back home. If they go down here, our country won't stand a chance. I hope you'll all follow me." He began walking toward the front line, deciding to dispense with the command APC.

"Sargento! Not on point, Sargento. Let a private do that." Gomez waved a soldier forward, then brought the rest of the platoon alongside Stark at a trot. "You ain't goin' over there alone."

"Thanks, Anita."

They moved up and over the low ridge, giving them a direct view of the dead zone. "They say it gets real cold in the Leavenworth stockade," Gomez mused. "We'll have to pack overcoats and stuff. Bet it's not as cold as here, though."

"No, I bet it ain't. Of course, I'd probably get a firing squad, not a prison cell."

"*Verdad.* But they say hell is real warm. You won't have to worry about no overcoat. You can pack light."

Stark laughed. "And I'll have plenty of friends waiting for me there. Nice to have you along on this walk, *compadre.*"

"*De nada.*"

Vic Reynolds came on, speaking in a rush. "Ethan, I've got the shuttles loaded. The handiest force was Milheim's Battalion. I think he's still reeling from the orders he's got, because he hasn't screamed bloody murder. Yet."

"Looks like the enemy's still sneaking up on the Mixing Bowl. Good thing they're moving slow."

"Ethan, they don't expect us to do anything, even if we spot them. I've just given the shuttles their launch orders. We don't know anything about the layout of the base inside the Mixing Bowl, so I'm dropping the shuttles on the north flank where I think the heaviest attack is going to be staged."

"Got it. Sounds good. When will you activate the worm?"

"At the last minute, when the shuttles are approaching the front. We don't know how long the worm will last before the system watchdogs over there axe it."

"I sure hope it works."

"Stacey promised."

Stark laughed again. "We're depending on a promise from Stacey Yurivan. Great God Almighty. We must be insane."

"Must be. The shuttles will be overhead of you in four minutes."

"Roger." Stark picked up the pace, watching the companies and battalions around and behind him match his movement. They were all following him, again, believing as he did or just trusting that he had made the right decision. *Four battalions. Is that enough to stop the attack on the Mixing Bowl? No, five battalions, since we're dropping Milheim's people in there.*

A few minutes later the shuttles shot by overhead. Stark looked, trying to count, and noting the symbology for his three remaining armed shuttles among them. "Vic, are those armed shuttles there as escorts?"

"Partly. It was Chief Melendez's idea. He says the armed shuttles can fire their point defenses on the surface, using manual targeting. I think he's looking forward to trying it. Uh, I just activated the worm."

"Is it working?"

"We'll know it's not if the Mixing Bowl opens fire on the shuttles. Cross your fingers, Ethan. What's your plan for getting over there, by the way?"

"It looks like a nice day for a walk, Vic."

"I'm sorry I asked. Good luck."

"Hey, I got Gomez, Murphy, and the others with me. What could go wrong?"

"Don't get me thinking. Movement on the flanks of the Mixing Bowl is almost gone. The enemy must be about in position."

"Understand." Stark increased his pace again. Not far ahead, the fortified line awaited, and beyond that the appropriately named dead zone separating the two opposing forces. Stark had never liked venturing into it. He didn't like it now, but he couldn't see any alternative that wouldn't give him nightmares for the rest of his life.

On scan, Stark watched the shuttles hurtle over the dead zone without being engaged by defensive systems. *Whadayya know. Stacey's worm worked. Good thing I didn't fire her.* In the Mixing Bowl, officers would be going ballistic, wondering where the shuttles came from, how they could be friendly, and why they weren't responding to orders from whatever headquarters was operating inside the valley.

"Vic, give me a relay on the distress frequency. I want to talk to the people in the Mixing Bowl."

"That's a misuse of the frequency. You can go to jail for that, you know."

"I'll risk it."

"Relay's on."

Stark took a brief moment to gather his thoughts, then started speaking on a circuit that every soldier's armor, every ship, every comm system monitored by law. "All personnel in the official American force, inside the valley we call the Mixing Bowl. This is Sergeant Ethan Stark. You are being attacked by your allies. There are strong forces on both flanks preparing to hit you even as I speak. I have sent a battalion in via shuttle to reinforce your northern flank and will lead more units across the dead zone into your base to help you hold. I repeat, my forces are being deployed to help defend you from those enemy attacks. They will not attack you. We are advancing to help—" Harsh static buzzsawed through the circuit.

Ouch. Jamming that circuit's illegal as hell. Of course, so is using it to broadcast speeches. On scan, Stark watched Milheim's battalion deploying from the shuttles and heading for positions near the north wall of the valley. Scattered symbols near them marked official American forces who were apparently either confused by the worm or unwilling to fire on Milheim's soldiers.

A moment later, red symbology surged over the rim of the valley. Stark held his breath as his ground soldiers raked the attackers. Threat symbology radiated from the three grounded armed shuttles as Chief Gunner's Mate Melendez and his crews provided heavy covering fire. *How's it feel to be surprised, you bastards?* The red symbols wavered and fell back in confusion, leaving numerous casualty markers glowing in their wake.

On either side of Stark, the bunkers of the Colony's defensive perimeter fell behind. Stark increased his pace to a low gravity trot, covering long stretches of ground with each step. He'd be a perfect target during those periods out of contact with the lunar surface, but he had to get his troops across the dead zone in time to make a difference.

"Stark? Stark! What the hell are you doing?"

"Vic? Where's that transmission coming from?"

"Official force source, Ethan, somewhere inside the Mixing Bowl."

"Huh. This is Stark. Who's this?"

"Rash Paratnam, you flippin' idiot. What's with dropping troops on us. You *want* to fight us?"

"No, you moron! Didn't you hear my transmission?"

"Yeah, but—"

"Open your eyes and look around. Check your scan."

"Scan's being sanitized by our headquarters, Stark. We can't see a damn thing."

"Aw, fer pity's sake. Rash, you've got enemy troops hitting you on both flanks. Your people on the south are being rolled over. We've managed to stall the attack on the north side, but can't keep holding there without reinforcements. You've gotta get your people moving and set up defenses."

A pause, then an agonized reply came. "Ah, jeez, Ethan. What're we gonna do? Our orders are to engage *you* guys. I asked my officers about the enemy forces, our beloved allies, and they said nothing."

"Rash, listen to me. We're on the same side here. I'm not gonna let the majority of what's left of the American Army get overrun while I sit safe behind my defenses. Hey, can you link to my scan?"

"Uh, I guess so. But you could use that back door to drop a worm into our system."

"Rash, we've *already* got a worm in your system."

"You do? That's why my scan's showing you as friendly? Damn." Another pause, longer this time. "You never lied to me, Ethan. Never. Okay. I'm linking to your scan, and I'll link everybody else over here into it. Then we'll be able to see what's going on. At least until the system watchdogs over here figure out what I'm doing and try to kill the link."

"Thanks, Rash."

Halfway across the dead zone, maybe, the new berm shielding the Mixing Bowl looming ever higher before them. If the forces manning those defenses were going to fire on Stark, they'd open up soon.

Another transmission came in. "Stark, we can't keep this up!" Milheim called, anger and fear edging into his voice. "My Battalion's getting hit from two sides at once."

"Who's hitting you? Enemy or official force?"

"Enemy. The ones coming in on the south aren't facing much resistance."

"That's gonna change. The official forces are redeploying to stop them."

"Thank God. We can't keep this up much longer, even with those armed shuttles tearing up the landscape."

"I hear you, Milheim. We're almost in ourselves."

The berm was directly before them, rising upward steeply. Rock wouldn't have held that slope unaided against Earth's gravity, but against the moon's puny pull it stayed in place. Stark began bounding up the slope, cursing as loose rocks broke free beneath him and simultaneously grateful for lunar gravity that let him almost run up the slope.

Over the top. Stark paused to catch his breath. A few soldiers occupied a nearby weapons pit, watching him silently. Most of the defenses on the top of the berm sat empty, their occupants presumably sent off to defend the flanks. He scanned the small force of defenders quickly, frowning as the names evoked memories. "I know you guys."

"Yeah, you know us," one of the defenders acknowledged. "We used to be in your Fifth Battalion, Second Brigade."

The mutineers he had sent back to Earth. "They left you in charge of defending the berm?"

"That's right. I guess they figured we were the ones most likely to shoot at you."

"So why didn't you?"

"Because you could have shot us when you put down the mutiny. You could have sent some of us to firing squads after. You didn't. If you wanted to kill us you could've done it a couple times over by now. We decided it was about time we paid more attention to what you were doing than to what the people who didn't like you were saying."

Stark couldn't suppress a grin. "I take it Kalnick ain't up here."

"He's up here. At headquarters. The guy ain't a good field soldier, if you ask me. Poor judgment. Sorry we didn't realize that before."

"Better late than never. How's your scan? Is it showing the enemy activity yet?"

"Not the official scan. We're backdooring an accurate picture from the guys in contact with the enemy." A brief hesitation. "I guess we're surrendering to you."

"Hell, no, you're not. Why would you surrender to people who're on your side?" He pointed back down the berm, toward the battalions coming up behind him. "Your old unit is on its way. They fought good just now. When they get here, you fall in with them."

"A second chance? You're giving us a second chance?"

"I'd give the devil himself a second chance if I thought I could make a good soldier out of him. But don't plan on asking me for a third chance." *I'm spending too much time here. Got to get moving.* "Come on," Stark ordered his own soldiers as more came over the crest of the berm. "Second Battalion, follow me to the south flank. Third Battalion, I want you to head for Sergeant Milheim's position and go where he needs you. First and Fifth Battalion commanders, as soon as you're over the ridge head your unit for whatever point you think you're needed at. Fifth Battalion, you've got some of your people waiting for you up here."

His Tac scanned the surroundings, trying to build a picture of the base to guide his progress. Unlike the almost entirely underground Colony, the Mixing Bowl base contained many low buildings, rock piled over them to provide protection from other rocks falling to the surface. "Can you see this, Vic? There's a lot of surface structures in here."

"I see. They probably did that to reduce the amount of excavation necessary during construction. This base is surely planned to be a temporary facility."

"I bet you're right. I got a feeling it's gonna be a lot more temporary than they planned on." Stark ran, annoyed as he realized his old squad had formed up around him as a moving human shield. *Just a big target. But I can't order 'em away.* Scattered groups of soldiers came into view, Second Division soldiers milling around uncertainly. "Follow me, you apes." The other soldiers were swept up by Stark's force, then the low buildings all around were falling away and combat was suddenly right before them.

The enemy forces coming into the Mixing Bowl from the south rim had apparently rolled over any attempts to form a defensive line and were in the process of rushing forward triumphantly when Stark's battalion came out from among the buildings and hit them in the flank. The enemy assault collapsed like a house of cards hit by a basketball, their soldiers unprepared to form any organized defense themselves. Stark swept through them, leaving the prisoners to be secured by following forces, keeping the pressure on as most of the enemy soldiers ran toward another enemy force advancing a kilometer downrange. The panicked soldiers burst into the formations of the other force, disrupting the enemy effort to turn and confront Stark's counterattack.

"Hit 'em!" Stark kneeled, aiming and firing carefully at the confused mass of enemy soldiers. From all around him, accurate fire lashed at the enemy. More of them started running, breaking away from attempts to organize a response to the unexpected assault.

A small force of American soldiers rose from their position around a wrecked bulldozer, catching the enemy forces in a cross fire. Resistance broke, the enemy forces openly fleeing as fast as they could back toward the south rim of the valley. *That should buy us a few minutes.* Stark gasped for breath, winded from the long stretch of exertion. As far as he could figure, he'd been essentially running for several klicks. Even on the moon, that kind of exercise added up, especially after a day already spent in combat. "Second Battalion, keep after them. Try to run them over the rim so you can set up a line there. *Don't* follow them over the rim."

He approached the small force around the bulldozer, waving in greeting. "Hi. Nice day for a war, ain't it?"

"Nice as any." One of the soldiers stood forth. "Sergeant Pericles here."

"Pericles?" Stark nodded, trying to remember where he'd heard the name before. "I'm Stark."

"Didn't think I'd say this, but I'm damned glad to see you."

Another soldier came up to them. "Lieutenant Fox. I'm in command here." The lieutenant's voice was slightly shaky, which wasn't anything unusual in someone who'd just been engaged in what had looked like a hopeless battle.

Stark glanced at Pericles, who made the small gesture used to provide shorthand descriptions of officers. *He's okay, huh?* "Pleased to meet you, Lieutenant—"

"Sergeant Stark, I'm afraid I must place you under arrest."

Stark couldn't keep his eyebrows from raising, an expression fortunately invisible behind his face shield. His guardian platoon leaned forward, their hostile attitudes clear. Before Stark could answer the officer, Sergeant Pericles stepped in. "Lieutenant, this ain't a very good time for that." As if to underline his words, armor alert systems sounded warnings as HUDs tracked incoming artillery. "I guess our 'allies' have decided the surprise is over and it's time to get real nasty. We all better go to ground."

Stark shook his head, his body already in motion again. "I've got to link up with my forces on the north flank. I got a battle to run. Lieutenant Fox, Sergeant Pericles, I'd appreciate you lending my Second Battalion a hand, especially if they have to coordinate action with your people." Any response from either soldier was drowned out by a brief burst of static. *Jamming? That strong and that effective? Got to be the work of official forces. Somebody's not with the program yet.* "Can anyone pinpoint the source of that jamming? I want it off the line, now."

"It's off line," an unfamiliar voice responded. "We killed the transmitter power. Sergeant Stark, things are real bad up here on the north side."

"You with Milheim?"

"Uh, I dunno. Everybody's sorta intermingled. I . . . hey, here comes a whole bunch of new guys."

Stark cursed under his breath. "Are they friendly or enemy, soldier?"

"Friendly! Sorry, Sarge. Scan says they're from, uh, First Battalion?"

"That's my people. Can you link me to your scan?"

"Affirmative, Sergeant. Here ya go."

Stark paused, resting again, while artillery thumped into the rock behind them, studying the picture he could piece together from the fragments of scan he was picking up. The northern flank was a mess of intermingled forces, in some places advancing against the attackers and in some places falling back. At a dozen places, smoldering wrecks marked what had been the enemy armored support. Either Milheim's antiarmor teams or the weapons on the armed shuttles had blunted that portion of the attack. On the left side of the flank, fresh forces were pushing in and shoving the enemy into stubborn retreat.

The south flank looked better, at least temporarily. Second Battalion, augmented by growing numbers of Second Division troops, had been able to chase the fleeing enemy most of the way back to the valley's rim, but fresh attackers had apparently stopped the counterattack short of the rim.

"Vic? Can you copy?"

"Barely. There's serious jamming from the enemy forces to either side of you. What kind of picture have you got over there?"

"It's a mess. Can you copy my scan?"

"Uh, wait one. Yeah. Wow. What a goat-rope of a battle."

"Tell me about it. Can you tell if anything else is moving up to hit the flanks?"

Instead of replying directly, Vic linked him to the command center scan again. Reinforcements were clearly moving up, in large numbers. Stark whistled involuntarily. "We can't hold here, Vic. The position's a death trap."

"Agree. I guess that's why the official force got offered it."

"I gotta find the headquarters here and coordinate a retreat. You get some APCs across to the foot of the berm to help move people." He switched circuits, calling on the general tactical frequency. "Anybody from Second Division know where your commanders are? I gotta talk to them. Fast."

"Stark?" Rash Paratnam somehow radiated anger through the comm circuit. "Stark, you're crazy. No, you're stupid. What the hell are you doing in the middle of this?"

"Trying to save your stubborn butt."

"What do want with our commanders?"

"I need to coordinate a retreat, Rash. We can't hold this position."

He could feel Rash's uncertainty, now, and the agony of contemplating retreat under fire. "Okay. Here's a dump of the base map. I'll meet you at the main entrance."

"Thanks." Stark was off at a run again, Gomez's platoon following, their weapons restlessly probing every area they passed for threats. Stark wove through a maze of small buildings, coming finally to a low, wide structure with heavy lunar rock berms on each side and a single armored figure waiting near the entrance. "Rash?"

"Yeah. Ill-met in the Mixing Bowl, huh? Come on." Rash led the way inside, past pale-faced sentries with confused expressions fingering their weapons. "In here. Our command center."

Stark strode in, wondering at the image he presented in battle-scarred armor, rifle in his hands, a platoon of mean-looking soldiers at his back. Several officers in battle armor were gathered at the main display, their postures proclaiming various states of bewilderment. "Sergeant Stark here."

"How'd you get past the sentries?" One figure off to the side gestured violently. "Surrender yourself—"

"Shut up, Kalnick. I don't have any time for your crap today." Stark scanned the others. "Who's in command?"

A moment's silence, then one of the figures raised one hand and waved it around the group. "That's what we're trying to decide."

"Excuse me? I hate to push things, but we've got a real mess out there," Stark made his own gesture toward the picture shown on the main display nearby, "and we cannot hold this position."

"Sergeant Stark, with the additional forces you've brought—"

"No. Sir. I'm sorry. You can't see it from here, but from the other side we can tell there's a whole lot more enemy forces moving up. This place is nicknamed the Mixing Bowl because once an enemy occupies the rims he can scramble anyone crazy enough to try to maintain a position here. We learned that the hard way years ago."

"I see. Thank you for your assessment, Sergeant. I am Major Kutusov."

"Major? You're the senior officer here?"

"One of the senior ones left. You probably didn't notice several shuttles blast out of here a short time ago." Kutusov didn't try to conceal her bitterness. "Our commanding general pulled a MacArthur on us. He decided the situation was hopeless so he told us to fight valiantly as long as possible, while he ran for safety. Those shuttles that lifted out of here held him and most of the rest of our highest ranking officers."

Stark shook his head. "So now the senior officers are just throwing their young to the wolves. Does anybody here doubt that we're all on the same side?"

"He's lying! Don't—"

Kutusov turned her head slightly. "Shut up, Sergeant Kalnick. So far your advice hasn't proven very valuable. What are you suggesting, Sergeant Stark?"

"A truce. Between us. We're on the same side here, and we're gonna need every soldier we've got to get our forces out of here in one piece."

"Sergeant, I don't—"

Major Kutusov was interrupted by another officer running into command center. "Lieutenant Colonel Hayes, Sergeant. I'm senior. Thank you, Major."

"Colonel, I was just trying to convince the major—"

"I know. Save it, Sergeant. I've been out there, and it looks really ugly. You know the Moon and this particular position. What are our chances of holding here?"

Stark smiled at the lieutenant colonel's brusque, no-nonsense manner, as well as the knowledge that he'd been trying to organize a defense while others fled. "Chances are slim to none, sir."

"What's your alternative, Sergeant? We don't exactly have any place to go."

"Get out of here. Evacuate everything you've got inside the Colony's defensive perimeter. We'll cover you."

"There's two problems with that, Sergeant. One, we can't get everything out. Not in any reasonable length of time. There aren't enough shuttles and heavy lifters."

"Fine. Then we blow whatever we have to leave. I assume you've got a lot of ammo stockpiled?"

"We do, though I doubt that course of action will be looked upon favorably by the next promotion board. The second problem is more basic, Sergeant. I cannot in good conscience surrender this force to you."

"I understand, sir. I won't ask you to do that. Withdraw everything you can inside our perimeter, and we'll give you and your forces direct passage to the spaceport. You can go home with all your weapons."

"Why would you do that, Sergeant Stark?"

Stark, feeling the surprise and suspicion his statement generated, spoke quickly but respectfully. "Because we're on the same side, or we ought to be. We know what's going on back home, how they stripped bodies out of the other two brigades in Second Division to bring your brigade up to strength. That leaves too damn little to defend America. They need you back there."

"That's it? You're willing to risk your forces to save us, then let us inside your perimeter, with all our weapons, for the good of the country?"

"Uh, yessir, that pretty much sums it up." Stark checked his scan once again. "We don't have much time, Colonel." The officers huddled, debating urgently among themselves.

"Ethan? Am I getting through?"

"Vic? Yeah. I guess somebody finally linked the relays."

"What in hell is going on? I'm trying to get more units activated and over there, but it's taking time."

"We don't have the time, and we don't want to hold here, Vic. I'm talking to the acting commander right now . . . wait a minute. Yes, Colonel Hayes?"

"I'll probably get to share your firing squad, Sergeant, but we're taking your offer. I'd welcome your suggestions on how to carry out this operation."

"Vic? It's a go. We're all pulling back into the perimeter. I'll need somebody screening our flanks as we retreat through the dead zone."

"Roger. Are you going to sort out forces there or wait until you get back here?"

"We ain't got time here."

Stark turned back to the colonel just as another officer rushed off. "Our senior combat engineer," Lieutenant Colonel Hayes explained. "He's going to see how much he can destroy with a lot of ammo and very little time. I've already ordered all noncombat personnel to head for the berm with everything they can carry."

"Good. There'll be APCs waiting at the bottom of the berm. You can load those people on them. Any of those damn Jabberwocks left?"

"You mean the autonomous robotic combatants? No. Every one we had went in on that last attack. I take it you didn't save any, either."

"No, sir. Though there's probably enough pieces lying around to slap together a few, not that we're so inclined." Stark faced the main headquarters display. "Vic, have you got the map for this place yet?"

"Yep. This is going to be hard, Ethan." Reynolds began sketching out a withdrawal plan, speaking hurriedly as Stark shunted her words over to the rest of the Mixing Bowl base command center. "That's the best I can offer off the top of my head."

"Colonel?" Stark indicated the plan now visible on the display. "That okay with you?"

"Yes, Sergeant. I hate doing it, but I can't see any holes in the plan. Let's do it."

Stark trotted out of the command center, his escorting platoon and Rash Paratnam still in attendance. "Listen up, everybody. All soldiers in all units inside this valley. Copy my Tac." Bright lines glowed across the map of the base on the tactical display, lines crafted to take advantage of what defensive shelter existed. "Everyone west of Line Whiskey take up blocking positions. You will hold until I say so. Everyone east of Line Whiskey begin falling back in good order. Pass through Line Whiskey and keep going until you reach Line X-Ray. Sergeant Milheim."

"Here."

"You've been beat to hell, but I want you to cover getting as many wounded onto those shuttles that brought you in as you can. As soon as they lift, pull back fast."

"I understand." Milheim sounded exhausted but determined. "Will do."

"Chief Melendez."

"Aye."

"Chief, you've done one helluva job, but your shuttles will be sitting ducks without infantry cover. I want you in the air along with the shuttles carrying the wounded."

"Ain't no air up here, mud crawler, but I copy. Aye, aye."

"Ain't no mud, either." Stark shifted circuits, catching Lieutenant Colonel Hayes confirming the fallback orders to his units. "Rash, I expect you've got a unit that needs you."

"I do. I'll see you inside the perimeter, you big ape."

"Look who's talkin'." Stark checked his scan again, watching the enemy beginning to tentatively follow the American withdrawal, no doubt fearing a trick. As he watched, first one, then another shuttle blasted away from its position near the north flank, followed by the rest of the cargo shuttles and Chief Melendez's armed shuttles. Other shuttles shot up from the Mixing Bowl landing field, following Stark's shuttles toward the Colony with cargoes of whatever personnel and matériel could be crammed into them on short notice.

Despite the size of the valley, a large number of soldiers were inside the Mixing Bowl now, their numbers concentrating toward the east end where the berm sat. "Sergeant Stark."

"Yes, Colonel."

"I've got equipment that won't get down that berm face, and I really hate to leave it. What happens if we drop it in this gravity?"

"If it has enough mass, it still gets messed up at the bottom, but I guess that's . . . oh, heck, where's my brain? Use the tunnels."

"The tunnels? Of course. How could I have forgotten? Those tunnels we excavated to allow covered egress for the autonomous robotic combatants are plenty big enough to handle all but our largest lifters. I'll send the equipment and as many of my people as I can out through those."

Stark checked the scan again, scowling as he saw enemy forces pressing close upon the withdrawing Americans. With their units hopelessly intermingled, the Americans were having trouble maintaining a coordinated fire and fallback operation. "On my command, everybody east of Line Whiskey stop withdrawal, face front, and fire like hell. I want to get those attackers to back off. Standby . . . fire."

Stark was moving again, watching scan with one eye and the terrain before him with the other. He saw threat symbology suddenly surge from the Americans as they unleashed a concentrated barrage, and saw the pursuing enemy recoil in response. "Okay. Fall back again." Units were passing through Line Whiskey now, moving more rapidly once the troops in the defensive line could cover them. The enemy forces, closing in again, once more got stung by a burst of fire as they hit Line Whiskey.

Stark came through Line Whiskey himself, finding he was near the Mixing Bowl command center once again. Soldiers were coming out of the building, some ready for combat and some hauling vital equipment. He wondered for just a moment if Sergeant Kalnick was retreating as well or had decided being captured was preferable to owing his freedom to Ethan Stark. The thought vanished as more artillery came in, impacting all around, many of the blasts confined by surrounding buildings. Stark and his accompanying platoon headed west, instinctively hunching over as they ran, as if it were rain falling around them instead of high-explosives and shrapnel. More shuttles rocketed past overhead, followed closely by a warning over the command circuit. "We're about to blow everything around the landing field."

Stark checked his position, finding himself still entirely too close to that area. "Let's go, people." Line X-Ray was solidifying into a jumbled but strong defensive barrier. "Everybody on Line Whiskey start falling back. Pass through Line X-Ray and take up defensive positions on Line Yankee. Milheim, how're you doing?"

"Clearing Line Whiskey."

Stark, checking scan as he talked, exhaled in relief as he saw the battered but steady soldiers of Fourth Battalion falling back. From Milheim's voice, and the number of casualty markers glowing among his force, the unit had been severely stressed. "Okay, Milheim. Keep going. Take your people all the way back across the dead zone. You've done enough today."

"If we're needed—"

"If you're needed I'll call on you. Just get back inside the perimeter."

Milheim had trouble hiding his relief. "On our way."

Stark found himself and his escort mixing in with other units falling back. As the scattered portions of Second Division's Brigade Combat Team gathered into the defensive lines their numbers became more apparent. At some point, their numbers would exceed those of Stark's remaining battalions. *Don't worry about it. If they're gonna double-cross me, they will. It's too late to second-guess things now.*

"Fire in the hole!" The dead lunar surface suddenly rippled like a thing alive as shockwaves ripped through it. Scan highlighted debris flying high into space, as multiple detonations tore through the stockpiled ammunition near the landing field.

Stark wondered briefly how many of the attacking enemy forces might have been caught in the blasts, then mentally shrugged. *At the very least, that blowup will take some pressure off our withdrawal.* Indeed, the enemy forces bearing down on them had slacked off, concerned by the fury of the destruction at the landing field.

It didn't last, of course. Enemy commanders, apparently sensing their prey were escaping through an unexpected exit, appeared to be driving their soldiers hard. The withdrawal from Line X-Ray proved to be hard fought, with exchanges of fire at nearly every step.

Stark and his escort, pausing while Stark tried to puzzle out the situation on his scan, came under fire. He dropped, rolling to bring his rifle to bear as the platoon laid down deadly fire on the attackers. Aiming points glowed brightly on armored figures pressing ahead. *Aim. Squeeze. Fire. Aim. Squeeze. Fire.* The attackers fell back, leaving several of their number dead. "Come on, you apes, let's get out of here."

They moved fast, merging once again with the crowd of retreating forces. Line Yankee loomed suddenly, an invisible line on the map made concrete by clusters of soldiers forming interlinked zones of fire. "The enemy's right behind us," Stark advised.

More detonations added to the chaos as the combat engineers destroyed all the equipment and ammunition stockpiles they could. A fine rain of Moon dust kicked up by all the explosions drifted slowly, dreamily down around the masses of retreating soldiers, punctured by the path of bullets pursuing them and artillery shells dropping to the rocky surface. The ever-dark lunar sky seemed even blacker, with the dust screening out most of the stars overhead. Stark heard a deadpan chuckle close at hand, turning to see Sergeant Sanchez. "What's so funny?"

"I was thinking of Napoleon's retreat from Moscow." From Sanchez's bland tone, he might have been explaining the joke in a rec room back at headquarters. "I studied it recently. This is our version of snow. It seemed amusing."

"I'm in hysterics, Sanch. How's your Battalion holdin' up?"

"Like all the other forces, it is mixed in with so many other units I cannot sort out the status of my soldiers. But I have seen no indications that morale is breaking."

"Me, neither. Thanks for the escort, by the way."

"Stark, if I had tried to assign Corporal Gomez to any other duty, I would have had my own mutiny to deal with. I will see you inside the perimeter."

"You got it, Sanch." Line Yankee held just long enough for Line Zebra to begin forming, then started falling back. Stark moved through a mass of soldiers and equipment, all slogging steadily toward the berm at the entrance to the Mixing Bowl, the debris of battle now thick enough to begin fogging sensors. A heavy-lifter stalled up ahead, its cursing driver bailing out and hurriedly rigging an explosive charge to the vehicle as the crowd of foot soldiers separated to pass around the barrier. Light glowed from several points behind the retreating soldiers as stockpiles of fuel burned, supplying their own oxygen to keep the blazes going.

Stark checked scan again, cursing as enemy jamming and the fallout of battle broke up his picture. "Lieutenant Colonel Hayes. I want to drop back to the berm."

"We're still getting people over and under it. Can you hold inside the valley a little longer?"

Stark measured the soldiers around him, standing up on a nearby piece of abandoned equipment to peer back as if he could gauge the enemy pressure better that way. "Sir, I don't want to. I don't think I can stop the withdrawal at this point. I will slow it as much as I can."

"I understand, Sergeant. I'll be waiting for you at the berm."

Stark paused, surprised. *I guess I figured he'd be already halfway across the dead zone to safety. Good on you, Colonel Hayes.*

Acting Corporal Murphy was by Stark's side, one hand steadying him and the other urging him down. "Sarge, you're awful exposed standing up there."

"I gotta see what's goin' on, Murph."

"Uh, Sarge, what would you tell one of us if we were doing that?"

"I'd tell you that you were ten kinds of idiot and to get your head down." He surrendered to Murphy's urging, dropping back into the mass of retreating soldiers. "Since you're thinking so good, do you have any ideas on how to hold off the enemy a little longer?"

"Gee, Sarge, didn't you always tell us to make sure we were using everything we had to pound the enemy with?"

I'll be damned. He did listen to me when I lectured the squad. "That's right. Vic, can you copy?"

"Your signal's weak and broken, but I hear you."

"Good. I need artillery."

"You're inside the enemy perimeter, Ethan. They'll knock the shells down before they get to you."

"That's what I was thinking, too, because I forgot they pulled their defenses out of this area when the official American force moved in."

Stark thought he could hear Vic's hand slapping her forehead.

"Yes. Of course. Somebody loan me a brain. Where do you want the artillery?"

"As close behind us as you can manage. I want to discourage the pursuit a little."

"On its way."

It took a few minutes, nonetheless, until Stark's sensors spotted the incoming shells and his HUD cried an alert. Heavy shells began impacting not far behind the mass of Americans, the shock of their detonations dimly transmitting the fury of the explosions through the soles of armored boots. Stark paused again, trying to assess the results of the artillery screening fire, but gave up as the friendly artillery tossed further junk upward to cloud scan and sensors. "All soldiers on Line Zebra, begin withdrawal to the berm." He switched to speak only to his accompanying platoon. "Let's head for the berm, too, people. Murphy, you just made permanent corporal."

Breaking out of the buildings of the base should have been a relief, but the soldiers and equipment all around maintained the feeling of claustrophobia. Soldiers were jumping down from the berm, braking their progress by grabbing rocks as they dropped. Some, obviously Second Division troops new to the Moon, had tried dropping the whole way, discovering at the bottom that even one-sixth g could add too much velocity to a falling armored body.

"Vic, we need ambulances."

"They're shuttling back and forth, Ethan, along with the APCs. Is there any organization at all intact over there?"

"I've got Gomez's platoon with me in one piece. That's probably it."

"That's what I feared. I've brought up two more battalions and placed Sergeant Shwartz from Second Brigade in charge of the covering force. She's moving those two battalions out into the dead zone to provide cover. Just tell everybody over there with you to get over here as fast as they can."

"Sounds like a plan." Stark triggered the command circuit. "Lieutenant Colonel Hayes."

"Yes, Sergeant."

"I don't know exactly where you are, sir. Scan's being seriously degraded. The situation's a mess. My second in command recommends we hightail it inside the Colony perimeter."

"What if the enemy pursues us?" It was a nightmare scenario, fleeing troops intermingled with enemy forces, so that defenders on the Colony's perimeter wouldn't be able to stop the enemy without firing on their own soldiers.

"Our artillery slowed them a bit, and I'm having two fresh battalions sent out into the dead zone to cover the withdrawal. Colonel, sir, I hate to be pushy, but—"

"Sergeant Stark, from all I've heard you've always been pushy. And usually right. Give the order. I'll accompany the rear guard off the berm."

"Yessir. All personnel inside the Mixing Bowl. Get your tails across the dead zone and inside the perimeter. On the double. Anybody who leaves their weapon behind will get to come back here and retrieve it."

The traffic over the berm doubled, then redoubled. Shots began falling along the berm as enemy forces braved the artillery to close in. Stark and his escort traded shots with pursuers as they fell back, threat alerts and detections appearing and disappearing like ghosts in the dust-shrouded valley. *I don't want to climb this side of that berm with people shooting at me, even with the dust messing up visibility. But I guess . . . who's that?*

An armored figure gestured urgently near the base of the berm. "You guys the last down here?" she demanded.

"As near as I can tell."

"Then get through this tunnel." The combat engineer swung one arm to indicate a patch of deeper black among shadows. "And make it snappy. I'll be right on your heels, and I'm blowing it as soon as we're clear."

Stark finally noticed the gapping entrance, hesitating for only a fraction of a second before hurling himself inside. "Stay with me, people!" Even though Stark figured he'd need explosives himself to pry the platoon away from him, he didn't want to risk anyone losing contact at this point.

The tunnel was totally black inside. Which made sense, as the Jabberwocks wouldn't have needed lights. His armor automatically activated the IR sight and a light of matching frequency, revealing rough walls on either hand leading onward into more blackness. Comms stuttered and broke as relays failed or were destroyed inside the Mixing Bowl. Scan shut down, showing nothing but the area right around Stark, the platoon's soldiers, and the combat engineer urging them onward. The silence, the isolation, would have been eerie under any circumstances, but after the prolonged pandemonium of battle and fighting withdrawal it was almost frightening.

It seemed to take forever, but abruptly the tunnel curved upward, star-spangled black sky standing out against the dead black of the tunnel walls. Then Stark was standing on the surface, comms and scan active once more, soldiers streaming by enroute to the Colony perimeter.

"Ethan!"

"Here. Damn, Vic, you don't have to yell."

"Where were you? We lost you completely."

"I took a tunnel out. I don't recommend the trip, but it did the job." Stark paused as the combat engineer triggered her charges. A moment later, a long narrow stretch of lunar rock leading away from the foot of the berm bowed upward, then collapsed into a trench as it filled the tunnel. The engineer gave Stark a thumbs-up before trotting off toward the perimeter. "I'm coming in now."

"Thank God. Watch out for the enemy artillery. I've got mobile defense units in place but they can't stop everything."

A huge beetle shape surged silently past Stark, then came to a halt, its weapons facing toward the berm. "Hey, Commander Stark, mind if I join the party again?"

"Be my guest, Sergeant Lamont." The pursuing enemy couldn't bring armor over the berm, and their antiarmor teams had to have been as scattered by their pursuit as Stark's forces had been by their withdrawal. The mobile fort the tank represented would be a nasty surprise to anyone following the retreating infantry too enthusiastically. "Don't stay out here too long, though."

"Not to worry. I'll get my hogs back. There's a whole grunch of fresh infantry screening us."

"Good." Stark began walking, suddenly feeling too weary to run any more, despite the enemy artillery shells that sometimes made it through the defensive umbrella Vic had improvised over this area. Soldiers and equipment came along with Stark, no one running, just plodding steadily onward. On the flanks, enemy forces along their own front line fired on the retreating forces as well, but since they stayed close to the middle of the area between the Mixing Bowl and the perimeter, few hits were scored.

Behind, scan reported firing as enemy forces tried to occupy the top of the berm. Lamont's tanks and the fresh battalion peppered the berm with fire, driving them back repeatedly, then as the stream of withdrawing forces slackened into a small trickle, the armor and the infantry began slowly backing away, taking care to blast away at anything showing itself above the top of the berm.

Stark kept walking, finally noting with dull surprise that he'd reached the perimeter, scan displaying the comforting symbols of once-again occupied bunkers standing guard along the front. He kept walking a little longer, down a long slope until he reached near the bottom, then stopped and watched visually and on scan as soldiers kept coming. He watched until the last of the withdrawing forces had passed, and Lamont's tanks and fresh infantry retrograded inside the perimeter, then breathed a silent prayer of thanks. "Vic, you'll need to provide some marshaling areas for the Second Division people to sort out their units."

"Sergeant Manley is setting them up, now. What kind of security should be posted in those areas?"

"No security. Just escorts to help the Second Division guys find their way around. Okay?"

"Okay. I was going to say, we couldn't post enough guards to prevent those official forces from doing something if they really wanted to. We have to trust them."

"Yeah. Thanks, Vic." Stark switched circuits again, finding the simple task unaccountably difficult due to his weariness. "Corporal Gomez, get the platoon home. Thanks, you apes. It's been real."

"Maybe," Chen noted with a voice that cracked from fatigue. "But it ain't been real fun."

"You gonna be okay, Sargento?"

"Sure thing, Anita. You apes done good. I'll see ya around."

"Gracias, Sargento. Vaya con Dios."

The platoon moved off, toward the rear, its duty done. Stark stood silent for a moment longer, savoring the security of the perimeter and the Colony's heavy defenses. "This has been one helluva day. Does anybody know where my APC is?"

About five hours later, fortified by generous quantities of caffeine and an hour-long catnap, he was at a conference room near the spaceport, saluting Lieutenant Colonel Hayes, who returned the gesture with ill-concealed surprise. "Sergeant, I thought you were a mutineer."

"I am. Technically. But not by choice. I render military courtesies when appropriate, sir." He indicated the others with him. "These are my senior staff. Sergeant Reynolds, Sergeant Manley, Sergeant Lamont, Sergeant Gordasa, Sergeant Yurivan, Chief Gunner's Mate Melendez."

"Yurivan?" Major Kutusov questioned. "There was a case study about a Yurivan in my military legal course."

Stacey Yurivan somehow managed to register astonishment. "Must've been somebody else, Major."

Colonel Hayes nodded to each soldier in turn. "Sergeant Reynolds. That was a fine withdrawal plan you came up with on the spur of the moment. Sergeant Lamont, we certainly appreciated your armor helping cover our withdrawal. And, of course, Sergeant Stark. Your handling of the defensive end of the withdrawal enabled us to concentrate on getting everybody out." He rubbed his neck, looking around ruefully. "I begin to understand how you've done so well defending yourselves. We kept getting told you were a mob led by opportunists. But you're an army being led by professionals. It's nice to see what such a force can do. Thank you again for getting us out of that trap."

"Speaking of getting out of the trap," Vic inquired, "have you heard from your commanding general?"

"Yes. He's on a Navy ship. He expressed his regret that the Pentagon ordered him to personally evacuate so that the enemy wouldn't score a propaganda coup by capturing him and his staff." Bev Manley coughed suddenly to cover up laughter. "The general is . . . surprised our force is intact and ready to evacuate. He's left that evacuation up to me. I've been in communication with the Navy ships maintaining the blockade. They'll be sending down shuttles to assist in evacuating my personnel and equipment as soon as they finish coordinating with your anti-orbital defenses. I'll be going up with our own shuttles in a few minutes."

"What about your wounded, sir?" Vic turned her palm unit to show the names listed on it. "We've got a fair number of Second Division personnel who shouldn't be subjected to the extra g's of a shuttle flight. If you insist on them being sent along with the others we can—"

"No. Thank you, Sergeant. Leave them in medical. I'll ask the Navy to have them evacuated when their medical conditions permit." He paused, looking distressed. "I'm going to be frank, Sergeant Stark. You've tempted the hell out of me."

"Sir?"

"I've got forces inside your perimeter, you've allowed them to retain their weapons, and they're once again organized. What would happen if I ordered them to seize control, Sergeant Stark?"

"I'd rather not speculate, sir."

"Me neither, Sergeant. That action might make me a hero. Technically. But I owe you all too much. All the soldiers from Second Division owe you."

"Thank you, sir. How come your general didn't order you to try to take us?"

"I probably forgot to mention to him that we retained our weapons. I'm sure he thinks we've been disarmed. In any event, I've no interest in repaying you in that fashion. Instead, I'll see what I can do on your behalf when I get home."

"Colonel Hayes, sir." Vic gestured upward. "You're likely to be in a lot of trouble when you get home."

"Oh, well." Hayes managed a small smile. "Thus ends my career in a burst of failed opportunities."

Lieutenant Conroy entered, saluting. "Colonel, Major, your shuttle is ready for loading. I'll escort you to the loading dock."

Lieutenant Colonel Hayes nodded, then glanced over at Stark. "Good-bye, Sergeant Stark. Perhaps we'll fight alongside each other again someday."

"I'd like that, Colonel. I didn't know anybody like you got promoted anymore."

"A few of us slip through the cracks, Sergeant." Lieutenant Colonel Hayes saluted again, the sergeants returning the gesture, then he and Major Kutusov left with Lieutenant Conroy.

"Looks like we did the right thing," Bev Manley announced.

"Yeah. Maybe we did." That night, for the first time in memory, no dreams of lost battles haunted Stark's sleep.

"You *are* one for grand gestures." Colony Manager Campbell was leaning back in his chair as Stark entered his office the day after the battle to save the Colony and the follow-on battle to save Second Division's Brigade. "It's all over the vid. Here and back home. How you broke the robotic combatants who were supposed to break you and then went on to save the official American force when their own alleged allies turned on them. Anyone who doubted your earlier promises not to attack the U.S. has to be convinced now. Are you interested in running for president, by any chance?"

"Hell, no. I'm a soldier. I don't get involved in politics."

"Too bad. You'd be a shoe in right now."

"I thought felons couldn't run for president. I'm charged with a lot of crimes."

"*Convicted* felons, Sergeant. You're still okay on that count." Campbell checked his display hopefully, then shrugged. "There still hasn't been any official reaction to what happened up here yet, but I'll let you know anything we find out."

"Same here."

The reaction, when it came, had Stark and Campbell calling each other simultaneously. "Did you hear?" Campbell asked first.

"I heard the Pentagon's ordered the disarming and confinement of every soldier from Second Division that we saved. They claim the soldiers are unreliable now."

"For their purposes, they may be right."

"What do you mean?"

"I mean the government has declared a state of national emergency. In light of which, the national elections have been postponed indefinitely."

"What?" Stark felt his jaw literally drop at the news. "They can't do that. Can they?"

"No. They can't. Even during the American Civil War, national elections were held on schedule." Campbell sagged in his chair, suddenly looking worn out. "This is a naked power grab, Sergeant Stark. The people in power are afraid to relinquish it, and since they know they have zero chance of winning the elections, they're taking the only action which would protect them from having to relinquish power."

"They won't get away with it."

"Who's going to stop them, Sergeant?"

"I don't know. Yet. But I do know something I can do."

Campbell perked up, eyeing Stark. "What would that be?"

"The troops we saved up here have been disarmed, so they can't participate in the defense of the U.S. Some parties on Earth may figure this would be a good time to take the country out. I want everyone to know that if someone tries that, my troops will be there to stop them."

Campbell didn't hide his startlement. "You'd send some of your forces to help defend the country? Some of *our* forces?"

"Uh, yessir. I assume that wouldn't be a problem with the civil authorities in the Colony?"

"Speaking on their behalf, I can't imagine how we could turn you down. But how would you get soldiers back down there? They'd have to get through the blockade and past strategic defenses on Earth."

"I'd find a way."

"I'm sure you would." Campbell nodded. "Don't worry, Sergeant. We have a lot of ways of getting information down to Earth, ways which can't be blocked. I'll make sure what you just told me is known to every human on Earth within twenty-four hours."

"Thanks." Stark clenched his hands. "I wish we could do something about this election garbage, too, but we can't."

"No, you can't. But, Sergeant, there are people who can. We just have to encourage them."

A week later, the demonstrations in American cities had grown so huge that large segments of the cities were shut down. Stark and his staff watched vid from back home, marveling at the size of the crowds. "How long can this go on?" Sergeant Gordasa wondered.

"More to the point," Bev Manley asked, "what will the government do? They can't put the demonstrations down by force. They haven't got the force available. Besides, they couldn't justify that because the demonstrators aren't using force themselves, except for the fringe cases throwing rocks. Everybody else is just marching."

Vic nodded. "True. Stacey, do you have anything new about the situation back home?"

Yurivan smiled. "The economy's shutting down. How's that? Heard from your friend Jones again lately, Stark?"

"Not a word. Why?"

"Oh, just that the corporate bottom lines are getting nuked right now. It's all about profits, Stark, and I bet there's a lot of corporate boardrooms talking about how to get the country working again fast."

"Turning over the Colony here wouldn't help that," Manley objected.

"That's not what I'm talking about. Corporate loyalty is to the bottom line. If they have to jettison a few old friends, friends who happen to hold political office but are fast becoming major liabilities, they just might make an offer for our help. At the very least, they won't stand in the way of anybody who tries to toss those guys out of office the hard way."

Stark shook his head. "I haven't gotten any offers like that, and I won't take them if I do. None of our soldiers are going to Washington, D.C., to act against the government."

"But sending troops there might be the right thing," Vic suggested.

"Vic, we don't change governments at bayonet point. We never have, and I won't be the one to set a precedent. Period. This isn't a military issue."

Yurivan smiled again. "I understand we're planning on sending troops down to help defend the border, though. Have you worked out the movement plan for that?"

Stark glowered at her. "No, Stace. Hopefully we won't have to do it."

"Well, foreign militaries have staged a few exercises and provocations in the last couple of days, but they're being real careful. No one wants to be the first to find out if the American eagle has really had its wings clipped." Yurivan gazed upward as if contemplating the stars beyond the metal ceiling over them. "I do have some contacts in the strategic defense forces, Stark. They've let me know that if we do send people in to defend the country, the strategic defenses are likely to suffer some critical system failures if they're ordered to fire on us."

"Do tell. We'd still have to get through the blockade near the Moon, though, and survive the trip back to the World." Stark shifted his glower to the table surface, unable to sort through conflicting emotions. "I hate to say it, but I don't think there's anything else we can do right now. Nothing but wait on events. It's out of our hands."

"Whose hands is it in, then?"

"The ones who should've been deciding things all along." Stark pointed to the vid, where masses of demonstrators clogged the streets of a city. "Those people. They didn't vote better or often enough in the past, because they figured it didn't matter what they did. Now they want to vote, and I don't think they're gonna let anyone prevent them from doin' it."

Several hours later, Stark was roused from another quick nap by his comm unit. He'd been unable to sleep through the night the last few days and had to grab snatches of sleep whenever possible. "Stark here."

"Ethan, this is Vic. I need you in the command center. Immediately."

"On my way." It took only seconds to straighten his appearance, then Stark was out of his room. Vic stood waiting for him in the command center, her entire attitude uncertain. "What is it? An attack or something?"

"No." She turned to face the secure communications module, a small room off one side of the command center whose walls were lined with devices designed to ensure no human eavesdropper could hear conversations inside it, no matter how sophisticated the technology that eavesdropper might employ. For reasons lost in the mists of history, soldiers normally referred to it facetiously as the Cone of Silence. Reynolds nodded toward the module. "You have a call waiting in there."

"A call? The only people who have access to the gear needed to call into that room are official U.S. forces. It's for tight-beam, sealed communications, right? Are you saying the Pentagon's calling me?"

"No." Vic shook her head, then pointed to Sergeant Manley standing nearby. "You tell him, Bev."

Manley cleared her throat, then also indicated the module. "It's a Marine."

"A what?"

"A Marine," Manley repeated. "A United States Marine. You've heard of them, right?"

"Well, yeah." Many a late night vid had featured Marines. Stark had never forgotten one in particular, with an old star named John Wayne charging across beaches. "But I thought they were gone. Downsized out of existence a long time ago."

"Almost. The Marines are Naval infantry, and the Army brass never liked the idea of the Navy having infantry. So, when push came to shove at some point, it came down to the Navy choosing between paying for a space fleet or paying for the Marines. Guess what the Navy chose? The National Defense Reform and Readjustment Act basically put them out of business."

"If they were all that great, how come they got downsized so much?"

Manley shrugged. "From what I heard, the Marines were too focused on mission accomplishment. Getting the job done, you know? So while they were busy putting out little wars all over the place the leaders of the other armed services outmaneuvered them in the budget battles. The politicians only kept one company active. They're stationed in downtown Washington."

"D.C.? Why there?"

"Protection. Marine guards are special, so the Congress and the brass in the Pentagon kept a few to guard their precious little behinds. That's all there's been for some time, but they're still Marines. The one waiting to talk to you is a Sergeant Major Morrison."

"Sergeant Major?" Stark questioned. "The enlisted ranks were 'rationalized' a long time ago. All the different grades of sergeants were consolidated. How can this Marine be a Sergeant Major?"

Bev smiled. "Marines do things their own way, Ethan. It's one of the things that makes them Marines."

"What else makes them Marines?"

Manley took a moment to answer this time. "They're different. They look like grunts, but they're different. Don't forget that when you're talking to this guy. Marines aren't like soldiers. They're more like some sort of cult."

"So what's this cult been doing for the last few decades? Besides ignoring the rules about enlisted ranks, that is."

"Guarding D.C., like I said. Putting on ceremonies for the tourists and the Very Self-Important Persons. You know the drill."

"Yeah. So these Marines are just show troops? Guys who know how to look pretty but can't fight?"

Manley shook her head. "I don't think so. I've met a few. They'd been kept in Washington, they'd never seen combat as a result of that, but they weren't show troops."

"Okay. Thanks for the info and the assessment. Guess I better see what this guy wants." Stark strode into the secure communications module, seating himself gingerly in a seat that would have been well-padded on Earth but was ridiculously overstuffed for lunar gravity. After studying the panel for a moment, Stark hit the control accepting the transmission.

A hard face stared back at him from the vid screen. Well-groomed, in an immaculate uniform, but something about him didn't strike Stark as being typical of show troops. *Manley's right. Whatever the politicians have tried to do to these Marines, they've stayed professionals. At least the one I'm looking at has stayed a professional.* "This is Sergeant Stark. I understand you want to talk with me."

A few seconds elapsed as the light-speed transmission made its way across the distance separating the Earth from the Moon. Then the hard-faced Marine shifted slightly, his eyes looking directly at where Stark's eyes had been a few seconds previous. "That's right. I'm a Marine, Stark. You probably never met one of us, so I'm going to tell you what that means. Our motto is Semper Fidelis. Always Faithful, it means. We've fought everywhere on Earth, and we've kicked butt in all those places. We're Marines. You can kill us, but you can't defeat us. Understand?"

"Yeah. I understand. That sounded like a threat."

A few more seconds. "What if it is?"

It felt odd, exchanging macho threat talk with someone who took seconds to reply. *Maybe it's not that odd, after all,* Stark reflected. *There's been many a time in bars that both me and the guy I'm talking to have been so drunk we took a while to think up responses.* He looked over the Marine's image again, taking in every aspect of Morrison's bearing. *Yeah. He's real. So I'll treat him like a fellow soldier.* "I'd take it seriously. The only place I want to fight Marines is in a bar."

"If you get into a bar brawl with us you better have the odds on your side, soldier. Heavily on your side. But you might end up fighting us for real, Stark, depending on what you do."

"What's that supposed to mean?"

"The word is your troops are planning to come down here. That right?"

Stark pondered his reply for a moment, trying to guess at the Marine's motivations. "What if it is?"

"We're here to defend the country, Stark. The Constitution. We won't sit back and let anyone take over. Anyone."

"I won't discuss operational plans, but I will tell you there's only two reasons I'd send troops down there. The first is to help defend the borders of the U.S. If anybody tries to come over those borders, we'll help hold 'em."

Morrison nodded. "Fine. What's the other reason?"

"The Constitution. That's what you said. We took the oath to protect it, too. You know what's going on. The national state of emergency crap. The big demonstrations. If a bunch of civs decide to march on the Capitol and toss out some politicians who are trying to tear up the Constitution, then my soldiers will defend those civs from anyone trying to stop 'em."

Morrison's eyes narrowed, his face hard as granite now. "Spell it out. What exactly are you saying?"

"I'm saying if any military force tries to shoot at those civs then they're gonna find themselves facing my troops. Understand, Sherman? Any military force. We'll take you down if you start shooting the civs." It was mostly a bluff, Stark knew. He had no idea if his soldiers would fire on other Americans, even Americans defending the corrupt politicians trying to secure themselves in power. But he meant every word of it.

Instead of glaring, Morrison grinned. "You could try, Stark. What you just said, it's on the level?"

"You have my word on it. Soldier to soldier."

"Soldier to Marine, you mean. Listen, if you send a single soldier or a whole division down here to take over, to set yourself up in charge, we'll stop you or die trying. Clear?"

"Clear."

"But if you come down to help the civs, to protect them in the exercise of their Constitutional rights, then you won't run into opposition from the Marines. Marines don't shoot civs."

Stark paused, taken aback by the unexpected declaration. "I didn't ask that of you."

"You don't have to. We took the same oath you did. 'To protect the Constitution of the United States of America against all enemies, foreign and domestic.' And we'll be faithful to that oath. To the death, if need be." Morrison hesitated. "There has to be a reason we take an oath to the Constitution instead of to the government. Somebody must have figured something like this might happen someday."

"Yeah. There's a real good reason. Thanks, Morrison. If I ever run into you, I'll buy you a beer."

"As long as you're buying, I'll be drinking. Headquarters, United States Marine Corps, out." The image broke into a million fragments of jiggling colors as the secure link dissolved.

Stark walked slowly out of the communications module, only gradually becoming aware of Reynolds and Manley staring at him. Manley spoke first, indicated the module. "What'd the jarhead say?"

"Jarhead?"

"Yeah. That's slang for a Marine."

"Why? What the hell does 'jarhead' mean?"

"Hell if I know. Sounds like an insult, though, doesn't it? So, what'd he say?"

Stark looked around to ensure none of the watchstanders was listening. "He told me the Marines wouldn't fire on the civ demonstrators and wouldn't try to stop us if we came down to defend the civs."

Reynolds's eyebrows shot up. "The Marines are ready to take down their officers?"

"He didn't say that. No, he just said the Marines wouldn't do it. Like he was speaking for all of them."

"The highest ranking Marine is only a major," Manley noted. "We've heard a lot about junior officers being fed up with the system. Maybe . . ."

"Maybe," Stark agreed. "I've got a feeling things are gonna be happenin' soon back home. Keep your fingers crossed."

When the news arrived, it still came as a shock. Campbell appeared stunned, as if unable to accept the information he was passing to Stark. "It's over."

"What's over? What happened?"

"The government has, for want of a better word, fallen. A mass demonstration simply occupied the Capital and the White House, demanding elections be held as scheduled next week."

"And nobody stopped 'em?"

"No." Campbell shook his head as if dazed. "Apparently, there was an attempt to call some local military force in to turn the demonstrators back."

"The Marines."

"Yes. That's right. But they stayed in their, uh, barracks. So, it appears we will have elections after all."

"Who's running the country until then?"

"Some senior statesmen have been given the job. Men and women who are long retired and still well respected." Campbell smiled. "None of them wanted the job, Sergeant."

"Good. I'll have to send them a sympathy card."

Stark rubbed his face with both hands, trying to order his thoughts while his staff waited. "Okay. The elections have come and gone. The new government promises to make things right. Everybody's happy, except the people who've been running things for the past few decades. According to Campbell, there's a lot of folks heading for the hills. He says foreign countries will soon have a larger number of recently retired American politicians living in them than the U.S. will."

"That's their problem," Bev Manley noted. "What's happening with the mil?"

"Every officer above the rank of O5 has been retired. Effective immediately. Officers below that rank will be reviewed for competence. The government claims no political litmus tests will be used."

"I'll believe that when I see it."

"Yeah. But, maybe . . . Campbell said the same thing happened once before, sort of. Back when Jefferson was president and there were a lot of excess officers. Anyhow, here and now, everybody above O5 is gone." He looked over at Chief Melendez. "Man, that's hard to imagine. Navy captains are O6s, right? So there's no captains in the Navy now. Weird."

"Of course there's captains in the Navy," Chief Melendez insisted. "Commanding the ships. They just ain't captains."

"Huh?"

"Someone commanding a ship is the captain," Melendez explained. "But that don't make 'em a captain."

"They're captains but they're not captains?"

"Right. They're, like, commanders."

"Navy commanders are captains?" Vic questioned. "Then why are they called commanders?"

"Because they ain't captains! They're commanders who are also captains."

"Uh-huh."

Melendez frowned. "Look, it's like you ground apes. You got captains, right?"

"Right."

"But they ain't captains."

"Sure they're captains. That's why we call them captains."

"But they ain't captain captains!"

The soldiers exchanged glances. "Okay," Stark noted. "I guess that point's settled, then." *Squids.* "Here's the other news. Campbell says the new government wants to negotiate with everybody up here. I mean really negotiate. They're talking about adding another star to the flag."

"A new state?" Gordasa perked up. "They want to make the Colony a state?"

"That's what they're talking about."

"What about us?" Vic wondered.

"Campbell said he'd look out for us." Faces hardened with instinctive skepticism. "He promised. The negotiating team from the new government will be here in a week. We'll know for sure soon."

Manley reached backward, as if searching for something between her shoulder blades. "Hmmm. Looks like I forgot to wear my armor. I better get it, just in case somebody tries to stick a knife back there."

Stark didn't laugh even though the others did. "We stuck by the civs when they needed us. Now they're promising to stick by us. I've got a meeting with Campbell this afternoon. We'll see what he's got, then."

Campbell seemed subdued when Stark entered his office. "Please sit down, Sergeant."

"Thanks. Something's bothering you, isn't it?"

"Something certainly is." Campbell shifted as if his chair was uncomfortable. "I've been talking to the negotiating team from the new government, as you know. They've been asking some questions which only you can answer."

"It doesn't sound like they're great questions."

"They're not." Campbell tapped his display, bringing up some notes that Stark could only make out as blurred lines from his angle. "There's no way to ask this but bluntly, Sergeant. Crimes were committed up here, by you and by me. Depending on how our actions are interpreted, we could both be charged with rebellion."

"I've known that from the beginning, sir."

"Then how will you react if the government insists on trying you for your crimes?"

"You roll the dice, you pay the price, sir." Stark saw Campbell's surprise. "I know. We've fought real hard to defend ourselves up here, and I guess that sort of sounds like I'm surrendering. But it's all about fighting for an objective. Mine was to fix things and to save my people. As near as I can tell, things are fixed as well as they'll ever be, and as long as I know my people will be taken care of, I'm willing to accept responsibility."

"You don't need to think about this?"

"I've been thinking about it for a long time." Stark sat back, spreading his hands. "Sir, it's . . . oh, hell, the fact is I don't have any real choice. You understand that, don't you? If the government needs a fall guy, somebody to hang so everybody else gets off okay, I'll be that guy."

"Sergeant, you realize the word 'hang' may be literally true."

"Yeah. Don't think I haven't thought about that. But all those grunts trusted me. I've gotta live up to that."

"I see." Campbell pondered Stark's words for a moment. "What if the new government wants more, Sergeant Stark? What if they also want your staff? And anyone who took command positions?"

Stark stared back silently. *What if they do? Hey, Vic, want to come along to my firing squad? She trusted me, too. All those guys who took command positions trusted me.* A vision came to him, of sergeants like Reynolds, Manley, Milheim, and Lamont, walking with him up a long empty slope toward waiting machine guns. *That's what it comes down to, doesn't it? Are we all willing to die for the troops? It's usually the other way around. The troops are supposed to be willing to die for you. But are we willing to die for them?* "Yes."

"Yes?" Campbell questioned. "Yes, what?"

"Yes. If they want my whole staff, and they want all the people who took command positions, we'll go. Just trade that for amnesty for the troops."

Campbell seemed lost for words for a moment. "Are you certain you don't need to discuss this with them first? I mean, we're talking . . . well . . ."

"We're talking marching to our deaths. Yeah. I know. We can do that. As long as it means something, sir. As long as we know it means something."

"What if the government doesn't even offer that? What if it simply demands you accept lawful authority once again, with no promises about what will happen to any military personnel up here?"

Stark tried to conceal his distress. "Is that what they're talking about, sir? Is that what the government wants?"

"I don't know. They're clearly trying to determine what we want, what is necessary to end this situation."

"But they're coming to offer you colonists statehood, right? And they did get rid of most of the officers who've messed things up in the military lately?"

"Yes. That's all true."

"Then, sir . . . how can I say no? To anything? It's not my call. You give the orders. You do what's best for everyone. That's your job. My job is to do what those government representatives tell me to do. I'll spend my last breath asking them to treat my people right, but there's no reason left to justify mutiny."

"There's your own self-interest, Sergeant. Self-preservation."

"Hell, Mr. Campbell, if that mattered so much I wouldn't go out and get shot at on a frequent basis. Look, I did what I figured I had to do. I did it all the best I could. Now I've got to pay whatever price my actions demand. I know that."

"Speaking from the perspective of a colonist, and a person you've helped defend, I'd think your actions demand a reward, not a punishment."

"Thank you, sir. You do what you can for us. Get the best deal you can for the troops. But whatever comes out, we'll accept it."

"Are you sure, Sergeant? Are you sure all of those troops will follow you this time?"

Stark paused again, remembering the events that had brought

them to this point. "I can't be certain right now, but I'm pretty sure. I'll talk to everybody. Make sure they know what we have to do, what's expected of them. We want to go back, Mr. Campbell. We're American soldiers, no matter what's happened."

"Then I will do whatever I can in the negotiations, Sergeant. Are you sure you don't want to participate directly in those negotiations?"

"That's not my department, Mr. Campbell. I don't want anybody thinking I'm using my firepower to influence what you decide. You do your job. I'll do mine."

Vic took Stark's news without any apparent surprise. "We always knew when the bill came due we'd be the ones paying it, Ethan."

"You think everybody else will feel the same?"

"Everybody I know. Well, Yurivan is a question mark, as usual, but she'll be certain of her own ability to cut a deal no matter what happens to the rest of us. It's the average grunt you've got to worry about."

"That's what I figured. I've got to talk to them, but there's not enough time for a face-to-face with everyone. I want you to set up something for tomorrow. A big room where I can talk to, oh, say one representative from each company in person. Everybody else will be linked in."

"You're going to give a speech, Ethan?"

"Yeah. And then I'm gonna answer questions. You got a better idea?"

"Nope. I'll set it up."

Stark spent a restless night composing his speech, running words through his head time and again in a futile effort to order them in just the right manner. He was still trying as he walked to the briefing room Vic had prepared, pausing just outside the entrance. *Hey, this is the place where we got that briefing on synergy warfare. Never thought I'd be here again, like this. Well, I've been rolling with events long enough. It's time I took charge of myself.*

Soldiers filled the room, corporals and privates sitting in the uncomfortable chairs that were standard issue on the Moon. Someone yelled "attention" and they all sprang to their feet, standing respectfully as Stark strode to the center of the stage.

"At ease, everybody. Seats." Stark stood for a moment,

frowning, then shoved aside the podium and gestured down to the first row. "Pass me up a spare chair." Seating himself, he looked out across the audience.

"You all know what's been going down. You all know that reps from the new government are coming to settle this mess. And I know you're all wondering what that means for you and me. First off, I'll tell you straight: I don't know. Everybody's still talking. But I do know what we should do. We should take whatever's offered. The civ colony is gonna be part of the U.S. again, all legal and official. We should be, too."

"Look, you apes. We did something wrong. Mutiny. Bad word. Bad thing. We did it because doing anything else, or doing nothing at all, seemed to be even worse. That's how bad it had gotten. You remember. It wasn't just losing our friends, or losing one battle, or even losing a war. Everything was being lost. We didn't trust our officers, we didn't trust the civs or the government, we were watching people die for nothing and knowing inside that we'd be next and then everything that still mattered to us would be gone, too. So all we could trust was each other, and all we could do was try to stop things from getting worse. But was anybody happy about it? No. Because we knew it should've never come to that. We never should've had to choose between duty and honor, between bad and worse. It seemed the only way to save things was to make that choice, but it wasn't one we ever liked."

"But things have changed. We've worked with the civs up here. They've helped us, and stuck by us when they could've screwed us over. They're doing it now, I promise. Talkin' to the new government about how to fix things. You all know that new government got rid of an awful lot of officers, right? They're gonna screen the ones who are left, make sure they can do the job, make sure they stick to military stuff and stay out of politics. Regardless of what happens to me or any other senior noncomm, the mil is gonna be better tomorrow."

"It's gonna be better if you guys stick with it. You know how it should work, now. Treat your people decent, focus on what's important, get the job done right. You can pass that down, and apply it yourselves when you become senior noncomms. And teach it to the new officers."

"I don't know what the new government's final offer is gonna be. I don't know if they'll let all you guys remain in the military. I told 'em you should, that you've done what you were told and done it well. But that mission's over and you got a new one, now. You know what it's like, when you've been on a really difficult campaign. It's hard, it's ugly, but at some point you realize you're over the crest and everything is downhill from there because you've done what you needed to do. Okay, that's here and now. The Colony is safe. The war up here's gonna end, they say, for at least a while. The rot that was tearing the mil apart is finally being ripped out. Most important, there's a new government, one that looks to be by, for, and of the people again. So there ain't no excuse for not following orders anymore. We're U.S. military. We don't mess with the Constitution. We defend it. Whatever the new government offers, we take it. That's our job. Any questions?"

A long silence descended, then a corporal stood. "Commander—"

"Sergeant. Let's keep it regulation from now on."

"Okay, Sarge. What happens to you?"

"I dunno. Probably something real serious. I started it, I ran with it, I commanded it. I already told 'em, if somebody has to pay, that's me." A low murmur came from the soldiers before him. "Responsibility, soldiers. That's the way it works. Don't do something if you're not prepared to live with it."

A private stood next. "Sergeant, are you saying we really might be able to be official again? Go back home and everything?"

"That's what I'm hoping for. I can't promise it, though. That's up to the government." Stark watched unhappy expressions settle onto the faces before him. "It's a legitimate government, people. They've got a right to tell us what to do, and we've got a duty to do what they say. *I'm* gonna do what they say, and anybody who thinks I'm gonna get a better deal than they are is welcome to swap places with me."

Another corporal. "Sergeant Stark, what if you're talking a prison sentence for all of us? It could happen."

"Yeah, it could. They'd have to build some more prison space, but they could do that. I don't think they will. We know they've let the Second Division people out and rearmed them, so the new government's not as stupid as the people they replaced. They know they need you. To keep defending this Colony. To help defend the country. But here's the catch; if you want them to trust us, we're gonna have to trust them. That means taking orders, whatever they are."

"What if they tell us to shoot you, Sergeant?"

"Then you do me the favor of making sure you hit clean. I don't want any lingering death scene. Understood?"

A second private. "What if we don't want to, Sergeant? We tossed out a bunch if idiots who were telling us to do something stupid. This sounds stupid, too. What if we don't want your deal?"

"Then head for the perimeter and offer your services to a country that wants that kind of soldier. Become a merc, fighting for a paycheck. I don't care. We fight for our country, not ourselves. As long as I'm in charge, we'll take whatever's offered."

A third corporal stood. Anita Gomez, her face hard. "I ain't got no question, Sargento. I just want to say I've followed you for a long time, up close and personal, and I ain't never regretted doin' whatever you said was right. I'm gonna follow you now, too." She sat, leaving silence in her wake.

Finally, a fourth corporal came to his feet. "Sergeant Stark? When will we know what's gonna happen to us?"

"The representatives from the new government are arriving in three days. They've got a meeting scheduled already at 1400 Thursday. That's where we're supposed to get our marching orders."

"So I guess we all oughta have a beer Wednesday night, huh, Sarge? Just in case it's the last one for a long while?"

Stark grinned as the other soldiers laughed. "Sounds like a plan. Save one for me. I'll try to drop by."

"Sure, Sarge."

Vic waited for him off the stage, nodding at Stark as he left. "Good job, soldier."

"You think they're gonna do it?"

"I'm sure of it. They'd follow you to hell right now, Ethan Stark, trusting you to somehow beat the devil once they got there."

"Hah! How about you, Sergeant Reynolds? Would you follow me to hell?"

"Let me think about that. I am willing to follow you to the nearest bar, though."

"Let's get the rest of the staff together for that. Just in case we don't get another chance."

Thursday. 1400 in military time, or 2 P.M. as civilians measured it. The same conference room where a succession of government and military representatives had threatened the lunar soldiers and colonists numerous times. Now representatives of a new government, with new military guidance, were waiting inside. Stark and Reynolds came to a halt at the door, where Campbell and Sarafina awaited them. "Not a big group this time, huh?" Stark observed.

"This time the negotiating has been done in advance," Sarafina advised. "We only need to review the agreement."

Stark extended his hand. "It's been nice working with you, Mr. Campbell. You, too, Ms. Sarafina."

Campbell shook hands, his grip firm on Stark's. "That sounds like a farewell."

"It might be, sir. I figure there's real good odds I'll leave that room under guard."

"Sergeant, I don't know exactly what the new government will offer, but I've done my best for you."

Reynolds stepped forward. "You really don't know what their offer to us will be? Even now?"

"Sergeant Reynolds, I only know that they've asked a lot of questions and wanted to see a lot of records. They've listened to what I and the other representatives up here have said. But they've kept their cards very close to their chests."

A few moments later, Stark found himself sitting at the familiar conference table, looking across it at the representatives of the new government. He'd somehow expected them all to be young, full of fire and idealism, which had caused him some considerable concern. Young idealists tended to do really dumb things in the name of their ideals because they hadn't the experience in life to know better. But many of the representatives were middle-aged or older, seasoned veterans of their own campaigns. Down at one end of the table, Lieutenant Colonel Hayes sat along with a couple of junior officers whom Stark didn't recognize. Hayes nodded in silent greeting to Stark, his poker face not revealing any emotions. *I guess here's where I find out if I did the right thing saving that guy's butt.*

A civ woman stood carefully, wobbly in the unfamiliar gravity. "As a first point of order, we must be certain of the status of the military forces here. We are all too aware that nothing can be done if the military resists."

Stark stood, ramrod straight, and saluted. "The U.S. military forces assigned to the defense of the American Lunar Colony are ready to receive orders from the government's representatives and our superior officers."

"What exactly does that mean?"

Lieutenant Colonel Hayes spoke up. "I believe Sergeant Stark is telling us his forces are no longer in a state of mutiny. Is that correct, Sergeant?"

"That is correct, sir."

Instead of replying directly to Stark, the woman looked over at Campbell. "You are surrendering prior to reaching an agreement?"

"Not exactly," Campbell advised. "We still need to reach an agreement. But as I have advised you, Sergeant Stark has told me in no uncertain terms that he, as a soldier, cannot negotiate with the government. He feels he has to accept your orders."

"I see. Sergeant Stark, if this is the case, why did you fail to accept orders for so long?"

"Ma'am, things happened that nobody wanted to happen. If someone, anyone had been willing to just listen and think . . . well, it's a long story, but we've been trying to straighten this out ever since then. I accept full responsibility for all acts—"

"Yes, yes, I'm sure you do, from all I've heard," the civ woman interrupted. "It appears we may proceed, then. You may sit down, Sergeant. As our second issue, I am authorized to apologize on behalf of the government for past actions against you. You, Mr. Campbell, and the colonists you represent, and you, Sergeant Stark, and the soldiers you have led in the defense of this colony." She made a gesture, and one of the other representatives tapped in some commands on his display. "Here is our offer. Please take a moment to read it."

Stark glanced at Vic, then they both turned to their displays and began scanning the text. Stark read rapidly, skimming in search of key words and phrases. *Amnesty for past actions by civil authorities . . . restoration of civil rights within the Colony . . . vote on statehood during the current session of Congress. Fine. Wonderful. Where the hell's the part about my people?* He read on, finally finding the subsection dealing with the military forces. *Amnesty for all enlisted personnel for all acts committed during a period of civil unrest . . . reaffirmation of oaths of fealty to the Constitution . . . all acting officer assignments formalized and confirmed by appropriate promotion.* Stark blinked, looking back over at Vic. "What about me?"

"It says 'all enlisted personnel,' Ethan."

"That can't include me."

"I don't believe it, either, but how about that bit about officer assignments being formalized?"

"I didn't think about that yet. Why? What do you think it means?"

Vic spoke so only Stark could hear, her voice hidden by murmurs from others at the table speaking to their neighbors. "It means, Ethan Stark, that I'll have to start calling you general."

"What?" Stark scanned the text, his eyes wide. "No. That's not possible."

"That's what it has to mean, Ethan. You will be formally appointed to command the division and promoted to the appropriate rank for that position."

"That's ridiculous! There's no way—"

"Is there a problem, Sergeant Stark?" Stark looked up to the see the civ woman eyeing him.

"Uh, ma'am, I was just attempting to determine the meaning of the document."

"Which specific portion?"

Vic spoke up as Stark hesitated again. "He's wondering what the phrase 'all enlisted' means."

"Exactly what it says."

"Ma'am, Sergeant Stark and I are also enlisted personnel."

"So I have been informed. Are you saying you don't want to be covered by the agreement?"

Reynolds stared at the woman. "Are you actually granting him amnesty? As well as the rest of us?"

"That is our intent."

"Then your offer is extremely generous, ma'am. Frankly, it surprises us. A great deal."

The woman smiled back. "I'm sure it does. I understand you've been told to expect the death penalty for your crimes."

A man near her nodded. "We reviewed your actions very carefully. Had you committed crimes against the United States or her citizens, you wouldn't be getting this offer. There have been deaths, on both sides. In one case, you executed a soldier for his role in an attack on you." Stark tried not to let his distress show at the words, a reference to Private Grant Stein's betrayal of them and his subsequent court-martial. "That particular case was of special concern, and even though we found you acted with every appropriate formality to ensure a legal outcome, we wish that had not occurred."

"Me too," Stark whispered too quietly for anyone else to hear.

"But the documentation surrounding that court-martial was complete, indicating you were personally willing to accept responsibility for your actions and decisions."

"I still will," Stark declared, louder this time. "Nobody else has to be blamed or punished. It was my call."

The man shook his head. "In light of all that has happened, we must add that particular case in with all the other deaths and events which everyone wishes had never taken place. Otherwise, everyone believes you all acted always in the highest traditions of your service. I believe that's the appropriate phrase?"

"It will certainly do," Vic replied. "I must confess, at best we expected dismissal from the military. Yet this offer says you trust us to continue on active duty."

"Of course it does," the woman stated. "You had the ability to do anything you wanted, eventually, including what might have been a successful attack on the United States herself. Yet you have kept the Colony safe, you have followed the instructions of civil authorities in the Colony and your actions have been directed toward the protection of our country and our citizens. We are well aware that some of your number died heroically as part of that effort, such as the Wiseman and Gutierrez individuals and their crews who we see have been recognized in the new name of the Colony spaceport." The woman nodded toward Lieutenant Colonel Hayes. "And, of course, we cannot forget the risks you took to ensure the survival of forces which were here to attack you. Actions speak louder than words. If the last few decades of experience with national leaders have taught us anything, they've taught us that. Your actions, especially those on behalf of others, speak for themselves."

"Thank you, ma'am."

"Don't thank me. You earned this amnesty, and the ranks you are being offered, by your actions. Had you acted differently, you'd be under arrest at this moment. But I believe if you'd acted differently our country would have faced a far worse crisis. The government owes you a debt as well as an apology, and it's about time we started acknowledging our debts."

Campbell smiled, his happiness at the outcome clear. "You're saying that while Sergeant Stark was winning the military war, he was also winning political battles? That's ironic. I've never met a less political individual."

The woman smiled back. "I assume that is meant as a compliment to Sergeant Stark. The politicians in this room will try not to take it adversely. But, you're correct. Sergeant Stark, by your actions you won another war, one you apparently didn't know you were fighting."

Stark nodded, his brain feeling numbed, but something nagged at it nonetheless. *Something I didn't see. Oh, yeah.* He checked the wording of the offer quickly. "Ma'am, there is a problem. This offer only talks about the enlisted personnel up here being given amnesty. We have some officers as well. A few combat troops, some chaplains, and some doctors. They stayed, too, by choice. They ought to be included in this."

"Sergeant Stark, we've familiarized ourselves with your military record." Stark tried not to wince in reaction to the words. "You do not appear to have had an overly high opinion of officers. Are you saying you would now refuse this offer in order to protect the interests of a few officers?"

"I can't refuse it, ma'am. I have to do what you say. But those officers are my officers. I look out for my people. I'm asking you to include them in the offer."

The woman glanced over at Lieutenant Colonel Hayes. "I see no reason to deny Sergeant Stark's proposed modification," Hayes stated. "The officers of whom he speaks have participated in the same actions which have motivated us to offer amnesty to the enlisted personnel."

"Very well." The woman looked around at her other companions, who all nodded in assent. "Our offer is amended to include the officers serving with your forces, Sergeant." She turned stern. "There will be no more amnesties from this date. Our country has come through a serious crisis. It needs to develop confidence in its leaders once again. And in its institutions. You do realize that henceforth you will be expected to follow orders from superior officers?"

Vic barely stifled a laugh, murmuring so low only Stark could hear. "He never has before. Why start now?"

Stark glared at Vic, then nodded to the civilian. "Yes, ma'am. Mr. Campbell can tell you I understand my place in the order of things."

"So he has already informed us. As I told you, that played a major role in our offer to you, Sergeant." She eyed Campbell in turn. "I suppose with the military under our control once more we wouldn't need to even offer you better conditions, would we? But being able to do something doesn't mean you should. Our offer stands. Is the civil segment of this rebellion also willing to accept it?"

Campbell looked over at Sarafina, then nodded. "Gladly. As representatives of the Colony, we are happy to accept."

"Then welcome back to the United States, all of you."

Stark shook his head, drawing a surprised glance from the woman. "Ma'am, we never left. Not really."

The civilian woman seemed perplexed for a moment, then nodded. "It's strange. Americans have always feared their military to some extent. We've seen you as the greatest internal threat to our democracy. Instead, you turned out to be among its staunchest defenders."

"We could've told you that, ma'am, but at some point the military and the civilians stopped talking to each other."

"That will surely change. There will be no more televising of combat for entertainment purposes. You won't be dehumanized in that fashion any longer. When we gained control of the government we finally learned the extent of military personnel casualties in the last few years. It was a considerable shock. There is simply no way to rebuild our military forces without enlisting large numbers of citizens who did not grow up inside the military."

"Good." Stark grinned over at Vic, who looked as if she was suffering from a sudden attack of indigestion. "That'll cause some culture shock on both sides, but it'll be good for everyone."

More talk, more handshakes, then Stark was standing outside the conference room, a dazed look on his face. *What the hell just happened? The troops are okay. That's what's important.* He jerked himself back to alertness as he became aware of someone approaching him.

Stacey Yurivan stood before Stark, admiration plain on her face. "Reynolds broadcast the deal while you were still in there. Stark, I really underestimated you. What a plan! What a scheme! Raise total hell with everyone and everything and end up smelling like a rose. Someday I'm going to insist you show me how to work scams that well."

"Stace, it was never a plan. Never a scheme. It all just happened because it seemed like the right thing to do at the time."

"Sure. Right. Whatever you say. You, Stark, are King of Scams. I salute you, sir!" Yurivan's hand came up in a rigidly correct salute, which she held until Stark returned the gesture.

"Stace, get out of here."

"Yessir, yessir, three bags full."

"Congratulations, General Stark," Vic offered as well, rendering her own salute as she did so.

"Don't call me that."

"Sorry. Military etiquette, you know." She indicated the shoulder of his uniform. "You'll have to pull off those sergeant chevrons and put stars on instead."

"Don't wanna do it."

"Terrible things happen to people, Ethan. Some get shot, some get promoted to general. You were one of the unlucky ones."

"Can I still get shot, instead?"

"Not by me."

"Of course not." Stark grinned. "Colonel Reynolds."

"Excuse me?"

"You're second in command. That means you'll be at least a full eagle colonel." Reynolds frowned, obviously trying to think of a response. "Maybe now you'll treat me with more respect."

"In your dreams, soldier. What you need, Ethan Stark, is someone giving you constant reality checks!"

"Which is something you happen to be real good at. I never would've started this if I'd known—"

"Ethan, I went in there with you ready for both of us to walk out in chains. Maybe wanting to do right finally counted for something for once."

"And look at our reward."

"What? You still want a firing squad? Look, the troops have always known they could count on you. Now the government feels the same way. And it's not because you're handsome or smart or articulate—"

"Thanks."

"—it's because of what you did when you could do anything you wanted. Right? That's the measure of a person, Ethan. You done good. You saved us."

"I . . . guess I did. No. Anybody could've—"

"Yeah. Right. Tell it to Kate Stein next time you dream about Patterson's Knoll."

"It's a funny thing, Vic. I haven't been dreaming about that battle lately. It used to be every night. Every night."

"Maybe your subconscious is trying to tell you something. Oh, by the way, a friend of yours came up with the negotiators. Wrangled himself a position as an assistant." She pointed down the hall, to where a large sergeant stood. "Come on over, Sergeant Paratnam. Say hi to the general."

"Don't call me that," Stark repeated, then smiled at his friend. "Rash. Long time, no see."

"Not that long. At least this time nobody's shooting at us." Rash grinned, reaching out to slap Stark on the shoulder. "Damn. Glad you're back on the same side."

"Me too."

"I got one question, though. You're gonna be in charge here now, right?"

"Of the mil, yeah. Hard to believe."

"That's putting it mildly. So, Stark, if you're the big boss, who the hell's orders do you disobey?"

"I still got Vic. I ignore her advice all the time."

Vic nodded in agreement. "Most of the time, anyway."

"So," Rash continued, looking from Stark to Reynolds, "you two gonna get married now, or what?"

"Married?" Vic apparently couldn't decide between amazement or laughter at the question. "Me and this goon? What've you been smoking, Rash? You seriously disoriented by the gravity? Got some bad air on your shuttle?"

"Nah," Rash protested. "I mean, it just seems right, you two together always."

"Always?" Vic questioned. "All the time? With Ethan Stark? I fail to see just what I've done in life that would merit that kind of punishment."

"Vic, you two were made for each other."

"If so, the Maker sure has an odd sense of humor." Vic shook her head. "See you around, Rash. I've got to make sure everybody's got the word that we're all official again. Take care of yourself, you big ape."

"Likewise." Paratnam watched her walk away, then turned to Stark. "Ethan, I will never understand that woman."

"That makes two of us."

"Can I still call you Ethan?"

"Call me anything else and I'll slug ya."

"Want a beer?"

"Sure. Rash, what the hell am I gonna do being a general?"

"Hmmm." Rash considered the question for a moment. "Maybe you could do somethin' so outrageous they'd haveta bust you back to sergeant."

"Really? Yeah. That might work. I could—"

He was interrupted by Vic's voice booming back down the corridor. "Don't even *think* about it, Ethan Stark!"

STARK'S COMMAND

A STARK'S WAR NOVEL

by John G. Hemry

After overthrowing the ranking officers, U.S. military forces on the Moon have placed Ethan Stark in command. Now, in addition to fighting a merciless enemy on the Moon's surface, Stark must contend with the U.S. government's reaction to his mutiny . . .

penguin.com
JohnGHemry.com

THE STARK'S WAR SERIES

by John G. Hemry

STARK'S WAR
STARK'S COMMAND
STARK'S CRUSADE

Praise for the Stark's War novels

"When it comes to combat, Hemry delivers."
—William C. Dietz, author of *A Fighting Chance*

"Sergeant Stark is an unforgettable character."
—Jack McDevitt, author of *Firebird*

"A rip-roaring race through tomorrow's battlefield."
—Mike Shepherd, author of *Kris Longknife: Daring*

penguin.com
JohnGHemry.com

M966AS0911